THE HAWTHO

Glyn Hughes was born in Cl................ Welsh parents, and has lived in Yorkshire for many years. He is
the author of a non-fiction book on Yorkshire, *Millstone Grit*; one on Greece, *Fair Prospects*; three volumes
of poetry, *Neighbours* (a Poetry Book Society recom-
mendation and winner of the Welsh Arts Council
Young Poets prize), *Rest the Poor Struggler* and *Best of
Neighbours*; and a play, *Mary Hepton's Heaven*. This
was commissioned for the Oldham Coliseum Theatre
and based on Glyn Hughes's first novel, *Where I Used to
Play on the Green* (also published in King Penguin),
which won both the Guardian Prize for Fiction and the
David Higham Prize for Fiction for 1982. Writing in the
Guardian, Hilary Bailey said of this work: 'Glyn Hughes
provides all the tensions without for a moment losing
sight of the humanity of his characters or the landscape
in which they live . . . We can only praise the author for
his complete imaginative command over a whole period
of time.'

GLYN HUGHES

THE HAWTHORN GODDESS

A KING PENGUIN
PUBLISHED BY PENGUIN BOOKS

Penguin Books Ltd, Harmondsworth, Middlesex, England
Viking Penguin Inc., 40 West 23rd Street, New York, New York 10010, U.S.A.
Penguin Books Australia Ltd, Ringwood, Victoria, Australia
Penguin Books Canada Ltd, 2801 John Street, Markham, Ontario, Canada L3R 1B4
Penguin Books (N.Z.) Ltd, 182–190 Wairau Road, Auckland 10, New Zealand

First published by Chatto & Windus · The Hogarth Press 1984
Published in Penguin Books 1985

Made and printed in Great Britain by
Richard Clay (The Chaucer Press) Ltd, Bungay, Suffolk
Typeset in Sabon

Forget this rotten world; And unto thee
Let thine owne times as an old storie bee...

Look upward; that's towards her, whose happy state
We now lament not, but congratulate.
Shee, to whom all this world was but a stage,
Where all sat harkning how her youthfull age
Should be emploi'd, because in all shee did,
Some Figure of the Golden times was hid.
Who could not lacke, what ere this world could give,
Because shee was the forme, that made it live;
Nor could complaine, that this world was unfit
To be staid in, than when shee was in it; ...

Shee, shee is gone; shee is gone; when thou knowest this,
What fragmentary rubbidge this world is
Thou knowest, and that it is not worth a thought;
He honors it too much that thinkes it nought...

from *The Second Anniversarie*
Of The Progresse Of The Soule

JOHN DONNE

⑴

Through the passageways of Lady Well a mob of weavers and other
artisans, of women, children and youths, chanted at Anne Wylde,
throwing stones at her, chasing the seventeen-year-old girl (called 'the
'Awthorn Maiden') from the enclosure where she had been scything
oats for her father, a stonemason. All her pursuers looked the same.
Their common emotion and purpose transfigured them with an identical mask. It was as if looking at Anne Wylde turned them to stone.
Whilst their shouting was like the banging of hammers hitting stone:

> 'GOD made MAN! MAN made MONEY!
> GOD made BEES, the BEES made HONEY!
> GOD made the DEVIL, THE DEVIL MADE SIN –
> GOD MADE A HOLE TO PUT THE DEVIL IN!'

they shouted. And,

> ''Awthorn, 'awthorn, burn in t'fire!'

Anne was a tall, dark, untamed, careless, *conspicuous* girl with mud
on her from scrambling about the Yorkshire hills. Her form was lean
and beautiful, her eyes exceptionally dark, her nose was sharp: all her
features were pointed, expressing her menacing (for so they thought
of it) curiosity. She was considered 'careless', because she adored
things to which other females did not lend their attention. She showed
an unwomanly love of learning, and with it an unbecoming quickness
in answering back. Partly, this was why they chased her. Her cotton
apron was smirched and frayed, she had lost her cap and her un-
combed hair writhed in thick black snakes which were described as
'intolerable'. For about her appearance she did not care, not in the
usual way. (Sometimes she dressed her hair with flowers – trefoil, and
the unlucky may.) She loved wild animals, flowers and birds, especially the skylarks, whose songs warmed gaps in the skies on spring

days. From early childhood she had nursed lame creatures. With little splints, with drips of milk, or by holding them to the warmth of her breast (the sort of attention that most of her female neighbours only gave to the pigs and calves upon which their livelihoods depended) she succeeded in bringing them back to health. She shared with all that was hunted a readiness to bolt, even when still and safe. And yet, though the child had all her life been such an animal at bay, she did not whine or show fear. On the contrary she was often annoyingly casual when reprimanded. Today, for instance (knowing that her long legs gave her an easy advantage), she found time to observe a butterfly's beauty, and then to insult her breathless persecutors with a long, contemptuous stare.

'Get out, you witch! You sinner! My uncle's cow ran dry because of you!' shouted Amos Culpin, a thin weaver embittered by the death of his wife and baby. He flushed when Anne Wylde stared at him.

'Our dog went blind last winter!' Joshua Binns, also a woollen piece-maker (married to a fair lady, but having a dark one in his heart), complained to Dick Whitely.

Whitely was the constable, the innkeeper, the owner of the slaughterhouse, an (unlicensed) preacher, and the chairman of the Society For Prosecuting Felons. He let Methodists meet in his rooms so that through preaching to them himself he could sell ale, and he was nicknamed 'Dick Almighty' – 'sin-catcher, thief-catcher, innkeeper and doctor'. A man usually of many words who at the moment could not answer, for he was overweight and had been running. His narrow, worldly-experienced lips were quivering and frothing in the largest, roundest, reddest face in Lady Well, upon it the tallest hat, bright yellow. All that was worldly was settled in beefy weight on him, and the keys of the town lockup dangled and rang from his belt. One further reason why they could not catch Anne Wylde was because no one dared to step in front of him in the chase, even though he was the slowest, windiest runner in Lady Well.

He was also a widower; and, despite his worldly windiness, his little eyes, like Binns's, like Culpin's, expressed his instinctive tender desire for the woman of his soul and imaginings; for a goddess who lurked hidden within himself, and who in reality directed his life – his foolishness and creativity, his secret ambitions as well as his public ones, his 'accidents' as well as his choices. This yearning for an inner woman, as in all the other pursuers, was mixed with hatred and fear.

'I took Wylde's mad daughter t'other night!' Amos Culpin intended to whisper, but it came out loud and boastful, and he rolled his tongue with a hungry expression over his lips.

'Has she a large mole with hairs upon her stomach?' Dick Almighty panted. (But with that steady interrogating look in his eye that came when he was about to catch a rogue.)

'That she has! I saw it clear.'

'Well, thou'rt lying, for Stott took her and says she is as fair as a new mushroom!'

' 'Tis Stott who lies! Jabez'd never get near her, he's afraid of his own shadow!'

Jabez Stott, a carpenter's apprentice, timidly changed his mind at fear of being convicted of an untruth by Dick Almighty. 'She did have a mole, an ugly lump like th'old mound upon Raven's Hill,' he said, and bashfully struggled to appear manly.

But to Anne it seemed that there was not one *man* amongst them: not one similar to the Apollo of her imagining, whose kindly face was flown direct out of the sun, and was of shining brass, like the name-plate on a clothier's pew.

'Mole or not, she can read like a parson! There's no chance of Grace with 'er in Lady Well, and so we are inflicted with such curses as seditious nocturnal assemblies of paupers and other cheaters of innkeeper and King,' sin-catcher Whitely said, spluttering over each *s*.

Esther Kershaw (who almost dared to step in front of the constable) threw a stone. As always, she wore an apron stained with three drops of blood; this was because, having said that times would not mend until the 'Wylde witch' had been driven from Lady Well, she had received in her lap the drops of Christ's life-fluid which had dripped from the roof of the church. She had screamed like an owl, alarmed in the dark-time forest that was her soul. The people rushed to her, examining aghast the splotches of fresh crimson spreading upon her white apron. Then they searched Esther's nose and teeth, but found nothing except scraps of grain from her bread, shreds of greens, and oats which she had been nibbling and casting before the painting of Saint Uncumber which was on the wall of the nave. As the stains had not come from her orifices, they were forced to believe that, for having abused Anne Wylde, and for telling everyone that the mason's daughter was truly the witch out of the may-tree, Esther was blessed with the sight of the shadow of Christ amongst the roof-beams.

'She should be excavated from the church!' Esther's voice was high and sharp. 'The church should excavate and whip 'er!'

'Go fuck your sheep!' the virgin yelled and set off running again, her lengthy stride making a distinctive clatter that brought others to their doors.

'You hear 'er, Amos Culprit! Dick 'Itely!' Esther shouted, 'The loud young witch should be stocked, lest she pollute all our souls on our certain road to Heaven!'

Lady Well, in the eighteenth century of *Our Lord's* reign upon earth, was populated by weavers, tradesmen and artisans, a solemn party of whom at the time of the Reformation had filled in the Well (that miraculous shrine – 'Our Mother Mary's ever-flowing womb in the ground', as the last Catholic encumbent had described it – that cured everything, warts, civil-war, childlessness and disease) and cut down the nearby hawthorn. They had thanked God afterwards, 'declaring his counsel' in a meadow, and (their diarist recorded) 'gone quietly home', there to deliberate and, upon concluding their meditations, build a commemorative workhouse. People had now forgotten the site of the Well and the tree, whilst they settled down content with their lot in the century to which they were called to live; as if to show it, they proudly had the mason, John Wylde carve the date and their initials over their lintels.

Though prosperous, the town was haunted by this loss, or by some other. The inhabitants seemed in mourning (though they did not know what for). From time to time they guiltily took consolation in some victim such as Anne Wylde; in music and dancing on the few remaining saints' days; in legitimate inns, or, if they were both poorer and more radical, in 'hush-houses', as they were called, where were brewed sedition, as well as untaxed liquor – both of these being the despair of Dick Almighty.

Lady Well had originally been made of wood in a forest clearing. Now that the hilltops had been cleared and burnt, the forest creatures vanquished and wealth manufactured, it had a heart of the local stone

4

(which was dark and gritty, but a brilliant gold if you split it open) and a crushing ravel of stone intestines in which the wind fluted and there was not a blade of grass; instead, there were those many reminders to fear God, carved over doorways, and taught also by man's experience of the fickle market.

A stone landed at Anne's feet and she put out her tongue. Swaying on her long legs, she sang a rude song, then ran again. She fled by the shops of wool-combers, carpenters, loom-repairers and other artisans. She went by the workhouse where sixty silent children, dressed in uniform gowns and under the eye of a taskmaster, were spinning coarse wool (at threepence a pound) and where the old quiet paupers were labouring in the orchard. (It was the silence of the poor that had always frightened Anne.) She passed the apothecary, who was loquaciously filling his *magic rubbing bottles*; water from the spring in his kitchen was tinctured with laudanum and with his own mysterious brown extract of herbs. 'Use it on your chest night and morning, miss! Or – madam! – take a spoonful upon judicious occasions to cure piles, rheumatic fever, or any other pains, and to excite your husband's venery. Yes, madam! – it brings children to the childless and Grace to the Godless, wi' a golden vision!' he shouted. Anne passed women who had their doors open (it being a fine day), and were spinning on their doorsteps, complaining that the huge furnaces in the wool-combers' shops caused fires; or they were discussing, more wisely than apothecaries and physicians, cures for the men and children in their hands; and now were wondering (seeing Anne Wylde flying by) when the mason's mad daughter might be subdued sufficiently to deserve being made party to female secrets.

(Men and boys were often shy of walking past. So they suffered the greater embarrassment of being laughed at; some developed a lifelong fear of women from the experience. It was assumed at the men's inns that the talk was of babies, of secret dyes for cloth, and of magic for the fidelity and potency of husbands. Yet they must endure this freemasonry of women; for spinning encouraged it, and they could not do without spun thread.)

Anne, careless, dodged by a string of packhorses, bandy-legged under rolls of cloth and waiting to labour over the hills. She went by the dilapidated church's north wall, that the witches and beggars haunted. She passed troughs overflowing with rapid glittering water, and up steep alleys that led her above the roofs to look down upon slopes of stone tiles, golden or bright green with moss, and across the deep gorges brimming with trees that surrounded Lady Well. From this height she could fling her glance across much of Yorkshire.

In its menace it was unique among landscapes. It inspired murder and madness. Sheer hillsides – a sense of the rough stone even underneath the green slopes – rose into cliffs with wind-and-rain warped rocks leaning over them that at will took on the forms of various monsters: at dawn, they were huge heads, and by evening they had turned into birds or lizards. (Or so it seemed, at least to those who had taken the apothecary's laudanum or had been drinking liquors brewed in hush-houses.)

Amongst those who now watched Anne, one was on the side of caution, thinking that something must be done to prevent the persecution; a second believed in innocence, saying, 'The Devil takes care of his own!'; a third had moral anxieties, and was for reporting to the Reverend Doubtfire; whilst a fourth was tortured by nostalgia for his own youthful pleasure in chasing witches, beggars, preachers, itinerant soldiers and other outcasts.

'There's nothing to surprise us 'bout folks wanting to hunt after her!' an old woman, spinning on her doorstep, told her grandaughter. The woman spoke with a rhythm picked up from her wheel upon which the yarn was hissing and humming. 'She is descended from Lady Sybil who changed herself into a white doe that slept under a hawthorn bush – she wished t'escape her vile suitor, Lord William, and be free for ever to roam the crags and moors. But another witch told him to go hunting on All-Hallow's Eve, and he surprised the white doe. Lord William and his dogs they chased all day upon them hills and did not catch the fair beast, until at evening they were joined by a strange hound, his witch's familiar – that soon had the animal by the throat! Lord William he attached an enchanted leash and brought the deer home and confined her in a tower where in the night during a thunderstorm she was changed back to the Lady Sybil, so he was able to lead her to altar and had many children by her, from whom the Wyldes come. It is because she is descended from a doe that she has such long legs and is always running.

'They say that after a few years Lady Sybil used to go frolicking wild on the moors again in the shape of a white cat, until a miller caught her and cut off her paw. Next morning Her Ladyship would not leave her bed. Then the miller came to the castle door with a hand which was shown to be Lady Sybil's by its fairness and the diamond rings upon it. Though it was re-joined to its proper body by magic, there was always a red ring around her wrist. Prevented from racing wild upon the hills, she pined away and died, leaving her children orphans. 'Tis a sad story.'

'Doesn't Anne Wylde want to go to Jesus?' The little granddaughter, light-haired as thistledown, stared unbelievingly at the flying 'witch', and merely breathed her words, hardly daring to disturb the air with such heresy. 'Parson Doubtfire tells us allus to pray to die and prepare for't in our sad life by being modest. Grandma, why hasn't Parson teached Anne Wylde to be modest?'

The grandmother, being asked such dangerous questions, reached for a *magic rubbing bottle*, a spoonful of which sent children to sleep.

Meanwhile Anne heard the voices of Culpin, Binns, Stott, Dick Almighty, Esther Kershaw and others coming closer, chanting with a loud heavy rhythm, as if they were a new sect of dissenters determined to dominate the town with their hymn.

'GOD MADE THE DEVIL, THE DEVIL MADE SIN, GOD MADE A HOLE TO PUT THE DEVIL IN!'

So off Anne set again, cursing upon her neighbours' disgusting offspring – two-headed babies, or sons with toads' legs, – that she had heard talked about amongst woolcombers, carters and soldiers returned from the wars, or amongst the tribes expelled from their distant homes because parks were being built there, and who now camped amongst moors or marshes.

Going through the shadow on the north side of the church, and then under the east window, Anne came out by the school. A fiddler and 'vagabond' known as 'Dick O'Lovely', whom Dick Almighty could never imprison or move on as he was so popular, was calmly trying a melody, tuning his strings, then plucking the air again. Because of his 'profane' tunes the Reverend Joseph Doubtfire had come out to glare from the school portal, though Dick did not seem to see him.

The Parson was a tall man with a long face and a hooked, lecherous nose. With his hands gripped tightly together, he clutched his groin as if he feared that his bag of seeds might fly away or roll to the ground. Because the fiddler smiled in a kindly way in Anne's direction, and as she smiled back, Doubtfire glared at her also.

He had first noticed Anne Wylde when she was fourteen and they had chosen her as Queen of the May. How all winter they had waited for this day! The thorn trees, so long gnarled and black that they looked as though they could never live again, in a week or two had their cragginess swallowed first in bright green, then in the consuming globe of creamy flowers. The young people had gone at midnight to the brink of the woods to light fires, and had played, touching Anne, decorating her with flowers that looked blue in the moon. When the sun rose and painted in daylight colours her cascades and wreaths of hawthorn, she still hadn't given in to them. So they attached long ribbons and led her like a captive spirit into Lady Well, where she wept a trail of petals and the warmed, wilting may-blooms gave off a strong, female smell. It was now affirmed that, like her mother, she would become pregnant with the Devil, or by a hare, goat or moorland beast. They brought her to Doubtfire expecting he would bridle, purge and put her in the stocks, or have her dressed in a white shift to confess before the congregation.

What was she truly like, 'this monster, this infant Gorgon, this Eve, this witch-terror-scourge, this curse and punishment for our sins, this profane polluted Graceless being' whom he had been led to expect? Before him had stood but a sensitive girl-child, who had a tendency to bolt, her long too-sensuous animal-legs aquiver. With her 'intolerable' locks of black hair, her suitably named *wild* look, her stance improperly proud for a female, and her unmaidenly cleverness, he could not think of her as *beautiful*, but she was definitely affecting and striking. And, though she was as certainly wicked as any other child of Eve, she was a child still – who dreamed of maypoles and of apples coated in sugar, no doubt; and yet one conspicuous and loud, who did rant too much for a woman, for her 'father' was a dissenter (a curse of this Realm!) who had taught her to read, and she in consequence lapped up knowledge as a starved mare gobbles oats. Captivated by her appearance and her cleverness, Doubtfire had been unable to punish her.

Releasing one hand, he now beckoned her. As her footsteps passed

8

by, Dick O'Lovely played her on her way. She entered under the great porch of the school, where was carved a sun, flames writhing out of it, at its centre a round, grinning male face with underneath in weighty letters:

Rich'd Horsfall Facit. A:D: 1660. FEARE GOD

Anne was afraid, all right – both of God and also because the grammar school was a boys' empire which she had never entered before. (The domain of the Yorkshire woollen-traders' God and that of the boys' grammar school where she had been taught not to trespass being the same thing in Anne Wylde's mind.) But 'God made a hole to put the Devil in!' still pierced the alleyways.

Doubtfire addressed her with vanity and confidence: as one who knows that his opinions are well thought-out and cogent, but does not recognise how prosaic they are. 'You are too Conspicuous, Anne Wylde! Woman's flesh is the house of the Devil and must Submit to Godly men or be flogged, lest she Pollute us!' (The Parson naturally spoke with capital letters.) 'It has always been my own daily care to Crucify the lusts of the Flesh, to cut off and cast away Sins as dear to me as my right hand or eye. I have desired to be a Mourner in Zion, and to grieve for the Abominations of the place in which I dwell.'

Anne's mouth was silently open with amazement, like a simple girl's, and she was for a moment stilled.

The cheeks of the willowy, truculent priest were purple and twitching; he'd been at the brandy. Disappointed that the young witch did not answer him back, Doubtfire led her into the very interior of the forbidden building, as if he intended to instruct her further.

The boys had left an odour of leather, sweat and dust. She saw a chart of the Greek alphabet, maps of the Holy Lands, sculptured mementi mori as in church, and frightening steel engravings of exemplary deaths or martyrdoms, and also of the ruins of Italy and Hellas. There were some stinking relics of anatomical investigations into birds, animals and even humans – the Vicar's pastime. Windows showed the green summer paps of the hills, which seemed so far away, and the stocks, which were horribly close.

Doubtfire made her sit down. Her legs sprawled carelessly and the priest stared, just as other men did. How could she be resisted? – long thighs shifting eloquently beneath her grimed apron and gown, suggesting therefore also smirched behaviour, and treacherous too for a man of Doubtfire's years. Those things which wasteful youth took for granted excited with a sad useless longing a man who felt that his lusts were ugly (even had he been capable of fulfilling them) and who preached to the young that they should pray for death to come.

With drunken stumbles he closed the shutters (although the pursuers had melted away before the Vicar). '"Man that is born of woman hath a short Life full of trouble! He is born unto Trouble as the sparks fly upwards".' Whilst he misquoted his Bible he nervously played with a child's skull: pale, almost transparent, as fragile as a bird's egg, it had been washed out of its grave on a steep and stony hillside in a rainstorm. He sheared away from his thoughts, and asked, 'Is the mason at home ... have you spoken together?'

Anne nodded, and her response made him still more apprehensive – she did not understand why.

'Reading Deists and French philosophers, is he? There are such nonconforming Devils amongst us today ...'

'No, for my father often foolishly forgets his proper hopes and ambitions. He is all the time now thinking of a new kind of building, to be filled wi' spinners – not paupers, but with women coming daily from the cottages. He says that in future times the weavers'll be weaving by steam. Sometimes he reads his books at night and I hear him through my sleep raking the fire, sir.'

Evidently the mason and his daughter had not talked together, and the Parson was relieved, whilst Anne felt that some secret was being kept from her.

'I am surprised that with your sins you enjoy any sleep, Anne Wylde!'

She laughed, and Doubtfire frowned as he closed another shutter: there were six of them. Before the last one he lit a candle, and inspected the wick closely, as if the poor woman who peeled rushes for candles for a living had not done her work correctly. 'Fire is so admirable a Servant but so Terrible a master! Pestilence, sword and famine do not make such outrageous Havoc. Some day you will be going as a servant, you ought therefore to be warned of the accidents which happen by Fire. Chimneys too long unswept ... great blazes in the Fireplace ... a candle brought into a hay-loft. Where the floor is grown spongy with age, a spark may fall on it. In going to bed use a short candle and a large flat candlestick, taking care to have an extinguisher. These observances regard as thy Duty to God and thy neighbour.' There was an excited gleam like a small candle-flame in Doubtfire's eye.

Anne stared thoughtfully, and not listening. Her expression had changed from that of a young woman who enticed him to that of a small child; changes typical of maidens, he thought, as a sky in spring switches between clear sky and cloud. She then asked a question which had been on her mind for a long while, whilst she baked bread alone in her father's kitchen, scythed oats or, equally alone, roamed the moors, the cliffs and the enclosures: 'Mr Doubtfire, do angels eat in Heaven?'

This was too trivial a question for a Theologian to answer. Doubt-fire instead replied, 'I, too, am weighed down by Sin. Oh, I have indescribable thoughts! If you are persecuted, console yourself with how much more tormenting it is to wait until the Fires of Purgatory to be purged. We all are such terrible sinners in Lady Well, in this horrible violent district, this terrible exile from Eden, awaiting the awful Judgment!'

Doubtfire came up to the schoolmaster's desk. Impulsively, as if to do it before wiser thoughts pursued, he snatched up the birch. His hands trembling, his eyes tearful, he approached Anne in a cloud of brandied breath. She saw a pitiful, broken, pleading, sin-wrecked man. 'Oh, Anne Wylde! I am able to beat the schoolboys for their acts of Wickedness, but who is to Birch me to make me clean and whole? Oh what Sorry sons of fallen Adam we are, in need of Correction!'

His second thoughts winging near, Doubtfire hurriedly turned his back, raised his cassock and leant over his schoolmaster's whipping bench. His reddened face between his toes, he waved the bundle of birch twigs impatiently; for Anne was grasping neither his meaning nor the birches. But at last, with a child's wondering and accepting expression, she took hold of the implement, gingerly, as if it was a poker out of the fire. Doubtfire's lips dribbled, and his upside down, staring bulging eyes were like those of a calf in the slaughteryard. She cautiously tickled the naked bottom. 'Harder! Oh Anne, I have so many Sins!' Then Anne made up her mind and blindly laid it on, purging, if not him, at least herself of what she had suffered in Lady Well. She was a practical girl, with firm hands and strong limbs, and used to work.

Doubtfire groaned, 'No! ... No! ... Oh for pity!' so Anne paused, aghast at the livid red bottom streaked by her birches.

'Go on!' Doubtfire hissed. 'Don't stop now!'

Anne swung her birch twigs again, just as she was commanded. Seeing that it didn't seem to be doing the Vicar any harm, she started to enjoy it. He began to writhe and yell, with sudden fear of the pain which he himself had willed. He rolled off the bench, putting his hand out to stop her, and she obeyed. The horrible priest was now grovelling at her feet. 'Anne, oh Anne, such a weight of Sins lie upon us poor mortals! Now I feel cleansed pure and whole.'

During Anne's childhood men had once or twice stopped her in passageways and shown her their parts, yet she had not been as disgusted as she was at this moment. 'If 'tis true that it is as difficult for a rich man to enter Heaven as f'ra camel to pass through the eye of a needle, how can a bishop be admitted?' she asked. 'Do you want this punishment because if you are not treated as a beggar you are too rich to enter Heaven?'

'Yes! Yes!' Appealing eyes were turned up to her. For he was not yet satisfied. He was not at peace. She thought of King Nebuchadnezzar, condemned to crawl amongst stones and eat grass.

'I don't believe you,' Anne declared. She moved away and, with confidence now, began to unfasten shutters. She hung up the birch. Doubtfire, returning from darkness and fantasy, fastened his clothes, feeling the weals beginning to smart and swell.

'Mr Doubtfire, how can women ever go to Heaven when they are cursed because they betrayed and deceived Adam?'

'They can be forgiven in life by honestly coming to God and Jesus, conscious of their sin against man and purging themselves through submissiveness to father and husband.' He stroked himself tenderly under his gown.

'When we go to Heaven, Mr Doubtfire, do we stay the same sex as on earth ... as men and women?'

'We remain men and women, yes.'

'Then what does God do to satisfy our desires which, you tell us often, are so wrong in His sight?'

'Shame on you for speaking of them! In Hell we suffer our Lusts and are Degraded, but in Heaven we do not have Them.'

'Are we then so old there? I would like to stay young in Heaven.'

What impertinent, foolish questions the child does ask! Doubtfire thought.

'We are ageless,' he added, crossly. 'You mustn't tell anyone about This, you know. God will never forgive you.' She paused, uncertainly. He waited also; he had finished with her. 'You may go now.'

Anne walked out through the alleyways, carefully as a hare comes into the evening dew. But all her enemies had disappeared and she returned safely to her father's house.

Anne's home was a comfortable solid building which had a handsome porch of carved pillars. The lintel was carved in the form of a heavy, sensual lip, and the door within echoed this same design. Above was a date-stone: FEARE GOD 1700.

Its master, the mason John Wylde, was, like the house, a large secure man, of substantial philosophy and dreams; a person who did indeed need over his entrance a reminder that there was One mightier and more secure than himself. He was a rationalist, and God's world seemed to him nothing but a huge stone ball like the ones that he carved for gateposts and gable-ends. He regularly journeyed around all England, staying with groups of artisans who disputed the Bible and about Greek philosophers, 'substituting Reason for superstition', as they put it. He also had visitors, which made him seem strange (like his daughter) to his neighbours. Radical dissenters or 'lunatics' came; working men whose philosophies were driven into the mad, twisted channels of *enthusiasm* through lack of any ordinary conventions of society to express their ideas. Scottish, even French, philosophers, whom John Wylde had met in Edinburgh, called on him. Also, other ambitious masons. Some had set themselves up as architects, or planners of estates and gardens, and their books and diagrams of parks laid out on the classical pattern, or of lavish interiors, inspired Anne Wylde, by the way, with exotic dreams of luxury – of palaces, gilded beds, silk clothes, blackamoor servants, and libraries of books that had gold and leather bindings – a life utterly unimaginable in bleak Lady Well.

Nowadays, John Wylde enjoyed more time for dreaming. For he had half abandoned the sheds where with his apprentices and journeymen he carved traditional heart-shaped dripstones for windows, or figures for door lintels and corbels. He had also ceased his wandering. Instead he would sit poring over charts, calculating the strengths of beams and floorboards, the spans of arches and the means of lifting the stones for a great manufactory that would surely make a fortune for his patron, Nicholas Horsfall, and himself. But at this clerkish unfamiliar work his eyes grew tired (though the Vicar had presented him, in return for his 'amiable repairs' to the church, with a pair of spectacles), and he would slip back in his chair and dream. He thought of God, the Great Craftsman, fondling in his hands the stone ball of the world; and as he turned it daily, the light crept over one side and the shadow in the opposite direction slipped along the other; a wave passed around it, of men waking up to the dawn, whilst another went along the far side of those going to their sleep.

This vision had been amazing John Wylde when the Vicar disturbed him, earlier in this day. The mason did not think that Joseph Doubtfire was much of a man: he was one of those victims of Nature who fill their lives with unnecessary misfortune. Moreover, Wylde liked to synthesise his thoughts; whereas the Parson's interest was in analysis. (Like Death itself, thought Wylde, which breaks down bodies, plants and all the seasons.) So John, instead of offering serious matters, bantered with the Vicar.

'What sort of winter will we poor sinners be enjoying, Mr Doubtfire?'

'It is, like all else, in God's hands.'

John Wylde glanced at the Parson's elongated, twitching, 'useless' fingers, stained and pale with the formalin he used for preserving 'specimens'. Fingers which, if a stone was placed in them, would surely drop it; and Wylde trusted that God's hands were not like those. The mason, holding *his* world of charts and calculations in his own firm grasp, looked outside carefully and slowly. Then, with his superior knowledge of the seasons and of all practical things, he put the Vicar in his place. 'Nay, we'll not be getting any weather yet! I don't know when, though ... I thought maybe God would tell you what he has in mind for us poor artisans.'

Wylde was easy with and respectful of all, even a generally unloved Parson, so his mocking and contempt were gentle compared with what Doubtfire suffered from other dissenters: some threw mud at him, let dogs into his church or carved lewd symbols upon it, and stamped their boots through his sermons. Certain nonconforming children even burnt little images of him on secret bonfires.

'It does not seem to me that *you* have to fear the winter's Savagery,' the Parson answered.

'Horsfall has it in mind to put the spinners all under one roof in what he calls a *manufactory*. Whilst they are in their cottages, the master cannot rely upon them to deliver their yarn and has to go in search of it himself.'

'And you think that the women will come to your "manufactory" every day, just as if they are resident Paupers? Surely they will not suffer the Indignity willingly!'

'Many are quite poor and lonely enough long before they reach the stage of dependency upon the Parish. If they are paid a small wage, they will think that better than falling to the state of imprisoned paupers, yet doing the same work. Or so our Captain Horsfall reasons, after talking with some great "economists" and "improvers". Such men are exerting a great influence on the proprietors of estates all over England, I am told. Well, it is at least a shelter.' Wylde paused. 'But as soon as we escape Nature's anger, it seems that we have to face the scorn of men.'

'You are thinking now of your daughter? The reason is, you have given her too much Scope for a woman's upbringing. How can she follow the instructions of Saint Paul after such a rearing? "Wives, submit unto your Husbands, as unto the Lord. For the Husband is the head of the wife, even as Christ is the head of the Church: and He is the Saviour of the body." Since you have Polluted her meek nature with so much freedom, you have made it impossible for her to be a good wife and servant. So those who perceive her to be Wilful chase her through the streets.'

'She's all right! "There's nothing wrong with right folk," as we say - her nature is kindly. And they are guilty men who pursue her, treating her as they feel they deserve to be treated themselves. For such is our human nature.'

Nonetheless, insight was no answer to a practical problem. So John Wylde listened to the Vicar's proposal of a way to 'remove' Anne, and now he was ready to face her with it when she came home.

Anne slipped oftenest through a back gate into the mason's yard, because there she found men who loved her – the old stone-cutters and dressers who when she was small had put her tenderly upon their knees whilst they took their cheese and ale squatting against the wall, and had told her, for instance, about the Great White Cow, who succoured everyone upon the moors, and about her 'ancestor' Lady Sybil.

At its centre the yard was golden-white with dust, and around the perimeter were damp sheds. The stones were a purple-black colour, except where they had been cut to show the bright gold. Many had the beginnings of carvings: dragons, fawns, interlacings, and column-flutings.

The place now echoed with the sharp, dry, regularly repeated sound of a chisel striking stone, like the call of a harsh exotic bird in a thicket: two apprentices were squaring up a block for a 'Grecian' column, such as was called for by gentlemen these days. The lads were laughing at it, thinking it feeble work compared with the bold rough stuff they were used to. Next, they turned to sniggering at Anne Wylde.

Anne went into the kitchen. The scrubbed stone floor, the broad and thick single board of the table with two wooden platters upon it, washed; a clean pot hung over dead embers in the fireplace, and around it a tidy hearth. There was no house-servant. Anne did the work herself, and fed the mason's journeymen and apprentices. She had been brought up as an only girl, indeed as the only woman in the house, resourceful and learning what she knew of domestic economy from aunts and neighbouring women.

She burst into her father's parlour in her usual 'excessive' fashion: like a calf that has been let loose over a moor and, dazed and amazed by the breadth and wonder of the world, has found itself again baffled in the gloom of its barn. So suddenly entering it, the room gave her an impression of brown stillness, as of peaty water lying upon a moor. The oak panels, the clock with its carefully oiled machinery ticking and snoring, the books and charts, and above her father's head the large brown painting of that group of seven frighteningly-still and patient men, standing in Puritan clothes and hats, who had filled in the Well; their rigid arms all pointing to one spot like a grave of new earth before them on the ground, and behind them a bonfire made of the famous Lady Well hawthorn tree. (A curious picture, given – like

16

the spectacles – to Wylde by the Parson in return for what he had done for the fabric of the church.)

John Wylde loved his only, motherless daughter; who fussed over him, making him camomile tea, pestering old women for herbal medicines more effective than the apothecary's 'rubbing bottle', trying different diets for him, worrying when he lingered in stone-yards and quarries through the cold and wet. ('Thou'll not find a husband by spending yourself on your father!' had remarked the foolish old hags and the wise-women – who in any case doubted Wylde's paternity.) John had transferred to Anne the love he had felt for his wife, who had died in giving birth. Following closely on the death of his own mother, this was a blow that seemed to destroy everything feminine in the world. It was as if for him Nature herself had died. The air was no longer pure and sweet, nor the grass, trees and earth. So he compensated by smiling upon Anne, whilst she grew up running free everywhere – a girl who did not lower her eyes nor keep silent because men were speaking; yet still he gave her everything that she wanted.

But at sight of her with bits of thistle and grass in her hair he placed himself imperiously before the fire. In a manner typical of him when deliberating he raised both hands to waist level, held them the span of a building-stone apart, spread his thick fingers as if balancing some heavy thing and put his words together carefully, quietly. He could have been building a cathedral.

'And where's the sickle thou's been cutting oats with?' he demanded.

She had forgotten all about that when they chased her from the enclosure and now could not remember against which bank, stone or tuft of grass she had left it. Whilst Anne was careless with such things, to John Wylde all tools were precious objects, to be nursed and coddled as a mother with a baby. More than anything else, her neglect of this put him in a rage.

'It'll be rusted and useless when thou finds it,' he said at last.

She dared not answer. She merely stooped her shoulders more, for she was taller even than her father, and at the moment this seemed improper.

'It'll need taking and grinding. 'Appen you've already broken the edge off it by catching it on stones, in your usual fashion.'

17

He was silent, waiting for the retort that might excuse the release of his anger. But she did not answer.

'And I've no time to do it!'

Silence, still, from Anne.

'All our neighbours are orderly, obeying God's commands, but thou goes about like a savage beast! However, Doubtfire came today, offering to arrange for you to be civilised at Makings where he said they'd be able to make a good servant of you.' (So that was what the Parson had been hiding from her!) '"To get her out of the way of folks throwing stones and calling her a witch?" I asked him. "You know what they did to Alison Wooler, tied to the tail of a cart," he answered me. It seems that Benjamin Greave wants to build a big family vault in the church. Our local clothier, though his father was nothing, plans to stop being a maker of rough kersey woollens for soldiers and hospitals, and to become foppish, weaving worsteds – callimancoes and shalloons for lining ladies' dresses. He says that is the "future". He thinks that making cloth for the gentry will turn him into a gentleman, and so our Parson believes he has influence over him. "I must be grateful that you take such an interest in my maid," I answered him – with sarcasm in my response. "I think you favour her because she was the youngest hereabouts to learn her catechism!" "She does catch on to things fast," he said. But I told him, "I taught her to read and write for more than to pay lip-service to folk."'

The mason spoke quickly to prevent his unruly daughter interrupting him. But now, at last, Anne herself broke out angrily. 'Doubtfire's getting rid of me because he's feared of me! You're all feared!'

'Making Hall is a grand place,' John Wylde said, trembling. ''Tis a grand sight, like the Parthenon was of old to the peasants of Greece.'

The mason normally hid his deepest feelings, as if to show them would attract an evil demon. But all afternoon he had balanced his desire to have Anne with him, against what her fate might be if she remained in Lady Well, and now his pain at the thought of losing her twitched in his face.

Anne felt as though she had been suddenly dropped into a hole. What could she imagine at Makings? Surroundings of elegant mirrors and gilt, a stream of visitors from far away, foods such as she could hardly think of; but her pride humbled, like a nun's.

Her expression, so distant from him, neither assenting nor disagreeing, made her father exclaim impatiently, 'Sometimes I think you are not my daughter!'

From then on, events seemed to belong to Anne's past the moment they were born. Everyone behaved differently towards her. When she went to the apothecary's or the grocer's, the women would usually stop their gossiping. Anne was annoyed only because they did not obtain their goods on first entering the shop, thus saving her having to wait through silence whilst half a dozen or so obtained their purchases. Now, however, the shopkeeper immediately said, 'What may we do to help you, Miss Wylde?' and this was even worse than having to wait, for she was being even more deliberately shunned and hastily got rid of.

When she passed the Vicar in the street he blushed and looked elsewhere. Out of embarrassment, he whom she had beaten might become angry with someone, or make excuses to rush away; whilst Anne grinned back, direct and fearless, making him cower.

But he could not avoid her eyes in his church of Saint Mary the Virgin.

John Wylde used to please himself which churches he visited and took his daughter to. (Or even whether he would go at all, for often they stayed at home and read their Bible to one another.) Though loyal to the tiny chapel of his own sect, sometimes Wylde liked to taste a new theology. Every Saturday evening and Sunday morning father and daughter bantered over which place to visit. The weather often decided the matter: if it was fine they enjoyed crossing the moors together, to startle some remote hideout of a rare sect where the mason indulged his greatest joy: friendly dispute with clever strangers. When the weather was wet they showed their faces at the parish church – the place where as a child John had first marvelled at sculpture. (Or what battered remains there were of saints, devils, gargoyles and kings.) On these next Sundays, though it was fine and warm, Anne wanted to stay in Lady Well to tease the Vicar.

As usual, she got her way with her father. She sat, her expression innocent of any intention to disconcert, demure with her hands folded upon her prayer book and with flower-like calm, even though the people tittered around her. Above and behind on the balcony were the Greaveses and their flock of servants, with Captain Horsfall, his mother and some of their servants. Enjoying ample space there, they were also hidden in the high-pews that were their own gift to the church, so that they could sleep undetected. Not even Dick Almighty – much as it offended his dignity – was allowed up there, so close to Heaven. The humble congregation, in smelly kersey-woollens, crowded into the earth- and damp-smelling nave, whilst Almighty, being a churchwarden, stamped up and down the aisles, ringing his keys and banging his staff as if he was Saint Peter himself, clouting round the ears those who were not sufficiently bent in prayer, kicking out the curs and mongrels: why, he even interrupted sermon and anthems for these important duties. Because of Almighty's edict, those such as Dick O'Lovely, who paid no rates or taxes, must miss God's words altogether and stay in the churchyard. (Where however Dick often played his own tunes, that were wilder and more thrilling than hymns, in order to collect pennies from the thankfully departing congregation.)

Anne felt glad to see her persecutors bowed, even though she knew that it was their stooping to them that gave fire to the Parson's sermons. She, like her father (who had first pointed out the beauties of the church to her – so unlike other fathers, who took them for granted), loved the atmosphere of the building: a wrecked and rustling forest of dark columns, numinous shadows and mysteries, throwing her into a vertiginous spin when she peered into the roof at the carved angels with rubbed-out faces and damaged limbs. Sunday after Sunday the child had sat here, like other children and their parents trying not to be noticed by Dick Almighty; wondering what her female fate would be, and why, and whether she would be able to bear it, with Christ and Saint Paul as her masters; or whether she would be different from others. At the age of thirteen, on the verge of menstruation, she first became aware that a female's whole world was one of shadows and mystery: of muttered secrets, of careful calculation when to be silent and when to affect a temper, of devices to manipulate menfolk without their realising it – even of magic potions (slipped into the men's oatmeal porridge or beer) to make them active or sleepy, quarrelsome or passive, according to a woman's devices. She saw that men, though they never admitted it, were afraid of women, who had such secret control of what went into their mouths and their homes.

So, in thoughtful dreamy hours in the church, Anne swung and kicked her legs, scared of how fast they were growing, wondering if she were turning into a monster, just as they said she was; week by week getting used to being shunned, sometimes scared by her fate, sometimes silently arrogant, sometimes screaming and raging about it.

The church was drilled with shafts of coloured light. The window-glasses, which were left undamaged from the old days – red for warriors, blue for saints and yellow for Heaven – were a view not into Lady Well but into another world, where Anne's imagination loved to wander and wonder. The statues (many of which had the wrong heads, because after the Puritan soldiers had gone through, lopping them off at the necks, pious people had crept in to place the heads back again, often on the wrong trunks). The paintings, with their pale colours faded or scratched off the walls. Saint Uncumber, patron saint of unfortunate women, depicted crucified upside down so that her long red hair fell from her tormented body like a river of blood; a scattering of oats on the floor below, placed secretly by unhappy wives to bring true their prayers to be rid of their husbands. A picture of the scourging of Christ. Jesus did not look like a man being whipped – except for his beard, he was more like a dreaming virgin girl. Perhaps Christ enjoyed the scourging! Anne, elected, with irony, to be God's agent, His punisher of sin, now asked herself if she had done her birching properly and for assistance she looked at the pictures of the expert scourgers on the walls; but they, like herself, didn't seem really to mean it.

Sunday was the most important day of the week for everyone in Lady Well. It was when they came down from lonely places on the hills and could gossip with their neighbours. It was when they heard what had been aired far away in newspapers and what had occurred in parliament (so long as Doubtfire was disposed to tell them about it). It was when the young people met, showing off whatever fine clothes they had. Here one could rest, once one had developed the trick – for Almighty's benefit – of seeming at the same time to have an ear cocked to the psalms, anthems and sermons. It was when one could daydream.

And so, whilst Doubtfire preached about Mary Magdalene, the 'natural woman' humbled to the feet of Christ, Anne's mind drifted into a blasphemous fantasy: in this, it was not the Parson, but Christ Himself whom she had whipped.

Anne tried to depart secretly from Lady Well. On the eve of Lammas Day she sorted her belongings (her mother's clothes, her Culpeper's Herbal, a Bible, a copy of Homer translated by Mr Pope, so full of exotic beings) and before dawn her father took them on his mason's cart to Making Hall, leaving her for a short while alone at home, where she prepared a table-load of baking to leave behind.

Many claimed later that they had heard during the previous night the eerie whistling known as 'Gabriel Ratchers'. (Amos Culpin said it was like the sound of a piece of timber hurled through the air, whilst another described it as the yelping of a pack of dogs.) Joshua Binns saw two stars fighting. But at the time, nobody especially remarked about Anne Wylde, who had with such great pride maintained her apparent indifference to her destiny.

After her father returned from Makings, Anne hesitated over kissing him goodbye – unsure whether or not she had been taught that it would be unseemly. She decided that it was bound to be another sin upon her head, and she walked off, alone, unhampered, along the route already followed by her belongings.

It was close to the end of a fine August morning when most had abandoned their looms and spinning wheels to make hay or go hunting for rabbits or hares. Those who watched might have thought that she, too, was taking a stroll to the enclosures and the hills. Yet she was washed, combed, dressed in her best gown of sky-blue wool with a bright white apron, and with tears dampening her eyes because of that missed embrace.

The Vicar, though some had begged him to cut the first corn, was poised in the schoolroom. He cast one quick glance through the window before turning back to reprove his tittering pupils. A dunce turned out for misbehaviour, who lingered in the doorway with a fool's cap on his head, stared lustily and he momentarily turned cheerful. Housewives, washing clothes at a spring, cackled after her.

Dick O'Lovely, alone and playing his fiddle outside a hush-house (the drinkers paid him to do this; if he stopped it was a signal that Dick Almighty or some other busybody was approaching) paused, though only for a second until he recognised her footsteps, and blew her a friendly kiss. He looked hungry, she noticed – even though it was summertime.

In the small stone-walled fields cramped around Lady Well – their bright grass like emeralds mounted within the dark moorland – weavers stretching their cloth, and women rolling hay, laughed and shouted, sure that now their milk would not turn sour, nor their pups be born blind, nor their rabbits devour their young; that the harvests would not be storm-beaten and that future winters would not kill the poor.

At one point a group of villagers, some grinning but most silently trying to hide their fear, gathered to watch her passing. They showed the usual embarrassment caused by the sight of a tall woman and she decided to scare them by running forwards, waving her arms and cursing. 'I'll pick thee out ... oh, yes! You who are mean from the generous, and the kind-hearted from the cruel!' she shrieked. Unbelievably, these hard weavers and farmers shuffled quietly and guiltily before the girl, who appeared to be driving them before her like a flock of hens. They gathered sullenly, and in truth frightened, in an enclosure corner to watch her pass – this alien spirit who had been born amongst them for their sins – and only when she was out of hearing did they fall to muttering again.

Meanwhile, with joy Anne leapt into sunlight beyond the last house. She saw the quiet hills and valleys draped around and below her: grey soft lips pursing upwards out of the dense woodlands. The smells had changed, from oily woollens and urined passages to hayfields and flowers, and some lane-banks were already scented with ripening blackberries.

Rooks rose off a plateau. Reaching the edge, they played with the breeze that scattered them over the skies. Their wings were shot with glossy blue, purple and green, like coal or iron settling and cooling out of the furnace of Creation. At other turns, the birds became an insubstantial colourless glitter; they were transformed to mere air, or water. Time and again they flew into the wind, full of pleasure.

A flock of larks twisted and skimmed over the slopes, their backs gleaming like fragments of glass, as if some brightness up there had been shattered and pieces of mirror were cascading, enjoying their descendings. All this turning of light wings inspired Anne with freedom, with an impulse to be also scattered in bright pieces about the Heavens.

(Anne Wylde's pleasure in the birds and flowers was unusual in being unpossessive. Others liked blossoms because they anticipated the fruit to be eaten, or they thought of decoration to their persons or houses that would impress their friends; hearing a lark sing they wished to cage it. But Anne hardly wanted to touch them – except just sometimes, she would bring a jar of modest wild flowers indoors, but not to make an effect on anyone, and she would occasionally put a blossom behind her ear.)

For several miles she followed a track along the spine of the hill. It overlooked two sun-filled valleys on either side glittering with streams and throwing up a warm smell of drying hay. The moors were smouldering purple with heather blossom from which Anne sometimes disturbed a thunder of bees. The countryside was busy, with gangs of men and women building enclosure walls and extensions to farms which were prospering with the trade in woollens; with travellers also happy at the sunshine; weavers leading their bowed packhorses, merchants, carters with their vehicles laden with wool and a drover bringing a flock of sheep. Scared of the eyes of these people, Anne used her shawl to flatten out her beautiful breasts. Meanwhile she stepped forwards with a simple desire to make her life happy.

A seven-mile clamber upon the hills was no effort to the long-legged girl. She burst over the brink of another valley, out of which these tradesmen climbed in their continuous ant-like file. Unlike the rock-strewn gorges that dropped away from Lady Well, this place was broad, shallow and fertile, the trees cleared, the land cultivated and enclosed, with the menacing moorland held back. It was evenly scattered with weavers' cottages, neat and as carefully placed to avoid touching one another as nonconformists ranged in a chapel; surrounded with ruffs of enclosures and linked in a web of small streams. The higher up the hillsides were these walled green oases, the more they were threatened by vast sombre areas of surrounding moorland. The lower part of the dale narrowed and steepened abruptly where all the spouts of water funnelled into one that rushed through waterfalls and was banked with the dense trees of Blood Wood. From the foot of the wood, Anne could hear the mechanical banging of ham-

mers in the fulling mill at Lower Laithes, which belonged to Benjamin
Greave.

At the head of this valley, which he virtually owned (as well as
controlling the livelihoods of his tenants) stood his home, Making
Hall, where he had first use of the water oozing out of the hills above.
Everywhere in sight was prosperous and it was clear that Makings
was the reason; for all the roads led to or from it, as sheep-tracks over
a field radiate from the place where the sheep are fed. Benjamin
Greave's clothing trade kept two hundred weavers in employment
and a thousand women spinning for them in this valley, the next one
and the one after that. It promoted a quarry industry, also carting,
loom-repairing, carpentry and land-clearing. Children were found
work (fitting the wires into the wool-combs) as soon as they could
walk, whilst old women were engaged to their days' ends in brewing
dyes. Anne could see the industrious weavers, their women and children, carrying on ponies or on their own backs their pieces of woven
cloth to Making Hall. Others were returning with wool advanced by
Benjamin Greave, whilst yet more were journeying to and from the
fulling mill.

Anne walked down the slope, crossed the stream by a stone bridge
(worn like an old tooth after a lifetime's chewing by the traffic that
had passed over it) and she climbed the steep hill to Making Hall,
hanging above her like a fortress. It had been built during Civil War
days, when despite burnings and destruction the clothiers sensed a
better time for tradesmen coming with Oliver Cromwell. Three huge
broad barns stood around it, and there was a clutter of well-made
outbuildings. The walls of the enclosures here were more grand than
anything that could have been built by an ordinary farmer and were
heavily capped with semi-circular stones, the gateposts thick, proud,
and carved in a herringbone pattern, with globes on the tops of them.

Anne entered beneath a great archway into a crowded paved yard
ringing with the noises of hooves, iron cartwheels and shouts, whilst
over it hung a pungent smell of dyes, wet wool, yarns and fleeces.
Weavers who had brought their 'pieces' (but who today would rather
be scything their hay) were grumbling about having to take so much
trouble making the fine worsteds that Benjamin Greave wanted now,
when for centuries they had got by through weaving rough kersey-
cloth. A couple of wool-combers had left the furnace-side in their

overheated outhouse, just to come out and argue (as travelling combers notoriously would); they were also flirting with the weavers'
wives and daughters, a small crowd of whom had gathered around
the door waiting to take home the combed wool and spin it. The aloof
Anne Wylde was a gift to them as they looked for sport on a summer's
day. Noting the fine blue shalloon wool of her dress, and the laundered
white of her apron, it seemed to them that though she entered as a
servant yet she was not of that class – perhaps she was some rich
daughter playing at being a simple girl!

They laughed whilst Anne climbed a flight of stone stairs to a
kitchen, the door of which had been left open for the summer air to
dry up the damp. She entered a room that was larger and loftier even
than Lady Well church, with sun and firelight glittering on pewter and
brass, high passageways leading off it, and many female servants busy.
Mechanical contraptions – gears and pulleys – turned meat against
the huge fireplace, before which some expensive, young-man's linen
underwear was drying. Rows of kitchen implements shone against the
walls, and a large clock was placed in an important position. There
were pies being baked, smoke curling around the shelves, cats hissing
and screeching over bones, a girl spreading a mop over the flagstones,
and other maids arguing and gossiping.

But the first thing that Anne noticed properly was that here she did
not need to stoop. Secondly she observed that the kitchen had been
built over a well and she thought, with relief, that on dark rainy nights
she would no longer have to cross a yard to get water.

(2)

Making Hall, everywhere apart from the kitchen, was a male house, and its dark rooms and passageways created like a ship under the weight of their transactions. The place smelled of tobacco, alcohol, snuff, ledgers and money. The talk was of money, trade, weather and the woollen industries of foreign countries. If God was mentioned he seemed but another prosperous clothier, His interest being in trade and His Heaven being a great 'piece-hall' where the finest materials were bought and sold. The visitors were male also: throughout the summer there was a stream of bankers, clerks and merchants from Holland, Russia or Spain. They came after difficult journeys and expected to be given splendid dinners eaten with silver implements and served by liveried lackeys. Much of the wealth of the countryside was gobbled into the maw of Making Hall. Whole flocks of sheep and geese were swallowed; carts laden with pots of honey; trout, salmon and pike; strawberries coddled to ripen in early summer; and presents from abroad sent ahead of the visitors.

But Benjamin Greave offered soups, oatcakes, boiled nettles and roughly-hacked sides of beef or mutton, to be eaten out of wooden platters at one end of a huge oak table, with the servants at the other; who were dressed in the same modest but good kersey-woollens (hidden under aprons of leather or cotton) as their masters; and who simply rose with their mouths full of their own food to bring further dishes. There was no elegance, and the house was without privacy. Foreign merchants, the Greave family, their servants, artisans and workmen, were thrown together promiscuously for eating, sleeping, conversation and entertainment.

One day a visitor – coming for the first time and badly (that is, foppishly) dressed for this part of the country – raised his white lace cuffs to save them from being touched by an ill-shaped, heavy lump of coarse bread and inquired, disdainfully, 'What ... is ... that?'

'A cake!' Benjamin Greave shouted back, dragging the 'a' so that it sounded like the bleat of a sheep. His visitor did not understand, so, 'An oat c-a-a-a-y-k' the clothier repeated, loud, impatient and grumpy. (He knew that what the man wanted was his cloth, which was the best in the world.) 'It's what we eat!'

Pause, and only the sound of the stranger swelling his chest. Greave thought his customer a fool and the customer considered Benjamin an animal. (In other words: this was a quite usual meeting between the clothier and the purchasers of his cloth.)

'The Duke of Buckingham' (the visitor pronounced it 'Back-ingham') 'deigning to call upon an inn at Marlborough, required the utmost decorum, all the servants to be in his own livery, though it was but an overnight stay. And he paid the bill.'

'Then the man had more money than sense!' Greave was small but made up for it by barking in a dry, commanding voice, like a dissenting preacher who behaves always as if he is in the pulpit: to shout was his normal voice, even for intimacies. 'He couldn't have worked hard for what he had. It would have been better for him to spend time thinking on Eternity. Or at least on a thought for 'ow we poor folk have to manage in t'North.'

So, without feeling (except for fine woollens), Benjamin Greave shovelled into his mouth oatcakes, blood puddings, stewed nettles, choice dandelions from the garden, or oranges from Italy. All vanished untasted through those thin pale voracious lips, as into the mouth of a pike.

The spectacle distracted his son Oliver, a man of twenty-four compelled to live here because he was a widower and had a sickly daughter to care for. He would, by holding a strawberry delicately in his mouth for a moment and melting the cream off with his tongue, try to show that life was not intended for the greedy swallowing of everything in sight.

'I've bought Upper Spout this week!' Benjamin Greave yelled at his son. (Ignoring his sensitive feelings, as usual.) 'I told 'em it was poisoned water up there and they believed me! They're fools and gobslutches at Spout, and one of them – though he's nowt but a weaver like the rest of us – has, so I believe, been reading a book. Novels and political philosophy'll be the ruin of us. Anyway, I was telling you 'bout the water. There's sulphur in t'spring! It's the best cure there is in these parts, they tell me. We'll have ladies coming from all over to take their baths in it, and we'll be rich as dukes afore we die! There's no more than one or two gaps in our possessions at that end of the valley now. I plan to shift the cottagers by building them better places up the moor over a pump, so they can wash their cloth without going out of doors. That should please them! Give them more time for reading seditious volumes, though!'

Possessions became merely acres written into deeds, whilst gifts were locked in cupboards by the housekeeper. Though so much silver, plate, linen and lace was never used but only regularly counted, though so many rooms were permanently fastened and those that were open lacking the continuous change that a mistress brings, with fresh flowers, pictures, new curtains, or a shifting around of the furniture, yet it was not that the two widowers who were its masters had such mean temperaments. It was because for them both the place was the shell of past lives. It was a dried-up womb without female blood pulsing through it – leathery and colourless.

Oliver Greave had from childhood been open-hearted, restless, desiring and inquisitive. He was fond of drawing; he learnt the fiddle, had written songs and verses from an early age. But his composing came to a pause when his father sent him to the grammar school (to learn just sufficient spelling and arithmetic to save him from being cheated by lawyers) and where the Reverend Doubtfire fought with birch and lexicon to impose dead Latin Grammar upon the chaotic stream of Anglo-Saxon that tumbled through the mouths of tradesmen's sons. Doubtfire taught that only the classical languages were perfect and that Oliver's native tongue was a midden, a muck-heap, of polluted heathen speech. Whilst it had always seemed to Oliver that the people of his own background had a lot to express, in their bitter, comical, abbreviated fashion, now he learnt that he had come out of a silence with, so far as elegant modes of expression were concerned, 'no more language than grunts in a farmyard', just like those of their own animals, and shouts across the moor. In their speech, 'Greece' meant *stairs*, an ant was a 'pissmole', a 'bandyhewitt' was the word for any man's *canine companion* or *fidus Achates*, 'beleakins' or 'farrantly dame' was the complimentary diminutive address for a lady, 'off-cumbling' was a stranger or indeed anything strange, 'laikin' was both to laze or to write poetry; and a 'basting' was the beating that a 'gobslutch', or dunce, got (or rather, *received*) for laikin instead of struggling with the off-cumbling language under the tutelage of his ecclesiastical vocabularian, orthoepist and orthographer, the Reverend Doubtfire.

Though Oliver at first got hottering mad with it, he struggled until in the end he fell in love with Hellas, and instead of laikin with old men, gobslutches and fiddlers, he spent time mooning over Thucydides or the ancient myths, gazing at and drawing maps of the classical lands or dreamily playing in puddles by the stream where he constructed archipelagos modelled on the Isles of Greece.

One day, some 'demon' (so Benjamin Greave put it) inspired an ingratiating customer to give the boy a copy of Pausanias's guide to ancient Hellas. Through its engravings, pernickety as an old spinster's needlework, Oliver entered that dry brilliant land of sun-bleached temples upon headlands overlooking the glittering sea – his Eden of ineffable wisdom and proportion. Now the Yorkshire hills began to close him in, and he ached at the thought of the huge distance that separated him from Greece. He imagined that the local dark rocks were white Greek ones, and that the mist sometimes flooding the valley was Homer's sea ... 'wine-dark' though it was not, but the colour and texture of phlegm.

Whilst his son for hour after hour with his lexicon fenced his native speech and poetry in Latin Grammar, Benjamin Greave enclosed moor and marsh with stone walls and hedges of hawthorn; or he discussed with parsons and Methodists ways of disciplining and encompassing the barbaric natures of weavers. All were occupied, one way or another, with enclosures. With prisons for language, land and people.

Yet the similar crucifixions of the souls of father and son did not bring them together. Oliver's new words and languages which could not be used in 'normal' conversations lay between them, like icy plains without the warmth to fertilise spring growth.

When Oliver was thirteen and finding his half-literate father unbearable, Benjamin apprenticed him to Joshua Binns, a manufacturer successful enough to pay a subscription to *The Society For Prosecuting Felons*, and who possessed six looms – Benjamin thought the lad had better learn of the sweat, noise and dust out of which fortunes are made, even though he'd never need to practise weaving. (Oliver

Greave had received his Christian name in honour of Oliver Cromwell – the father of modern trade, and especially of opportunities for English clothiers.) So both at home and in his apprenticeship, Oliver overheard trade, and the work of its Industrious God, often discussed. He slowly realised how this man's world of woollens, and all other trade also, depended upon an empire supported by battlefields and slaves; by forests burned and ploughed, or savage tribes exterminated; and it repelled him. Yet repulsion made him listen harder, and come close to inspect it (as he had once sniffed at the leather bindings in Doubtfire's library). He was further disgusted. Then he ran off, into woods, fields, moors, or to scribbling in the back rooms of inns. A shy, gentle, uncertain boy, who was sometimes full of fun and sometimes tongue-tied.

Binns was soon declaring that the lad was the worst apprentice ever to have come his way, wasting hours writing those verses imitative of Pope, Dryden, Milton and Horace. All that saved Oliver from beatings and fines was the position of his father, with whom Binns sought an advantage and (whilst the great clothier looked with contempt over the rough kersey-cloths that satisfied Binn's ambition) lied to him, 'Why yes, Mr Greave, your son will make an excellent weaver!' During the rest of the time it was curses and threats – the truth being that Oliver was not only feckless himself, but his fiddle, dreams, wild talk and escapades influenced the other apprentices; he flung open a magical door in a dark prison for them.

They were, in fact, locked in a dormitory. Oliver found how to break out. Taking his violin he led the way to moorland inns where they spent the nights singing, dancing and, occasionally, fighting: though Oliver when sober had a quiet nature, yet if someone angered him when he was drunk he might well hit out viciously or throw bottles at the walls. Sometimes Oliver was still playing as he led over the moors at dawn; an eerie sound and sight in the grey-green twilight. During the day, Oliver's weariness exasperated the master. The lad's aristocratic distaste for weaving, and for all manufacture, expressed in scornful satires, jokes and couplets, also set Joshua Binns against him. Moreover, the mistress, Binn's dissatisfied wife, a large kind-hearted beauty who fed the apprentices beyond the weaver's generosity, further annoyed her husband by siding with Oliver because he was a good-looking entertaining boy who treated her gallantly and watchfully (as no doubt a poet behaved towards his muse).

At last Benjamin Greave understood what was going on. After their quarrel, Oliver one night crept finally out of his master's house. (Mistress Binns from then on would not speak to her useless husband, whose love-making was like the bundling into her of a goosedown pillow – though she rejected him less for this than for his more important impotence, his meanness.) Meanwhile the remaining apprentices, feeling sadly abandoned by the rich spirit who had dwelled amongst them, were bullied into becoming commonplace weavers.

For seven years, whilst the melons of Mistress Binns's full bosom heaved sorrowfully through those same silent nights in which Benjamin Greave tossed and turned in anxiety for the future of the turd-piles of his wealth, no one knew where Oliver had gone.

Oliver Greave had always felt (perhaps he was born with the feeling) that he was in the wrong place at the wrong time, in the wrong age and the wrong class, doing the wrong thing, with a destiny he could not escape, never satisfied, but driven by a secret nature not expressed; a conflict which made him think that if he was indoors he should be outside, or if he was enjoying the open air that he should be toiling in his study. Now he was maddened into searching for he-did-not-know-what over the moors. Occasionally Benjamin Greave received a letter (one so poetical and metaphorical that it made no reason or sense to him) from an inn, but Oliver would disappear before a messenger could be sent there. Occasionally he was briefly glimpsed in Lady Well, where he called for laudanum or a *rubbing bottle* to ease a toothache; finding also that it eased the deeper ache in his heart.

He left across the hills a legacy of village schools set up in barns and unused sheds to earn money by teaching children to write, fiddle, scan verses and long for a dream Hellas. Also a trail of infants fathered to console maidens for the loss of 'their' poet, after Oliver had grown tired of his occupations and of them. There was something about women that he could not face. Though he felt weak and humble before them, yet he did not believe that it was right to express it, and instead he set off across the wastes again. He was avoiding himself, and therefore found that he yearned for something though he did not

32

know what it was. When he heard hedge-preachers talk of vanished Edens, he felt that he understood what they meant.

But he did not comprehend why, when duties beckoned or even when things that he loved called, he would *flee*, for months or, as he was now doing, for several years. The more compellingly he felt himself addressed by his obligations, the more dilatory he was in obeying. He had not yet met anyone else who had this wayward characteristic, and he was confused and grieved by it. It was as if he was nursing himself in that womb of removed silence where poetry is nurtured, and to which both duty and happiness can be a threat. He was seeking that state in which a question might be raised from a mysterious source, the struggle to answer which is the stuff of poetry: one was as it were the warp, to the weft of the other.

Yet because he was such good value if in a laughing humour, and stayed capable of creating music and fun at those remote morose inns in return for his nights' lodging, they put up with him when he was so despondent that no kind word – no word at all – could be dragged out of him.

He was tormented by the struggle to articulate, in the iron mould of classical verse, his own complicated nature; and to bring to 'proper' speech the silence lying under the wounds of his ancestors – of dissenters whose tongues had been torn out, and of farmers' wives who had their bones broken for being 'witches'. Oliver's ambition was to make those who had been dumb for centuries, speak. He stared so deeply into the scars marking the history of his forebears that they turned into flowers: into pentameters and hexameters. The rhyming couplet, the muscular iambics leading majestically to the final syllable – these were life itself for Oliver.

But his workaday habit of exercising with words (or of 'flowery talking' as they called it) irritated tradesmen who were content with limited language – who were more than content, were proud of their narrowness and regarded Oliver's sprinkling of sentences with Latin, Greek, or references to myth and legend, as worse than vanity: they thought he was deliberately trying to offend them. They begrudged him both words and experiences.

Oliver soon felt his natural heritage, especially that of local language, as an impediment to his ascent of Parnassus; whilst his grip high upon the cliffs of Poesy separated him from all below. He could go neither up nor down, and yet must choose whether to soar or to fall.

He fell. When he met Zillah he was brought home at last to settle in marriage at Lower Laithes, a house his glad father built near Makings. It was Zillah's prettiness and her expensive fashions that captivated him. From his marriage onwards Oliver's days were spent in his father's trade, earning to provide for his wife, whilst his muse was in hiding somewhere up on the moors, and his fiddle was secreted in a cupboard because he could not bear its reproach, asking to be played. The engine that drove Oliver's true nature was a desire for wider experience, and greater means of expressing it. (For him, language was synonymous with experience, and using words was the same thing as going to foreign countries.) But now the engine was choked of fuel and his gay character dimmed.

A daughter was born, who was christened 'Betty'. Oliver doted upon her, in a way that is common amongst fathers; he liked to talk of the silkiness of her hair, the blueness of her eyes and so forth, at inns and parties, whilst leaving the practical care of her in the hands of nurses. Soon, Zillah died of a consumption. Oliver returned, in his dispirited state, not to wildness and wandering but to Makings, although also to writing verses; whilst continuing to search for the physical embodiment of that shadowy yet certain figure who always haunted him, seeming to hide behind the twigs of the wood or on the moors: his muse. It was his devotion to the unspoken woman of his imagination that made him appear, in the eyes of others, a flaccid, ineffective and indecisive man: though he was, in fact, merely an absorbed one.

Since childhood he had shown an extreme curiosity about women. He was fascinated by their scents, as of banks of different flowers; by their movements and their mysteries, their haughtiness and humility. But the only women at Makings were servants and these, even the young girls, showed a hard, dry, deliberate, take-it-or-leave-it, blunt manner. Most of these females had been in the one employment for so long that they even menstruated at the same time, as they say long-immured nuns do.

(Oliver had seen them washing their monthly cloths together in the Making stream: the water already arrived a dark brown colour out of the moorland peat, and at certain times it left the Hall the colour of

34

dried blood. Thus enriched, it ran downhill to feed the weavers' starved lands in the lower part of the valley, just as the male Greaveses fed their bellies with trade.)

In this company, Oliver's whole being ached for one whom he had never met. He imagined her so strongly and tantalisingly, that often he was sure she must be lingering behind those bushes, or that he would meet her beyond the next turn in the street.

One day Oliver glimpsed across a yard at Makings a tall dark girl with wild snake-like hair protruding from her cap. She was singing, her skirts tucked up for work so that they added volume to her hips and displayed her ankles. The poet instantly felt his inside turn to water. A cascade of pleasure ran through him, swept everything else away and left him clean. His eyes doted on her movements and the shifts of her dress, his back stiffened, his penis stirred and his ears took in the excitement and unbearable longing for some ancient past, or mystery.

The spontaneous notes seemed to surprise the girl herself as they came into her mouth. She sang as a lark, robin or thrush does in winter sunshine, when it amazes itself with a scrap of exquisite melody – the music opened moist and sensual, as a woman before a man she loves (so the poetical Oliver Greave pictured it), or as a dewy rose before the sun. (Though the tune would have seemed 'impolite' to most of his circle, and the words of the ballad would have shocked members of established and dissenting churches alike.)

His attention stopped her singing and she looked at him.

'However did you come to our establishment?' he asked, apparently mildly, because of the severe self-control he was practising.

As he was one of the masters, Anne Wylde defended herself by adopting vulgar speech and delivering it coarsely. 'I come straight up Swine's Lane, sir, same as everybody else does. I come from Lady Well on Lammas Day.' With a modesty not shown whilst she sang, she sagged her shoulders so as not to embarrass him with her height.

'Swine's Lane? Which is that?' he teased her, amused at her 'rude simplicity'.

'Straight up from th'mill.'

'I have heard it named more poetically "Swaine's Lane".'

She now wore the innocent face that she often used to disguise her cleverness. 'I think we common folk call it "Swine's" because it is so filthy and dirty, sir.'

Though he bantered plainly, as her patron and her master, yet from this moment Oliver was in reality her servant. His attention became as helplessly fixed upon this girl as a prisoner's is on the window of his cell at dawn. It was in an instant revealed to him that every beautiful freedom that gave meaning to life lay through her.

Anne Wylde was never sure whether a new person would turn out to be a friend or a persecutor; whether, or when, he would change from one to the other; and she was always uncertain in discourse whether she was unintentionally offending against a God whom she did not understand. Instead of speaking much, she looked searchingly into a face that stared like a child's in wonder, yet wasn't absorbing the outside world. For an instant his eyes would focus brightly, like an ignited candle, and then would turn inward, snuffed; his lips having for a moment trembled with eagerness for some new thought or opportunity, then become still and unexpectant. He dressed with some vanity, she noticed – silk cravat, bright waistcoat, cutaway jacket of fine bay wool. Following the fashion of republicans and radicals, he did not wear a wig, but his thick hair was carefully dressed for an appearance of wildness. So evidently he did have some show to make to the world. Anne guessed that he had been many times disappointed in converse, which was why his speech was mannered and stiff. She saw that there was something else on his mind, and that it was inexpressible. She decided that he was a gentleman (despite his rude father). A little bit weak, because of the refinement of his feelings, and he could never truly become a tradesman. But it was a weakness she found attractive, just as many girls did: he appeared helpless and in need of women, and was smaller than herself. She entertained for him some of that tenderness that she gave to frail wild creatures. Yet he also had something powerful. He showed both the capacity and the weakness (though Anne did not realise this was what she was looking for) to sacrifice himself for her.

Oliver Greave still took museful ramblings around the countryside – especially when business should have been transacted, or when worldly men called. Nature was for Oliver (as for many sensitive men) wholly feminine; in his case she was also identified or confused with that mental mistress to whom he was devoted. He had always sensed the presence of the goddess of Nature. (Parallel to that vision of the other one: She who especially belonged to himself, the secret one; she whom he was bound to meet one day in the street. Or were they both the same person?) But he had wasted much of his life, for the sake of the conveniences of trade, pretending that She was not there; She had to be ignored, for if She distracted his thoughts, then huge volumes of trade were lost and the whole valley suffered. So her lineaments became as tarnished and faded as those of Saint Uncumber in Lady Well church. Whilst at other times – on his rambles, or when he stared out through a porchway at the moors – the femininity of nature's forms overwhelmed him. For Oliver, She was softly-rounded hills, trees exploding with green, and other pregnant forms. Tempting rustlings, lithe and liquid movements; and the inspirer of exclamations from his inner voice that could only have been duplicated by raptures addressed, if ever he became forgetful of himself through passion, to an actual woman.

So what loneliness he endured on returning to Makings, where his father and acquaintances (Benjamin had none to describe as 'friends') saw Nature as a different kind of female – as man's handmaiden; they measured Her as yards and acres, yields and prices, obstructer or beneficial servant of 'progress'.

One day Oliver watched a young woman removing stones out of his father's enclosure. She was bent under the boulders like a straining ox; a beauty was turned, by a stone, ugly and peasant-like. Oliver was detachedly delighted by her classical profile, her statuesque posture, and for a moment wanted to sketch her or commit her to memory for his verses. But then a second thought came: those with such classical form had lost their appeal before the unconventional appearance of that servant-girl in his father's house, who seemed to be his Nature-Muse Herself.

By such revelations Oliver realised that he was in thrall. For so many years since the death of Zillah there had been in his heart a blank feeling upon the throne of happiness. But Anne Wylde had the effect of a powerful icon in a dim church. She transformed him from an unowned, unwanted wanderer in the wilderness into a worshipper and slave, but one whose dependency brought a happiness and stea-diness that had been unimaginable in his previous freedom. She was hardly a real person to him, since he knew so little of her. And his instinct kept her an inscrutable icon. If he had faced her it would have sent ripples across the mirror-surface of that still pool of idealised womanhood, in which Oliver was in fact staring at himself. But of course he didn't recognise the image. She was the looking-glass which reflected his deepest hidden self; she was that mirror of fairy-tales which answers riddles, if you ask the right ones, and if you can understand the inscrutable answers.

He had glimpsed the one love of his life. He was standing before the open temple, on the walls of which his visions were painted. He did not dare to hope, for surely the girl must have a sweetheart in Lady Well. Yet she had placed a glow over nature, such as he had read of amongst the most modern poets. Encouraged by his reading and by his image of her, for a time Oliver Greave sought no company other than landscape and his own thoughts.

One evening sitting amongst his books and drafts of poems before the fire, smoking his pipe and drinking common ale in a little room where he went to be alone (to the bafflement of his father), Oliver found himself staring at the cupboard where his fiddle had been entombed for so long and he was moved to root it out. It lay under discarded weaving patterns, clay pipes and waistcoats, buried in a black case like a child in a coffin. He raised it lovingly, blew the dust off, and opened it; he had almost forgotten its once-so-familiar pattern of scratches and stains, acquired at many inns and farm kitchens. Delicately he took out the corpse, which was as light as a butterfly, ran his fingers over the mellow brown body, tightened strings, lifted the bow and tried a few notes, tensed the strings again and in rapture played an air.

The housekeeper, Patience Helliwell, using the excuse of serving beer, interrupted to find out what was happening.

'You have come to help renew my devotions at the shrine of Bacchus!' Oliver remarked.

Patience always had a bedraggled, despised look. It was as if someone had recently thrown a bucket of water over her. She was short, dumpy, whiskery, with heavy boots, other mannish clothes, a male manner and a Methodistical accounting memory watchful as the big kitchen clock, ticking with the number of silver spoons and pewter dishes that were locked away. Above all else she disliked fiddle tunes. And she hardly understood a word of her master's 'flowery nonsense' (though accepting it, as appropriate to one of his superior class). So she did not answer him.

'Who is the new servant-girl, Miss Helliwell?' Oliver asked, more severely, but still playing. She looked at him shrewdly, wondering how to get him to tell more than he intended. 'The tall dark-haired girl,' he added.

Patience Helliwell pretended that she couldn't hear because of the 'noise' of the fiddle. Oliver put it down.

'The crazy one with a mad look and a terrible cough?' Patience answered. 'It'll be Mary Ingham, she's from such a poor cot! I've many times had girls who've barked like that. It is the Lord knocking on her chest as on a door and she'll not be absent from Him for long.'

'No, it's not her! The one I saw looked particularly healthy.'

'Are you meaning Jane Oddy? The young widow?'

'Oh no, she can't be a widow! She is as fresh and untouched as an apple coming into ripeness on a branch.'

'Her father a mason? I hope it's not Anne Wylde you're carried away with – a terrible witch. They used to throw stones at her for her sins in Lady Well.'

'This one has a look of complete innocence and beauty ...'

Patience could not think what had happened to make him so light-hearted and merry. 'Then it cannot be Anne Wylde! Mr Greave, sir, being a poet you do not understand the schemes that young women in need of prospects get up to.'

'Why do they call her, "The Hawthorn Goddess"?'

'That girl is of the Devil's brood and bound most certainly for Hell! We common folk say that every few generations one like her is born out of the sins collected amongst our forefathers – as flies are born out of filth. It is a purging or bloodletting that we must suffer, for one like her to be born. A temptress – she shall like Jezebel be eaten by the dogs. You must pray, pray, pray to the Lord for strength to snatch your eyes off, for she has bewitched you!'

'Ah, Miss Helliwell, I am confined to these moors as Prometheus chained to his rock, torn by the eagles of learning and poetry. What can I do for sport?'

The housekeeper looked puzzled. 'Sir, you are in need of a true wife to care for you ... not Anne Wylde. Look for some Godfearing woman to be a helpmate for Betty and yourself. Turn your mind that way. As we say ... "Only get thy spindle and thy distaff ready, and God will send the flax"!'

(3)

One rainy dark autumn day, when the moorland was blotted out in a mist of seething porridge and when candles were lit indoors, Oliver met Anne Wylde again. She was cleaning a passageway and he could not avoid her, though now his feelings made him nervous. Besides which, his daughter Betty was clinging to her skirts, and the warm association that had developed between these two demanded that the father remark upon it.

He delicately fondled Betty's head. He often found that to touch the hair and skin of infants revived his joy, his sensitivity, his desire – in a word, his belief in the world. After a moment, the child, sensing perhaps an incipient, exclusive conspiracy between the two adults, skipped off into the shadows of Makings, which were so familiar to her, leaving the young clothier and the girl facing one another.

'Do you like it at Makings, Anne Wylde?' Oliver asked at last.

'It's somewhere to be.'

He pulled back his shoulders. 'I hear they were ganging up on you back home.'

Oliver found himself smiling with the open countenance that he had not shown for years. One moment later, these two near-strangers were magically extracting laughter out of each other. It was as if she was drawing glittering water out of an overgrown well.

He was carrying a leather-bound folio in which were mounted duplicates of the sample-sheets given to agents to sell the Greaves' cloth, and, 'Would you like to see our wool patterns?' he asked her.

All about Makings there were little desks for clerks to scribble at. Oliver rested the volume on one of them and lit the candle that waited there. (Clerks were always careful about such things as candles, quills and tidy account books.) The girl came close to his side, her face as waxy as the taper in its wavering light. Her gown (of blue stuff, smelling of dampness; she must have been in the yard), brushed his sleeve. Their faces were close. As he opened the book, she placed her

41

hand upon it and he noticed how large were her palm, fingers and knuckles; and also a curious red line around her wrist, as if she had been wearing a too-tight chain.

Shaking because of her proximity, Oliver forced himself to turn pages and explain patterns in a matter-of-fact way, just as he would to a client.

Meanwhile, Anne's breath was taken away by the beauty of the samples. Gems of brilliant dyes. Strips of glowing red, blue, orange, chrome yellow, deep purple, velvet green. Beyond the window were the familiar tones and colours of the landscape – soft grey-greens and browns melting in the rain. But here, distilled out of its herbs, heather and roots, did she walk through some garden of brilliant flowers? There were strips of 'amens' – woollens embossed with minute suns, flowers, or with geometric designs like formal summer gardens. One page showed a dozen shades of mauves, purples and blues mixed with yellow, like gorse flowers amongst heather on the Yorkshire hillsides. The first pages were of old-fashioned kersey-cloths – strips of plain colour so heavily fulled that they had lost the nature of woven things and had a nap on them like moss. Next were the new callimancoes, delighting with the delicate grain of their threads and so closely woven that this woollen was like silk. Most beautiful of all, there followed the materials worked in small detail with stripes and patterns in many colours; with minute hearts, leaves, flowers and what looked like clumps of trees. Then came pages of tiny samples forming together the rich delicate beauty of a moth's or butterfly's wing. Around these were fine sepia engravings of ships, anchors, mermaids, and of Greek temples, which Oliver had designed.

Affected by Anne's breathless mood, he handled the pages in greater reverence and silence, as if turning a holy book in a monastery. He would never have thought that a volume dedicated to trade could be so transformed merely because of her attention to it. Time was suddenly passing in ecstacy and at great speed. Both wanted to grasp and slow down the minutes, but were also impatient for the next stage of happiness to arrive.

Anne Wylde was overcome. She could not believe that the dour weavers who threw stones at her and went about with clenched teeth and bowed shoulders, the postures of defending themselves from the malevolence of man and weather, could from their shuttered hearts, in their dark stinking noisy cottages, produce such beautiful things. They were like the local stone, the 'millstone grit'; dark and rough outside, but when you broke it open, it was bright gold. And Oliver Greave in her eyes appeared to be the mastermind of a great art.

From dealing with merchants who did not find it in their interest to praise the cloth that they bought, he had forgotten that it could inspire such warmth. He was dazzled and amazed. 'Would you like to look into our barns and warehouses?' he asked.

So there they suddenly were, the two of them, with the rain singing for them in the yard – a soft hum as if a hundred spinners were working. The cobblestones shone, polished by hooves and carts, whilst the wet made the walls dark purple. Further away the weather was rougher. Clouds were torn off the valley rim like ragged fleeces upon a fence. They evaporated, re-formed, and swept away in torn screens, or looking like the underbellies of sheep. To ease their intense feeling, Anne broke into a run. Leading merrily, she splashed in the puddles. Reaching the porch of the barn, they together shook off the rain drops, as two birds on a branch.

They went into the building. It was a vast shadowy cathedral with a cart-road down its centre and ponderous arches letting the light in at either end. The rattle of carts and echoes of voices were muffled in the huge bales of finished cloth, where servants and weavers sifted through the multitude of alleyways. They passed a Dutchman with a clerk, thoughtfully fingering samples. The next gentleman was Russian. Oliver read off the names on the bales, tapping each with pride but otherwise, Anne thought, unfeelingly, having now come back to earth and trade. 'Everlastings. Kerseys. Grograms. Callimancoes. Moreens . . .'

'I can read for myself, Mr Greave! My father taught me.'

'I didn't mean to offend you – I know that you are educated. Why don't you want to make something of yourself? I am surprised that you are not ambitious.'

'In Lady Well they believe there is a Great White Cow upon the moors and that whoever meets her will be fed with an endless fountain of milk. I think that life is too sweet to spoil it with foolish longings, Mr Greave. I am mostly well-off where I am, though I didn't like coming here at first – I suppose it's the same for gentlefolk when they're sent to university?'

'I've never been away, though I've travelled about our own hills in a period of my youth when I was ...' He paused. 'My father thought the grammar school in Lady Well a good enough grounding in the business he supposed I was meant for. But I am glad that I learnt Greek and Latin there, he continued.'

'You don't sound happy about being confined at Makings.'

'Kitchens and passageways packed with artisans and weavers in unwashed stinking kersey-cloths! Evenings with Patience Helliwell conducting a howling meeting for Methodists in the kitchen! Yards and sheds wi' greasy pieces bleached in vats of piss!'

'A place where you cannot move for the gifts that folk send,' laughed Anne.

'Worst òf all I lack the privacy for my own thoughts – which my father does not understand at all. What I enjoy about Yorkshire, Anne, is the wind on the hills, the scent of heather in my nostrils, and the crack around the fire at a moorland inn. But I also wish sometimes to travel to the places our cloth goes to. Most of all I would like to go to the cradle of our civilisation, Hellas, where the sunlight shines in endless calm on time-worn monuments and all men are civilised.'

This was a strange way to talk, Anne thought. It was as if she was reading a novel. 'You are a poet, aren't you, Mr Greave?' she suggested.

Oliver realised that she asked this because he was being pompous, with 'flowery talking'. He looked crestfallen, the corners of his mouth turned down, dimpled. But this too charmed her – he could do nothing wrong.

'To what school of verse do you belong?' she asked, to put him at his ease.

'Schools of poetry! So you've heard about them, have you? For real poets there's no such thing, despite what is said by writers on the art. It's only dead ones who are herded into "schools". In real life there's just people like me struggling with the unkind climate of Yorkshire and its even unkinder philistines. The true poets, the real makers, are always alone, they are the victims of the muse to whom they must be sacrificed in love, as Adonis to Venus or Hippolytus to Artemis – these myths are parables of poetic creation! Tim Bobbin says that God nowadays is only on the side of clothiers, and that he curses all true poets.'

44

'Who's Tim Bobbin?'

'My old friend and a true maker, in love with the muse. His real name is John Collier. He's the son of a parson suddenly struck blind as Homer, lost his living and could not send his son to Cambridge, but apprenticed him to weaving, where we first met side-by-side on the hard wooden bench of a loom. His verses are in the Aristophanic vein, satirical-comical by way of analogies to the animal kingdom. His blackbird is a magistrate, his goose a parson. So he must flee about the hills with a pack of angry worthies at his heels. When he is not running before these persecutors, he labours unhappily as a schoolmaster. Tim admires his native speech best, deeming the common language of men and women to be also that of the muse, and so for the use of future poets he has compiled a dictionary of our local words, stating whether their origin is Anglo-Saxon, Belgic, French or Teutonic. I'll tell you properly about him some other time – I hope you don't believe I am being enthusiastic.'

Anne noticed that when Oliver spoke about poetry he became animated, as if a burden had been lifted. 'Say me some of your verses then,' she demanded.

'Now from her chamber Chloe smiling comes
Like summer's empress decked with airy ...'

'Plums!' Anne instantly felt sorry for having made fun.

'... plumes!
The Cyprian goddess whose transporting charms
Calms furious Mars when in her snowy arms ...'

'That's Aphrodite,' Anne remarked. 'My father taught me a lot of things,' she added, for the knowledge possessed by one as humble as herself needed explaining.

'Showed no such beauty when for golden fruit
Juno and Pallas did with her dispute.'

'What admirable verses.'

45

Because of poetry, their conversation had run to an embarrassing halt. 'Why do you make so many kinds of cloth?' Anne asked.

Oliver now spoke dully – as one who has been running a race afterwards walks drearily. 'Father and me, we have to find new ways to keep the weavers occupied and interested lest they desert for the new manufactories. You have seen the new buildings erected along the river? There is a lot of discontent today, father gets very upset about it. He feels sick after dinner and I think he's decided to invest in the Americas. When I was a boy the weavers were very satisfied with what they had. They were forever able to build on to their houses and put in new looms with the money gained from us. But now they send their girls into manufactory sheds, with which the home-workers cannot compete. My father does his best to keep things in the old way, which benefitted every weaver under his care. He keeps trying out new kinds of cloth so as they'll think that something fresh will make them prosperous again. But I do not think he will succeed. I think he'll have to go and profit out of the black folk from Africa. Or invest in a ship bringing sugar from Cuba. Or in the East India Company, who anyway take our cloth ...'

'Sometimes I lie in bed and try to imagine Africa. All that jungle, and no God. Perhaps the negroes are lucky.'

'But they suffer badly. They need our missionaries.'

'Other folk suffer, too – because of their souls, which black men do not have, the Parson says. It isn't missionaries they need. I think they are luckier than us if they are out of the prying eyes of God. Women don't have souls either, Mr Doubtfire tells us. We are formed to be man's servants, out of Adam's rib. If most men are free, why cannot women be so, too? But I think if we are slaves it is because of our natures, so I could never be turned into one.'

'What seditious talk, Anne Wylde!'

Walking the alleyways amongst funereal shadows and oily smells of wool Anne noticed that the labels on the cloth were enscrolled like tombstones, and that in fact many were called after those in the Greave family who had died. An 'everlasting' bore the name of Oliver's mother, and a 'flowered amen' that of his dead wife Zillah.

'You must be sad for your wife who died so young, Mr Greave?'

Oliver remembered how he had held Zillah whilst she coughed, the bark echoing in her chest like a small animal stirring in a deep box or burrow. His eyes glistened wetly. 'She was but nineteen and we had only two years of married life. And one sickly child.'

'I'm sure that one day you'll not be melancholy.'

'I don't think so. I *always* feel that I am in mourning, yet I do not think it is entirely for Zillah, since I experienced it even before I met her. I have always felt it. I think it has something to do with the age and the place in which we live. As if we have lost something that was there in the past. That is why so many people are melancholic these days. Only last week a carpenter in Lady Well simply walked himself to death upon the moors. He had always been melancholic, and brooded over the literature of the subject – Young's "Night Thoughts" and the rest. A farmer at a lonely cot murdered his wife and children and then he hung himself. Such things are happening all the time in our district. Our housekeeper tells me one can only be happy from "knowledge of sin and redemption" which has to be daily sought for fresh sins, but I don't think such a carry-on would suit me.'

'I haven't noticed that Methodists are so joyful. They have tormented souls. I've seen bands of them about the countryside or preaching by our church wall and coming to the kitchen here. Happy folk leave others alone to enjoy *their* pleasures. But I don't think I could ever not be happy. If I was one of your manufactory spinners or your black slaves I would find ways. Mr Greave, I was told that you too used to be a jolly person, always playing your fiddle. They say in the kitchen that you were performing some sinful airs the other night!' Anne made his face break once more into laughter.

But they were interrupted by Benjamin Greave entering at the far end of the building. He was accompanied by a tall young man in a cavalry officer's uniform which, amongst the subdued colours of the barn lit only by the grey rainy light, was a vision of amazing magnificence: white woollen trousers tucked into polished cavalry boots, sword and spurs glinting, and a cockaded hat exhibiting the white death's-head of the 27th Light Dragoons. The wearer of this costume moved as carefully as a cat so as not to be touched by the oily bales belonging to the clothier. His affected indifference showed that he was used to making an impression. He was indifferent to Old Man Greave, and also to the poet who could not keep from ogling. Anne keenly observed that Captain Horsfall had straight-looking handsome eyes, but a spoilt slack mouth – a contradiction expressing to her that

47

he was used to having others provide for him, and was not aware of difficulties in life. Yet she could not help but be stirred by the magnificent bold sight of this Apollo, all his colours glowing like the sun.

'The greatest benefits and wealth of civilisation come from mutual trade!' Benjamin Greave shouted in his usual hard dry voice, as if his listener was on the far side of a moor.

'But you need us warriors and seamen to give you the advantage in the bargain, my friend.' The officer spoke quietly and was courteous because he wanted a loan from the old fellow.

'Nay, an exchange benefits both sides.'

'Though we give trinkets to an African king in return for all that he has?' The soldier laughed. 'I think we must force such exchanges upon them by keeping them ignorant through our strength of arms, otherwise what will happen to our wealth and our civilisation?'

Benjamin Greave was puzzled by the argument of his travelled and educated acquaintance. He scratched at his small, bony, scampily-haired head. 'However it is, if your fellows command sailors who wear low-priced kerseys I can send them from twelve pence a yard, or the equivalent in blacks from Africa. But I'm bound to tell you I love worsteds best!'

Oliver had heard this type of conversation before, before, before, and how it repelled him! He noticed again with what delicate feeling his father handled pieces of cloth, but was bluntly insensitive to everything else: which Oliver could not comprehend, for he himself followed the Renaissance ideal, that perfection in one thing made for a wholesome perfection in everything else. Yet despite his criticisms, when his father was within hearing Oliver's tone became like his.

'These kerseys are for Christ's Hospital, Miss Wylde. We send t'Amsterdam, Rotterdam, Utrecht, Antwerp and Bremen. Father and I have managed thirty thousand poundsworth of trade this year, all woven in our valley. This is soldiers' cloth for Saint Petersburg. In one year we have sent them a thousand bales. We post the same to France, Prussia, Holland and Spain – there is so much fighting and growth in their armies on the Continent that they go through a deal of cloth, which turns out very good for Yorkshire! We make enough to be spoilt by both sides in their wars; and we don't leave our customers, when they have finished with our woollens, to lie useless on their foreign battlefields, Miss Wylde. You must have noticed the fine grass we grow? We're bringing their bones home to fertilise our enclosures – cartloads over the sea through Hull in exchange for our woollens. Even if peace comes, I think we'll survive the inevitable recession.'

Oliver was no longer true to himself, instead he was hiding behind the opinions of a commonplace tradesman. This inspired not anger, contempt, or impatience in Anne Wylde, but tenderness for him. Yet because Mr Greave had come up, Anne, knowing her place, turned aside. Before her was a bale of fine red material, its rich colour glowing like glass in the church window. She thought of all the young manly chests, like the one of the soldier before her now, that it would cover, then she imagined the cloth spoiled and muddy on a battlefield, and the vision was so ghastly that she could not bear it. She winced so that the captain suggested to the clothier that perhaps she was being overcome by a witch-fit.

As a way to indicate that the girl was not worth much attention, the officer shook and flicked the rain daintily off himself. Dismissing the rain was a metaphor that he expected Anne Wylde to appreciate. Benjamin Greave on the other hand let the water soak down to his feet – in his shaggy clothes he was as indifferent to it as sheep are in a field. Anne Wylde saw all the difference between them expressed in this.

The father put his arm round his son. Oliver cringed away from the gesture, resentful of being spoilt – of his father's blindness towards his failings as well as to his talents.

Benjamin Greave noticed how keenly the tall girl was taking this in and he gave her a glance which made Anne feel as though she had been hated by him all her life. It was not for her, merely. It was for the force that he sensed was poised beyond her: he recognised one of those women who appear before us as messengers out of our own deepest fears.

Was Oliver Greave blind to all this? Blind as poets traditionally are? For he announced, blithely, 'Father, this is Anne Wylde. She is a girl educated well above her present station.'

Benjamin cut his son with a long stare – as when he confronted a competitor, 'eyeball to eyeball'. Then, totally ignoring what had been said, 'Captain 'Orsfall is kind enough to take an interest in our making and to further it through his regimental influence abroad,' he snapped back.

'Father, I'd like you to take notice of Anne Wylde ...'

Benjamin Greave, seeing there was no way out but to confront the matter, gripped Anne's forearm. (How tightly he gripped things – ledgers, bales, a gate that stood in his way, the arm of a customer, or of a girl he might be about to hurry off to the witch-pond – as if in need of securing his grasp on the world!) 'You must be the madcap then? The one with books in her room? Do you know what they do with such girls, considering them no better than whores? I'd say you'd better burn them before it's you they come and set fire to! Before you preach about destroying wealth and property, you'd best give a thought to how it acts as a cement to the whole neighbourhood. And what will you have to replace it?'

'A six-foot wooden box is all we need in the end, sir.'

'Seven foot, in your case!' the Captain said.

So far Anne had been smiling, her nature stirring in admiration for his figure, but now her expression was wiped clear – she did not like this Horsfall, her father's patron.

'It's also beneficial to have something to leave to your heirs so that wealth might prosper in the future, thou impudent girl,' Greave continued.

'All books are not about destroying wealth. You are confusing me with my father's way of thinking.'

'Then you must be reading novels, that all offend against decency!'

'I must go back to my work, sir.'

Benjamin Greave watched her departure sullenly, Horsfall as if he would have liked to strike her (or something else violent), whilst Oliver was perplexed to see the joy, that had been gently flowering, cut down.

Benjamin Greave said, 'That girl is a spy! She's been seen with you today taking a great interest in our trade designs and patterns. For what reason does a girl speaking Latin better than a parson come here, my fool of a son? I'll send her back to Lady Well! They know what to do with her there and will soon throw her in the pond for being conspicuous.'

'If she leaves, I'll go the same day.'

Oliver flushed.

'You always were a rascal for roaming with women. The worst of 'em could easily make an ass of you! Forget the witch, and come and see the curiosity that Mr Horsfall has brought us from the Grecian Isles.'

Horsfall waved his arm, producing a flash and clatter of the metal variously about his person. 'It's nothing – merely a token of my friendship with our ambassador to Turkey.'

Whilst Benjamin Greave wanted to rush back to the house, Horsfall was aristocratically refusing to be hurried and he lingered, as if thinking of following the servant-girl. It was in fact he who in the first place had suggested to Greave that she be brought here, expecting her clashes with the old Presbyterian clothier to provide amusement. Waiting for Horsfall to catch them up, Benjamin Greave paused in the yard where the rain had now stopped and the weavers with their packhorses and pieces, the women with their yarns, the woolcombers from Somerset, Wiltshire and Norwich, now for Greave's benefit pretended to be busy. When the Captain joined him, the clothier shouted across the surrounding hills, and as if defying Nature Herself, 'Ever since she could walk and shriek, that one's been causing trouble in Lady Well, until I offered to the Vicar to find her a home!' (As usual with ideas, Benjamin Greave had forgotten that he himself was not the inventor.) 'A most generous kind benevolent offer I made, so I consider it; for all the worldly-wise were reminding me't brings misfortune into a home to tak' hawthorn into't. I am not a superstitious man, Mr 'Orsfall, and ours is reckoned to be a reasonable age, yet I find that now I'm doubting, for there might be some truth in their omens. 'Appen we do need charms and safeguards, even in our present state of reason. Captain – yon carving's a fair warning to 'em, depicting t'proper fate of such witches! I'll have it over my porch gable.'

For once Benjamin Greave avoided the kitchen door; though that was his usual entrance, even taking stylish guests that way – his principle being whenever possible to 'kill two birds with one stone', and route his journeys so that he could at the same time supervise his servants. That was the policy that turned a halfpenny into a penny! But not wanting to meet Anne Wylde again, he went through a small side-gate into the walled garden at the front of the house.

They reached the main porch. It was thick-walled and deep, giving the impression of a burrow safe from the weather. Benjamin pushed open the oak door and they were in a passageway lined with dark furniture and gloomy stone. But the scrubbed paved floor was the colour of honey. The sculpture was propped on a sideboard. It was in low relief, fifteen inches high, of sun-bleached and sea-washed marble: a carving that, after long scouring in the elements, seemed never to have been touched by man.

'Perseus slaying the Gorgon Medusa!' the Captain said in that arrogant way of people who have picked up a little knowledge for the purpose of dominating others with it. 'Instead of teeth, the Gorgon women, representing barbarous untamed nature, had the tusks of boars and whoever looked at them was turned to stone. But the handsome Perseus, as brave and clever as he was handsome . . .'

'He might have been a Horsfall!' Oliver interrupted.

'. . . averted his eyes. Afterwards he gave the monster's severed head to the goddess Athene – the patroness of Athens in its golden age of Socrates and Plato. No doubt it signifies that Reason can be born only after such witches have been slain.'

On his galloping horse, Perseus, though 'brave and clever', yet looked over his shoulder frightened of the pursuing women, the Furies, whilst in his right hand he dangled the bleeding female head. The decapitated Gorgon sprawled beneath him – her knees collapsed, her arms and wings plaintively outstretched, blood seeping out of her neck. But this particular Gorgon, who ought according to the Captain's claims to have been grotesque and ugly, was beautiful. She wore a girdle of snakes and her transparent draperies rolled gently over her form as the small waves of a calm sea lap the sand. One artist, at least, had evidently loved her whom he was supposed to have found horrifying!

'It's a crude carving, my friends, probably made by some illiterate local mason such as our own, and much surpassed in elegance and proportion by the products of our present age,' Horsfall opined.

'Perseus looks as furtive as a cut-purse,' Oliver commented. 'As well he might. For the murder of Mother Nature has given birth to monsters of Reason and Progress!'

((4))

Winter grew close. Doors and windows were shut tight and the passageways became mouldy. Stone floors, greasy with the damp, were a sombre colour, exhuding a moist chill. The heather was first dusty, then faded and bleached by the autumn rains. In fear of winter, and oppressed by the darkened hills, the weavers grew mutinous or bullied their wives. The memory of summer's business at Makings made the winter desolation seem bleaker. Anne's fellow-servants were bad-tempered. The leaves that drifted into wells, troughs, and against walls, the wet areas that spread over ceilings under damaged roofs, and winds in the open yards that needled you like the Devil's stings, all annoyed them. Plasterers blamed carpenters, dyers cursed fullers, chambermaids blamed kitchenmaids, who threw their slops over the cats. People died in the countryside, in ditches where the frost turned them to stone, in cottages where they had been forgotten, or on moorlands where 'reasonable' men walked overcome with Melancholy.

During the nights Anne Wylde often read her *Iliad*, or in her Bible – loving those sensuous passages that were like a pagan undergrowth to it. '*A bundle of myrrh is my well-beloved unto me: he shall lie all night betwixt my breasts.*' Secret beneath the words, it seemed to her, unreasonable, subdued Nature had once laughed, screamed and sang – before the Prophets put an iron cage about Her, and an iron brank upon Her tongue, as a dangerous witch.

Whilst Anne read and pictured Nature laughing and dancing with her children in Eden, Patience Helliwell and her friends (also desperate, it seemed, about the Expulsion from Paradise) in the kitchen beneath howled and groaned for salvation. Under the hams and salted meats hooked to the ceiling like God's flayed condemned victims hanging in Hell, they cried, they wept, they openly and loudly accounted for their faults (going so far as to enter debit and credit for their sins and their piety, in a ledger first intended to be the clothier's account book). They sang and prayed, even if the good God could not hear above the roar and rattle of the wind at the latch. At other times it had been the odours of cooking that had risen through Anne's floorboards; now it was prayers and hymns, a steam of misery seeping up between the oak planks – high intense beseechings, the most ghastly hymns of the Wesleys:

'Signs in the Heavens see,
And hear the Speaking Rod;
Sinner, the Judgment points to Thee,
Prepare to meet thy GOD!

Terrible GOD! and true,
Thy justice we confess,
Thy sorest Plagues are all *our* due,
We own our Wickedness,
Worthy of Death and Hell . . .'

and:

'Constrained by the Stroke of thy Rod
I pour out a Penitent Prayer:
Ah! do not abhor my sad Moan,
Extorted, alas! by Distress,
But hear, and with Pity look down,
And send me an Answer of Peace.'

One day Anne suddenly thought: these are cries to a *mother*, not to a father! They express the feelings of a whipped child in terror of being cut off from female care, burying himself in his mother's lap!

They were, literally, the howls of those poor little boys, John and Charles Wesley, who had been beaten so savagely by their mother Susanna. *These* had become the harrowed wails of clothiers, farmers and tradesmen who felt guilty of an offence against the green moorland world. Who were also thrilled by their own guilty natures:

'A deep Revolter I,
And ever to my Vomit turn . . .'

In another part of the house, Benjamin Greave (who tolerated the Methodists because their orderly principles were useful for disciplining the weavers but who himself clung to the Presbyterians, the 'Old

Dissent'), schemed over the wars and revolutions of the Continent – butcheries, iconoclasms which he could hardly imagine – thinking of where he could next sell worsteds.

(The news of each crisis was hastened to him from the stagecoach by the Vicar, who always wished to consult with Lady Well's prominent gentlemen over whether or not it was advisable to announce these matters to the general populace in church. Doubtfire, also, sometimes overheard the crying in the kitchen – and wondered whether, after all, there might be some Righteousness spoken by these Methodists with their songs about *the speaking rod, the stroke of Thy rod*, and *the scourge's o'erflow*.)

Or Greave fussed over his tomb – that flock of marble angels intended to block the nave of Saint Mary the Virgin.

Whatever the clothier might have to offer in the form of an erection in the nave and passageways to the Virgin, as he grew older he was losing his potency with his own household. Despite his threats, Anne Wylde was still at Makings. For she had proved a good and careful servant, surprising her colleagues (who had expected little of her) with her knowledge of how to brew and bake, milk cattle and churn, tend poultry; how to prepare cheeses and take care of winter provisions; also (so that her hands should not be idle in the evenings) she had learnt to spin, to card, and the secrets of dyeing, from her aunts. Because she now had a protector in the young Master Greave, she was becoming a happy young woman, and her look was less savage.

Yet she was different from the other women, for she saw into their fates. Having got free of squalid cottages, it was only to spend years in another's house, hoping for marriages that would make them mistresses and also slaves again of just such grimy cots as they had in the first place escaped from.

Here, in this house that was without a mistress, where all the women were servants, she especially noticed how men could work with broad and easy gestures – handling large sums of money, travelling, making decisions, moving stone and wood easily, quartering the land and enclosing the hills with brute strength and physical command over nature. But women's labour was tight and cramped. From earliest childhood, females made thousands of tiny stitches upon a few square inches of 'sampler'; and small fingers remained necessary to do most of their tasks in life. The cut of their clothes confined them to small and ritual movements. In the production of wool their main work was in spinning, dyeing or otherwise preparing the material which their menfolk, the weavers, finished and sold – so that males alone held power and control. The women listened to men, and obeyed. If in some – perhaps many – instances they ruled in bed, this was kept secret and not referred to even between the couple themselves during the day. And if a woman held subtle command between the sheets, the land outside the window always lay passive to the men, ready for them to do what they wanted to Her, though it was a scouring, a burning, a poisoning and robbing for profit.

Anne often found it difficult to talk to the women; whilst men could hardly be addressed at all with any intimate conversation, without it being compromising. She was always glad to be sent out of the kitchen, say to feed the poultry and dogs in the yards. She felt more at home with the amazing abilities and agilities of animals. She watched a cat strip the discarded remains of a fish and discover a complete meal out of it: ravenous, yet still delicate, and nicely poised, the animal would leave a complete, neat skeleton behind. The beauty of its movement thrilled her to the point of tears. Whilst if Anne threw the remains of a meal over a wall, then a crow, with incredible eyesight, would fly from half a mile away to eat it, pecking carefully, gobbling the bits, and turning its head watchfully, in one alert stance and movement that was in contrast to the muffled and lazy apprehensions of humans.

As an alternative to Methodist meetings to cheer some of the winter evenings, a barrel of ale would be opened in the kitchen. Then music was made, out of coarse voices; violins and clarinets; the rattle of dry bones, the vibration of stretched skins, or plucked catgut, or breath in a trembling reed. Oliver described Hellas, and played his fiddle, often joining in a duet with Dick O'Lovely, or some other. Oliver from his wandering days had a network of 'rascally' acquaintances, whom he knew from their hours – or days, or even weeks – of relaxation at remote inns, where they lived passionately for their music or song. Apparent ne'er-do-wells, who lived as scavenging cats do and on the watch-out for Dick Almighty; who thieved and cheated unblushingly over taxes and tithes; they were in fact, in their souls, true artists, giving dedicated labour to their music. They knew how much they were hated in some quarters, being considered as 'barbarians'. Yet 'the young master' welcomed them to the Makings kitchen, and so there at least no one asked them where they had slept the previous night, or who with, and they played their music with joy, until later they melted back into the moorland landscape.

Oliver performing was a man possessed. His passion made his instrument physically part of himself – as impossible to imagine them being parted as to take away an arm or a leg. He would close his eyes tight and his foot went tap, tap to the melody – cascades of music filling the great stone room where smoke and the fumes of ale hung in rosy firelit clouds below the ceiling, and where the furniture was pushed aside to make way for dancing. How he adored drawing his bow across the strings, from the first bars that tested the acoustic of the room – a thrill like that of plunging into a pool and sensing the water – to the last that sighed confidently away through some improvisation of his own. In this circle of rascals and musicians, he, too, was loved and admired as he could never hope to be through his father's business.

Anne took glass after glass of gin. This, and the music, and the knowledge that the artist who produced so much of it – who was the admired golden centre of this company – had sworn himself her sweetheart, inspired her dance. Dance was her element, as the swallow possesses the air or the trout commands the stream. 'Look! Look at Anne Wylde!' She became isolated on the floor. Oliver's tunes made her feel that she was weeping deep inside herself. Yet in this mood melancholy was so mixed with joy that it was indistinguishable from it. Her stomach seemed to fill with air, rise and float through her throat.

Meanwhile the poet-musician showed only a stone-blind face, his feelings turned in to his music, captured and captivating. Everyone would then be reminded that Anne and Oliver were a couple – whatever Anne did it brought envy, admiration and spite. And everyone took notice of her.

One night Anne first met Mr Tim Bobbin. Oliver, in a burst of energy which new love had given him for prosecuting his life, had rescued Tim from his schoolmastering to do the Greaves' ledgers, 'because he wrote the best copperplate in the district', he told his father. Tim, though no more fond of being a clerk than of acting as schoolteacher, yet recognised a sinecure in idleness (or thought he recognised one: he forgot that he would have to reckon with Benjamin Greave) that would be fruitful for his poetry and for his favoured companionships.

Anne saw a small man with bright little eyes and a sensual mouth flowering in a pale face above double chins. Not a handsome face, but a beautiful one because of the happy and adaptable temperament that shone out of it. With great impertinence amongst traders and clothiers, he wore a revolutionary's blue woollen 'cap of liberty'. He was a serious clown, and to express the latter aspect, his breeches were made out of the leather of his old mare, 'to immortalise her by making her the second skin of a poet'.

He put his arm around Anne, but she slipped out of his grasp.

'You are studying to be a clothier, sir?' she asked.

With the arm that had been rejected he made a gesture to express his hatred of such interests. 'I am averse to learning anything of worldly use, I prefer my savage liberty!' He swayed, glass in the other hand, and his extravagant words were delivered in a high-pitched voice. His mere presence brought merriment. 'My greatest living fault is what th'old Greeks called "hubris",' he squeaked, tipping some of his drink on to the floor. 'I gave up being king of the birch when I found I had nothing of the mundane sort to impart. One day a fond parent discovered me asleep on my bench, even the brawling of the infants unable to wake my slumbers. (Though I could have flogged them, as the Parson does ... "God is love!" Wham! Wham!) "What does thou teach the little ones, my good man?" quoth my visitor. "Nothing, sir." "Nothing! Why *nothing*?" "Because I know nothing myself," answers I. "Same as Socrates, who thought he was the wisest man on earth, because he knew that he knew nothing." '

Anne laughed, unmaidenly-loud and suddenly. Then she noticed that Tim was not shocked by it. It surprised her, for most men were.

'But you have no family to care for?'

Froth dropped excitedly from Tim's lips. 'An unhappy wife and some brats to fetch into Benjamin Greave's kingdom when I have found them a cottage!'

'There are plenty of cots in the Greaves' domain. Why did you marry her if it was to make her unhappy?' She easily fell into teasing him – many women did.

As Anne Wylde would not dance with him, the clerk manfully

puffed clouds of smoke out of his pipe – imagining that this added to his dimensions, although the disproportion in size between pipe and himself made him seem even smaller.

'That's a question I have often asked myself. Why make one woman unhappy when I could make many women happy?' Tim answered, pretending extreme thoughtfulness now. 'One day whilst we were courting we saw a maid driving two swine to market. "Those are very pretty, clean pigs!" my Mary remarks. "Then," says I, "we'll each purchase one and the first to draw out of the promise to wed shall forfeit a porker to the other." Mary grew so fond of her porcine companion that she married me rather than lose it. Don't look so fretful, Miss Wylde! We soon got through the fortune she brought into our partnership, and then we were happier, for it tamed my *savage liberty* and I had to seek employment, which kept me at home for a while.'

'Say her some of your poems, Tim,' Oliver encouraged.

Tim set himself up grandly. He held his hands out like a priest, made scything gestures to count the rhythm, and rolled his eyes around the ceiling. The fact that so many in the crowded Makings kitchen were noisy with drink and were ignoring him did not put him off his recitation.

'Some write to show their wits and parts,
Some show you Whig, some Tory hearts,
Some flatter knaves, some fops, some fools,
And some are Mister Greave's tools!'

His dramatic rendering or (more accurately) squealing of his verses arrested many of the drunks. They listened to him with mouths agape in amazement at the very existence of poetry.

Anne saw that Oliver adored Tim, as the only committed maker whom he knew. But she did not like to think she was walking out with a man who did not believe himself to be the best one in the world. So she sought distraction from, as she thought of it, Oliver encouraging her to play fickle with his own friend. And there was Betty, Oliver's daughter who – small and sickly though she was and used to scurrying pale as a lost bewildered ferret about the passageways, cared for by the housekeeper or whoever would take charge of her – had come into the arena of music and conversation where she struggled to imitate Anne Wylde's dancing. It was obvious how much the child admired Anne. Laughing, Anne took the hands of the girl and led her through steps that were an erratic caricature of her own.

Afterwards Betty sank back into her weird, watchful silence, her expression turned both inward and outward at one and the same time, and with a curious adult patience. It was as if she had already rushed quickly into maturity because she knew that her life would be a short one; and yet still she was unable to comprehend these people, these adults, who had lived already for such a long while.

On the following mornings Miss Helliwell would return to where she had been expelled by the gaiety. With a hymn on her lips; resentments and loathing on her teeth; *clunk, clunk, clunk*, on her stumpy legs, and a rattle of keys, her first task was to turn sore-heads out of doors. Sulky apprentices and other rascals who had sat through drunkenness to become sober again, and then in blind stupidity swallowed more drink until they collapsed, were woken roughly from corners and trestles and thrust out to face cruel daylight, rain, wind or shine, over their own vomit which they had forgotten having left on the doorstep. 'That was a good night!' they assured one another, reeling and unable to bear the too energetic stirrings of moorland air and light. For them, it would be too bright even on the gloomiest winter day. Meanwhile the kitchen was scoured and aired, whilst guilty eyes were ducked from those who had Methodistically taken themselves early to bed.

'You affect conviviality as happily as if you had thrown a jug of water on a fire,' Tim Bobbin told Patience Helliwell. His waving hands and arms seemed to threaten the housekeeper. He was addicted to making extravagant gestures with his limbs.

She ruffled and puffed like an aggravated sparrow with the wind in its feathers. 'I am one that walks the right road to redemption! Oh what a weight of sin lies on those poor mortals that at night do so much to scourge themselves for i'the morning!'

Thinking of those in need of the *scourge's o'erflow*, she would fix especially on Anne Wylde. The housekeeper would look the girl up and down as if she was an animal in a pen at a fair. Anne realised that Patience's dislike could easily transform into its opposite; she was as one who has been spurned, rather than one who hates. She would shift unpleasantly close to Anne and seem tongue-tied, then move off briskly with pursed lips. Brush close again. Rustle her keys as if they opened the gates of Heaven.

'There is none without hope!' Patience whispered softly one day. 'I've witnessed as many as twelve wicked sinners awakened all in one day by the preacher Elkanah Beanland at a crossroads. This is a time of miracles in Yorkshire – eight of them were redeemed, and not one backslider later amongst them! You could join us still, if you've a mind. What a victory 'twould be for the Lord! There is still time to escape the eternal fires. Just imagine them eternal fires, suffocating, flaming, choking thee, burning for ever and evermore again and through Eternity always!' As she gloated, her eyes had a moist shine, like those of someone in sickness.

Patience was driven crazy by Anne's ignoring of her, so on the next occasion she spoke not apocalyptically, but bitterly. 'You hope that your ways will turn a few heads, believing that men never understand what goes on in the hearts of maidens, thinking them as pure as snow. But the Lord has his surprises in store for you, Hawthorn Maiden!' Her voice rose bitter and high, to an edge of terror like an animal trapped. 'The Lord, I am bound to tell thee, *will* visit with the scourge, whips and rods of His judgment! There was a foolish woman fro' Lady Well scoffed recently at a preacher who was giving out the Words of Light on the river bank. A week – no, I lie, a fortnight – later she was wringing her mop at that same spot when the Good Lord sucked her into th'waters and drowned her. Took her straight t'Ell – she was found in Huddersfield. Drifted down t'river and caught on a bush. Another thing! There was an ungodly parson delivered a sermon against us Methodists and was overcome wi't'plague . . .'

The rebuffed housekeeper revived Benjamin Greave's desire to get the servant girl out of his son's sight. With the master-clothier's approval, Patience set Anne the most unpleasant work, in the cellars and remote rooms, or sent her on errands in the fiercest weather so that she might catch pneumonia, come near death, and realise how little time there was to repent and save her soul.

Despite her good works, Patience was troubled and guilty, even in her bedchamber, by the questioning judging presence of the Lord. Sometimes He took on the outlines of a black bull, looming out of the darkness, setting up a great pounding as if about to stampede. At other times He was formed like a raven; or the dark bird's-wings were, in her dreams, His spread-eagled cloak as He scoured a thousand devils out of the corners of Makings just as she herself did for spiders. Sometimes she even felt His beard tickling her between the sheets.

One windy night she lay questioning whether a noise was her visiting God, or a rat, or a loose board banging in a draught; and though she dozed off once or twice, she soon awoke, more nervous than before. Was a thief prowling? Terrified, grasping her prayer book, Patience raised the household. Servants with pistols, carving-knives, meat skewers and half-rusted swords rushed to the landing outside her room. There had not been time to light enough candles, and many others were blown out in the draughts, so her panicking defenders fell over one another. Those who fancied that they had deep manly voices shouted fearfully at the ceiling. But one of them had to dare the rafters and to avoid being chosen most busied themselves comforting Patience, who broke down under the unaccustomed attention, stuttering and wailing as if (Tim Bobbin said) the Devil already had her by the toe.

Tim was the only one to brave the roof. He felt in need of some opportunity to display his virtue; for Benjamin Greave had been complaining about his fecklessness, had been quarrelling with Oliver about the 'clerk', and though Tim didn't 'give a pig's whistle' for the old clothier, it pained him to compromise the young one who was his friend and patron. So in virtuous gallant defence of the housekeeper he crept, balancing on the ceiling joists, crouching beneath the filthy slates, dodging sharp gusts of wind that threatened to blow out his light; knowing how easily he could miss his foot-hold, break a rotten timber and fall through a ceiling; startling rats and mice, and truly scared.

At last, 'Your thief and demon's nothing but a chimney-flap blown in the wind!' he shouted and he came thundering down.

A group of menservants, to cover their shame, now claimed that he had tackled the disturbance wrongly and that they themselves knew better and braver solutions which the poet's rashness had prevented their executing; whilst the maids converted Tim Bobbin into a hero and giggled as they led him away to wash off the soot.

'I who have never dreamed of robbers nor slept with a door closed in my life, come t'a rich man's house and have to be raised up to crawl in the rafters like a bat, for fear of a chimney-flap!' Tim shrieked. 'You all tremble with an ague fit. Do you think the Devil with his cloven-footed squadrons is after you? You can keep your wealth, if it brings such fears!' he spluttered through gobfuls of cold water. 'I've seen enough to satisfy me that he who has a bare living and can sleep soundly at nights with his door open is the only happy man. I've had enough of you! I've spoilt my best hat wi' taking it off, sticking it under my arm to bow and cringe to piece-makers! My neck's grown crooked and my chin turned into my shoulder with obsequious humility! From the worries of being a clerk I can carry large quartos in the breast of the jacket I could hardly button a few months back. I'll be off to retrieve my savage liberty!'

Tim was one who dealt in poetic, not in mundane truth; in other words, so far as merchants were concerned he was a liar. But in matters of change and movement he meant what he said. Also, his account books were in a muddle. Tim left Makings as thoughtlessly and unpreparedly as he had arrived. But it was to the envy of Oliver, who had found in Tim the only other person with the same feckless and unreasonable instinct as his own for wandering.

Oliver sometimes, on mornings of fine weather, could also get away, though only to travel the cottages seeing what progress was made with spinning and weaving. He was then offered, here a jug of ale, there an artisan's views on poetry, on rational philosophy, on Calvinistic predestination or on the easier more-magical redemption offered by Messrs Wesley. But on most days, with cold compresses over his forehead, inside which buzzed regrets and resolutions, Oliver designed labels for woollen goods: surrounding 'Amens. 28sh. per yard', and 'Bays. 18sh. per yard', with wreathed Ionic columns and lewd drawings of the love of Adonis for Venus, or he laboured over correspondence to persuade merchants to take his father's worsteds. Both the clerk to the governors of Christ's Hospital in London, and the factor who supplied soldiers' cloth to the Empress Catherine of Russia, could not understand why the clothier was so little interested in their requests for rough woollens, instead wanting them to bring shalloons to the attention of their clients. Oliver hardly cared what types of cloth were sold nor whether it was suitable for paupers or for ladies.

But his father was always at his elbow, insisting that the only way to 'defeat' the clothiers of Somerset and Gloucestershire, and 'raise-up' a Yorkshire industry, was to make finer and yet even finer woollens.

So Oliver wrote: '*If you would be pleased to accept our calliman-coes you will benefit from the best making in England.*' Then he added a more persuasive afterthought: '*I also trust you will find to your satisfaction these sides of pork from our own native hills.*'

His mind wandered constantly, but settled longest on the subject of Anne Wylde. In the idle drift of his thoughts, he often considered what a dismal place Makings must be for such as her. For that was how he himself found it to be.

And that, obviously, was how it appeared to his daughter Betty. Oliver was sad that, being a widower, he could do so little for her.

Betty drifted amongst the temples of wool bales, the dark tombs and ziggurats of its piles, as detached as her father was from the woollen industry – sitting and swinging her legs here, dashing along that warehouse alley, darting between a surprised Dutchman's legs, then peeping out scared but interested from some burrow made of kerseys and callimancoes. She was like a kitten, or like a scrap of winged seed that had blown in and was puffed hither and thither, having nothing to do with this place and possessing nowhere to take root. When she was bored with the barns, she played with the fowls and the dogs in the yards.

But always eventually she had to join Patience Helliwell, who was responsible for her.

'All this will be hers someday!' Patience remarked to Oliver – disapproving, envious, but putting on the measured air of one who is wise and sagacious. 'Well then, she must be brought up to her responsibility.'

'How?' Oliver asked in surprise. For he had never thought about the subject of educating a daughter, and no one else had ever suggested that it was of importance.

'So as to devote 'er wealth to good works and not bad ones, she must 'ave a clear knowledge of the dark world of sin that surrounds us. She must learn to fear God, for only 'E can save us. The spectacle of *funerals* is most instructive to children. She should be taken to one, instructed in the awful fear of death, and then to make the lesson stick brought home, whipped and locked in a cellar to meditate on our earthly lot.'

'I will have no such thing done to my lovely daughter! It is preposterous!'

Patience touched his arm, and let her fingers linger there. 'Maybe it sounds harsh to your ears, but trust me it is the only way. "Spare the rod and spoil the child", Mr Greave. 'Twas done to me and it did no harm, as you can see. 'Twas the method by which Mr Wesley himself was brought up and it made him a saint. One of our own brethren is to be buried next week, Mr Greave. It should be an instructive occasion . . .'

'Miss Helliwell!' Oliver interrupted – but could then think of no reasonable arguments against her monstrous suggestion. So, 'Where is Anne Wylde?' he asked, to change the subject.

'She is cleaning a cellar.'

He grasped the opportunity for diversionary anger. 'Such a Venus, such an Aphrodite, set to clean cellars! I will not have it, Miss Helliwell!' He threw down his quill so that it splattered on his letter. 'I think you are in league with my father to keep the fair maiden from me! I say I will not suffer it! This is the last straw! Like Mr Bobbin I am sick of heart, and I'll be off to Athens tomorrow . . .'

That evening he went to Anne's room. She was snipping her hair. Her scissors slipped so that she cut her neck, and he rushed to mop it with his handkerchief.

'I cut myself because you came upon me! They say we women are to blame for our troubles, and that we mutilate ourselves, seeking suffering.' Oliver lingered with the handkerchief. 'I have been waiting for you, Oliver.' There were tears in her eyes.

Her tenderness released his hands. He began lightly, touching her knuckles, her wrist encircled by the strange red line that never faded, then up her arm, across the back of her shoulders, lingering with delicate fingering at the pit of her neck, feeling the flesh thrill; whilst with the other hand he held her waist. This first occasion that he came really close to her, he with relief discovered that her breath was fragrant and he tried to kiss her. He fingered her breasts, and he ached for those white fluttering doves.

Anne was used to hard graspings or fumblings, and no one had ever fondled her so delicately. She had never imagined that a man who was hardly touching her at all, his fingers doing little more than rest and flutter upon her skin like a butterfly, could melt her thus.

But she also had her reasons for not trusting men. From what practice with other women had he learnt to do this? she thought. The acquirement must have involved many deserted maidens. So when his hands played near her breasts, 'Ah no, sir!' she said.

'Anne, do you know what a passionate creature you are?'

'Do not touch me like that.' As she moved his hand, she felt something harder pressing into her below. 'Do not do that,' – although she was absorbed and lost in desire for him to do just *that*.

Over his shoulder, she caught the eyes of Patience Helliwell in the passageway. Anne put two hands on Oliver's chest so that he turned to see what alarmed her. Patience after glaring for a moment, her hands grasped together – not as if making a prayer, but tight and trembling as if pulping something, flower or insect, beyond recognition between them – disappeared into the shadows.

The housekeeper felt that just by showing her presence she had issued sufficient warning. What she had actually achieved was to bind the lovers together in the common purpose of having to do something about the housekeeper; and, far from being parted, they found they had now reached that state of closeness in which they did not need to speak, for a touch and a meeting-of-eyes would communicate enough.

Patience Helliwell returned after Oliver left. Full of jealousy she stroked Anne's hair. Anne could see no way of escape. Patience smiled sweetly. 'Attractive young servant girls are soon tempted – especially when they think themselves intended to be more than servants. But thou's bound only for eternal fires along yonder road. Why do you never seek redemption along with the rest of us at our joyful hour? Those who were at Upper Spout, 'til Master Greave opened sulphur springs have joined recently, not cast down by the loss of their home but secure o' their reward in Heaven. Elkanah Beanland has preached, wi' fire in his voice. Richard Whitely a time or two has delivered eloquent sermons telling of the deceit o' scamps and wicked travellers. Binns has called upon us, and Amos Culpin, and others you'll know from Lady Well. You stay aloof from the right-thinking folk, with your fine ways, when you could be so happy with us! There are all classes visit. Many of the most rejected of mankind come in to hear the Good Book and the sermons sent to us by Mr Wesley and others.'

'The scourings of the countryside enter because the room is warm! You can sing and shriek and write your "rules for conduct" in your ledger like weavers' clerks, but it'll never make me believe that is the way to Heaven!'

'Oh, there can be such Heaven for us poor sinners and I am one who is already 'cquainted with the taste of it!'

Patience was swooning. With desperate roughness she took hold of the girl's hand and forced it to stroke her own thigh. Then she abruptly raised her dress and thrust Anne's fingers into her opening, although it was quite dry. The girl sprang away so quickly that for once she forgot to stoop and caught her head on the low ceiling. Patience withdrew into herself. But she was shaking, like a cat that has been rudely swept out of doors.

'And what does thou think Mr Greave will make of your evil tempting of his son? You're a servant still and nothing'll turn thee into anything else, Miss. Be glad of the Lord's will, if you would escape the Everlasting Fire!'

The housekeeper moved to the far side of the room, turned her back (which was shaking violently, a frightening sight in its lack of self-control), opened her legs and desperately fingered; forgetting Anne Wylde, she was lost in a dream of her own.

Snow tumbled over the hills. A sharp wind followed and raised it in clouds of white smoke above the walls, laying drifts upon the road-ways. The West Country was quite cut off, and so was Norwich, they learnt, before Yorkshire too was isolated in an ocean of silent pillows. Even the goods and presents already sent away would arrive late and damaged from having stood on snowbound wharfs at Hull.

The more Benjamin Greave's imprisonment and damaged trade became unbearable, the more he attributed it to a bewitching of his household by Anne Wylde, was sure that she brought nothing but ill-luck and must be got rid of. All the weavers if they could get together through the snowdrifts had stories to tell about Anne. Through alcoholic fumes in the early hours of the morning her shape or her spirit loomed out of the smoky shadows of dozens of hush-houses and inns.

Oliver was distracted by her. When she walked out of a room, it was for the poet as if darkness descended. When *she* was not there was when he felt a prisoner. He was immured in his room simply because there was nowhere he wished to go; all freedom was taken from him because there was nothing he wished to do without her. In a house in which he had access to all the keys, he paced his room as a prisoner does, trying to think of some way out of his dilemma, or of some diversion from his desire, and wondering (because, after all, he was no young fool in love for the first time!) whether she was with equal impatience thinking of him. Was this the true 'happiness' of love – this mixture of the sweet and the sour so intermixed that you could not tell which was which?

Meanwhile the thought of Anne Wylde's 'spells' upon his son and indeed over the whole valley preyed upon Benjamin Greave's mind whilst he was in his barns, brooding amongst the stranded and growing mountins of cloth. The snow, which like his cloth was piled up uselessly everywhere, and the frost, which seized the springs, the milk in the jugs so that they cracked, and even the piss in the chamberpots, was, he decided, the curse laid by this evil pagan spirit who had been born in the hotbed of a community's sins. After days of sulky temper, he came out with his thoughts to Oliver.

'I'm deeply troubled! If that girl gets into our family she'll go through my fortune like a knife through butter. And thou'd never be able to maintain thy superiority. It'd be silks and fine dresses and trips to London to choose them and a king's ransom spent in candles for her balls every winter!'

'If Anne Wylde leaves, I'll go with her.'

Benjamin realised that he could not prevent this if it arose. Yet even the mildest threat from his son gave the clothier a desperate fear of being abandoned – an apprehension that he kept to himself as much as he could. He swung his arm at Oliver, who stepped back, trembling at his temptation to strike his father.

'Now look how she has set father against son as well as servant against master!' Benjamin shouted, frightened of the loneliness he saw looming. 'I tell you I'll not have her here! And I forbid you to see her!'

Nonetheless the lovers did meet. In the frozen garden a single rose managed to flower. Nobody noticed it but Anne, who intended to pluck it for Oliver when the petals opened in perfection. She fluttered with anxiety lest they became frostbitten and black. Each morning and evening she strode out, stooped in the snow on which frost glittered, and she cupped the fragile crimson in her hands, blowing gently upon it until she grew stiff with cold. The petals seemed each morning gratefully to open a little more, and each evening to close gladly upon her own warmth that she had sacrificed for them.

She hoped she was unobserved. But Horsfall (who was always hanging around Makings) saw her. 'Look, my friend,' he confidingly told Oliver, 'I'll find some way to keep the Old Man busy whilst you go out to your sweetheart.'

Oliver, torn between love for Anne and for his father, was glad of the ruse. It succeeded. As the couple met, snow whitened the northern flank of the house, whilst trees were as thick with frost as they had been with leaves all summer, and it looked like a white, bridal blossoming. Everything about the lovers, even their speech, was frozen; they were mute with the silence of a couple newly meeting who believe any converse too mundane a vehicle for their mutual gifts of love.

Oliver wanted to lead Anne towards a stone belevedere (one which had been built by her own father; though his buildings were so common about the countryside that she never took notice of them), and she, not wishing him to detect her business with the rose, let him take her there. 'Anne, before I met you I lived like someone sickening. I saw no reason to climb out of my bed. I could sleep until noon and yet still be tired. I saw no purpose in any conversation. In my father's business. In poetry, even. I remembered that beauty does exist, but I could not feel it . . . perhaps such memories, such numbness, is Hell itself? All my comforts meant nothing to me. I was trapped here, yet without the strength to move. And now because of you all the light and beauty has flooded back into the world! How can I explain it? I am in love with you. I am your heart's slave.' As they sat on the frosted bench, his *own* heart was thumping with fear and excitement at the consequences of her accepting his love.

Anne had previously been wooed with stones and catcalls, so she yearned for such tenderness as he had shown her; such spiritual and artistic refinement, as was the cause of Oliver's weakness. Now this 'weakness' shone at her with sun-like Apollonian radiance.

'You say that you are my "heart's slave", but I want you to be independent, as you deserve to be, free as the sun and the air.'

'It is a poetical figure of speech.' He flushed. 'I am quite free.'

'But you are not free of your father. He keeps you confined when your desire is to travel.'

'I told you that I would leave Makings if you were forced to!'

'I would want you to leave for you own desires, not because of mine. Poor Oliver, you are not free, because you understand so little of the cruel results of human frailty. We poor folk and servants see much more. We have to, to survive.'

'You are like some ancient priestess from whom flows a fount of sensibility!'

'Tim Bobbin said I am a Celtic Queen who should be decked in jewels and flowers. Why cannot I be just a *woman*? In truth I am no wiser than many a washerwoman. It seems there are as many clever washerwomen as there are parsons, who should listen to what is said in kitchens before they write their sermons.'

Her apparent lack of sympathy with his sentiments was so equably expressed that it was unnerving. For the first time ever, Oliver felt cut by the razors of her cool quick answers. As the Reverend Doubtfire, as his own father, as *her* own father, and many others so reasonably opined: her cleverness degraded male dignity and superiority. At this moment he thought that he understood why they stoned her. Yet when he looked into her face, he realised he was staring into a mirror: his muse. This woman was her own self. He felt helpless.

'No one is like you – I would like to lay my fortune at your feet,' he answered, weakly.

'And I have always wished merely to be left alone.'

They could talk, talk, talk about love for ever. But it was becoming unbearingly cold. The rooks, that scavenged daily in Greave's well-manured enclosures where the dung-straw now lay upon the snow in golden tresses, were returning to their roosts and were speckled across the last strands of the sunset. Darkness and frost would fall tonight as sudden as an executioner's axe; as the trap of the notorious guillotine in the nearby town of Halifax. They walked back through the bare and frozen rose-garden whilst the lamps and candles were lit in the mansion and they could hear from beyond a wall the clatter of hooves and wheels as workmen prepared to return home.

'Oh, Oliver, though I feel so much for you yet I cannot give myself into the care of someone so foolishly trusting. In Horsfall, for instance . . .'

'He is helping us to meet now! It seems that suddenly no one can see any innocence – even you, who are yourself full of innocence. My father suspects you, you suspect Horsfall, though he tells us that he is our friend!'

'A man like that never does anything that's not to his own advantage. I don't know what there can be in it for him to bring us together, but his desiring it is no good omen. Look. I want to show you something.'

She raced him back to the garden, plucked the rose and pressed it, a token of her body, to his breast.

When Anne looked at flowers, it was as if *they* gazed even more intensely at her, he noticed. Staring flowers seemed to undress her. Birds and animals were the same; they peered, fascinated, straight into her. From the way she held the rose, Oliver realised that for Anne Wylde every plant and creature, wind and water, rock, hill and valley, had a living spirit. It was a pagan sense with which she had been born and she was not aware of it. If her attention was fixed, even upon a mere glass of water or a half-frozen rose, her nature responded appreciative of the living, separate being. She loved, but left alone. There was no division into demons and the children of God for Anne. The Universe was a harmony to her.

Restless in her bed, Anne overheard the Methodists beneath. '*Oh God Thy Righteousness we own,/ Judgment is at the house begun/ With humblest Awe thy Rod we bear,/ And guilty in Thy Sight appear!*' blistered the floor. '*Our Sin and Wickedness we own,/ And deeply for Acceptance groan!*' cut through the passages and stairways, out over the hills to join the harsh, stony calls of starving rooks and winter-thrushes.

Anne could not sleep for it. She huddled herself into a shawl to hurry through the damp stone passageways, where in some places icicles and sheets of ice hung upon the walls, and she went downstairs. The kitchen door was open and no one saw her enter the crowded room, with most backs turned to her. They were packed even upon the long table, which an hour or two ago Anne had scrubbed, and were holding on to one another like shipwrecked people clinging to a storm-tossed raft. At the far end of the room the faces ran with sweat for there a huge fire licked the black cavern of the chimney. To Anne, it looked like the gate of Hell. To Patience Helliwell, it offered the same symbol. That was why, smiling upwards with nervous self-satisfaction next to the visiting preacher, and twitching her fingers around her keys to Heaven, Hell and Benjamin Greave's knives, forks and pewter, she stood before it: because all, whether sweat-tormented at the front of the room or frozen white at the back of it, were turned towards this reminder of th'eternal furnace, and its infernal machinery for roasting souls or sides of bacon. Betty crouched there too, hesitantly afraid to warm her toes at the 'fires of Hell'.

When they became aware of Anne, it was as when she used to walk into the apothecary's at Lady Well and the women were gossiping; there was a silence, and a feeling that nothing further would be prosecuted until she had left. Only Betty ran to her, relying upon finding warmth and comfort in the folds of Anne Wylde's gown.

But Patience had been preparing for such a moment as this, and she struck up the hymn that she had saved for it. She conducted by holding a large kitchen-knife in her hand. Anne noticed how fiercely this 'humble and meek' woman clutched the handle, and how viciously glittered the blade which, Patience insisted, must always be razor-sharp. Her congregation – the servants dried up from a lifetime's service to the clothier, the shuffling wanderers out of the countryside defeated of all hope except for a last sad reflective anchorage in God the Father (as interpreted by this kitchen-evangelist), and those tradesmen who saw advantages in Methodist doctrines of regularity and sobriety, or perhaps thought it worthwhile to use any means to get inside Benjamin Greave's house – whilst seeming to ignore Anne Wylde and avoid her sensual eyes, yet they wailed more loudly for her benefit. They howled in the pitiful way of beasts who have seen that their life's journey is but to the slaughterhouse, and who find perverse consolation in their own helplessness:

'Abandoned to the Fury's will,
I prove her utmost power,
And twice ten thousand deaths I feel,
Yet live to suffer more!

With me the ghastly spectre walks
In every secret shade,
In all her horrid forms she stalks
Around my sleepless bed

My poor despairing soul she racks
With agonising smart,
Her whip of knotted vipers shakes,
And tears my bleeding heart!

My soul shrinks back – but oh! to whom
Or whither shall I run?
Will God, the just, reverse my doom,
And hear my latest groan?'

Their bowed, guilty shiftiness! Their spiritual ledgers, their clasped brown books of horrid verses – verbal enclosures similar to those stone ones that imprisoned the moors, to those hedges that gripped the pastures, and that kept out life, light and the wild creatures of moor and woodland!

Anne with her hands clasped over her ears tore away from the surprised, hurt Betty and ran from the room, hunted again, this time not with stones, but with hymns. These tore like Patience Helliwell's knives when they rended the flesh of hares, rooks, salmon, sheep, cattle and pigeons. Along the passageways, not knowing which ones she was following, Anne fled shrieking. Often she ran through darkness, yet some spirit seemed to save her from collisions. Back and forth, on different levels of the house, shrieking.

The Methodists paused in silent awe and horror listening to this ghost, this banshee. Anne's pained scream travelled, louder, softer, louder, softer. It was like a trapped bird's cry: a lark baffled in a cage of hymns.

At last, the preacher calmly said, 'She is a mad woman that must be confined in irons. Makings and our useful countryside must be purged, must be rid, must be saved from her – praised be the Lord!'

'Confine the witch! Lock her up! Lock 'er in Bedlam! Praisèd be the Lord!' the other Methodists exclaimed. And then (with more vigour than they had shown all evening) they chanted:

'GOD MADE THE DEVIL, THE DEVIL MADE SIN,
    GOD MADE A HOLE TO PUT THE DEVIL IN!'

Whilst Betty, stinging from Anne's apparent abandonment of her, raised her thin voice mercilessly with the rest of them.

Escaping before it was Dick Almighty who came jangling chains and keys to remove and confine her, Anne returned to Lady Well in April. On her walk there she saw a clothier's barn that had burned down. It was a recent event, for it had melted a bright green patch out of the snow, and there was still a smell of wet ashes. The stone roof-tiles had broken and fallen, except for one or two perilously hanging over the edges of walls and clinging to the charred timbers that poked into the sky. Poor children, women and discharged soldiers making their way across the country – winter starvelings – were picking amongst the ruins, risking their lives under tons of collapsing masonry in the hope of finding rags or some corn. Half a mile further on Anne came across a once-fine building erected by John Wylde, and now also burned to the ground. These destructions were the only changes in Lady Well, although she naturally expected the rest of the world to be as much transformed as she herself had been in the past eight months.

She was menstruating and the blood was uncomfortable, making her irritable. The stone-upon-stone of the town oppressed her once again; stone underfoot, stone portals framing God, the sky, and the greening moors. Even the familiar tap, tap, tap growing steadily louder as she approached the mason's yard did not seem a welcoming sound any more, bowed as she was by her sense of failure, feeling wearied and cold because of her menstruation. But as she came up the pathway, sadness was at last overborne by a glow from her father's house, where she noticed that the snow had disappeared off the roof because of the warmth within. Yet, on entering under its low ceilings, she was forced once more to stoop.

Her father had been reading Lavater's *Aphorisms on Man*. He did not expect her and had received little news; only sometimes a passing weaver or workman had brought a message. When he glanced up and saw his daughter, he could not speak. Something, that could not be contained within Reason (though to the mason this was 'God's greatest attribute'), overwhelmed him. His spectacles grotesquely enlarged his eyes and their welling tears, until with shaking hands he put his lenses on the table. 'I was just thinking of you,' he said (but he was always thinking about her), and he flushed, with (Anne sensed with alarm) what might have been an incapacity of the heart. He was of those middle years when a person who leads a tiring worrying life seems on certain days to grow old suddenly, and Anne was stabbed with compassion for his helplessness, large as he was.

John Wylde felt for his daughter something akin to a mother's love, so purified was it by self-sacrifice. He led her gently into the parlour where his charts and treatises were, scattered just as when she had left.

'Father, you should not be alone. I ought to be here taking care of you.'

'But I've got me a servant woman!'

'At last!'

'At last, as you say. She's a poor thing, who'd not otherwise have survived the winter. Martha!'

Anne heard a shuffling in the passageway. It did not seem to be a person walking on two feet, but was more like an animal brushing against things. There entered a small crippled woman apparently about forty years of age. One side of her hip sagged uselessly. Her face was pale, blotchy, stupid. Even so it expressed loving tenderness and she looked at John Wylde adoring him.

'Martha, this is my daughter, Anne.'

'Please t'meet you, Ma'am.' As the cripple attempted a curtsey, it looked as though her bones would collapse into jelly. It made Anne feel sick and she turned away.

'That's all right, Martha, you lay out oatcakes and soup and we'll join you presently.'

After she had left, Wylde explained, 'As a baby she was dropped at the door of the hospital and when she was nine they put her out to service for seven years. The mistress beat her and broke her bones so she was little use to man or beast. They would have killed her and when they wanted to be rid it was only kindness to take her in. You know I do not like to have servants about the house. But this is a good one. She is still only fourteen years of age and there is no one more willing.'

Anne suffered a jealous pang, seeing the willingness with which her father brought a stranger into his family (though according to gossip she was herself adopted). 'A thing like that cannot care for you! Th'ospital can take her back and I will stay here!' Anne shouted angrily.

Wylde looked startled. Then he understood. 'Something's happened at Making Hall. The truth shows through no matter what pleasant lies you send ahead of you to soothe me.'

She was silent for a while. Then she said quietly, 'I saw two buildings burned down on my way here, Father.'

'We have discontented weavers or some of that sort, "having a mind to bring revolution by setting things afire", so Dick Almighty says. "Folk i' moorland taverns and hush-houses who drink untaxed brews, sell stolen game, and enjoy night-long suppers of their poachings over which they discuss elections, poetry, Reason, or the downfall of the innkeeper and the King," that is the way he puts it. "Subscribers to penny libraries." I believe Dick thinks that I'm one of them. This week he's hunted out the Rhodes family that once lived at Upper Spout, who have been hiding books i'Greek and seditious pamphlets in a coffin that was supposed to be awaiting the passing of a sick grandfather.'

'I've not heard anyone but our housekeeper at Makings and the Vicar talk of fire. I remember he wanted an artist to depict the flames of Hell eternal upon the church walls but the wardens wouldn't have such "Popery". Nor could they understand why our Parson was so interested in such depictions, for he had always shown hatred of art and graven images before.'

'Doubtfire used to think so much of you and now he can't say a good word! He tells folk that you've bewitched them at Benjamin Greave's and are spreading sedition there. "You know what your lass is like," he says. "They'll be after her for a witch there, too. They'll be looking to her as the cause o't'fires and will be setting *her* upon a blaze".'

Anne in shame pressed and rubbed her fists into her eyes. 'The housekeeper didn't like me because she's a Methodist and she gave me the worst work to do! Old Man Greave thought I was after his fortune. I cannot go back. Father, I have been so unhappy – but for one person, a fair good man, I have been made so unhappy! You know how you may sink to such depths of misery that you become too weak to alter it and appear to choose to continue in your state, in spite of yourself you go on, confusing those around you? That's how I was.'

When his daughter was upset, it evaporated John Wylde's temper. 'Well, perhaps there's no need for you to return. We'll think of something. These are not the Dark Ages, for we now know that all problems can be resolved through Reason. I've been reading some of our greatest philosophers this winter, to pass the time on. The Universe, I've discovered, is but a great rational instrument like a clock in which, once set in motion by God, one thing brings about another. As in a mill or a manufactory, after the raw wool is fed in it continues through due process, all hands obedient to Reason and playing their part. We have but to accumulate enough knowledge in order to set everything right. God is our mill-master. Abundant Nature is as it were the handmaiden of Man, serving him with materials to exploit; whilst Reason is the manufactory through which he puts it, turning it into goods for his ease and prosperity. It's proven that every single thing is caused by another. So now we can sit peacefully by the fireside and trace all your misfortunes to one original cause, or to one misuse of the clockwork of knowledge – so I've learnt from the doctors – and correct it. Come now, go and tell Martha to serve oatcakes and we'll settle down and adjust your nature to the facts.'

'I don't think you can understand everything from philosophers.'

Her father grew impatient. He restored his spectacles and spoke more emphatically. 'God's universe is such a marvellous balanced instrument that if so much as one thing or person is out of step, the whole is by that degree, be it ever so small, upset, just as with an unreliable servant in a manufactory. I have always tried to teach you, believing that it is everyone's birthright, but it seems the result has only been for you to show too much independence for your female station! A woman that is wise as well as clever should ever struggle to be modest – a lesson you have never taken to heart, though you have learnt so much else. Be taught that, and I'm sure all else will follow, when you are less conspicuous.'

John Wylde angrily left the room, returning himself with the food. They ate in silence. Then the father read aloud from Lavater's *Aphorisms*. ' "Forwardness nips affection in the bud." And here's another

77

wise saying for you to think on, now. "If you mean to be loved, give more than what is asked, but no more than is wanted." Your main fault, Anne, from which all your troubles spring, is excess.'

'It is the world that is mean and timid.'

'So you blame the world now!'

'I am very unhappy.' She played clumsily with her hair that tumbled stiffly about her head like thorns. 'I think I will go to bed.'

'We'll bring your things home tomorrow. The day after we will go to church with Martha. I have a bacon joint for dinner and we can wash it down with ... with something that Dick Almighty knows nothing about.'

'You will not want me in church. I am unclean.'

'Oh.' He smiled, with tears pricking his eyes. 'Well, then – here's a last thought from Lavater. "Whom smiles and tears make equally lovely, all hearts may court".'

She laughed again – her father and his philosophers talked such nonsense. Once more comforted by this familiar house and the memories of soothings received in it, she climbed the oak stair, the very dimensions of it making her happy. The big carefully oiled clock ticking in the passageway. And the shape of the hill outside her bedroom which seemed to her like a crouching hare, gladdened her, lying under stars in the snowy dusk.

She stripped, and as Martha had thoughtfully put a bowl of water ready in her room, Anne spent some time cleaning up her blood.

It led her to staring at this desirable body of hers. In the candlelight it was long and snake-like, smeared at the top of her thighs. She twisted this way and that, watching fascinated as different bones projected. She squeezed her freckles, counted them, traced the pattern of a scar, then she pulled at her mouth and eyes. She rearranged her hair. Put two hands under her breasts and tried how they looked when she lifted them. Examined that opening amongst the bushes where in a fountain of blood the Devil was supposed to dwell. She pictured him, with his little ram's horns and impish eyes, peeping out of the well of blood.

She stopped caressing herself when the feeling of something uncanny outside made her look through the window. The tradesmen and artisans mostly went to bed at seven, to save the expense of candles, and even the Constable did not find it necessary to make any rounds; instead he attracted the rascals to listen to his 'sermons' in his public house. Yet there was Doubtfire, presumably on his way to visit someone who was sick. His eyes glittered impishly in the light that he carried. Realising that he was seen he vanished amongst the walls.

When Anne came down the next morning Martha was babbling about another clothier's house that had been fired. It pleased her greatly and she was chuckling to herself as she served oatcakes.

The burned house belonged to the family of Esther Kershaw who like a Papist kept a holy relic in her bedroom – the apron stained with blood which had dripped on her from the church roof during one of Doubtfire's services and which she believed was the blood of Christ. (If it was not, then what else was it?) Esther was the only one to escape the flames, clutching this garment, and now was to live without father, husband, children or home. 'All my years living faithful in Holy Monotony gone to waste!' she had cried. 'We grow a rose in a garden only for our menfolk to pluck it, and soon as 'tis plucked, then all is gone . . .!' She was half mad, walking up and down Lady Well shrieking this, tearing at her hair and her apron, and claiming that it was the Reverend Doubtfire who had set the fire in revenge for her making a holy image. Esther said that henceforth she would wander the moors wearing the apron as a 'sign' and would go only amongst poor people, there to look for the true Christ whom she did not find through the Lady Well Vicar.

'Esther is I suppose slandering our Parson because he will not raise an appeal in church for her relief – she being something of a Papist,' John Wylde said.

'Everything that Esther says is not foolish, Father.'

John Wylde took no further interest in Martha's and Anne's talk of Doubtfire and magical spots of blood. His face was shut. Anne now cared only about her father's expression. She felt guilty at remembering how irritable and selfish she had been, and at not having inquired about *his* affairs, and she thought he was sulking because of this.

Yet as so often she said the wrong thing. 'You cannot consider a person as being like nothing more than a spinning machine – or even a shed full of machines. Our natures are not so mechanical and we do not accumulate understanding like money added to a store, for often one thing that we think we know conflicts with another...'

'Doubtfire watched you display yourself at your window last night!' John Wylde burst out. 'When they went to tell him about the new fire he thought it a small matter compared with what he had seen of "The Lady Well whore", as he called my daughter!' Quivering, breathing heavily, he was removing his belt. 'No wonder they call you "whore"!'

'That's not reasonable, Father...'

'To Hell with reason! All of Lady Well is looking to find fault with my daughter! Almighty's *Felon Society* has met to discuss ways of apprehending the fire-raiser and even there the Vicar had to tell 'em that their time'd be better spent rooting out witches and sinful women. Yet still you taunt them with your wickedness! I'm thinking that folk are right and thou'rt truly a demon from the Old Religion sent to plague us. Something bred like a gadfly out of the manure of our sins. Oh, what a daughter! I've always been too gentle with you, thou's done untold harm to my business, and folk are laughing at me. The Constable will be coming to *us* before long!' Wylde was swinging his belt, one end wrapped around his thick wrist. 'It seems that rough timber must have many blows to hew it even and fit for the Lord's building!'

'No!' Anne screamed. Or rather, a scream possessed her – a sound not human but intense as the cry of a vixen or a peacock: all her being was consumed in that yell.

John Wylde, who had been unnerved by this unearthly howl once or twice before, shouted, 'Thou'rt no daughter of mine!' and, afraid of what he heard both from himself and from Anne, he chased her down the path. Then, so that no one would witness his tears, he returned indoors.

As Anne fled, housewives cackled, artisans whistled and shouted, and the young ones again threw stones, thinking that the old days of baiting their scapegoat had returned. ''Awthorn! 'Awthorn! Burn in t'fire!' they shouted, and the familiar:

'God made the Devil! The Devil made sin!
God made a hole to put the Devil in!'

Hurtling through the flowerless stony narrow streets, where the hard echoes cruelly mocked her flight, Anne recalled the many occasions when she had escaped. But this time she had even deserted her father's house.

Beyond town she kept on running, through an air tainted with last night's ashes, and she made for the moors, where there were no people. She was already on Black Hill before she remembered that there lived her Aunt Pity, with whom she could take shelter.

It was said of Pity that she was so old, she had been around at the time of the earliest Christians. One thing at least could be truly said of her: she offered comfort and healing, not only to her neighbours, but even to vagabonds, wandering soldiers, gypsies, and other travellers with cut feet who called on her. So Anne ceased to rush or sweat and she peacefully climbed the slopes looking lovingly about her. Most of the snow had vanished in the morning sun. The urgings of grass or buds could be felt and primroses were straightening after the burden of snow. Moisture necklaced the plants with pearls, and upon them light trembled, whilst dappling further hillsides with broad sheets that were flowing with shadows. Tentative robins and thrushes were singing to test the coming spring. She saw a wren. Bright tongues of water licked out of so many enclosures and banks, it seemed that all the hills and valleys floated upon it: as if everywhere underneath was the one substance, breaking out with a voice cheerful as the bird-song.

Meanwhile the road was growing stonier and there were more, larger patches of snow. On Black Hill she could look across other hills stretching silver and dark grey for miles. The moor was animated with a scattering of boulders shaped by wind and rain into forms seeming full of dormant life. There were vast purple-dark pregnant stomachs balanced on slender stalks. Rocks like old molar teeth, or like tiny virgin breasts popped up out of the grass. You could imagine anything. The stones were alive, and changing constantly, as she walked by, from one form into another. Here there was no grass, only withered rushes, their tips capturing the gold given by the sun so that there seemed to be swarms of dancing sun-spots around her feet. The hilltops and slopes, too, leaped about under the delicate touches of light. It shifted from one peak to another, brightening them momentarily with the special yellow-green of the Pennines, set against blue watery pools of shadow in the valleys.

The moortops were governed by a different god from the valleys.

Everything on the hills belonged to infinite light. In the distance, rock and moor, such heavy things, dissolved into the milk of the hazy sky. As intoxicated with height and space as a skylark, one wanted never to descend. The few people living here showed reluctance to come down into the towns and hamlets, even though they might starve because of it. From isolation, they experienced different lives; they were harsher, according to the philosophy at each solitary farmstead developed in response to the God of bleak weather, sky and dark stones. Without realising it, they dressed differently. They experienced different dreams. Their speech grew clipped and brutal. Everything was thinner – their bodies, expectations, purses, poultry and cattle.

After Anne Wylde disappeared, she was talked about even more than when she had been present. Travellers returned to Holland and Spain with tales of a giant gorgon who haunted the English moors and had adopted the shape of a maidservant in a clothier's household, in order to destroy him. According to various accounts Anne had three, four or five breasts which poured forth honey under a full moon and she went about dressed in a girdle of snakes, like the figure of the Medusa which Captain Horsfall had given Benjamin Greave to put over his door. Or they said that Anne was a form of that wandering White Cow which still gave milk even after being sucked by a regiment of men. It was hard to believe that the maiden Anne Wylde of Lady Well, a mason's daughter, had ever actually existed.

Benjamin Greave was impatient of these superstitions. He agreed that the girl was a witch, and that in his youth she would not have been tolerated; but foolish laws had come in for the defence of such. However, the form that her witchcraft took was not worth his bothering his head about. He was too old and wise. He was too busy. Not wanting to travel south so often to buy wool, nor to trust factors, he was experimenting with keeping his own sheep. Modern improvements in the management of grassland indicated that even Yorkshire's sour hilltops could be grazed if the land was cleared, an enterprising visitor had told Greave; and the clothier joked back that maybe one of the useless hawthorn trees that he was destroying was the vanished devil, Anne Wylde, so he'd rid Yorkshire finally of her and deserve to be knighted for't. If the old heather was burnt, it would leave a layer of fertilising ash. When he had been setting fire, the district hung under drifting smoke. The Making's food, bedding and clothes were tainted, and the people, already with lungs full of wool-dust, coughed through work and sleep. Greave's whole life had become a dream of selling worsteds to the Empress of Russia, of burning useless heather and hawthorn from the moors and of planting straight lines of cuttings from the old wild chaotic hawthorn trees to make enclosure hedges.

Gobbling up the hills and valleys, shovelling food rudely into his maw untasted in the smoky kitchen, he saw Oliver's distaste, his unhappiness and restlessness without Anne whom he could not trace, and he challenged it.

'What's th' matter? Thou's like someone that's lost sixpence. Thou wants a dose o' th' apothecary's rubbing bottle to raise thy spirits.'

This produced no answer, so Benjamin tried another tack. 'You think the Devil-woman might make a good wife for you – if you can find her! But I fear she's been spirited away, to save us. I'd not let such a one in sight of my pattern books! A young girl is filled with love as a cistern with water, she wants only somewhere to empty it. And then it is impossible to stop her, as when a dam is breached. Also, having such a strong purpose makes her blind to her lover's defects – though he's as big an ass as you!'

Meanwhile the clothier chewed noisily, like a horse, upon a turnip. It was the earliest one, plucked from his garden: he had a fondness for roots. Also, so as not to 'waste time' whilst he was eating, he fingered a small sample of weaving that had been brought to him. Turning it and turning it, like a Catholic with a rosary, he was perfectly self-absorbed.

Oliver burst out, 'Do not preach to me! If you will not be just to Miss Wylde. I will leave this house. I'll go to London ...'

Benjamin studiously nipped off the tail and removed a few green leaves that were sprouting from his turnip. 'Aye, I'm told you've only to know 'ow to hold a knife and fork for them to make a great man of you down yonder. Even thou should be able to manage that!'

'I'll tak' myself to Greece. Or to Russia. I'll mak' worsted for 'em there. I have heard that the Empress's court gives encouragement to strangers who wish to settle at Astracan, for the convenience of the woollen manufacture of Persia.'

Bits of turnip spluttered from the exasperated clothier's mouth. Then, anxious for his samples of beautiful cloth, he shook the scraps off it. 'Thou's forever restless to get by thyself somewhere! When a child you were always hiding in rabbits' or foxes' holes and by t'streams, instead of ganging to school with other children, though you risked a whipping for it. Never satisfied with us all working and living together, man and beast, to be prosperous and happy in *this* life. Thou'lt find the grave private enough . . .'

'I'll settle again at Lower Laithes, where I was with Zillah.'

'Wylde's girl'll not make a wife for you! She's about as domesticated as Genghis Khan!'

'She is experienced and skilled at every branch of domestic economy.'

'*When* thou can keep her at home!' Benjamin paused. 'She'll have no dowry, neither.'

'John Wylde is a successful man.'

'He won't be if he keeps on reading them books.'

When Benjamin Greave mentioned 'bewks', as he called them, it meant he had thrown his final argument – if the contentious subject was guilty of reading, there was no need to say more. (Especially if the reader was a female.) The word 'bewks' fell like a tombstone on a villain's corpse.

So Oliver said no more. Yet he had made up his mind. Through clouds of smoke rolling off the hilltops, hearing the tormented screeching of larks above their burnt nests, Oliver rode down through the oak trees, and the grey glacial boulders the size of houses, into the pit of the gorge below Lady Well. There John Wylde was erecting a big new spinning-building for Captain Horsfall. Along the river – a place which no one had been interested in before, except to chase wild duck or snipe through the marshes, or to graze oxen on meadows dry only for a few months in the summer – it was as if a new world had to be built overnight: though it was impossible to tell what sort of world it would be, there was such confusion. From high up Oliver saw a row of bonfires and black smoke where they were burning waste wood. When he came close he found oily putrefactions out of wool or timber, and the chemicals or oils used by engineers and carpenters, coiling in the water where until a year ago he had watched the grey muscular shadows of salmon nosing upstream and the trout, flicking into the currents, or bubbling peacefully from the depths. Barges carrying Russian pine were tied up under the sites for several long stone sheds, Horsfall's being the largest. Carts laden with fittings of iron and gleaming brass stood by.

Dick Almighty was standing there with gold to invest, and a greedy anxious look as he tried to speak to busy engineers or to the impatient bankers who had rolled up in their carriages. He flattered them by telling them what they already knew only too well: that they were *important Gentlemen*. As a reward for being this, Sin-Catcher Almighty offered to enrol them in to *The Society For Prosecuting Felons*, which was short of members (subscription a guinea per year). They answered him that they were from Leeds, 'an important universal city': a clear suggestion that they were not interested in a parish-pump constable. Almighty was apoplectic at being spoken to in this way, for such a thing had never happened before. Nonetheless he must control himself before such distinguished people. They off-handedly told him to 'see what he could for himself'; in fact nobody, not even the workmen, had time to bother with him.

Almighty could make out clearly only two things that were quite novel. Firstly, the delivery of pine for building. He had never seen anything but oak used before. Secondly, they were digging a canal that headed direct to the hills.

'So our river is to be as straight as the path to God!' he smartly exclaimed, to the only man he could at last find with the time and the will to listen to a fool. 'You cannot take water up a mountain! 'Tis against the will of Lord!'

He received the coyest of smiles.

'Sure you can, if you make a hole to put it into,' the Irish labourer answered.

They were going to dig a tunnel, which would destroy for ever the separation of Yorkshire from Lancashire! This alteration of God's ordered universe at a single stroke was the product of Horsfall's genius; he had sold the land for the waterway at a cheap price in return for other advantages from the bankers. (Another slight to Almighty; for the Captain had declared nothing, neither to him nor anybody else, about his plans.)

At sheds in which spinning machines were already installed were lines of women and girls seeking employment. They were a desperate kind to seek such work – drifters from other counties, turned from their homes because a gentleman desired a park there or was improving the land – and some attempted to be saucy because Oliver was one of the masters.

Oliver found John Wylde raising a huge flagstone, weighing several tons, for a machine-bed. Several men with pulleys had it balanced in mid-air. There was a confusion of noise all around – carts struggling through mud, saws and masons' hammers – but this circle was silent and tense as if concentrating on a ritual. Some of the labourers twitched with nervousness, afraid to move under the vast stone swaying precariously above their heads. Others, used to brutal work and boasting of their roughness, acted rashly. John Wylde calculated the whole action. With the same accuracy that he applied to stones, he balanced the temperaments of his workmen, anticipating characteristic reactions, and with a slight movement of eye or hand encouraging or restraining them. For half an hour Oliver watched the machine-bed inch its way ten feet across the sky, to rest one end on a wall and the other on a pine beam. By which time Oliver appreciated, for the first time, the delicate skills of these workmen compelled through every hour of labour to trust one another.

When the flagstone was safe, the slackened ropes sagged as if they were as glad to relax as were the workmen; two of whom sang bawdy songs (one brought out a fiddle), whilst the third took Plato's *Republic* from his pocket.

John Wylde smiled, not especially with pleasure at seeing Oliver Greave, but at the neatness of the operation. 'We use pine instead of oak for the spinning sheds because it is more supple and therefore does not have to be of such thickness,' the mason said. 'It does not matter that pine is not so enduring. Perhaps our manufactories will not be wanted for ever.'

Oliver seemed uninterested.

'The skills of my labourers would amaze many a gentleman,' Wylde offered next. 'Jeremiah Rhodes there can understand ten languages, yet until the age of twenty he could hardly read or write. He used to live at Upper Spout, but ever since your father told 'em it was poisonous to drink from the spring there – and they believed him, being ignorant, though Mr Greave, pardon my saying so, has made good use of the water – he has stayed up every night teaching himself.

Before that, he was satisfied to let Methodists preach at him. Though I suppose they have given him orderly habits.'

Oliver was not surprised by that either: he had met this type of fellow many times at Library-Subscription Clubs, Rhymesters' Clubs and Debating Societies.

John Wylde knew, of course, what Oliver Greave really wanted. The mason, following his usual manner with visitors, was simply keeping the conversation going in the hope of obtaining in return something instructive or entertaining from the clothier. But he saw that he was not going to get it, for the young man was distracted. At last, Wylde gave up the attempt. 'She's left home. Gone over the moors,' he said.

Wylde was reluctant to add more where he could be overheard: Dick Almighty and Doubtfire had already been to him, investigating a 'curse' upon the clothiers consisting of more fires, mysterious swelling in a child's body, a 'plague of sinfulness' with fiddlers playing night and day, and a woman whose mouth filled with blood whenever she spoke of the Devil. He led Oliver to one side and whispered, 'My wife had a sister lived in a cottage beyond Black Hill. She's another queer witch, maybe she's gone there. Anne follows her own rules, though. It wouldn't do any good for me to seek her out.'

Oliver ascended Black Hill, over the bouldered moor into thick smoke, hurrying and yet frightened of his horse breaking an ankle amongst ashes, tangled heather and stones. He saw his father's blazing hawthorns, which as they darkened to charred wood bled a reddish-yellow sap like blood. And as if to warn him (though of what he could not think) larks screamed from the advancing fire, and then returned arching over it to find that nothing was left of their nests.

When the smoke cleared Oliver saw a line of cottages circling below him where water burst out of rocks and rushes. Following the course of a stream he descended into a valley that had a different spirit; one out of Benjamin Greave's reach, unenclosed except by its majestic circle of hills, and with no 'useful' packhorse-route into it; unburnt, undrained, with bright patches of bog-flowers and freely blossoming hawthorn. Each cottage here gave forth a different, peaceful domestic smell. From over there it was of pigs, here of oily wefts, and in another place of horses. The odours rose to choke a calm afternoon, with the silver light melting the silk of distant hills, so that moor and light became sometimes one, and at other times indistinctly separate. Oliver tried to pinpoint the likely home of an eccentric spinster. But at one there were children. At another a weaver moved amongst rows of cloth spread out-of-doors on his tenter frames. A third had a horse nearby, whilst at a fourth, a man was digging drains.

Oliver approached a derelict-looking house that might be the home of a witch. But it held nothing except sheep. So he turned along the track linking the cottages. In the next, two or three looms were clattering. The father came to his door: a gaunt man, brusque and cheerful but not good at giving directions because he got lost in his memories of each place.

'You'll see up yonder a bridge!' he bawled, as if he was delivering a command. 'Just go over and thou'll find a rowan tree, for my Uncle Matt planted it. He had a home there, but it's tumbled now. There's still fruit bushes that he grew in yonder wild place. They seemed to find time for much more in the old days, didn't they! Then thou goes to the right – no, is it left? – up by a spout of water. "Foul Syke", its name. Or better still, stay this side of the bridge, though then thou'll miss where Uncle Matt lived. I wish I could go with you to see the old place again and show you the way! But you know what they say?' He nodded over his shoulder to the noisy looms. 'On Monday and Tuesday the loom chants, "Plenty of time! Plenty of time!" But on Thursday and Friday, it's "Thou's a day too late! Thou's a day too late!" So I'll have to be finishing my piece or time'll be catching up on me. Good day to you now!'

Oliver turned the corner of the hill, saw a flourishing rowan-tree and a tumbled cottage, followed the energetic little stream along Foul Syke, and reached the open space of a north-facing slope where hardly anyone wished to live. It was called, indeed, 'the Dark Side'. However, there was one dreary cottage. Its grounds were walled off, and a sign pointed into a bog: MERCHANTS WOOLMEN WORLDLY FOLK THIS WAY. Other crude boards declared: BLESST BE HE THAT TURNETH TO THE LORD, and CONSIDER THEE DOOM.

There came out an old man who Oliver recognised as one who went about preaching and who sometimes came to Makings. At first the man was fierce and hostile, just as he usually was when he visited the clothier's mansion. Then, because they were in the open air, the two of them fell into that relaxed understanding of those who recognise in one another that they both enjoy wandering the hills.

'Elkanah Beanland, I can't pass on my way through that miry trough!'

Elkanah's flesh was a tangle of veins standing out on the sunken scarred skin and of tendons that threatened to tie themselves into knots, as he shouted, apparently irate, 'Then thou shouldn't be one wi' the worldly folk! Let this be thy journey's end. Come in and pray with me. Aren't thou Oliver Greave, a poet and student, as they tell me, of the classics, that recommend sodomy and incest shamelessly to all?'

'Elkanah!'

'They write about nothing else! Follow that path and thou'lt end in antinomian piss-mires worse than any I can lay before ye! I've seen poets before and what Devil's piss-mires they fall into!'

'Mr Beanland, I'm looking for the cottage of a woman named Pity.'

'Another sinner! But a good one.' The 'preacher' mellowed his voice now. In fact he whispered, awestruck. 'She's up there. Well thou can take a short way through my garden if thou's a mind, Master Greave. And if thou wishes to arrive in Heaven wi' dry feet, carry this text in thy heart...'

Rejecting the text but thankfully accepting the dry way (to Pity's, not to Heaven) Oliver climbed the garden wall and pressed on through the cold shadow covering the moorside.

Just when he was becoming desperate he stumbled on to the sight of a cottage chimney-stack rising out of a crack in the moor like a hand drowning in Hades. From the lip he saw below a waterfall thundering through rowans, hawthorns and alders, and a garden where, in this place lit by only a few hours of sunlight each day, grew fruit trees, roses and other flowers, and the earth was freshly planted with seeds. Hens wandered and a cow was tethered near the water. As Oliver brushed down the hillside, even at this early time of the year he raised the scents of herbs and he imagined how perfumed this spot must be in late summer. It seemed both the entrance to a scented flowery paradise, and also to the dark secret underworld.

Before he reached the gate a fierce black dog leaped on its chain, as though to throttle itself. Its yellow eyes gleamed with malevolence, hair bristled on its neck and it gnashed its mouth of slavering teeth in frustration. Whilst Oliver hesitated, an old woman came out with a bucket and calmed the dog. She was so bent that her chin was close to her stomach, and yet she seemed very strong as she ducked her container in the waterfall.

'What a delightful place!' Oliver shouted. 'You must practise witch-craft to make so much grow here!'

The woman looked sideways at him and shaded her eyes, even though there was hardly any light. The little that Oliver could detect of her features was remarkable: weathered brick red, but without a wrinkle, it was a maiden's skin preserved within a mane of grey hair. Her voice was weak, but because of its authority one realised that it had once been forceful.

'I cannot see you, my dear! The sky hurts my eyes. Though it's a long time since I stared it in the face, it seems never tired of punishing me! I've never got on too kindly with the sun; th'old brass-face and I are ancient enemies. By the sound of your voice I'd say you was from Makings. Oh, yes, I'd recognise a Greave's voice anywhere. You will have come to find Anne Wylde, I suppose? The Vicar tolls a bell and all must come to church, a woman calls differently and men come hurrying to her ... She escaped from your clutches! But she's just inside. You can go right in, my dog won't touch you now and no one's unwelcome here.'

Easily carrying the filled bucket, the old woman hobbled down the path to her cottage door whilst she talked, her dim eyes meanwhile taking in a hazy view of the ground, snails, dirt, grass, weeds and spring plants sliding beneath her. 'I've planted dandelions there as'll be ready soon. How was the comfrey up the hillside?'

'I didn't notice, Madam.'

'You come right past it! Eh well, we don't all see what's under our noses.'

Aunt Pity stayed outside, tending her plants whilst Oliver entered. Indoors there was the hiss and flash of several cats. He noticed bunches of primroses and other spring flowers in jugs, a pungent smell of vegetation brewing and a large vat of dye. Aunt Pity, like many unmarried women and widows, made her living by colouring cloth. They used roots and herbs but kept their recipes secret, and Aunt Pity's speciality was that particular soldier's red for which Benjamin Greave and other clothiers had to come to her.

Anne was wearing a red gown, a white apron and a cap that could not control her hair. She was singing. The words glided bouyantly on an invisible current of air – a river of words delighting in its lightness. Seeing Oliver she became silent. And after such a long break, Oliver was too shy to touch, even to speak to his beloved.

'It is my birthday in April,' Anne said. 'That is why Pity fills our cottage with flowers.'

Oliver told her, nervously and bluntly, 'I have left my father's house and taken Lower Laithes and I need a housekeeper. Your father could live with us, as he grows weaker in the flesh. I will give you an interest in my affairs. Anne, I love you ...' He spoke of love so pitifully: as if it was as much a sickness as a joy, and as if he anticipated as much pain as pleasure from it.

For a few moments the heart of the hunted virgin drummed and fluttered, like a small bird cupped in warm hands, at the thought of being held by this gentle man. Then the alternative idea that had already kept her so often distant grew uppermost. She feared that he might begin to neglect her as soon as he was satisfied.

'I am happiest collecting herbs and whinberries with my Aunt, who has noone to look after her,' she said.

'You cannot live up here isolated in this bleak place! Your beauty was intended for palaces.'

Anne interrupted him. 'Aunt Pity came here when her sweetheart died in the wars. They said to her, too, that she could never make a life up in this place, and without a man. But you see she has done quite well out of brewing dyes.'

Pity came in then, kittens and hens around her skirts. She had an intimate consciousness of each one of them, the grey, the tabby, the speckled moult, even whilst she gave her attention elsewhere. When she turned to Oliver, she spoke with that certainty of being listened to which women who have been beautiful retain throughout their lives. 'Aye, but we have little choice in this world except to be as men wish it!' she said.

Lower Laithes, built as a home for Oliver and Zillah but according to Oliver's taste, was symmetrical and spacious in a classical style, with an extravagance of Corinthian pillars, pediments, statues and mottoes in Greek. Benjamin Greave always said that there were too many 'private' rooms for it to be a happy home, and that they were too high for anything except for a bird to fly in. Nobody had wanted to live there since Oliver and his wife. This was mainly because, the crafty father having planned that his son should at least overlook his fulling mill, the big wooden hammers clattered in hearing all day long and the stream roared nearby, tumbling over waterfalls and dams made by Benjamin Greave's engineers; who schemed and suffered sleepless nights to make Nature do what she did not intend. The place was usually wrapped in a damp woodland twilight and the tracks were muddy from daily traffic to Makings.

A week after Oliver had called upon Anne, inhabitants of Lady Well heard an eerie whistling, and Joshua Binns saw a pack of black hounds flying in the sunset. Or they claimed that they did: and this was, they said, because it was when Anne Wylde went down to Lower Laithes.

She walked lightly and smiling, with her usual challenging expression. The spring day and the sunlight were still. Patches of the moor were bright green with fresh whinberry leaves and the watery places floated crowfoot flowers. The smell of juices leaked out of the grass that was cut in the enclosures. Across budding trees cut a sharp edge of shadow, out of which mossy trunks rose in lit tapers and spread into delicate cobwebs of branches. Everywhere, in wood, field and moor, was a green reflected light.

Anne strolled around the unloved forgotten mansion, peering through dusty windows at bare boards and frozen-looking furniture. She wondered what curtains would best suit. Before long (remembering those volumes of engravings that architects and masons had brought since her earliest childhood into her father's house) Anne had in her mind carpeted, refurnished, altered the withdrawing room and peopled everywhere with a flutter of servants. The rank lawns and overgrown gardens – patterns marked out with low hedges of yew and boxwood – were at present unfashionably formal, so she 'planted' spreading trees (forgetting that they would take fifty years to achieve the proportions of her imagination). Peacocks on the lawns...

Nearby, engineers were tampering with the dykes, weirs and watercourses. They were experimenting to find out whether, by storing water in reservoirs at higher contours, its natural force could be submitted to machinery. Acquisitively they glanced up to scrutinise the invisible wind and wonder how that too could profit them. Thereby they caught glimpses of the strange young woman in the overgrown garden. One went to Makings, and said (in a blunt, challenging but humorous typically Yorkshire manner), 'Trouble's turned up again yonder, Mr Greave!' Whereupon Oliver rushed downhill to find it.

He surprised Anne as she paced back and forth tyrannising the desolation. Being withdrawn, her features appeared disdainful. But he knew by her air of possession of his house that he had won her. When she had focused upon him, she smiled, shivered slightly and then frowned, as if intimating that he ought to do something for her protection or comfort. So he lifted the shawl that had half-slipped from her and, boiling with desire, put it as slowly as he dared around her shoulder.

'It would take the women a week of scrubbing before you could move in here,' Anne said, coolly ignoring his manifest longing. She slowly plucked a forget-me-not, tumbled it in her fingers, and led him around the building. 'You must arrange for my things to be sent from Makings, for I am never going *there* again. Pay me what wages you like, but let me in charge and I promise you, you will be pleased. But you must not come here again for one whole month.'

They had followed the gravel walks around the house and had come to the front. A crack in one of the pillars of the colonnade, in which weeds and flowers grew, appeared ludicrous. That something so monumental should so soon prove vulnerable to time and the energies of an ordinary English spring! The whole classical façade was crumbling and the green light emphasised the moss on the building. Set into the pediment was a flaking inscription in Greek.

Oliver translated, ' "Know Thyself." It was a saying of Socrates, the Greek philosopher.'

'I can read that too!' Anne replied indignantly. 'I have met a lot of men who think that they can "know themselves", because the ones who visit my father always talk about it. Socrates must have been such a person as them.'

To find servants for Lower Laithes, Anne made her way to the camp of 'hardy ruffians', as everyone called them, in Blood Wood. For if she employed Lady Well people, she would be bringing her tormentors into her home, thus inciting envy; also, because their need was less, they probably would not work as hard as strangers.

The air was suffocating with the smell of the bluebells that had now reached their fullest blossom and lay like drifts of thick mist. Whitethroats and other warblers, robins and thrushes were singing, though faintly, because the end-of-May, summer-drowsiness was overcoming them. The first thing that Oliver had done for his house-keeper was to purchase the finest clothes that he could for her, and she wore a full and heavy walking dress of brilliant red wool – officers' cloth, the best that the weavers could make. She had delicate shoes, brought from London.

She found her way to the camp by the music. For in their savage tongues, Irish, Scottish, Welsh and Cornish, the outcasts sang laments for their homelands; melodies that rang mysteriously through this rocky northern woodland. Some of them had been wandering for years. Several children had been born on the unenclosed watery heaths, amongst treacherous rushes, alder swamps and willows. They had perhaps not left such places until they were in their teens, when upon bursting out of the brown and trackless wastes they had been amazed by the sight of bright green manured grass weeded to make fine and even pastures, and enclosed in squares of hedgerow or wall. A sight as amazing to them as would have been sudden glimpses of magnificent palaces of the Orient. Yet nothing had surprised them like the sight of this fabulous fine lady seeking them out.

Fiddles and flutes were silenced at her coming and the smutty derelicts rushed to hide what they had been cooking. Yet from a close look at Anne's weather-darkened skin and large hands, they saw that, despite her fine clothes, she was nothing special. When she asked for those who might be her servants, they answered her sarcastically, 'No one in this clearing is fit to dwell in fine houses, Ma'am, as you can see well enough.' (Meaning: 'Who are you to be wanting servants, and not dwelling yourself amongst brooks and stores?') 'Some of us unfortunates has spent th'ole winter in the countryside, *Ma'am!*' one added.

But when they realised that the lady meant what she said, the staring people behaved as if a load of beef or apples had fallen from a cart in front of them. They crowded around her, one or two horribly close to her face, or on their knees plucking at her gown, and some of the girls thrusting forward starved babies. Anne had come here disdainfully, thinking only of her own fine home. Now she could hardly speak, witnessing such misery.

'Madam, my husband came home to me drunk and threw our baby on to the fire. That was in Somerset. Then because I was angry and distressed it annoyed him and he did trample over my throat and breast until my crying brought a neighbour. Today he lies in the low jail in Bristol, though the lawyers say that it was my fault for opposing him, and now there is no one to care for us!'

(How do men come to describe the God who created this world as good and wise? He is neither! Anne thought and she felt ashamed of her fine clothes.)

'Madam, a farmer's son got me with child! The other women where I was servant whispered and searched my breast and found milk, so I confessed then and was given a licence to marry. My husband told me I would make a fine widow after he had gone. That is all he said to me, "Thou'll make a fine widow when I am gone!" On our wedding night he hanged himself in his father's barn. Oh Madam, what have I done to deserve such a sad hand of God? Give me work, please give me work!'

Anne could not cope with such unhappiness. Could not be expected to.

'Why is that one saying nothing?' Anne pointed at a lank-haired girl who sat sorrowful and bewildered by the fire. She was wearing camblett (a rain-proof worsted not made in the north), so Anne recognised another stranger.

95

'Bridie is from Ireland, where the soldiers burned down her village because it did not beautify an Englishman's estate. 'Twas not "picturesque" he told them. Some went west to the bare white rocks of Connaught – "To Hell or Connaught" as Cromwell said, for there was nothing to choose between the two – but Bridie drifted east to Liverpool. I do not think she knew which direction she was walking in. She does not speak a word of English and is too ignorant and stupid, like a beast, to learn.'

'I'll take her! You tell her what I want.'

'But she is pig-Irish, can't do nothing, Miss!'

It seemed that no one who had themselves anything to hope for would help the girl, because she was Irish. Then a huge uncomplaining woman, badly-scarred from the pox, gently led her over. The kind woman knew enough Gaelic to explain what was wanted, and the wretch was transformed. Her face took on a tranced look: it had the phosphorescence of those who have received an epiphany, or found themselves "redeemed" by a crossroads preacher. At last her lips quivered into speech.

'She says she don't expect to be paid, she'll be happy to work just for her food.'

The big kind woman who said this had once been amongst the merriest at fairs, wakes and saints'-days, until love and happiness led to the pox. Now the hair was almost gone from her head, and her face was marked as if with fire. Yet she was not ugly; and though she was large, she was not cumbersome; for her inner spirit vitalised her features. Perhaps because of embarrassment caused by her scorched appearance, she had a trick of not talking directly to one; she spoke as if addressing an invisible person at one's side, and would half turn away, laughing. The effect however was not of furtiveness, but as if she feared that her jokes might not be understood, except by some other, invisible, friendly company that she kept. 'As they write over the pillory in th'ospital, Ma'am, "Better to work than to suffer thus",' she remarked in her curious, sideways fashion.

Seeing that she wore a wedding ring, Anne asked the whereabouts of her husband.

'I'm Mary Pickles, Ma'am, and my husband was unjustly imprisoned. I know it was unjust and tried to prove it. When I could get no hearing from the lawyers, I seed no point in living, though we had a fine house and some acres with a pig and a cow, and I gave them up t'abide in the woods by the sun and the moon.'

'You gave up what you had because of love?'

''Twas for lack of justice, mostly. That wore me out, that did, for I saw no purpose in life any more.' She turned her cindered features appealingly to Anne Wylde – begging, not for work, not for money or bread, but for understanding. 'Yet it is only love that justifies us, I believe. And the only one to have seen and told us that is the Jesus who is so hard to find in the church. I have been turned away too often not to know that!'

'I'll take you also,' Anne said.

A man who by his grand diction, his purple skin and swollen nose Anne took to be a hedge-preacher or a renegade parson too drunk to preach, then shouted, 'Mary Pickles drowned her baby in the river to save it from getting the pox from its mother! Madam, you are choosing the most Godless sinners, outcasts from Grace, doomed to Hell, who will pollute the souls of your household on their journey thither!'

'The only outcast I will not employ is a God-fearing Methodist!' Anne answered, to almost everyone's laughter.

When gossip had spread that Anne Wylde – Anne Wylde! – was 'mistress' of Lower Laithes and taking on any rascal as servant, Amos Culpin came to her.

Though once he had been energetic enough to throw stones at Lady Well's scapegoat, now his doubts and sufferings had left him weary. It tired him of life to think that everyone was born of a filthy act which made us no fitter than animals to enter Heaven. He was amazed that men still dared to pray. Our sexual organs were our curse, for they prompted continual anxieties and, helplessly in the Devil's hands because of them, our eyes were directed away from God. Culpin's jolly maypole had turned into a cross upon which the Christ of his virtue was hung. His single consolation was the thought that the worst misfortunes proved that God did look into our foul hearts, sufficient at least to want to punish us, and so this was proof of His care. Such trials were our only hope of being purged. Culpin had at one stage turned to nonconforming sects, but these unsettled him further. Some believed in the abandonment of morality, saying they were born 'the Elect' and therefore would be saved no matter what

97

they did; or they thought that sin was the very road to freedom, before the world was destroyed tomorrow. Other groups of 'worshippers' were merely seeking a cover for radicalism and sedition, and they even sheltered atheists amongst their number. Then there were the 'magical Methodists' (as some called them); vulgar believers in miracles, revelations, manifest spirits, and mysterious vengeances.

These groups were all over Yorkshire. It was as if an ant-heap had spewed upon the hills. (A spawning of Hell or Paradise? Only time would tell which.) Amos, confused, on some days felt that there were now only a few untidy remnants of faith left in him; whilst other moments were full of the terror of God. His worldly affairs reflected the erratic state of his soul. He was notorious for being unable to keep any employment for long. So now he came humbly to Anne Wylde, who smiled at her victory, and made him her footman.

Next, Anne's inquiries for a personal maid brought her to one Jack Loveless, a widower, who needed to be rid of his 'hungry' daughter, whom he could not feed. He lived in a stone shack perched on a ledge on the edge of the moor and overhung with rocks. It took an afternoon's scramble to reach it. A richer artisan would have chosen a more sheltered spot but Loveless, in order to benefit from the nearby spring, had also to accept a magnificent spectacle of the valley and the maelstrom that often raged out of it. The cottage was backed against the hill out of which water seeped, or streamed, over the stone floor. The shelf of land was a wet, spongy green so brilliant that the eye could pick it out from far away. It was sufficient to feed a few hens, grow some oats, and keep alive an undernourished pony.

It was evening but Jack Loveless was still working the loom that filled the single downstairs room. The cupboards shook. The cottage was like a small ship with a huge engine in it. On the hearth squatted a small child setting wire teeth into pieces of leather used for 'carding' the wool. Michael Loveless spent all the hours of daylight thus and, frustrated of companions, adventure, play and the variety of the open air, he was muttering or laughing to himself. 'Jack o't'Crows,' he tittered. Like all children, he had been taught to distract boredom by naming the wires after people whom he knew, but Michael's self-absorption and self-made fun was slightly mad. He stared hungrily at the lady. 'I know someone who ate meat last Quarter Day, Ma'am,' he said, wistfully. Meanwhile his thirteen-year-old sister, Jenny, was bleaching the grease out of newly woven cloth by trampling it barefoot in a large shallow stone sink set into the floor, which contained the urine of the family and their pony.

The amazing product of this dreary industry was a stretch of blue weaving glowing upon the loom. 'They say that freedom glows brightest in prisons! That is blue wool for the French to make their "caps of liberty" from, God bless 'em,' the weaver explained.

Without removing her riding habit in the damp cottage, Anne went to the fire and warmed each delicately booted foot in turn. The child continued to set his wires, from which there was no release until he fell asleep over his work. Jenny Loveless had stopped trampling cloth, but she stayed in the sink, turned to stone by the sight of Anne Wylde who had risen out of the valley.

Jack Loveless proudly looked over his woven piece. This luminous stretch of colour, dyed-in-the-wool from roots of local herbs for the sake of *Liberty*, was the sublimation of all his sufferings.

But, though his loom had stopped working, its hammering continued in his head, and would do so all night even whilst he was singing, shouting and talking sedition at a hush-house, or whilst lying in his narrow box-bed; banging, although increasingly faint, until its noise was resumed at the hard wooden bench at dawn.

Jack was a small shrivelled man, crippled in his thigh and leg, and he had a closed expression; though, as Anne knew, such as he often have the deepest tales to tell when they have been prised open. So Anne remarked suggestively, 'If we fine ladies knew what was needed to manufacture our woollen dresses, I wonder how we should think of them?'

'You have furs also, for which another kind of animal other than a weaver has died in traps,' he answered drily.

'Where do you find all those beautiful colours and rich patterns?'

Loveless took a clay pipe from his pocket, stuffed it with tobacco from a tin over his fireplace, and lit it with many puffs before answering. 'I sometimes look at the church windows and take my designs from the bright glass. If there is a God, that is where He shines – in the pictures of the artists – for it is not in the homes of poor people, where parson and t'Bible and all our "lords and masters" tell us to find Christ and virtue. I've seen enough poverty to know. Designing cloth has been my undoing.' He ended his sentence bluntly, as was his manner, and he stared unflinchingly, to show he was unwilling to explain more unless she asked for it.

'How so, Mr Loveless?'

'Going too far with it. I made black "amens", with embossed patterns of yew and laurel leaves, for widows' cloth in Spain – the soldiers cause a lot of mourning there. I wove striped callimancoes for elegant ladies. Throwing away designs that didn't suit, wasting time whilst my children were hungry and my old wife coughing blood under a heap of blankets – it was ceasing to flow from one opening and now it came out of another! But when I took my work to Mr Greave, who aims to make the finest pieces in England, he'd say: "That's a grand cloth, Loveless, grand, but I'd be ruined if I made it." "Why so, Mr Greave?" I'd ask – tho' my own politeness stuck in my teeth. "It's *too* good and even in St Petersburg or down London they would not pay the price." Now *I'm* paying the cost, with my dear wife passed on and me living in this hut. I have heard tell that in Oliver Cromwell's day we were promised something better.'

'I think that what you weavers make is the most beautiful art and shouldn't be rewarded with poverty.' Poverty made Anne shudder with repulsion; she saw here a lesson in what her own fate would be if she lacked control of her destiny. 'But at least I can give you something in advance for the services of your daughter,' she offered.

'I'd be glad o' summat. But you are doing me a turn just in taking her away from here. Though we conceive 'em with pleasure enough and so are bound, by God! to take care of 'em, yet girls are nothing but a curse to us from birth until they marry. Are you not, Jenny?'

The maid did not answer. Obviously she was used to not answering. Anne ordered her to go and wash her feet in the spring, then she left two sovereigns with Jack Loveless and led Jenny away.

At Lower Laithes the girl entered a state where everything was different, yet she did not show surprise. There were large rooms, statues, paintings, and formal gardens. There were clocks. Although Jenny could not herself tell the time, yet she recognised that others did so, for they gave her orders by them. Also they rose from and returned to bed according to the numbers on the dial, instead of by when the pony stood up and shook himself in the enclosure, or when the raven settled upon the cliffs. She accepted all these, and other, changes in her life. She was too numbed to respond. The maid had a born slave's temperament. Contentment characterised her as she performed whatever task was set in front of her, and she never questioned it. She doted on her mistress, who knew so much about life and human nature. Only sometimes, when she was tired, Jenny would simply stare at the sky. It was for all the world as if a thought, a desire, even an ambition, was leaving its glittering track across her dark mind, and arousing the still waters of her eyes to look upwards for Heaven and God.

In her heart, where no one had ever looked, Jenny carried the image of a master, and this fantasy filled up those inscrutable, silent moments. He was not a small, dry, worried, embittered man like her father, but someone large, confident, powerful, certain of his position in the world, indeed in the whole universe, and expressing himself with large spacious gestures, with grand language and easy humour.

When Anne had peopled Lower Laithes with servants, she was occupied with them – singing around the house, keeping everyone cheerful, knowing her business as one who has herself scrubbed floors, and discovering that, even though she was of the same class, yet she was one whom servants liked to obey.

Because it looked as though the house might at last become as fashionably splendid as it was originally intended to be, the foppish servile tradesmen flocked around. Dealers in silk, damask and velveteens. Cabinet-makers with samples of mahogany or other new woods brought back by traders and explorers in Africa and the East, and with drawings of temples, Greek, Egyptian, Assyrian, which they proposed to apply to tables and chairs. Artists in plaster who made tinted cornucopias of grapes, chrysanthemums, oranges and the other newly discovered colonial benefits for mankind which Flora, or Mother Nature (a lady after Titian or Tintoretto with a swelling bust and fair hair swept from a broad brow like the wife of the weaver Joshua Binns), poured out of her capacious horn-of-plenty. Thanks be to the Lord who was giving us so much of India, Africa and the Americas! One artist wished to depict the personification of tea. He painted a nubile black woman rising from a steaming brew. Hairdressers visited Lower Laithes. Peruke-makers. Shoe- and stocking-makers. Traders with pictures of nature (or, at least, with *landscapes*) in the style of Gainsborough. (Those park walls, those deer, those golden oaks, were clearly *owned* by someone, which was why the limners were able to sell their paintings; and the artists expected to depict the Greaves' domain in the same style, for what else would a clothier desire? But Anne Wylde would have nothing to do with it.) They all came to scoop up Oliver's money, as mice gather round a tear in a sack of corn. They forgot that Anne was a 'witch'. It was no business of theirs, they now said (so long as they could conspire to cheat her), and they replied to questions with the invariable complaint of the worldly: 'What can I do? I have to live!' Three such tradesmen would secretly agree for two of them to ask an exorbitant price, so that the third could offer an apparently cheap tender. Smilingly offering credit, they anticipated turning Lower Laithes into a showplace of the new and unnecessary things that the whole of Lady Well, following a fashion set by the richest family, would have to purchase to replace their sound tables and chairs or the dowries already collected for their daughters.

Anne's father, loathing these parasites, stayed away. Whilst people he despised collected money that might have been his, he continued to build a manufactory for Horsfall. There was little understanding now between father and daughter.

Anne still held off Oliver's advances, fearing that if she gave in he would despise her and so treat her just as other men had done. Secretly it tortured her. Often when alone in bed, and imagining what that strange experience of copulation might be, she found herself damp for him. It further tormented her that he did not realise the degree to which abstinence was deepening her love, or at least her desire. Instead he of course thought that her feeling for him was weak.

To compensate him, she struggled to be a 'muse', even though she did not know what one was. She imagined herself one of those expensive plaster figures that craftsmen now hauled up to the Lower Laithes ceiling – all breeze-blown drapery, bottoms and breasts. At other times she realised that 'muse' was a gentleman's word for a poor girl's giving her life in order to make Oliver happy. Beneath her thoughts and actions was this simple ideal of a tormented village girl: that domestic luxury would make possible all other beautiful things, especially Oliver's poetry.

On the day when Oliver had arrived at Lower Laithes, holding Betty by the hand, he had been made speechless. The door was opened by the lugubrious 'unemployable' ex-weaver Amos Culpin, dressed in a livery of wig, blue frock coat, yellow stockings, and with a black 'solitaire' ribbon around his neck. He was now capable, apparently, of holding himself erect. The old carved black oak of the house had been replaced with walnut, mahogany and rosewood, decorated with inlay *à la mode*. A huge ill-featured woman with the pox was scrubbing the floor of the hall, on the ceiling of which buxomly cavorted all nine of the muses freshly painted *trompe l'œil* in colours of rosy flesh.

Oliver had then been ceremoniously conducted into the presence of Anne Wylde, his housekeeper (the scrubbing-woman, seemingly devoid of Reason, laughing crookedly after him). Dumbfounded, he looked this way and that, his mouth opening and shutting but speechless, and his movements indecisive.

After a few days this first and (when Oliver had reflected upon it) delightful surprise settled into an uneasy, constant feeling of truancy. It was a mood largely fed by Benjamin Greave, who found a hundred ways to express his disapproval of Anne Wylde, and his hope that his son's infatuation would not be serious, but only a temporary flight from reality. When in a jovial humour, the clothier addressed his son jokingly with new epithets, as 'sinner', 'malefactor', or 'condemned', so repetitively that it set Oliver's teeth on edge (was the old clothier, alone at Making Hall, falling fast under the spell of Patience Helliwell?). But if there was a hitch in his trading – a consignment of woollens delayed by storms, or some credit-notes proving too long in arriving – he argumentatively took it out on his son. So eventually Oliver refused to listen.

Introspection, also, was soon haunting Lower Laithes. The couple found a great deal of time, whilst sitting together for sweet long hours in quiet rooms, for studying one another in that different way that couples discover when they live together, and after other energies have spent themselves. (Such as the effort to overcome a fear that this liaison might be a mistake; and the making of practical arrangements for their career.) Oliver observed Anne as previously he had never done. He even noticed fresh things about, for example, her hands. Of course he had seen before that she was left-handed and he knew that in childhood she had been beaten for it. But he had not realised how practical that hand was for everyday life – as distinct from the right, which she used for caressing.

She would caress him, and expect him to stroke her, for hours on end. She closed her eyes and he felt the softening of her body, melting in waves – a sea of wax. Yet as the point was reached when he was sure he could approach her, she would stiffen and prevent it. He never understood to what extent this will of hers tortured her; this suspicion taught her by her experience of the threatening male. He merely saw that she flushed. She coloured partly with the violence of sudden frustration, though caused by herself, and partly with invented anger. As excuse she would pretend some alarm, and stiffen like a fawn in the grass.

Anne was waiting every day for Oliver to settle to writing poems. She believed that this would satisfy the desire which she was refusing to fulfil. With all her sensual longing hidden behind it, she laid out his ink, quills, lexicon, paper, pipes, tobacco, and placed his chair temptingly before his desk; all other services were available by tugging a bell-rope. And she waited.

But Oliver was used to penning his verses at inns, in briefly held schoolmaster's lodgings, or out of doors, and it took him a long time to settle amongst these grand surroundings. Around him it was too quiet, the very furniture menacing him with its silence. Or contrarily there was too much noise of squabbling servants coming from the kitchen. His fine clothes, worn to impress Anne, impeded him. Lace cuffs got tangled with his pen, tight trousers made it uncomfortable to sit, whilst his shoes pinched. Though it was his own home, he was more constrained here than he had been at Makings. And whilst the only place he would have felt free to play his fiddle was the kitchen, there it seemed improper, for his relationship to Miss Wylde was an embarrassment to him before the servants.

At last, amongst plush damasks, velveteens, silks, carpets, silver, china and mahogany, he got down to his verses. He hewed the marble block of poetry:

'When bright Apollo's flaming car had run
The southern course, and in our climes begun
To perfect blossoms and the budding flowers,
To paint the fields, and form the shady bowers...'

But his verses, like his surroundings, were a texture of rich furnishings within a crumbling classical edifice. (And 'perfect' didn't scan!) He could not push his lines forward. His mind was elsewhere, straying to the bosky embodiment of *tea* upon the ceiling, or to the bosoms of the plaster muses who roared across the ceiling like spirited English ladies engaged in a fox-hunt. He daydreamed of sitting with Tim Bobbin before the fire in some secret and convivial moorland inn (or wherever that ariel-spirit had now disappeared to), smoking a long clay pipe, his feet on the hob, and a scrap of paper on his knee to scribble down whatever was dictated by a flesh-and-blood muse, who was whichever lady brought jugs of ale to his elbow. Recalling his past years of wandering, when adventure and health had mounted to blossom out of his fiddle or his pages of verse, and progress marked every day, he could hardly believe with what zest and undoubting purpose he had lived, although he was then but a poor traveller about the hills. Nor could he disentangle 'the messy skein of time' that had left him, despite Ann Wylde, feeling bereft. What was it about himself, that – though he grasped the opportunities before him, and he had no *reason* to be dissatisfied with his tremendous good fortune – yet a demon of unhappiness, a constant cloudy shadow, would not go away? He longed and longed for Anne and was in various moods of torment because of this. But she was not the total cause. Was it some unrecog- nised part of himself that was unsatisfied?

Ironically it was Anne Wylde, his Nature Muse, who unwittingly drove him into anxieties about trade. He found himself repeating the mistaken pattern of his life with Zillah; for all this luxury had to be paid for, and because of quarrels with his father, mostly about Anne, his livelihood grew insecure.

Whilst Oliver was writing, Anne would often move restlessly around the room, picking up and putting down various things, want- ing to stay near but knowing that she upset his concentration. He had no conception of what tides and cross-currents were racing through her mind. She would be longing to 'give in' to him – some- times keeping her legs stiff to control her moistening, to make it possible for her to remain upright, whilst she imagined what it might be like. Next she forced herself to believe that the best use anyway for his energies was for them to go unadulterated into the permanent mould of his poems. The verse that he might write became her substitute for the man. She thought of all his gentle, warm character being poured into them, and this way she loved him possibly more than she could ever feel physically for an erratic living human.

When Oliver looked up, he saw only her inscrutable eyes staring at him.

'Poor Oliver! You wouldn't have these troubles if it were not for me,' she said, one day. (Almost Zillah's very words! Oliver reflected.) 'Perhaps they are right to throw stones and call me "witch", though I cannot help myself.'

Typical of his good nature, he did not even think that what she was doing was blaming herself for his sexual discontent. (If he had, he might have suspected her of teasing.) It was his opinion instead that she was worrying over the problems of the woollen industry. This, he thought, was preposterous. 'No! No! No! It is only that the weavers are so discontented,' he answered. 'Inspired by the Republicans in France they want more money than they truly earn from my father. So they do offhand workmanship, which means that our goods are returned. Now poor father is aged and does not have the control of his affairs that he used to.'

Oliver would then be soothing Anne and soon she would in her turn again be consoling him, convincing him of the advantages of life at Lower Laithes. She would move close and kiss his frown. He would kiss her in return, and try to do more. She would resist. Thus Oliver's scruples and doubts would dissolve into a mist of lovers' sentiments – as Anne intended.

Sentimentality, which always bears the promise of fulfilment *later*, was the perfect way of keeping Oliver adoring her: so Anne thought. The two of them caressed, fetched things for one another, fed titbits; until Oliver, with his author's detachment, thought that this spectacle of two people pretending to be one because they believed they were in love was ridiculous, and his frustration then showed itself once more in erratic anger. He felt that old instinct for violence rising in him, and he crushed it.

So love remained everything but consummated. When he was on the edge of impatience Anne kept one step ahead in making him amused or baffled. She always seemed to be changing her mind, and yet to be consistent to something deeper. Her sensibility was, like the spring season, full of surprises but underneath moving into fullness and blossoming. He grew dependent on her ever-resourceful faculty, tried to forget his lust, and doubted any opinion of his own until Anne had confirmed it. Often he did not understand her enigmas. But though he was confused and insecure with an unpredictable muse, he decided to be loyal to her sensibility. And always she was able to keep him afraid of annoying her, and of her despising his simplicity.

(7)

Once everything was running well and there was little for her to do, Anne Wylde found a dullness about Lower Laithes. It was without visitors. Despite her new fashionableness and the money spent, 'Society', no different from the more primitive people of Lady Well, shunned her, this time as an upstart. At first they paid some prying calls but these soon fell away. A few invitations were received, though only to the houses of tradesmen employed, or hoping to be employed, at Lower Laithes. Even these were at difficult hours, and the one visited was likely sick with an illness that kept others away. Anne made one spectacular effort to recover: she had an ox roasted out of doors, employing two men to turn it day and night. But no one of importance came to eat it and after a few days it stank, so it was given to the poor who lived, or who squatted in the woods, outside the walls of Lower Laithes. Anne and Oliver were finally too proud to accept this treatment and they became recluses, whilst their coachman grinned as he polished the equipage that was never required to go anywhere. Not only Benjamin Greave, but none of the Makings' servants either, would come near Lower Laithes. Those on their way to the fulling mill shunned the house, with its tall polished windows, its neatness as if it had nothing to do with trade nor any practical business, and its ornaments in the Greek style; it was the home of a witch. No one came to the kitchen door courting the maids. The only visitors were beggars wanting to look around and steal something. The menservants stopped going to the local inns, where the drinkers extracted tales, making grooms, gardeners and kitchen-boys afraid to return and face their mistress. So there was no feeding of stories back into the Lower Laithes kitchen either. The flow of life stopped and there was much brooding over petty obsessions.

Even Oliver was often not nearby. Either business genuinely called him away; or, to hell with the torments of desire! he thought and grasped excuses to be free of the strangling of his muse. Often he did not inform Anne of his comings and goings, assuming his freedom just as he had always done. He relaxed in an illusion, and returning reality only brought him ill-temper. He would come home smelling of alcohol, or sooty with pipe-smoking, and she met him reproachfully. The reproaches turned into quarrels. They became bitter.

Innocently, Anne had thus created loneliness around herself. She was without her father, and Aunt Pity, whilst Oliver had turned into a stranger; and there were no other friends in Anne's life. She missed especially her father as never before – imagining that he would have some wise solution to offer her, just as he had so often in childhood.

One Sunday morning she went to Lady Well to win him. Riding her handsome black gelding (a present from Oliver) she rushed so quickly clear of the wood that her blood raced, whilst the horse sweated in the clear dry summer air. The beast's incalculable temperament was very like her own, and both thrilled with a harmonious desire to get free of the stuffy house and the moist dark trees. For a few moments Anne felt that she never enjoyed with humans such love as was now between herself and this animal.

Enclosures and farmyards were empty of people, who instead shuffled towards parish church or to one of the scattered chapels – Congregationalist, Methodist, Baptist (Calvinist or New-Connexion) and Quaker. Sealed in their separate Sunday tribes, they communicated to those of another group only silent glances of pity, contempt, hatred, fear or incomprehension. What did they share as humans all together of God's great, glossy, open summer day, though it fell so powerfully and equally upon them all? They agreed only on this: that the impatient arrogant woman whom they saw, dressed in 'Jezebel's red silk' and clouding them with dust, was hurrying to Hell itself. They said that she was surely at one with the secret moorland spirits which fled as larks through the blue dome of air, and they cried for her 'justified undoing'. Some even chose to blame her for 'taking her trade to foreign parts' by purchasing genteel silk instead of local wool. Some were also jealous because today was an excellent one for making hay and if they were as bold as she they would be doing what in their hearts they really wished, and be scything grass, or bleaching cloth in the sun.

At Lady Well on marshy ground on the north side of the church Anne found a small crowd making a great noise. She peered over their heads and saw Esther Kershaw digging out heavy spadesful of the clogged wet earth. When they tried to stop her, Esther lifted up her magical apron and waved it in their faces. The charm worked, for even the staunchest Protestant stepped back. Anne guessed that Esther was either burying, or digging up, an unbaptised illegitimate child that had been sneaked into the holy ground – perhaps one belonging to another woman whom she intended to prosecute. But Jabez Stott (less adoringly shy of Anne Wylde, now that he was a journeyman carpenter with his own sweetheart) told Anne that Esther, after a long, long search, had discovered the ancient well and was going to make it flow again. Since her father's house had burned down Esther had, as she promised, wandered the moors in her apron that had been blessed by Jesus. (Some thought, not in search of Christ as she claimed, but to find and tether the Great Mother Cow.) One day at an inn she had heard a drunken old man toasting the servant (who was named Mary) saying 'Here's health to *all* Marys,' and Esther realised that he was a Papist. So she asked him if he knew the whereabouts of St Mary's Well in Lady Well, because she wished 'to look for the image of Christ in its clear water', and he had told her to dig on the north side of the church.

By the time of Anne's arrival, Esther had uncovered a circle of stones on some uncommonly wet ground, within it a tip of old cooking pots, 'superstitious' carvings that had been broken from the church, bits of tiles, and broken crutches. Also some coins. Thereupon the well performed its first miracle, reminding several that the gold belonged to them; for, 'come to think of it', their 'grandparents had thrown them in long ago to buy wishes'. Esther, frantically excited, hoped to reveal the crystal water in time to lead Doubtfire to it, that he might be resurrected by the true image and pure spring of Christ before beginning another drunken sermon. Meanwhile her neighbours, who were in horror thinking that she had turned to that scarlet blood-beast, the Pope, and was trying to satisfy his thirst for magic wells, were throwing all sorts of rubbish at her.

'This should quench thy doubtfire!' Esther screamed. 'Will you stop throwing stones and slutch, all you sinners, for I am no Papist dressed in carnal!' and she flapped her apron. 'I tell you, there are some things that I know. There are some things that I know even though I was never in a school to be learned to read, write and menstruate!' She was up to her knees in mud. It daubed her face, arms and dress, 'like a painted pagan savage', someone said; whilst her limbs jerked with brisk madness like a showman's doll.

'Let the poor woman be!' Anne shouted, so that all listened to her and Esther could at last straighten up.

Anne's cry silenced everyone. That the woman who had stones thrown at her since birth should not be relieved when a different scapegoat was found! 'Anne Wylde! For you to defend me! Here is the second miracle!' Esther's voice was breaking with emotion.

The mason's daughter, sad at this never-ending persecution, moved off to her father's house. What madness and un-reason swarms outside, he was thinking, in his brown sober rooms, though he said nothing. He only, with great patience, *looked*. When Anne met John Wylde's eyes, she thought how rare it was to find orbs as level and unflinching as his. That steady gaze, resting without embarrassment upon its object, could measure a stone or just as accurately weigh up a disputatious parson or philosopher.

Anne found that, during her absence, John Wylde and the fifteen-year-old ancient-child-servant-creature Martha had grown close together. Both had relapsed into taking old persons' diets of dry crusts, oat biscuits and bodiless soups, and to picking bits off one another's plates. Anne saw that Martha had replaced herself in the house, perhaps also in her father's affections, and she felt jealous. Meanwhile the servant girl prattled about the doings of clergymen: one fell asleep in his pulpit after being out hunting since dawn, another insisted on being buried on the north side of the church (reserved for witches, criminals and heretics) because it was in sight of the ale-house, whilst a third composed what Martha called 'jeering verses' and threw them upon a rival, nonconforming, parson's coffin as it was being lowered into the ground . . .

Anne interrupted, 'I see that Esther Kershaw thinks that she has discovered our well, father. I saw a great crowd who had no will to abuse me because of their throwing stones and rubbish at her.'

'It is no wonder that the innocent and vulgar of our countryside lapse into superstition, when Joseph Doubtfire is in his pulpit not one Sunday in four, but raking around the countryside in search – he says – of "specimens". When he returns he has nought to show for it but a mutilated badger, or the swollen liver of a dead pauper. He never has a concise thought to offer us, or even a well-constructed phrase. He rarely has a sermon to take into the pulpit. He is most often drunk, and too incensed about the burnings to preach the gospel of Christ. And all the clergymen of our district are seemingly hewn from the same rough quarry!'

'Parson's importuned all t'time to give relief for those that's lost everything i'fires,' Martha said.

'Do you still go to your chapel at Clay Slack?' Anne interrupted again.

'Martha likes to remain faithful to the town church.'

'I did not ask you about our servant!'

Once again Anne's bristling unsubmissive speech scalded his ears. John Wylde looked wearily at her. 'You, my daughter, do not change, though Lady Well becomes the home of pagan beasts and is burnt to the ground.'

''Tis awful, the fires, and there's more and more of these wool-combers opening their shops with furnaces, a danger to us all. 'Tis the new worsteds that ruin us,' Martha said.

When they were about to set off for Clay Slack, Martha put on her bonnet, but Anne firmly sent her to the local church of Saint Mary the Virgin, alone. Anne was determined to have her father to herself. Yet she felt regretful, for she had come to woo him softly and here she was already creating anger, dispute and irritation once again.

John Wylde was not able to step out as briskly as he used to up the hillside. Yet he wanted to walk, savouring the old days. In order to give him time to draw breath and not insult him by it, Anne stopped to pluck bunches of heather, which was just coming into bloom. There was a large purple variety and some with smaller, tighter, white flowers. She chose the more luxuriant purple. The thin stems were tough, bending into supple knots before they would break; but her father (unusually) did not help her. Either he was too weak, or too impatient of her, or both.

'I do not know what our congregation will make of your dressing so immodestly,' he remarked.

'I do not care what they think.'

'It seems that since you became the seeming-mistress at Lower Laithes you do not walk in the ways of Christ as I have shown you.' He pointed to a cottage, standing alone and sheltering against some rocks. 'There is a witch yonder who blasphemes, saying that all females are cursed because of Christ's religion, which is for men. Even if women go to Him daily on their hands and knees. Now her mouth fills with blood whenever she speaks.'

'A tooth is bad in her head.'

'She hath become very wasted and lies in bed ready to die. I think it is her soul that sickens for her wrong-doing and is preparing for Hell eternal. No one will go near her.'

'I believe you are becoming a superstitious Papist yourself, my father. Your mind narrows because you do not travel so much and are staying in Lady Well building manufactories! You used to tell me, "Heaven is but this world when men laugh and are merry. Hell is also this world where they suffer grief and pain." Has all your reason left you? Has all your joy deserted you? What do your books tell you now?'

'My eyes are none too good any more, and I cannot read so many books. But I know that the ways of God are strange.'

The track was solitary, dreary, hot and straight. Wind-warped, weirdly shaped stones peered with foreboding over the skyline high above them; monsters leaning down out of a nightmare. A pair of curlews glided like disinherited spirits after the father and daughter. The birds moved heavily, yet took in a great deal of sky in wide easy sweeps. 'Cur-*lew*! Cur-*lew*!' followed by a gentler noise as of bubbling fountains came from their long scissoring fragile beaks, which Anne could pick out against the light. Upon Raven's Hill a flock of sheep grazed, their mouths making a loud drumming noise upon the turf. And, indeed, it was hollow beneath it; there was a great chamber, its entrance lost, where 'ancient people used to go to talk to their dead'.

Near to this, isolated and huddling next to each other as if for comfort, were two small plain buildings. One was the nonconformists' place of worship, the other the home of the couple who cared for it. The eye could not help but fix upon them in this empty landscape. Near one building were several hens and a pig. The other was fringed with small graves and had KNOWE GOD carved above the entrance in the heavy style of lettering that was now out of fashion (but followed by the mason) and seeming ugly to others' eyes. The doors of both were flung open and women in workaday aprons were carrying oatbread and ale from the cottage into the chapel.

'Well, mason, and what news has thou brought us from afar?' the visitors were genially asked. Amongst smiles and kindnesses, Anne and her father entered. They were confronted by a high wooden rail forming a horizontal passage for men to go to the right and women to the left. The Independents' clothes, of black or white wool or cotton, were tight at the throat, the wrist and the ankles, as if to say, 'Lord, how humbly imprisoned we are within our sin compared with your unbuttoned wrath and bliss about the skies!' The chapel's possessions were similarly confined, being locked in the many dark cupboards. The congregation consisted of weavers and spinners. They treasured cramped little enclosures that they had grasped out of the moor's bosom and had claimed with tight walls. Everything of theirs was brown, black or white, without decoration. The only strong colours were the tints of eggs, butter and hams which the community bartered before worship; the astounding red and green of some apples on a pewter plate; Anne's even more astonishing red clothes, and the purple of her heather.

She twisted her nosegay around the passage-rail. A moment later, one of the women with an angry expression briskly threw it out of the door, as if it was unclean. The hens came running but then stalked away, disappointed, whilst the woman muttered to her friend. She was a tough person, her piety surviving regular beatings from her husband on Sunday afternoons (before he took her to bed) for having attended the chapel, and her voice was hard and spiky.

Anne felt lonely, as if she had stepped under an icy deluge. Even in the Sunday presence of The Lord nothing was more important to these people than the trading of eggs for hams or the affairs of one who had deserted chapel because of a dispute over a pound of wool. Where was their serious discussion of God, the equality of man, the nature of the lost Eden and the future Paradise?

However, they did assume that all people were equal (so long as they had equal things to trade). Even women, though they had to enter at the left hand, yet were allowed to be equivalent intellects with men. And all, men or women, who wished to preach could do so in their turn. No one was more welcome for this than a stranger or one who had been absent for a while. So John Wylde – who shone with happiness in the community – was asked to give a sermon.

Gesturing firmly and still the solid mason even in the pulpit, he began, quoting fluently, and some passages by heart, from the Book of Jeremiah: ' "Say unto the King and to the Queen, humble yourself, sit down. For your principalities will come down, even the crown of your glory! The cities of the south shall be shut up . . . lift up your eyes and behold them that come from the north." '

The congregation had no doubt that this prophesied the supremacy of the northern woollen-traders over sinful, Bacchanalian southerners, especially those in London and Bath, and so they were as pleased to hear these words as the mason was to deliver them. Whilst John Wylde preached in his most careful, solemn voice, the chapel became so silent that, although Anne made no more movement than her breathing, yet a continuous rustling of her silk could be heard. When her father reached the passage, 'For the greatness of thine iniquity are thy skirts discovered, and thy heels made bare . . . Therefore will I discover thy skirts upon thy face, that thy shame may appear,' several turned to look at her, sure that the quotation signified that only *she* was an obstacle to their triumph and prosperity. Meanwhile the mason was squinting short-sightedly and unaware of the effect of his words. 'I have seen thine adulteries and thy neighings, the lewdness of thy whoredom, and thine abominations on the hills and fields . . .' Anne put out her tongue at the congregation, whereupon the staring women withdrew under their black bonnets and the men into coat collars, like retreating snails.

When the service was over and they were eating oatcakes washed down with ale, John Wylde was so bloomingly happy that he noticed nothing of his daughter's gloomy silence. She was wondering: what better things might be done amongst clever people in a chapel, besides praying and trading? She was also unhappy because her errand had been to ask her father to live at Lower Laithes, but now this seemed threatened with bad omens.

They were released at last on to the hot moor, which was brazen with sunshine and colour. The two curlews still swung in great interlocking circles over the barrow, and the people going home from chapel radiated over the sheep-tracks, trying to disperse without drawing attention to themselves, and lost in this huge bright bowl of space.

Between John Wylde and his daughter her question was poised, circling like the curlews in the air. 'Come and live with me,' Anne pleaded, at last.

For some time they marched silently upon the turf and the stones.

'And how is the young master – Oliver Greave?' John Wylde merely answered, slyly.

Anne knew what he meant, and realised from it how gossip about her must have spread. She laughed softly. 'Mr Greave is only happy when he is playing his fiddle and writing poems,' she told him affectionately.

'Are you together as man and wife?'

'No. Come and live with me, Father,' Anne repeated.

'Nay, I shall only be a trouble to you, and thy conscience will not be any happier.'

So Anne returned alone to Lower Laithes. There one servant showing pleasure took her cloak, another her shoes, and she moved through the high rooms feeling liberated after the cramped chapel.

But she found Oliver worrying (as so often these days) over his accounts and poring over wool-patterns. The sheets were covered with mean little figures and calculations: a clear sign of trouble.

'Let me have charge of the pattern books, and I will make you prosper,' Anne said.

'Why? Will you cast a spell?'

'Yes!' She came close. As he stared at her, Oliver awoke to an uncanny realisation. Anne Wylde was *himself*! She was not substance, but reflection. He was looking into a mirror in which his own feminine part was revealed. He was facing his own manifestation, his twin. Knowing each other so well was the reason why they loved deeply, but also why they were so intolerant of one another.

Or was it Anne who was real, and he who was her reflection?

Her wide-spreading gown (which showed off the money he had spent on her) swallowed him and drowned his revelation – or whatever it was. There was a rustling in his ears like a wood full of birds. Some new strong feeling, or instinct, also clothed her, invisibly, like a perfume. Was this *the* moment? Was it?

It had been such a long anxious wait that he was afraid now of being unable to fulfil it: or alternatively that he would 'fulfil' it too soon. He was tired from his worries; often he did not sleep because the screaming of Anne's peacocks woke him at dawn; and he gave in to her beckoning, offering the pattern books – the secrets of his and his father's trade – to her scrutiny and care. She then fell even further upon him and he realised that this afternoon was indeed his chance to take her. He was smothered by her dress, like a sparrow under a hawk.

He surfaced with the intention of leading her, his doppelganger, to his room. But she would not be led, and instead took him to her own place. 'You know I am a virgin,' Anne whispered, as if this explained all her remoteness from him.

His throat was too dry to answer. And it was she who undressed confidently in front of *him*, just as if she was used to men. He drew the curtains (she did not seem to care) and helped with her stays and underclothes – trying to look and yet not to look at her body. As she lifted her dress her arms were twisted behind her back, thus raising her breasts, and she grimaced.

'I cannot undress without my maid,' she complained. She was grasping at the commonplaces of life as if they were posts or rocks that she could cling to in an ocean. He realised that she was trembling.

'You must have managed in the past.'

'I did not need such gowns as these.'

'Need?' Oliver wondered. He himself stripped, producing a tiny pile of brown cloth next to her mountain of silk. The moment was held in a drugged aura and he could not believe it was happening. Because of his erection he felt ashamed to remove his intimate clothes.

She knelt before him. 'I want to see what it looks like before it goes inside me,' she whispered as if a louder voice would have frightened her. He blushed and opened his legs slightly. 'I have only seen a child's before, never an erect one. Except once Amos Culpin showed me his, in a dark passage, but I did not look.'

'Amos Culpin! Him you employ as your servant?'

'What better use for someone who tried to mak' use of me?'

Oliver opened his legs more widely. She touched with one finger delicately. He leant to put his lips in the valley of her breasts. His mouth travelled over the soft hills of her stomach that was white and slender, with the thin bones under the flesh, like the breast of a plucked bird. So they fell together on the floor. She turned over, encouraging him, saying, 'I want you to kiss me all the way up, oh so slowly, as the spring comes with flowers over the moors, so gently!' He moved his lips over her thighs and between her buttocks. 'Your kisses are like petals,' she said. He had never explored such secret places of anyone before. 'Along inside my legs,' she whispered, opening them for his convenience.

His mouth brushed the deep and shaded wood. Her hands reached down for his armpits and drew him up so that his penis, beginning to moisten, could enter her. He did not realise he had broken the hymen until she cried, a sharp sound like a disturbed bird.

Oliver wanted to hold himself for her pleasure and he waited for her thighs to start twitching under him, but they did not do so. He twisted her nipples and she took hold of his hand as if she wanted him to play with her more firmly, which he did. Oliver came, his eyes closed and crushed upon her throat.

He opened them and returned his gaze to hers, which had not left his for a moment. She did not even bother to look down, and she was calm, just as if she had done this before. 'Is that all?' she asked. Oliver did not answer. She was frustrated and angry, and turned her face away from him, with no interest in the blood and semen trickling from her body.

'Tell me about Zillah,' she said. She was crying.

He sat apart, trembling and ashamed of the failure. 'My father trusted and liked her, particularly when she gave birth. It was then that he shared his business with me, thinking that his wealth was now fertile. We Greaves are not gentry stock who are sure of their pedigree and my father's greatest desire in making wealth is to have someone to pass it on to and a memorial. It was a blow when Zillah produced only a daughter.'

'Was there much passion in your marriage?'

With Anne, even whilst she had held herself from him, he had felt immersed in the great bowl of all womanhood. So he had to answer, 'It was not an all-consuming passion. At the time I thought it was, but it was not. For I have learnt since what it is to be consumed. But you must be thinking that I'm saying this only because I'm with you!'

'No. I know you are not wayward and dishonest.'

Then, being unsatisfied, she was off on another train of thought. 'Oliver – there is such poverty, darkness and ignorance in Yorkshire. Couldn't we build them schools which those of any age might attend on Sunday when they have no work to do? They might say a prayer or two at the same time, to please the Parson.'

'What will you have them taught?'

He began to dress.

'Oh, reading and good breeding. They could learn to show me proper respect and be cured of their barbarous custom of throwing stones.'

He was engrossed in his own fulfilment and discovery. He was transformed. It was as if a flock of birds was circling inside the tower of his skull, looking for somewhere to settle. He felt that for so many years he had been living inside a womb, sleepy, like a snake that is casting its skin or a baby waking only for its food. Now he had woken alert, conquering, vigorous, and as if he had been given eyes with which to see in the darkness of our mundane world where vision is so clouded and obliterated. He felt that he had been purged in fire, or in ice. That he had been taken back, back, to the roots of poetry.

Conscience-stricken that he had failed to make her happy, he searched for an excuse. 'You are so strange, Anne Wylde. You do not seem to feel.'

Anne shrugged. 'I have heard that some women pretend to be happy, just for the sake of keeping their husbands.'

'And I have heard that you are of unnatural birth and that you have long legs because you are descended from a deer!' For the first time that he had seen, she looked confused, did unnecessary things with her hands, looked about distractedly. 'Is John Wylde your father? They say not. Culpin says not.'

'I do not know my father. Not in reality.' She paused. 'I do not know who he is.' Pause. 'I do not know him. I do not think I am of this world.' She paused yet again. 'I am from somewhere else, I do not know why I am here, and I do not like it!'

'Tell me who your father is, then.'

'I do not know.' That did not seem helpful, either. So just as confusingly, she added, 'I knew my mother.'

'But she died when you were born!'

Anne looked at him blankly.

'I still know her. Not what she looked like, only what she felt. I cannot explain to you, and you'd better go!' Because he did not move, she suddenly screamed out, *'Leave me alone and go!'*

'I would like to know who your father was,' he repeated, timidly.

A peacock screamed in the gardens.

She smiled. 'You can believe the stories, so long as you do not dare to do as others in the end and throw stones at me for it. My father came and went, and I do not know what he was. Ask Esther Kershaw, perhaps she has met him, for she wanders about as my mother did. John Wylde is a good man . . . oh, go away now!'

When he had left, Anne rang for Jenny and told her to bring water.

Jenny Loveless, as she bathed her mistress, watched with dark eyes that showed neither sorrow nor happiness – an expression that it was easy to ignore. If it had occurred to Anne to wonder what the girl thought as she washed away the stains, Anne might have imagined envy. A desire, too obscure to express, for comforts of her own, the privilege of rising late in the mornings, and for a powerful husband to provide these things.

Jenny silently raised the cloud of red silk and stood patiently upon a stool to dress Mr Greave's 'housekeeper'.

The following April Oliver arranged, through one of his father's agents, to collect a black boy from Liverpool as a present for Anne Wylde. The Negro was on the quayside waiting in the charge of a sailor, and clutching a small bundle, plus a Bible. He was smiling, in the way of one who always smiles, but he was bewildered. He had ended up in Liverpool from Africa by way of China, having been exchanged for some perfumes. Next he had been bartered for a horse. He expected only to be used again, and was waiting for a master because that was a law of life.

The boy followed Oliver down the street. He would willingly go anywhere so long as it was in the opposite direction to the clutter of tall masts along the quay: when Oliver for a short distance went that way, the Negro halted, gibbering and stubborn. So Oliver had to cheat him, seeming to turn only inland. At a crowded tavern he gave the boy a meal. The blackamoor scooped with his fingers and Oliver was amused, wondering at this queer creature's indeterminate position half way between animal and man.

Having the boy's confidence now, it was no trouble for Oliver to fix him on top of his carriage. Whilst Oliver read within, they set off across the marshy Lancashire plain. When they crossed a river the slave threw away his Bible, for the charm had done its work of finding him a kind master.

The first lesson the Negro learnt in England was about toll gates and the bad temper into which they threw travellers – although he himself was glad of the pauses because he was shivering and wet on top of the coach, his grin fixed to his face as if it was frozen there.

They stayed overnight in Manchester, where the Negro unfortunately lost his bundle, for Oliver might have learned from its contents something about him. Oliver, wondering how he might find the parcel again, raised his hand to scratch his head and the slave for the first time ceased to grin, cringing because he expected to be beaten. When Oliver quickly lowered his arm, the boy smiled again.

The next morning they climbed over the hills. It was a cold day. Whereas grass, flowers and tree-buds flourished upon the lowlands, the Pennine moors were still bare and dirty-looking with the accumulation of winter. Cold mists swept around the carriage. People who had never seen a black person before poured out to laugh at him, huddled against the mist. 'Put him into the river and set dogs on him!' someone shouted. Nevertheless the Negro, not understanding a word, kept on grinning.

Eventually he was standing, shivering, wet and dazed, in the kitchen at Lower Laithes whilst the servants formed a laughing circle around him. Oliver told them to get rid of the lad's rags, wash him and find better clothes, and he left.

Whilst Jenny went to scour attics and lumber rooms, Mary Pickles undressed him. She touched the boy as delicately as if she feared that he might fall to pieces in her hands. The others stood around watching silently, and wondering whether he was dark all over. They thought Master Oliver meant them to scrub all the black off, so Mary led him by the ear to the well. There she scrubbed harder and harder whilst the floor ran with water and everyone laughed or scolded because the black could not be removed. 'I've seen chimney boys before, but never one like this!' Amos Culpin grumbled. ' 'Tis a pagan sin to keep such a creature, dark as the Devil, and a mark of God's displeasure with him that he cannot be made clean!' Gardeners and stableboys came in from the yard to see what caused the laughter. The Negro still kept grinning, pleased to bring amusement. He winced only when Mary Pickles worked over-generously at his neck, which was marked and evidently sore. They tried poking to make him tell them why he was so black. The boy simply grinned and danced about in the cold water.

Culpin turned to the scullery girl, Bridie. 'It knows no more civilised English than you do! Try him in your Irish tongue.' At the word 'Irish' Bridie spoke rapidly but ineffectively in Gaelic.

Now Jenny appeared with some oddments of pantaloons and a tunic. The Negro was dressed and Jenny led him away. They were both children of the same age and she took him sympathetically by the hand to where Oliver sat with Anne.

The gift was partly for Anne's birthday. It was also to celebrate the fact that, by withholding himself powerfully, and with a great deal of caressing, Oliver had recently brought this apparently bold but in truth deeply shy creature, Anne Wylde, through to the full happiness and forgetful blindness of love.

How excited he had been that he *could* hold himself steady, feeling her eagerness and anticipation mount, the tension climb in her body, her head thrown this way and that. At the last moment she had wrapped her legs around his waist and pulled upon him tightly. He thought that he had *heard* the spasms in her body, growing louder. As Anne felt the semen spread inside her, she sank into a great peace. Her eyes had opened and, in harmony with her lips, smiled, a smile slow as though certain of itself that it was now to become a permanent expression.

When the lad entered the splendid room he rubbed at his skin and was frightened. Anne clapped her hands. 'You've brought me a slave boy!'

She looked at Oliver nowadays with a different expression. She was calmer, but above all she was more absorbed in him, and this was because ever since the first successful love-making almost every occasion had been happy – and when it wasn't, neither sensed a reason to be distressed about it. Whilst Oliver showed some pride in his love-making.

'A servant, not a slave. We don't do that sort of thing in England,' he replied.

'Your father is investing in them in the Americas.'

'But that isn't Yorkshire! I thought we would teach the lad, quite freely, to stand behind a carriage.'

Anne stroked the boy gently with one finger. 'What a lovely blue-black skin! What shall we call him? Earth! That's a name for a Negro, isn't it?'

Anne knew too well how the people might stone this vulnerable creature if he were set loose, so to protect him she planned to take him to the blacksmith and have riveted around his neck a collar which said, *Earth. Anne Wylde's Negro. Lady Well*. She chose her design from a volume delivered by a merchant: it was engraved with bunches of grapes, and with kneeling blacks offering up globes of the world. On the way to the smith, the Negro, though he did not know English, certainly understood the symbol of slavery which dangled from his mistress's fingers. He draggled hopelessly and helplessly behind, wondering where he could run to in these woods and hills, even if he escaped. Sometimes he refused to go on and hid behind bare trees and bushes, presumably satisfying needs of nature brought on by apprehension.

The blacksmith laughed as his big hands held the boy's head. 'Whatever will our Anne Wylde think to do next! It's just like a monkey. I've never seen anything like it!'

The resigned grin returned to the Negro's face, for he had known collars before and he did not even bother to put his fingers up to feel it. Some day, no doubt, another accident would cast him on a different shore into some other hands. Meanwhile these grey-faced people with their looms and their bandy-legged horses laden with wool were not bad masters and did not torment him, starve him or load him with chains.

Back at Lower Laithes, Anne had ready for him a newly woven blue livery and she wrapped upon his head a pale silk turban, which like his silver collar glittered against his dark skin.

(8)

The black boy broke the ice, for because of him curiosity overcame
Society. So that the Negro could be inspected, Oliver Greave and
Anne Wylde were invited where clothiers, merchants, artisans, school-
masters and parsons were not usually welcomed – to the Snawdens:
a family grand and old enough to know nothing of weaving and coal
pits. The event that inspired an invitation was a 'musical evening'. A
daughter was to play upon the spinet and a son, come from Oxford
('down' from Oxford, he called it, although everyone else said 'up')
would perform various pieces upon the flute, with eloquent intro-
ductions.

Anne was not so easily flattered. She realised that whilst the common people attacked with stones, those of a better class abused you
with their whims and sarcasms. They flattered and held out entice-
ments but when they had grown tired dropped you back again into
that pit of the lowest society, with contempt for your 'presumption'.

Anne and Oliver stalked boldly into the withdrawing room, just as
they would have done if they were stepping on to the carpet of turf on
a moor. Indeed, the couple always had a breeziness that was not
remarkable amongst clothiers and weavers who were always scrambling about moorlands, but which was most conspicuous in a genteel
drawing room. There was a stiffening of the faces of the Snawdens
and other people who lived almost unseen in the district. (They did
not even have to show themselves in church if they did not wish to,
for they were rich enough to be safe from Sabbatarians.)

All behaved as if the last thing to excite their curiosity would be the
black boy, who followed behind Anne without function other than to
be decorative. 'I believe that Negro attendants are commonplace in
London,' one said languidly, and at last. 'The practice is now discon-
tinued as being vulgar.'

A lady, with a ship in full sail rouged upon her cheeks, fingered the
black youth. 'I trust that he carries no diseases,' her escort warned.

Her alarm painted a sunset behind the sails of her man-o'-war, and she quickly withdrew her exploring fingers.

'Ah, Miss Crabtree!' another gentleman remarked. 'I believe the true position is that *we* are taking the diseases to *them*. Some tribes, I am told, have been quite wiped out after the coming of our sailors.'

'What kinds of diseases?'

'Too delicate to mention!'

'I believe that Miss Wylde is no more than the daughter of a mason!' Anne was allowed to overhear. 'She has such a *healthy* complexion. Quite weathered. Almost as dark as her Negro!'

'It is said that she is not popular with her own class. Quite notorious, in fact.'

'*Conspicuous!*'

'Though she sings trippingly, so I am told.'

Oliver turned aggressively. '*Trippingly?* What's that?'

A friendly hand soothed him. 'The young man is "up from down South", as you vulgarly put it. You should not take notice of our humour, for 'tis only fun.'

Some of the people, in the light of hundreds of candles, did have kind expressions. But it was inexpensive for them to give and they did it thinking it was all they lacked to achieve God's Grace. Others had found out, with pleasure, that riches made it possible to be cruel, and no one dared tell them so to their faces. As could be seen by their attitudes to footmen and maids, they acted without restraint or responsibility to those beneath them; thus they would do to weavers, tradesmen, old soldiers, artisans, lunatics and the poor. This was Anne's first experience of a gathering of her Betters. What a contrast these were to Anne's father and his friends, with their books, their humble desires for knowledge, liberty and expression! She did not enjoy their musical pieces either – realising that one was here not for true delight, but to applaud and feel satisfied with oneself for doing so, touching one's hands together softly.

Horsfall said clearly within her hearing, 'By God, my friends, you would not think her father-in-law was the old clothier with a dry wit and a tight grasp on his purse!'

'Father-in-law, you say? She is married, then?'

The young flautist, who had a polish like marble on his unweathered cheeks, looked gratefully down at his white fingers, for the thought had struck him that God's Grace could suddenly be removed and leave him with hands as coarse as Anne Wylde's. Then he remarked to her, 'Perhaps one could find at Oxford an engraver to immortalise one, so tall and statuesque, with one's Negro?'

He was sufficiently amused by this scandalous beauty-from-the-artisan-class to want to take her away from Oliver Greave and make her fashionable in London, Bath or Oxford. So his mother, sensing the threat of a dangerous liaison, interrupted, savagely and censorious, 'Miss Wylde, I have not seen you at our parish church!' Thus the thought was born in Anne Wylde: And why *not* visit one's parish church with one's Negro?

The next Sunday Oliver and Anne went to Saint Mary's, audaciously to claim a place in the Greaves' pew. They were laughing as they set out, although it offended their servants. On top of their carriage, Earth carried two prayer books on a green velvet cushion.

But when they burst from the Lower Laithes gardens into the changing landscape of burnt moors, cleared woodlands, drained marshes and new enclosures of stone or quickset-hawthorn that hurt Anne so deeply she would often literally close her eyes to it, their laughter ceased. Some wild thorn-trees still lingered, burnt or mutilated by the axe, in the open countryside. Mostly only their trunks remained. Some had grown fiercely contorted, as if registering the pain, or were twisted so tightly that they had burst into splinters: bright yellow jags leaking a bloody sap.

At last opening her eyes to see the destroyed hawthorns that had given up their last cuttings for the hedgerows – there intended not to blossom freely, but to enclose – Anne felt a premonition of ill-luck and disaster. Death of children and cattle, loss of fortune, parting with loved ones, were all foretold by the destruction of May-trees. Anne could not laugh again that day.

She timed her entrance into church to coincide with the beginning of the sermon. She had not been to Saint Mary's for many Sundays and she recognised its atmosphere with fresh surprise. A thousand years of bearing all the crises of Lady Well – births, marriages, sickness and death – had overloaded with weariness this tiny space, this theatre, as the scent of flowers that have passed maturity weighs down and sickens the air. Even the wedges of creamy light (or of multicoloured lights where it fell through the remains of the old glass) that carved the shadows, seemed made of a substance weighty enough to bow down the unexpectant congregation.

Anne alarmed this atmosphere with a daring clatter and squeak of the oak doors of the Greaves' pew, up on the balcony. The Horsfalls and the Snawdens, who had been preparing for a dozy Sunday and to take naps snug and hidden in their great wooden boxes, now peered out hoping to enjoy the first-ever comical incident in Lady Well church. There was a titter from the maids with whom Anne had once worked; whilst Patience Helliwell tightly gripped her prayer-book. Benjamin Greave, who had been daydreaming about the pile he intended to erect in the passageway to the altar of Saint Mary the Virgin ('The columns fro' the Greek, the angels carved by John Wylde so perfect you could hear 'em sing'), awoke to mutter boldly and sourly, 'Pride comes before a fall!'

Doubtfire was struck dumb. But, tipsy (as usual) though he was, he rallied himself to fight back. His lean face reddening above the pulpit, like a plum ripening in a dark orchard (or could it be a roasting soul in Hell?), he gripped the carved oak as if its enduring strength might lend itself to him, whilst he stirred his memory for where to find described in the Bible the *just deserts* of the *most execrable woman*. He also raked the pit of his own soul to discover shadowy female shapes, bringing them forth so that he might hate them. They were there, all right, like snakes in a ravine; ancient lurking vengeful mothers.

(Sometimes, in dreams, daydreams and drunken stupors, they rose, and seemed as beautiful as Anne Wylde. He recognised in himself then longings so deep that he did not know what they were, nor out of what well they had sprung. Desires for a goddess made flesh; for the ancient Mother. But before he could properly recognise her, she would vanish.)

Kings – that was where she was to be found! *Kings. Chapter* ... With fingers stained by the formalin in which he preserved his specimens of 'natural science', he ruffled the pages desperately to find Jezebel. Meanwhile the congregation was waiting. Anne Wylde coughed and sniffed. Ah! Kings 2, not *1*. Chapter 9 ...

' "And Elisha the prophet called one of the children of the prophets and said unto him, Gird up thy loins, and take this box of oil in thine hand, and go to Ramoth-gilead! ... And when he came, behold, the captains of the host were sitting; and he said, I have an errand to thee, O captain ... thou shalt smite the house of Ahab thy master, that I may avenge the blood of my servants the prophets, and the blood of all the servants of the Lord, at the hand of *Jezebel* ..."'

Then occurred something quite unknown before in Lady Well. The Parson, in mid-sermon, was interrupted by a woman! (Doubtfire was used to disturbances in his services: but by men, not by women.) That clever female, Anne Wylde, of course, who, questioner though she was, knew her Bible well enough to continue the Vicar's quotation and flaunt him with it. "For the whole house of Ahab shall perish and I will cut off from Ahab him that pisseth against the wall!" she shrieked. There followed laughter and whistling, whilst someone's dog, sneaked into the building, began to yap. Dick Almighty, confined down below in the nave of the church, could do nothing to control disorder amongst his superiors upon the balcony. He could merely grow red, turn his leonine angry head this way and that, and bang his staff.

Doubtfire retorted, viciously, ' "And the dogs shall eat Jezebel ... and there shall be none to bury her!" '

' "And he opened the door, and fled!" ' Anne Wylde continued the quotation, angrily.

This was too much for Doubtfire, and he did, indeed, flee from his church, amidst a chaos of ribaldry and laughter. Even the picture of Saint Uncumber was smirking, it seemed to Anne. As she glanced at the upside-down crucified face, with the miraculous smile upon its lips, the similarity of that gaunt crucified form to her own struck her. Except that Saint Uncumber's hair was red, she was an exact replica of herself. Whilst Anne gasped at this fact (which she had never noticed before), 'Bang! Bang!' went Almighty's staff, with the brass knob and the little eagle glowing on top of it. But he was impotent because Anne Wylde, with the other superior members of the community, had her own way out of the church, down a broad oak staircase and through a special door, that was definitely outside his jurisdiction. She slipped away, for one moment at least something of a heroine amongst her own people.

Before the next Sunday, Anne set afoot rumours that she was going to pay another visit to Lady Well. So people stationed themselves for a good view of her. Although recently they had stoned her, many

128

because of her wealthy connections, and the way that she had defeated Doubtfire, were now just as ready to curtsey and remove their hats.

Anne enjoyed making a spectacle of herself even more because Oliver was embarrassed by this gaunt, uncontrollable, sometimes menacing beauty with whom he had 'thrown in his lot', 'lived over the brush', or 'over the broomstick'.

'You are not God!' he tersely expressed himself at last.

'I haven't forgotten that God is a man!' she answered, primly.

That day, Doubtfire foolishly allowed the words, 'Christ has merely delivered us from mercy into misery,' to slip unguarded from his lips. He had lost control of himself, Anne Wylde had unmanned him.

Though it was an honest and deeply felt speech, one of Doubtfire's few, the congregation thought of it what he might have expected them to think (and did, later, when he had recovered self-control): though no one disagreed about the misery, yet if a clergyman is to tell us it is Christ's fault, then where are people to look for a saviour? So an angry crowd, Anne Wylde laughing amongst them, gathered at the church door, catching the heretical Parson before he ducked into the inn with Dick Almighty, Joshua Binns and the other churchwardens. Anne gaily shouted out her father's words, 'Heaven is only this world where men are merry, Hell is also this world, when they suffer grief and pain!'

'You talk like a damned Dissenter!' Doubtfire roared back, pulling his skirts about his stick-frame as he escaped, with Dick Almighty covering his retreat by waving the oak-and-brass staff of office.

Anne yelled after him, 'Your religion is only for those who have been cast out of paradise, where I still dwell!'

Through the following weeks Doubtfire appeared even less frequently in his pulpit. At the locked church door small groups of unhappy people, many of them old, begged Almighty to turn the key and let them in to pray even though there was no Parson. Or they drifted off to join the Methodists and the Baptists, perhaps never to return to the Established Church. Before what few services he gave, Doubtfire would be until three in the morning staring either into the bottom of a tankard, or through the eye of a microscope, to find the courage to face Anne Wylde's scorn. Finally, he spent almost all of his Sundays slipping across the moors, creating with tinder and flint his own fiery hells out of hay ricks and barns, or collecting 'specimens' –

paupers, or horses that had collapsed under their loads – whilst leaving his parishioners to what pleasures they could invent for themselves.

Jack Loveless's conversation with Anne Wylde had stirred his roots. Grievances rose to 'pollute' (as Doubtfire and others would have expressed it) the stream of thoughts which trickled through his head whilst at his loom. He remembered for instance when a traveller had turned up from South America with a piece of 'traditional Indian weaving' which Jack recognised as one of his own designs that had been taken to the southern hemisphere and copied by the Indians, its source in Yorkshire forgotten.

After his day's work Jack used to limp down to Lady Well and spend until the early hours in seditious talk with wool-combers and wool-croppers, these being the most radical artisans. Giving the password *Ezekiel* at the door (only for the sake of formality, since the guard knew Jack well) he entered a hush-house where illicit whisky, used to wash down a hare poached from Nicholas Horsfall's park, inflamed poetry and republicanism. Loveless soon realised that if his friends did not express themselves to such as Benjamin Greave or find an outlet in a written manifesto, the boil would burst more dangerously. Others already knew what the wool-combers were doing even though they swore one another to secrecy, debated mostly in darkness, and left their meeting-room on tiptoe. There seemed always to be someone to watch them. John Wylde would be up, squinting at a book by candlelight. (Though the mason had been a frequenter of hush-houses himself, in his time.) The Vicar might be slipping through the streets, 'keeping watch'. Or Esther Kershaw would be woken from where she often slept against the north wall of the church.

The wool-combers and croppers instructed Jack to ask Oliver Greave if he would write down their ideas in the form of a pamphlet and give them some money to print it. They argued that firstly Oliver was a poet, secondly that his quarrel with his father must at root have some grievance sympathetic to the wool-combers' cause, and thirdly that his woman, Anne Wylde, belonged to the common people. 'If he does not agree,' said one, 'tell the fellow we'll fire Lower Laithes, wi' his mistress in it.'

Loveless found the poet settled into a corner of an ale house, one of the many he went to in a futile search for Tim Bobbin and for his moorland muse. It was ironic that Anne Wylde, now in full sensuous happiness, and in a home furnished according to the best taste, still did not satisfy him. It was because she herself was not satisfied: he realised that Anne was even now not completely with him, but that part of her lay amongst the wiry moorland grasses. His muse still seemed out of reach. It was as if there was a veil, with on one side of it his elegant *verses* and on the other, *poetry*. The latter, in his imagination was identified with the moorland winds (whose variations he knew so well, from the soft breezes upon flowering heather to the shrill and cutting blasts of January), searching for expression in verse as the breath of a musician finds its true note in the mouth of a flute. But he, it seemed, was not the instrument. Or he was not the musician who was able to bring forth the sweet right air.

His failure to produce poetry angered Anne and even her sensual happiness was adulterated. In some violent arguments, she threw at him the questions that he must answer, the riddle, that he must solve, if he was to become a real poet. One was that of discovering that mysterious, shy wisp, who for a second would stand clearly embodied before him and then would disappear, convincing him only that what he had seen was an illusion: himself. There was also the question of feeding upon older roots, of growing in deeper soil, than what satisfied fashionable verses. It was all too much for Oliver. He took more of the apothecary's *magic rubbing bottle*. His feckless wanderings, seemingly irresponsible because he was obeying the mysterious voice of something he could not see, touch or understand, began again.

So when during his regained 'freedom' he rested the night at a moorland inn, he did not feel disposed to discuss money and materialistic grievances. 'Is it you combers that are setting fire to houses? You'll be hanged!' he briefly answered Loveless.

'We have done nothing so far. But it is not unlikely that the weavers will burn the new manufactories if they remain unsatisfied. In our work we know the necessity of trusting one another and acting as one, and with the strength that comes of it we will overturn – we will overturn every hindrance. We will also claim back our common land, before all England becomes private and enclosed. For then when they want someone to die on foreign battlefields for't, they'll be telling us it is *our* country that we are defending, though we'd be hung for trespass if we dared even to walk upon it, let alone enjoy its fish and game!'

Oliver waved his pot for more ale. 'The weaver and the wool-comber, the mason and the carpenter, are their own aristocracy, showing its virtue in a job done well and with skill. Instead of investing your pride there, you hunt worldly wealth as dogs pursue a hare and the longing you have for yellow dirt transforms you into galley-slaves! You should desire leisure and art more, not money.'

They burst out laughing at this last sentence. So Oliver shouted, 'Afore long you'll give up keeping saint's-days altogether! And when you do have gold you put on the haughtiness of Spanish dons and mix it with the meanness of Dutch merchants!'

'If you wish to discover the true poetic muse in these times, you should look for her amongst our radical causes,' Loveless told him, in a level voice.

One night, shortly after the wool-combers and the croppers had received this rebuff, the spinning mill which John Wylde had built for Captain Horsfall was ignited. Loveless realised that his friends would be blamed for it, unless rumours were killed at birth. Gossipers were already tracing a connection between the public threats to burn Anne Wylde in her own house, and the fate of the mill built by her father. Though it was two o'clock in the morning, and dark but for the flames in the sky, Jack hurried to tell his friends that they must quickly explain themselves to the Vicar and to Benjamin Greave.

A large crowd was already attracted by the fire. Not only the plotting radicals were there, but also many others who in their hearts wanted to see the new manufactories burned down, saw that this was popular, and were therefore ready to assume some credit for it if it was to their advantage. Binns thought it might bring him the renewed love of his wife, and Jabez Stott hoped it would make him a hero amongst the wool-combers. So it took Loveless some time to sift out trustworthy friends, and lead them across the hills. Others, out of curiosity, followed after.

Doubtfire, they discovered, was not at home, so they went to Making Hall. When Greave came into his porch he saw the sky on fire as if with the Apocalypse. It illuminated men with big fists and forearms developed from handling for fourteen hours a day the huge cropping shears that cut the nap off the wool. He saw artisans such as

Jeremiah Rhodes, who could read, and so, Benjamin assumed, could only be poring over Tom Paine and seditious pamphlets, or making some nonsense of their own out of the Bible. This he believed had inspired them now to burn down Makings.

Frightened though Benjamin was, he spoke to them calmly and jovially, his tone one of amazement that they should feel the lack of anything. 'Good evening, sinners! What can I do for you?'

'More payment for our pieces and longer credit.'

Loveless's unequivocal, unaggressive manner made the clothier feel secure. 'Thou'll not get that without working for it!' he answered, and (recalling the preaching he did during his early manhood at the chapel of the Presbyterians), he drew what breath he could in to his tight little chest and launched upon a speech. 'In the old days, men, how much we completed in a day! In the morning cutting grass, threshing corn, walling, or churning milk. Before midday we'd maybe weave six yards, weed a garden or spread dung. Fetch peat home, and still have time to listen to a preacher. That's the attitude with which I built my business, and you must be the same if you wish to succeed. Instead of that you're risking hanging by setting fire to property.'

'We've not burned down no buildings. But we've all worked as hard as you, Mr Greave. Only you're luckier than some, and you've built what you have on our backs,' Loveless answered.

Benjamin was flattered by this implicit celebration of his wealth, and secretly he was glad that the rival mill had been burned. He understood these men, for as a trader and their master he had cared for them like a pastor with his flock. They had pride in their craft, but also an unadventurous ungenerous attitude, simply wanting 'things to stay as they'd always been', though with more prosperity and less interference from 'incomers' and foreigners. So he wooed them gently. 'If thou'lt come along wi' me in weaving new cloths, though it seems strange to you and I cannot offer so much money at present, yet I'll make you in time the most prosperous weavers in England! A little sacrifice from you now will bring in a new age! You often hear folk preach of a new time that is coming. What *is* the "Heaven on earth" that you hear hedge-preachers and Methodists and suchlike talk about? I'll tell you: it is *The Period of Worsted Cloth*! Moreover ... Moreover! ... that its destiny, to prosper or sink in dismal failure, lies in your hands! We already 'ave the Empress of the Russians eating out of our palms, and I'm told she's a bit of a Jacobin like ourselves, believing in the rights o' the people. Think on that! Eh lads, what a prospect, what a destiny, what a future, what an opportunity lies before you! Mak' the new woollens, I tell thee, mak' a little sacrifice for't, and it'll make thee!'

'Mak! Mak! Mak! All you thinks of is new "making"! But it takes so long to weave, is so much trouble, and then you say you cannot pay us so much for it. If it's rivalry from Horsfall keeping the price down, that's settled for you now,' Loveless replied.

'I aren't giving up my children's food for callimancoes and such stuff, Mr Greave. We've been all right so far weaving kerseys. I cannot see *thee* sacrificing so much!' said Jeremiah Rhodes. 'You do whatever you've a mind to do. But, "The exercise of the natural rights of man has no other limits than those which are necessary to secure to every *other* man the free exercise of the same rights." That is what they said at the National Assembly of France.'

'I am, but I am tho'!' Some of them laughed at Benjamin, and he smiled back the stiff smile of one who is actually afraid. 'You're being short-sighted, friends. Where's your ambition? Oh, what a glorious vision, what a future, there lies before us wi' worsteds!'

Jack Loveless's hungry face in the light from the distant burning mill was like a flame itself, escaped to speak out of the fire. 'Citoyen Jeremiah Rhodes is right,' he said, 'Worsteds'll make one man rich for a hundred poor. And that hundred'll be those asked to make the sacrifices now! It's happened before in the King's England and for sure it'll happen again.'

'Nay, friends, how short-sighted you are!'

Benjamin was still genial. Then Jabez Stott mentioned his son and Anne Wylde.

'What about my son?' the clothier snapped. 'He is at liberty to do as he wishes. You say that you believe in Liberty. Anyone who has anything to say about him may step forwards!'

'You know they're keeping a black boy down there in illegal slavery?' Loveless asked.

'I'm told he's an indentured apprentice.'

'With a collar round his neck!'

'What's that to do with weaving pieces? I've always given *you* your dues.'

Joshua Binns answered, 'We cannot possibly live in this valley whilst they are at Lower Laithes. There's no hope of morality with their example. It is sinfulness for which they will burn for ever in Hell's fire.'

'Then let them pursue their Hell-bent course in peace! There are plenty of others have been courting Hell. You do not need to join them.'

Loveless continued, 'We think that the reason you have been unwilling to pay and give us work is because your business is impeded by your son's associating with Miss Wylde. She herself is all right, I wouldn't have no harm done to her. Yet because of her very nature, and where she is from, and the Devil that gave her birth, she interferes with the progress of trade. She is as unlucky as a woman taken on board a ship. No one can work without doing as she wishes, and Oliver Greave is like wax in her hands. So we shall go to Lower Laithes to make him answer for it.'

'He is not there, he has gone south to buy wool. Friends, your hardship is due merely to it taking time for a new fashion to catch on. Now we have to grab the business from them West Country clothiers by making finer woollens than them, and if we do not do so the whole north is doomed. It is fated right on the shores of a sea, of an ocean, of a great tide of prosperity. With our good sense we'll better them, you'll see! But first we have to defeat the machines that threaten us and I can only pay you more if I do not have to fear their competition. Though I would not encourage you to do what is not legal. What is not right within the law.'

'He talks good sense, he's one with us!' Joshua Binns said.

Most of the men now wished to help Benjamin Greave and therefore (they thought) themselves also, by going that night to fire another mill. Binns especially believed that the way to grow into a large-scale manufacturer was keenly to follow Greave's example. Loveless retired with them into the darkness. Whilst Greave returned thankfully and at peace indoors, Jack, sweating with fear, persuaded them that what the clothier really wanted was to get the most troublesome hanged, at the same time to be rid of competing manufactories, and also to redirect animosity from his son at Lower Laithes.

'You know how it is with magical conjuring doctors at a fair?' Loveless said. 'They tell you, "Look at such and such". But if you do, you never discover the trick, for you must search in the opposite direction to what you are told. So it is with the clothing masters. You must go in the opposite way to where they direct you if you would save your lives and liberties.'

Loveless managed to divert them from firing a manufactory. They went instead to Lower Laithes. There, the peacocks screamed like huge cats, and dogs barked through the darkness. The men left pale grey trails across the dew of the lawn; it was as if they had entered a carpeted room wearing muddy boots. Anne looked out of her window. For a moment she indulged the sweet thought that the 'mob' could not reach her any more, and then she returned to bed. Instead of her, Mary Pickles, Jenny Loveless and Amos Culpin went out.

'We are citizens who have come here in defence of our natural liberties,' Jeremiah Rhodes announced.

'You are right to think of freedom from wickedness. Our mistress here lives in savage, mortal sin,' Culpin lugubriously told the weavers.

Jenny Loveless added, 'If she were still in Lady Well they would squeeze her bubbies to see if there is milk in them! That is what they are like in that town. Mistress is sick every morning these days.'

They all looked up to the iron grille in the stable-loft where Earth peered out. At sight of the torchlight, the flames, the intense faces, the cries of exotic birds, and the outlines of woodlands, the slave was transformed with sweet memories of Africa.

'That one takes our bread, too,' Joshua Binns said.

Eyes gleamed in torchlight as they wondered what to do.

It seemed up to Joshua to think of something. 'We could treat her to rough music,' he suggested, disarmingly meek. 'A crowd of honest citizens banging drums and rattling sticks outside the window does a lot towards teaching respect to a shrewish female. When next Lammas Day Fair comes round there'll be opportunity for it. It's but a few months' wait until August.'

They were all silent for a while with horror.

'The light of the morning shames the work of the night,' Mary Pickles sighed, at last, and as if with the weight of a heavy stone in her breast.

Three days later Oliver returned, in a good mood because he had enjoyed a pleasant journey in spring weather. Southern landscapes had suffocated him with what he thought of as 'airless comforts'. The trees were thick, close, over-rich canopies. He was frustrated by lack of distant horizons. Occasionally he would cross through the heather, water, or oak trees of a heath, and burst out of them to see carved out of the distance a gentleman's seat, a park, some neat, hedged, drained, enclosed fields, or a town clustered around its church; though mostly he found himself drowned for mile after mile in leaves. But upon northern hills the spring (arriving late) was a slender, athletic, dancing sprite, rather than a plump spirit. Through clouds, scraps of light daubed the moors, for thrilling seconds only, and then were torn away restlessly to other places. The valleys and slopes were rinsed and wrung in the brisk hands of the rain showers, as a strong weaver rinses and fulls his green making. Oliver loved especially the sound of water gurgling in stone holes hidden under the grasses, and the positive feel of the land's structure beneath his feet. Here you knew what the rock was, because its dark stones in cliffs and jagged piles stuck out through fields and littered the rivers. It felt firm, you saw and sensed under your shoes what sort of land you trod. The elements were restless, the ground was stony, and the marriage of the two expressed the nature of the people and the society dwelling there.

As soon as he tipped Raven's Hill and looked into his native valley he saw anew the scars of burning. Down by the river was a charred manufactory. Speckled around Lady Well were little burnt spots of ruined farms. Close at hand, his father's men were destroying gorse bushes, heather and hawthorn with fire. Smoke seemed a permanent taint in the air. Lady Well is like a battleground, he thought. Oh, when will there be an end to conflagration and trouble? And he knew that the bedrock of it all was the dissatisfaction of the weavers and the ambitions of the clothiers.

'Your mistress Anne is in her withdrawing room, drinking gin,' Mary Pickles told him in the stableyard, in such a tone that he could not decide whether her words were tender or insulting. Certainly they were now too familiar. But he was sorry for the huge, bowed, once-happy woman and he never reprimanded her.

Oliver's southern business had largely been an excuse, understood tacitly by Anne Wylde and himself, to be free of one another for a while. Their arguments had culminated in one when he had *demanded* that she marry him. It was a preposterous thing to say in an argument.

Of course she would not: it was for his gentleness that she loved him, and here he was betraying it with roughness! Once she had feared to give her love in case it led to his despising her; now that was overcome, she was restrained from tumbling into marriage because she thought that once Oliver possessed her he would mistreat and neglect her as wives generally were. Because she could not give him this true reason, she would not answer him at all, which inflamed his anger, and – as sometimes in the old days – he had trembled with incipient violence.

But now, as they had both hoped, their love was refreshed. He could think of little else except being in her presence again, and she wished to be in his. He instantly tumbled into his old feelings about her. He was so happy, he was on the edge of both laughing and weeping at the same moment. He felt it in his stomach, and in his eyes which through sheer joy in life would water and glitter at something beautiful or sad. Oh, why, why, had they ever chosen separation? Some day there would be parting enough! Whenever they were to-gether, unsatisfactory days were turned into good ones merely because they touched one another or kissed in the first rituals of love that reminded them that another full day had circled into happiness again: lips, neck, hair, feet, then the pink rose and the bird nesting in its petals. Thus they embarked upon the long moon-voyage of the night, with whispering, fantasies, scents, touchings, and brief soft landings on the shores of strange dreams. When they turned from one another to sleep, they held hands lightly until tiredness loosed their clasp. On awakening each was conscious vaguely of lightness or darkness first of all, but next, they desired the assurance that the other was still there.

Whatever bad or unpleasant thing the day held for either of them, the other would be there. Sexual joy was not of the night-time only. Oliver was always aware of Anne. Even when she was in another room a constant inner voice would hardly let him get on with his book or his papers, for wondering what she might be doing. The simplest acts that they performed for one another were invested with sensuality. When he laid a shawl around her it became as full with sexuality as was the moist flower between her legs. So the whole day and night were sexual and he was always in a state of mild distraction. If he felt she was unhappy, he took it to be his own fault; and so he became quick to defend himself, bursting out in excessive blame of her, for which later he would hate himself. But for almost the whole time the background of his mind was filled with the happiest thoughts, such as of the way she moved about a room, or what she had said, or would she in a moment move just-so and show her liquid legs? For so many years now, he reflected, he had been bursting with an ecstatic readiness both to laugh and cry at the same moment.

But when they met they did not speak of this. She was drunk. Yet still he saw her love for him shining out and she saw his.

They talked about the insulting manner of the servants, of which Anne made light even though she had begun a habit of avoiding her household, complaining of headaches and tiredness, and staying in her room. The stories overheard amongst servants, to which she was previously aloof, now made her shudder. Noticing this, though at one time they used to grow quiet in the kitchen at her presence, these days they became garrulous.

'Martha Jolley at the Snawdens was washing clothes in an out-house. They saw she was heavy and slow, being with child, 'til she crept from her wash-tub and delivered herself in the garden, buried it and come back to her work. They searched her and found milk so she confessed, and they discovered the babe with earth stopped in its mouth, so she was sent to York and executed!'

' 'Tis nothing to what I'll tell you! Rebecca Pogson she shared a house with a woman but sent her off for a time. Rebecca was delivered and made it away. The other returning noticed the change in her and told neighbours, who forced a confession. At first she lied that she had thrown it into the brook, so the town was raised to search for it. When they found it not, she said it was in a coal-pit and there they discovered it laid upon a ledge, halfway down, upon a cushion. That mother was committed to die, also. Oh, the unhappy woman!'

The maids had contrived that Anne should overhear such tales as these. Anne knew they were suggesting that she herself would be producing a bastard, would do away with it, be committed to York – for they would see to it! – and executed. Once she fainted and Mary Pickles loosened her throat and carried her to her room.

When Oliver saw Anne's tiredness and sickness (especially in her eyes, which were heavy, moist, and steady with all the sadness she did not speak of, but that at last was weighing her down), he felt that she was not so much ill physically, as faint and listless with her premonitions of unhappiness and disaster. He had the image of an ocean of intuitions within her, formless, continuous, fathomless and uncharted, where he merely stood on the edge, timidly dabbling his feet.

Soon Oliver had to talk to his father about business. The son wanted to share his deepest worries, but he dared to speak only about his purchases of wool. As they both knew, it was going to prove more difficult than ever to get the weavers to make it into worsted cloth, after all the dissension in the valley. So Benjamin Greave after all raised the matter that was closest to Oliver's heart.

'What unsettles the weavers is not the prices we pay them, but your sinful association with Miss Wylde,' Greave said. 'As always she is at the bottom of all misfortune! She ruins our prosperity, and so it'll be until we are rid of her! I'll not have that woman thought a fit garden to grow an heir of mine in, and I hope you're not planting her with any bastards!'

Oliver flushed. 'She would have married me by now if we were not at Lower Laithes, which is too wet, gloomy and unhealthy for her to contemplate the prospect of spending a lifetime there. And the servants wouldn't gossip so maliciously if they were not confined to such a place. No art can refine it nor make it enjoyable or habitable, though we have employed the best craftsmen. You built it only so that I could watch over your fulling mill, and it was no *gift* for it brought on Zillah's ill-health in such a damp bottom of the woods. It is doing the same thing now to Anne Wylde, who is not well from these persecutions, but I will not desert her!'

'So you're ready to marry your housekeeper? What have you had so far with her?'

When Oliver would not answer, Benjamin continued, 'I have t'impart to you the saddest news of my life. But all our miseries have sprung from taking in a witch and the time is come to put an end to it. As you are determined to stick to this madcap who enslaves you, one without morals or decency, and you have become the same, then I will break my association with you. I will cut off my branch of the business and you and Miss Wylde can fend for yourselves. You may go to Hell together!'

'I will not abandon Anne Wylde, not for yours nor any man's worldly interests!'

In this moment it seemed to Oliver that whatever security with his father had existed had finally collapsed beneath him, like a wood-wormed floor.

At Lower Laithes Anne was white and sweating. He loosed her stays. 'I am with child,' she whispered.

He was certain that now she would marry him.

'You do not know Doubtfire as I do, otherwise you would not be so keen on his approval of our lying together,' she answered him this time.

'Anne! My father, his clerks, the servants, and the weavers, are all angry about you. If people see you with child they will not be stopped from setting fire to our house. You need protection.'

'Then let us pretend we are married, to satisfy them.'

'My station is not that of a gypsy nor an outcast! You cannot bear our baby unless we are married!'

'Then I will hide myself at my aunt's.'

He looked as though she had destroyed him. It quite deflated the impatience he had been expressing so far.

'Don't worry, I will not kill your child,' she added.

Her firmness made him weaker. He was overwhelmed by an irony: what his father longed for was an heir, this was the source of his hardness and bitterness, and yet Benjamin Greave was at enmity with the womb that grew it.

Oliver was weeping. Anne struggled to uplift him.

'The whole household would turn on me if I married you and stayed here, Oliver. I am used to stones being thrown at me, ever since birth, but if envious Lady Well saw that I was married to your fortune they would kill us both. They would find their way, for they have always wanted it. The only safe thing is to hide. The world's hurt is not as hard to bear as you think and we are both strong enough.'

He clung so pathetically to her that she had to snatch back her clothes and he fell to the ground. When she escaped he was weeping into clenched fists upon the carpet.

As Anne left her home, taking only Earth with her, the rain was
shuttling across Blood Wood, weaving lines of the pale undersides of
leaves across the green. She reached above, into even stronger rain.
Mingled with the showers came light thrown about the skies and hills.
Scraps of rainbow were thrust out of a cloud and blown away on a
ribbon of wind. Sometimes she saw a lark daring a fling, to be tossed
aside and plummet back on to the grass.

The Negro from Africa seemed to feel the cold and wet less than
herself, who was born here. Expressionlessly he carried her bundle,
whilst Anne shuddered and protected herself. Walking lankily, and
on the balls of his feet, even his movements made him different to the
weavers, who shifted along stolidly: a Yorkshireman put the whole of
his foot down at each step, as if asserting his right to the earth and
rock, his grip of it, and his defiance of wind or rain's attempt to
remove him.

As they climbed, Anne saw how the small valley, that had always
been the theatre of her life, lay bosomed in a larger dale, which was
in turn nursed by the slopes of a still wider depression, itself lying in
yet larger arms – layer upon layer surrounding, and all hidden from
those who toiled in Lady Well. How tiny in the scope of the moor
were her village, Makings and Lower Laithes. She was amazed to
think that these unimportant stony spots on the sweet earth had
troubled her so much. She imagined the people twisting through those
dark alleys, believing that their neighbours, their property, and the
walls shutting them in were all that mattered in the Universe, being
blind to the great space surrounding. Anne felt that Lady Well could
slip or blow off the hilltop in one puff and it would not make any
difference to the eternity of the hills.

Anne and her Negro climbed beyond Upper Spout, where set in the
black soggy peat was a small Greek temple made of black stones. It
had carved Nereids holding vases out of which tumbled Benjamin

Greave's cold, sulphurous spring. It was a bleak place. No fine ladies had yet come to bathe and the keeper, Israel Merrybent, in his inconvenient but majestically fronted cottage (based upon the Niké temple of the Athens Acropolis, to match the nearby 'Parthenon') spent his time (or so it appeared to his few visitors) reading his Bible.

Beyond these absurd erections were no more buildings good enough even to be termed 'cottages'. Yet still a few people lived in huts made of peat-stacks and reeds: squatters, rush-gatherers, 'moor-edgers', freaks of religion and politics, soldiers and ruffians of every breed. They did not go to church or village much and they had never before seen Anne Wylde with her black boy. So as these two climbed, groups appeared on the skyline. Many of them were drunk. At first the watchers were silent. Then loud cruel laughter followed after Anne and Earth. Behind the laughter and the drunkenness, she sensed the madness and misery of outcasts. A few years ago Anne had not guessed what deep oceans of feeling were brewing their hidden storms under the frozen crusts of most people's characters. Were these too – jeering now – in the secrecy of their homes called upon to navigate such gales as she herself had to weather?

Further on, amongst the mud and stones of Raven's Hill, nothing watched her but the larks struggling to sing against the showers. She descended unseen into the shadow on the far side and slipped – brushing by the scent of thyme, comfrey, mint, so that the smells clung and mingled upon her dress and skin – into her Aunt Pity's narrow tear in the earth where everything was moist and still. She had dropped through a rent in the roof of the Underworld.

The Negro, frightened of the snarling dog with hair raised in barbs on its neck, and of the moist shadowy cleft into which he was being led, looked desperately back at the view. Weavers' cots, clumps of trees, stone enclosures and streams, all standing out unusually brilliantly in a moment of sun, were now disappearing. The world was setting over his horizon. Soon there was left only a patch of light, brittle as glass, and becoming narrower, narrower . . . he was drowning . . . he would enter the jaws of the beast . . .

But the animal recognised Anne and calmly sniffed her hand, so she brought the Negro for a friendly smell at him, too.

He was happier still inside the cottage. Anne and Earth had it in common to be at home with bare floors, crude tables and chairs and the clatter of wooden bowls. Earth (as was usually expected of him) stood by the door but Anne this time took hold of his shoulder and steered him to the hearth.

Aunt Pity glanced at Anne's condition. 'Call upon Saint Felicitas, and hope to be blessed with a boy!' she remarked. The aunt ritualistically poked at the fire and tidied her things. More and more now she fussed over insignificant possessions that were by unnoticed degrees becoming tattered and unusable. The less time she had to live, the more of it she devoted to what would soon be thrown away. She continuously closed doors and curtains. She sat by choice in the shadiest corners, and she liked most often to be quite, quite still. It was as if she was preparing herself for being shut in a clammy grave.

Pity ran her trembling finger greedily over the black skin as though feeling the soundness of a vegetable or fruit. 'Can he chop wood and shovel snow? There might be some more up here yet. I couldn't open my door for three days a month since, and each snowfall I think it'll be the last one I'll see. Elkanah Beanland had to scythe my enclosure for me last year, and he brings me my bits and pieces. He's glad to do anything so long as I'll let him spend an hour now and then reading his Bible at me!'

The two women and the Negro lived off preserves of whinberries or blackberries, on oatcakes, and the trout that Earth caught skilfully, with boyish joy, in his hands. Having almost no English he lived very much either inside his own head, or amongst the moorland spirits, and he enjoyed an illusion that he had escaped – at any rate, he had never before been so happy. There passed for the three of them a short eternity of joy, peaceful and contemplative. Anne discovered that, contrary to what Parson Doubtfire told her, Negroes did have souls. Obviously happier than in his previous pampered and decorative existence, Earth before the women's eyes thickened into a laughing lusty youth, who was gradually picking up the language of his mistress, whilst at other times he gabbled forgetfully in his natural tongue.

Whatever was growing inside Anne began to stir, slide about and thrust out lumps. Slimy and formless it would then retreat into her like some monster sinking back into the deep. It was as if she had caught a slippery fish, a mermaid, or a dolphin. Her womb was a net which had been trawling through an ocean. When, some day, she dragged it finally out, she would find what was pulling at her so far down on the end of a line at the bottom of a dark and heavy sea.

Anne suffered violent pains. It was several months too early and she went to bed horrified at the thought of the dead creature, or the monster, she was about to eject. Witches gave birth to things with eyes in the centres of their foreheads or without mouths. A long while, an eternal moment of horror, passed as she waited for the next spasm – Anne was more conscious of minutes passing than of pain. There was time now for her to weep. She saw, swimming before her tears, this huge fish-shape that her imagination had given birth to. Now it seemed not a beautiful mermaid, such as Oliver was fond of drawing on wool-bales, not a playful dolphin all shyness and delight: it was something cold-bodied, pike-toothed and grinning, with expressionless glassy eyes.

Another spasm came. Anne clutched and rocked her way through it. She was being drawn through strange oceans, past weird creatures, and grappled by terrifying slimy weeds . . .

Afterwards she realised how quickly she had ceased to cry, and she was comforted to find that the rapid demands of her body could overcome both agony and sadness. Then a further pain announced itself, surprising her by its fierceness.

She saw coming out of herself a white ghostly sac, like a moon, and half-transparent. Within it was a beautifully formed arm with its tiny fist clenched. This little creature moved.

For a moment she was thrilled by the beauty of what was appearing from that bloody place where the Devil was supposed to dwell.

Then she realised that, born so early, it would be malformed, if it lived at all. It would be something black, horned and foul engendered in the 'womb of darkness' (as Parson Doubtfire called the origin of evil and of ourselves), and a hideous curse upon her and her lover. Before Anne could glimpse whether, inside the veined little moon, it was mouthless or eyeless, she fainted.

As she lay with strings of jelly, blood and wetness emerging pulsing from her, Aunt Pity cut off the mess that was Anne and Oliver's 'child'. Then she gave her attention to the mother.

Coming round, Anne saw that her baby was dead. She closed her eyes again in weariness and at the final numb end of grief. Aunt Pity and the Negro then buried the foetus in the garden. Both women tried to be glad at least that it was a dead thing and not a malformed living one; whilst Anne wanted not to know where its grave was. Yet the vision of that minute fist clenched in its sac, and its little movements, would stay with her for ever.

On the following day Anne suffered a rush of blood that drenched her bedding. More the next day. She still kept on weeping. Weeping. But after several weeks it gradually lessened.

Meanwhile the spring continued steadily upon the moor. Firstly a brightening green appeared at the edges of the stream and its surface was starred with crowfoot flowers. Then the air lightened. The wild birds recognised with delight that their calls and songs were not now crushed by the wind. The curlews returned to Lady Well, enjoying lazy sweeps across calm open skies. They seemed to be pursuing their own mournful cries, as if these were echoes of something they had lost. The larks drilled into the Heavens like dark sparks, melting in rapid flickerings of wings and pulsings of their throats; substance dissolved into energy which finally disappeared in the sun, the song still sprinkling down. Then the lark would drop, body restored to it and its wings folded, except for pauses when it spread and caught itself. It would fall like a pebble, glide before touching grass, and sing another short burst, clearly reluctant to leave the skies. At last it would hop through the grass just as if it hadn't done these things. But then, with crest raised proudly, it would look around as if for applause. Anne regained her strength by watching the larks, as she lay in ecstasies upon banks facing the radiance that stroked her with the sensitive firm fingers of a lover.

August came, burning, breeding hot tempers and rebellion. People smelled always of sweat. They were restless all night with the energies stored up in them out of the heat during the day when they had felt so sleepy. As the moon swelled more and more pregnantly, men and women increasingly roamed through its greater light, drinking, loving, picking fights, looking for release. But neither Dick Almighty's ale and sermons nor the apothecary's rubbing bottle could cure them. The moors wore a silk veil of heat. People every day expected them to catch fire and at night, if they imagined a smell of smoke, they left their beds. Surprisingly the conflagrations did not happen, but everyone was nervous.

The enclosures of wheat, oats and barley turned the colour and texture of cream. When the first was ready Doubtfire was made to take up a position next to Dick O'Lovely, who was playing his violin, and the two led a procession of men and women (who had been drinking for most of the day) out of Lady Well, where his black-gowned arm was forced to an unpractised scything of the corn. The cadaverous Puritan hated doing this, which he condemned as 'Druidic'. He found Dick O'Lovely's company frightening, because he never spoke, (the Parson believed in words). But his parishioners (who had chased him before) could be a frightening tribe also and the Church, as Doubtfire well understood, held a frail truce with their savagery.

Doubtfire was further employed (a group of big-limbed, threatening women and men standing by) to say a prayer over the first sheath, which was then taken (Dick O'Lovely's fiddle still playing) to start a Lammas Day bonfire, after the fair and at the height of what the Parson contemptuously called, 'the Lady Well Saturnalia'. For this, Benjamin Greave provided a pig and an ox to be roasted, Horsfall gave wood from his overgrown estate, Dick Almighty (anticipating revenue from ale) paid for the carting of it, whilst Esther Kershaw, Dick Almighty and Elkanah Beanland all supplied free preaching.

Whilst the afternoon of the 'Saturnalia' wore on, the dust that lay golden on the streets or, having dropped from corn and hay, gilded the enclosures, rose in a parching cloud that needed washing down with ale. No one realised how reckless it was making them – they being eager for the evening, and the bonfire. Elkanah, who had taken up his pitch early under the full sun, yet had few to listen.

John Wylde was one of these few. Since the burning down of Horsfall's mill, in which Wylde's capital had been invested, he had been reduced to labouring, working hard as he had not done since he was a young man. He, who had been sociable and popular most of his life, was now much alone. As his faculties dimmed he was no longer sought out by philosophers and radicals. He was without family and was remote and different from his neighbours, though they respected him. This morning he had been laying a stone floor in a kitchen. He worked with two careless unambitious men, yet what they did was dangerous, so John could not help but give advice. 'Thou's not set above us any longer, John Wylde!' they answered and had then acted more rashly than they needed, to 'show' him. Wylde hated doing anything in which craftsmanship did not count, and yet he was not nowadays fit for heavy labour. His tired body seemed detached from his awake spirit – his soul inhabited a strange dwelling, his limbs would not obey his will, whilst his spirit tried to wriggle free, as one climbs out of a suit of clothes. But today he rested, listening to Elkanah's description of how God had with His own hands once built the world perfectly, though now it had filled up with fools and sinners.

Nearby was an example of it, according to Elkanah. Four strong women were tossing Jabez Stott in a blanket. Each time he rose spread-eagled grasping at the air, the women shrieked:

'Jabez Stott!
What've you got
To make a woman happy?'

'Plenty!'
'Canst rise as high as this then?'
'Aye, and mo-o-o-o-re!'

'Will't'stop thy sinful doings and hear the sayings of the Lord?' Elkanah shouted. 'Then we all might be taken back with the words of the old preachers to the time when there was nobbut God, at the beginning of the world, which was a waste of darkness, water, and muddle. And there are some as say it hasn't improved much since!'

'We are resurrecting Jabez for his marriage. Cannot we do it for Jabez to be married after Lammas Day?'

The gypsies who had sold their goods and had spent the money on ale, horses, and trinkets for women, now dozed or copulated on the grass. Or they drank illicit whisky brewed by Israel Merrybent, lonely keeper of the Upper Spout waters which had been quite useless until he turned to using them for brewing. He brought the liquor down to the fair in two ox-bladders, fastened together by a leather thong, slung around his neck and hidden under his coat so that he looked like a grotesque woman. The only other female more ugly was his own wife who walked always five paces behind him. This was as much to keep out of range of his curses as for any other reason, for he continually swore over his shoulder at her. Israel was a poor conversationalist.

His only other addiction besides cursing and whisky making was for reading and rereading but one page of his Bible per day, and even for this little he had a bad memory. But his cheap whisky made him popular.

On this, the musicians got drunk with the dancers and the harvesters. Or with the boys and girls who had come to be hired, whose fortunes were now decided, and whose clothes that were so neat earlier had become ale-splattered and torn. During the late afternoon some girls ran a naked race because Captain Horsfall offered a dress to the winner, and she who might have won, had she not stopped to wipe her lover's stains from her thighs, fought with the victor so that the frock was torn to rags.

The one place where the elusive Tim Bobbin could reliably be found in his uncharted moorland wanderings was at a saint's-day fair, and he turned up at Lady Well. There he set a group of woolcombers' apprentices to creating a name for Dick Almighty's inn. This was an elaborate establishment, as befitted its many-sided owner: there was a slaughterhouse, a preaching-room (for which Almighty, being so powerful a man, did not have to bother applying for a licence), a butcher's shop and cottage, besides the brewhouse, wellhouse and drinking parlour. As it was said that Almighty Whitely feared neither God, man nor Devil, 'Fear Nought' was suggested for a title. But it was also believed that he had a pact with Satan, so 'The Devil's Friend' was put forward. Finally, inspired by Elkanah preaching about the Creation, Tim got Dick Almighty to accept 'The Adam and Eve' – saying that the original Blissful Pair would have got all they wanted here: meat, preaching or ale – and some painters, for free beer, designed a sign showing our first parents in shameful copulation.

But, as everyone realised, this was mere filling-in of time compared with what came next when the sheath of corn was carted in by some of Lady Well's chief revellers, Joshua Binns prominent in harness. Dick Almighty strutted in front. 'Mak' way all you honest sinners!' he shouted. From time to time he gave his huge belly a friendly slap with his carter's whip, or took off his tall hat and waved it to the ladies, whilst leading the singing of John Barleycorn. He winked and shook his whip as he passed three recruiting sergeants who were drumming up potential soldiers by the church door. It was as if these were the three men from the north who were described in the ballad, come for their victims:

'There were three men came out of the north,
They all did swear and say,
They greatly made a solemn oath,
John Barleycorn should die!'

At this moment, someone said within John Wylde's hearing, 'They've an effigy of Anne Wylde to burn in yonder barn.'

John, his stance fierce as in the old days, swung round to face the man. But the malicious gossiper had slipped into the crowd, who got in the mason's way when he gave pursuit. Meanwhile the rumour had trickled from its bourne and must spread through the flood of people.

'When is it to be burnt?'

'After dark.'

A calm twilight was already settling upon the hills and the sun was a trembling disc reddening more and more as it sank into a haze. The cart led by Dick Almighty creaked up the alleyways leaving, upon the stones, ears of corn which were plucked to wear in hats or button-holes, or stuck in a sweetheart's hair.

John Wylde was the only sober one, as he searched barn after barn. He scrambled over roofs, looking for access to locked places. He passed from group to group, trying to wring reason out of rumour and to save his daughter from such mockery that it would chill the heart of the most rational of men. He spoke to those by Dick Whitely's tavern and around the barrels of ale set up on carts. He went amongst the drunks who were leaning stupidly against walls, rolling in the grass or being sick. Nobody seemed to know in which place the effigy was stored, nor who its makers were, nor who was paying the bill, nor whose straw stuffed the figure, 'Nor whether 'twould take place at all, for it was only a joke and a rumour.'

There was an ugly moment when John Wylde grabbed Joshua Binns around the throat for saying this. Binns's fellow cart-pullers tried to help, for the mason could still be a frightening man. All that saved the weaver was that the cart swayed backwards down the hill, so everyone ran to stop it, and turned upon Wylde for 'spoiling a happy day'.

The corn sheath was stuffed into the unlit bonfire at the moment when the sun disappeared into Raven's Hill. Doubtfire and Benjamin Greave then came out of the Parsonage where they had spent the day away from the populace, and in discussions, over brandy. The tall parson and the small clothier paced about with smiles and patronising words. Then they led, not towards the great tithe barn as John Wylde expected, which was always locked and guarded, but towards a mere cart-shed – which the mason, though he knew intimately every stone building in Lady Well, had overlooked.

Torches were lit, the doors swung back and out of the shadows, on a hay-cart that creaked through the silence, was wheeled the effigy of Anne Wylde. Her red dress was of spoilt soldiers' cloth, her head made from a swede with a candle flickering inside (as Anne's eyes flickered) through the holes that were the shapes of her eyelids, whilst her black curls were of barley-straws dipped in tar.

Yet it was a calm and beautiful figure, for its makers had unintentionally shown their admiration by reproducing her lovely shape. But it began to shake as they wheeled it along. The head slipped sideways like an idiot's and the straw with which the body was stuffed shifted and made it lumpy. It was as if she aged from a young girl to an old woman in her journey from barn to bonfire.

They looked around for Dick O'Lovely to play an accompanying fiddle tune, but he had disappeared. It was amazing that Dick was not there when a fiddle was required. He must have disapproved of what he saw happening.

'Nay, that's not right! That's not right!' Elkanah shouted. But his voice was drowned by a tin whistle eerily played, by a cacophany of drums and bagpipes, and by the accumulated, drink-enflamed, bursting anger of weavers and wool-combers. 'We'd've prosperity in Lady Well without the witch! Burn the sinful witch!' they yelled.

'She has not deserved this! Let her good and respected father protect her,' Almighty pleaded. But (as his experience of being constable, innkeeper, and chairman of this, that and t'other had taught him), beyond a certain point one could not control a 'mob', short of using soldiery and cannon. If one tried, one's own authority was weakened. So he said no more.

They struggled to hold John Wylde back, for despite their lust to see his daughter damned and burning, no one wished to harm the mason, but only to have him removed. ''Twill sour our beer to have poor John around,' they said. So Lady Well's champion wrestler was called up to restrain him as gently as possible.

Meanwhile Doubtfire pointed his long finger to the tip of the unlit bonfire. 'Where the sparks fly upwards, there is man's salvation and destiny!' he declared. 'Not in such worldly Saturnalias as I see today.'

'Salvation is to the north!' Esther Kershaw shrieked back at him. 'For all our moors are mostly to the north, and that is where the Great Sweet Cow roams free, but you all go about mindfolded and you cannot see!'

'And for my part, the road to salvation is southwards, to Greece and Italy!' Tim Bobbin laughed.

'Thou Bobbin Never-Do-Good-Fellow, 'tis in the north!' Esther retorted and flushed.

'Don't thou gesticulate at me!' Tim answered, good-humouredly. 'I'll testicle-ate as much as I wish!'

Tim was so exasperated by this silly discussion that he snatched off his wig and threw it at the Vicar. Doubtfire at the same moment grabbed his own peruke and flung it at the poet because he was so ignorant of the geography of Hell and Heaven.

Seeing this, John Wylde could not help but smile at the stupidity of human dispute and at his own foolishness in bothering about it; and having no one able to understand why there was a *smile* upon his lips, he let himself be led away.

The wrestler was a man whose appearance could be described entirely by his aggressive-looking neck. His solar plexus was not for ruminating over philosophy, his spreading anus was not primarily for manuring God's earth: the first purpose of his whole body was to carry forwards that great neck, which was so thick that it would hardly bend or straighten, but was stuck obstinately at forty-five degrees, like a bull's. Yet his nature was gentle. He had a great love of children, who followed him about Lady Well as he brought out of his pockets small toys, rag dolls and nuts.

'Now, John,' he said calmly, 'Thou's been a good man in thy time – all the old folk say so – but that one yonder's no daughter of thine, is she?' Since no one ever argued with the wrestler, he was as confident as God Himself that everything he said was true and he spoke with that domineering certainty in his voice.

He left John Wylde on the steps of the church.

After Wylde had sat for a while he stood up and discovered his aches. The side of his face stiff from a punch. A deadness in his thigh from a kick. One eye beginning to close. He was like an old stag that can no longer hold its own; he was like his beloved church, with its war-smashed sculptures, its paintings and much of its glass destroyed by a parson who hated art.

Meanwhile dreaded Melancholy, or Reason's shadow, stalked up on him. As usual she came suddenly and unexpectedly. First of all she baited him with rational thoughts and fears for his daughter, or longings for those days when he had travelled and met interesting companions, when his eyesight was clear and his hand steady. But this was only Melancholy's entrance, in her outer dress – as he well knew, for she had opened his door and trespassed on him many times before. Soon she would disrobe and overwhelm him with her naked black self. John would not admit that something existed if it was not accessible to Reason. At most he would dub it 'a dark meditation of the Devil'. Yet this misery for which there was no antidote in rational thoughts was real enough in its effect. It often drove him to walk for miles upon the moors – not as in the past with the joyful purpose of seeking good society, but simply, he found, to *woo* this very Melancholy. And this he did not understand at all. How could he comprehend such an unreasonable thing? It was as if in suffering he copulated with her, in hope that she would give up her secret, and he would learn what he grieved for. But he never found out what it was, unless it be for the lost mother-garden of Paradise.

Saint Mary's Church, being at the highest point in Lady Well, was still catching the last of the sun. One ray speared a window, and scattered the blurred coloured lights of saints (surviving high up out of Doubtfire's reach) to dissolve on the pavement and over the half-cut stones and stacks of timber placed for the Greaves monument. Astonishing colours, like a garden packed with summer flowers, grew over the deathly-white marble angels lying on their backs in the grass, their limbs slack and sensual as if they had capitulated to love, their mouths open as if in an orgasm with death; upon the Greek columns in designs taken from engravings in the best textbooks, and over the stone blocks meant to impress with their vastness. (A monumentality not in keeping with the shrivelled little man who was to be buried under them.) The rest of the church was an enclosed mysterious purple-dark forest where pigeons fluttered and roosted, and John imagined that the sculptures, with their rubbed-out faces and limbs broken through the enviousness of war, religion and politics, had also retired to settle here one evening in the past.

'Call no man happy until he dies.' Aeschylus's words passed through John Wylde's head. For those who had been his friends, indebted to him, and whom he had served well, were now performing magical acts against his daughter.

Meanwhile two strong weavers were standing on the cart to lift 'Anne' on to the crown of the bonfire, which was then lit at the sheath of straw. The flames burst suddenly, driving people back. The fire climbed more slowly up rotten timbers, fetched from old houses, and decayed boughs from Horsfall's park. When it reached Anne's body it spurted quickly again. The lower part burned first, and flames licked at her head which was broken, like a hanged woman's suspended from a gallows, over the fire. The head dropped off and out of the neck sprang snakes of smoke.

'Let's have a look what's under her skirts!'

'Beware anyone that goes near! She's got teeth like razors inside there!' Binns shouted.

Elkanah Beanland felt once again the weight of his sadness at the foolishness and brutality of men that had in the first place turned him into a preacher. 'There's nothing wrong with the lass, she's right enough if you'd let her alone! There's nothing wrong with right folk! She knows more o' God's ways than most of you!' he declared angrily. He packed up his Bible and in disgust walked away rapidly towards the moors.

Joshua Binns whispered to Horsfall, 'That woman was of unnatural birth and so she should not enjoy a natural death. She was born from a hawthorn tree (though some say from a wild white doe) and is a curse to us. Oh yes, 'tis true enough! 'Tis certainly true. I know 'tis true. At six months of age she had to be churched and was brought forth a second time in mockery from under her mother's shift to make it legitimate after she married John Wylde. Oh yes, she was a bastard all right, for she was not John Wylde's daughter. The woman he married had been on to the moor and lay with a goblin that crept out of tree roots, and Wylde only married the woman out of pity!'

'She is definitely conspicuous and loud,' Horsfall very reasonably answered, 'so it is time to pull her down!'

He talked to some mummers. With Horsfall, these left the fairground, just as they were, in their animal disguises. 'You're not off to some nocturnal assembly?' Dick Almighty asked threateningly. He guessed where they were bound, but as it was Captain Horsfall who led he could see no way to stop them.

Rustling their bells and from time to time throwing out scraps of tunes with their flutes and drums, as sleepless birds do on light nights, they climbed Black Hill where moths blundered out of the heather. From the moortop, moonshine flooded the valleys and the spaces reeled about the drunken men. A slender moon stood above, sharp as a polished axe, and smiling. Binns pointed to it: 'When the man can fall out of his boat, it will bring foul weather. That moon is completely upside down - some dreadful thing is foretold,' he said.

'Nonsense, you old fool,' Horsfall answered him. 'Never mind the moon. Just watch where you are setting your feet.'

Here and there the lights of farms floated like luminous fish rising through dark water. A shadowy thing that they took to be a boulder turned out to be a great valley opening up before them. Streams rustled musically amongst the stones at immeasurable distances away or below. What they thought of as a short drop turned out to be one of several hundred feet. Such surprises jolted like explosions inside their drunken heads, and they were sick upon the grass.

They came to Elkanah Beanland's house. His candle flickered in a window as it illuminated a chapter of Revelations which he read over and over again to induce prophetic dreams. Because of the burning of the effigy, and what he feared might follow next, he was praying for Anne Wylde. Hearing noises, he looked out. He saw a fox-man, a Negro with vast antlers, and a huge trout - its mouth open and its large expressionless eye staring at the moon, whilst the silver head tapered into the body of a man. 'Good Lord deliver us!' Elkanah cried with sweat upon his forehead, and he fell to his knees. The 'creatures of the Apocalypse' laughed, banged their horrid drums, shook their wreaths of flowers and bells, and kicked over Elkanah's notices - '*Blesst be he that Turneth to the Lord*', '*D'sire Him to forgive thee sins*'. Then they pressed on into another broad swathe of moonlight.

As they came to Aunt Pity's, the dog barked from where he slept curled up against the Negro in the barn. Earth peeped out and saw the creatures on the skyline. He could have loosed the dog, but he thought instead only of defending it, his only trustworthy friend, from the monsters. The fish, the antlered black-man, the fox and the mummers with blackened faces and flowers in their hats, therefore freely circled the cottage, rattling and banging bells and drums, clattering on doors and window panes; the 'rough music' with which Binns had threatened Anne Wylde, a terrible tuneless noise. Tuneless and yet it gathered force into a rhythm, mechanical and pitiless as the march of soldiers, broken with piercing shrieks and with bleats like the noises of wounded animals. It was the rhythmic voices of an ancient terror. It was as if the tortured earth herself cried out.

It stopped, eerily.

'Come out Anne Wylde! We are here to see if you are hiding a bastard!' Horsfall, the fox, shouted.

Joshua Binns, who was the fish, mumbled through huge narrow lips, 'The good women of Lady Well are coming to tear you to pieces!'

As she did not answer them, the 'rough music' began again. The dog was howling and gnashing in the barn, where Earth watched. He longed to protect his mistress. He felt a deep pang when he realised she had been his one protector against a world that would destroy him as unfeelingly as sharks or wild dogs devour whatever strange vulnerable thing falls amongst them. But the habit of slavery prevented him from doing anything. He was a big lad but he stayed frozen in the barn, restraining the frantic dog, and watching in terror through a vent-hole in the wall.

Anne Wylde appeared at her window. The spectators saw a slender outline, craggy like a thorn-branch. 'We have come to squeeze your bubbies and see if you give milk, Anne Wylde!'

Horsfall climbed up, followed by the antlered 'Negro' and the huge trout's head under which two elbows appeared to prop it whilst it watched. The 'Negro' and the 'trout' stayed there, whilst the fox-man entered slowly, saying nothing. He lit Anne's candle. Pulled a dresser across the door.

'Where are your bubbies, Anne Wylde?'

She grabbed a knife and fell back on to the bed as if to dare him to come near the blade. She turned on to her stomach with her legs clutched together, hid her face and bit the pillow. Frustration and anger as well as fear raised the beat of her heart. The fox came close and she turned to slash at him. He caught her wrist and the blow that Anne intended to answer him with glanced sideways, catching her own neck. She cried as the cut began to sting and blood smeared her dress. The fox put his hands heavily upon her breast, but she pushed him away. She glimpsed his smiling face, whilst he dived for her clitoris.

Anne realised it would be less painful if she were moist and she suffered his fingers. When at last he entered her, she struggled to think of something else – anything but her beloved Oliver, in case that thought induced orgasm.

Thankfully, the fox-man soon came. Anne lay still, weeping, partly with gratitude that she had felt no joy, and turned her face into the blood-smeared pillow. The fox threw her nightgown over her.

'I know who you are!' Anne hissed.

As soon as she heard him and his companions descend the ladder, she rushed to the door, pulled the furniture away and shouted to her aunt. With tears and water the two women washed the semen out of her, trying again and again to rid her of every foul drop, whilst the mummers and the animals paraded around the house a few more times. The women washed and washed, though hopeless of ever quite removing the pollution. Neither of them slept that night. After their tormentors disappeared laughing into the moor, Pity built up the fire, then Anne cried and shivered for hours in her arms.

Oliver, one gentle sunny afternoon when he expected his child to have been born, came across the hills. The first trees in Blood Wood were turning yellow; a new glittering beauty shaking amongst the dark monotonous green of late summer. The bleached lank grass of the wood was incandescent, there was a clean yellow light in the sky and the stream, and he had no doubt that the greatest happiness awaited him. At one or two moments, as the breeze stirred the heather or a turn in the ground revealed a view so beautiful that it took away his breath, he felt about to become the instrument of his muse. But when he paused to write, the damned habit of mechanical jingles got in his way. He reached Aunt Pity's cottage wistful, dazed by what he had almost grasped, and longing for a few inspired lines which might be the first true verses of his life. But the words stayed locked in the stone of his breast.

As he heard no crying, he guessed that his heir was asleep in his cot. He expected Anne to have the milky smell of a woman who is feeding a baby, but that was missing too. Yet she seemed more matronly. She moved heavily and the virgin bloom was gone from her cheeks. He anticipated that she would be happy, but she was restless, even bitter. What was it? He went to kiss her, and she would not accept it.

'Are you pale and pining? Lovesick?' she asked, sharply. 'Not eating, in danger of falling into a consumption?'

'Where is my son?' he asked, confused.

'What is my father doing now?' she answered curtly.

'He still will not live at Lower Laithes – I have asked him. It is difficult for him to uphold his honour in present circumstances, and he is erecting enclosure walls on the moors until he recovers better prospects. It's rough work, but they say that his walls are better made than anyone else's and will be standing in a thousand years after all others have fallen. He is building for my father. He spends a lot of time alone these days and is hard to communicate with. But where is my son?'

'It is a daughter.'

'We hoped for a son, but I can love a daughter nearly as well. I want to see her.'

'She is sleeping.'

'I want to see her asleep. What did you feel when you found her at your breast? When Betty was born the first thing I did was to count her fingers and toes. The midwife laughed, telling me that Zillah had done the same thing.'

'It would be best if no one saw it for some time. We must hide it away for a few years here and then show her as a "servant's child" that we have adopted. You suffer so much already for us, I do not want you to have more to bear.'

'I see no reason why I should not see her! God, but this woman has a demon in her!'

'Hush! I am afraid of your feelings! You know that farmers never dare allow the cow to see her calf before taking it away from her.'

As much to give expression to his exasperation, as to search for his child, he paced the cottage, opening doors, going into rooms, and standing several times at the foot of the ladder which led upstairs, but not venturing on it.

'What about baptism? Suppose the dear one should go back as an unchristened pagan and be condemned to Hell for eternity, full of sin?' he asked.

'Hush you, "eternity" is so terrible a word! It can be done later. Your child is healthy and no more than a girl anyway, so why do you fret?'

She was leaving the room, either to get away from him, or for him to follow, he was not sure which. He came after, grudgingly.

'I hate the word "eternity",' she said, 'it makes me think of grave-yards and monuments.'

She led up the ladder to her bedroom. There she enticed him into a gentle fondling of her breasts and then to kissing slowly upwards along her limbs, the way she enjoyed love-making. Just before he was ready to enter, Anne imagined herself a hole in the earth, warm, damp with spring rain; and that he was a farmer about to plant seeds. She felt the cavity become moist. As he touched and sank into her, it seemed to her that she was nothing else but this opening.

Oliver had by now learnt to stir his penis inside her. He would almost remove it, then delicately touch around the mouth of the Paradise Garden, and go inside again, moving from side to side, which drove her mad with joy; try thrusting as deep in as he could; draw back delicately for a few moments, and when he was about to come, crush his mouth between her breasts as if to seek that blindness and obliteration which a second later consumed him. Thereupon she came with him, twisting, bucking against his spasms. She did not know where she had been or for how long, when she returned.

They both also loved the resting in one another's arms afterwards, her legs thrown across his thigh; usually a time when they spoke their deepest thoughts.

It was now dark outside. Oliver had lost his agitation and she walked quietly with him across the garden. They climbed to the ridge where sounds from beyond rose out of the wells of night-time. Bleats and bellowings were scattered over the velvet darkness. They saw lamps moving far away, as if they were distant luminous planets. Near at hand, Aunt Pity was calling her poultry by banging the bottom of a bucket. Then Oliver disappeared, over the bank into the darkness, as if over the lip of the world.

(10)

The following May, Anne Wylde gave birth to a boy. She kept Oliver
away with the argument that spies might follow him and discover that
he was hiding a bastard. He was not too difficult to persuade, for
while Oliver Greave was intensely sociable he had an incompatible
love of solitariness and irresponsibility, which he found necessary to
cultivate his poetry, and he was ready to grasp a chance of being
alone. By midsummer the child was weaned and Anne prepared to
leave this pitiful, sometimes helplessly loved and at other times hated
creature of Horsfall's, this hopeless baby, in the care of Aunt Pity –
buying three sheep to provide milk for him. The Negro filled the
draughty chinks in a small shed and made a cradle.

For the last time Anne walked the garden with her child, showing
him the midsummer flowers, (or was she showing the flowers, him?);
the tall white daisies and the buttercups. She fed and nursed her baby
in the shed. When he was asleep she laid him in the cradle, slipped
out, barred the door, and sat off with Earth back to Lower Laithes.

Over the hill-crest, and into the Makings valley, she saw that new
enclosure walls were drawing an ever-tighter grip. The sight of the
burnt stumps of oak, hawthorn, and gorse clutched with premonitions
of ill-luck at her throat. It choked her like the smell of burning itself.
Around Lower Laithes even Oliver Greave had been persuaded to do
some clearing of 'the wastes'. The ugliness of cleared woodlands, the
way water lay in pools or mud on the bared earth which later would
turn hard and uncooperative as stone, should have been sufficient to
show him its unnaturalness, Anne thought.

Her now-ragged dress, apron and cloak smelled of soot and herbs,
so she entered her home secretly and tried to disperse her tears by
going through her old wardrobe. When she had changed her appearance she noisily and bravely took command again of her kitchen,
passageways, larder, brewing-house and cellars.

She saw Oliver before he had spied her. He was arguing weakly with a Dutchman, who was wearing his hat and cloak as if unwilling to stay. 'You do not wish to see what I have been making, Mr Van Broyes?' Oliver pleaded. 'I have an officers' cloth, as smooth as cream ...'

'Forgive me, but I cannot buy from both your father and yourself. Also as the wars are for the time being over, soldiers are returning and therefore the woollen trade suffers. Perhaps I will purchase more happily from you in the future, when the son is not competing with the father. Maybe next spring. In winter my family do not like me to travel so far as Yorkshire. They think I should trade only in Holland where there is no sin!'

Oliver desperately chased after the departing Dutchman, who was waving his hand over his shoulder as one brushes away flies.

Anne meanwhile read a paper on Oliver's desk: 'Your Broad Shalloons having been shown to the Honourable Buying Committee of the United East India Company, I am ordered to acquaint you that they are too loose made and bare, therefore they will not have any at present. And please to send first a sample of any new makings, that the Committee might see your goods do not fall short in quality, as with previous bales.' Another letter read: 'Sir, your woollens have met with so many disputes about the quality and measure that I have now placed orders for next year in other hands. We must confess, that after your fair promises, saying that the face of your shalloons was more like glass than woollens, we little expected to have such complaints about quality and price of several articles ...'

'Anne!' He stood confused, torn between his unsuccessful pleading with the Dutchman, his joy at finding her, and the adulteration of that joy with her annoyance and dissatisfaction at what she had seen in his papers. For his sake she cleared her frown, and reassured him with her touches.

'The clothing trade does not seem to be prospering,' she ventured to say.

'Pooh! They care about nothing but work and trade in this valley!' Oliver tapped his ledger. 'This is their Bible now.'

The account book was indeed in size and proportion like a family Bible, with its light-brown cover of soft highest-quality calf's leather, greasy at the edges from being so much fondled. Anne remembered that it was an identical book which Patience Helliwell used at Makings for the Methodists to debit and credit their sins and good works before God. Anne opened it at the back, glanced at the index of customers, then turned to the front, flipping through until she came to the latest entries, marked by a sheet of blotting paper on which Oliver had made calculations. The early accounts were crowded on the page with many sorts of woollens listed for each customer, and cash totals of one or two thousand pounds per month entered in a minutely careful hand. The later entries were loosely scrawled and for low amounts. Often Oliver had abandoned a page in the hope that starting a new one would change his luck.

Anne saw how sheepish he was about his decline, and to cheer him she began, 'Our son is . . .'

'You told me it was a girl!'

'Oliver! Absence has estranged your memory!' She tried to distract and caress him, but now he would not be touched.

'Heaven knows, I am convinced you told me of a daughter.'

'Why should I lie to you? Oh Oliver, there is nothing to be gained from being quarrelsome! Tell me what you think of Peter for a name? "Upon this rock shall I build . . ." I want him to grow a secure, firm man.'

'I would call him Benjamin Tim.' Oliver was dreamy. 'I want to see my son.'

He was overwhelmed. Thinking of being an example to the boy, Oliver from this moment stood more firm and erect. How would he cultivate that good in Tim which, if it exists in a man, shines only upon others and is unrecognised by himself? Oliver saw ahead moments when, being turned to for help or advice, his own manhood would be tried, and he vowed to respond always with kindness. He reminded himself in all circumstances to behave generously, no matter what he felt at the time, that his acts might be a future example to the child. He imagined Benjamin Tim grown to manhood, sharing a pipe of tobacco or a mug of ale, and able to listen to Oliver's telling-over of his own trials and experiences.

Anne retorted, 'You know that cannot be! Stay patient for a year or two and then you can "adopt" him as your heir.'

Trade declined and superfluous servants were one by one dismissed. Mary Pickles and Bridie left, on the verge of winter, to be swallowed into the countryside. Soon only Amos Culpin, Jenny Loveless and Earth remained.

Culpin was burdened with the power of more responsibilities and honoured with confidences. Cloth-factors, bankers and weavers as well as the craftsmen and traders who had decorated Lower Laithes but were still without payment, and whom Oliver therefore did not wish to receive, were met by Amos, who was relied upon to give 'the soft answer that turneth away wrath'.

Many of these one-time intimates of Oliver, but now of Culpin, agreed with Amos about 'the weight of sin laid upon the English nation', and would meet him secretly to plot how to uproot it from the North Country. A 'hearty religion', they said, 'diverted revolution and rebellion'. Beyond their wages, men must seek God; whereas their present pleasures (in these days 'happily diminishing') of fiddle-playing, singing, and in the music of rattling bones, cows' bladders and the newly fashionable clarinet, brought them no permanent ease but instead engendered even greater dissatisfaction with their masters.

It was Culpin's duty to fetch the weekly mail from the stage-coach. On one occasion he appeared exultantly drunk (though it could not be with alcohol, for he never touched it), as he brought an exceptionally bulky sack to his master. Culpin waited, to see it opened.

'There is a difference betwixt my father and me over money, Culpin!' Oliver remarked. 'I am an artist, so I treat all that I receive as a matter of fate. In any case I am most likely to spend it on what husbands my poetry, and fall into debt. My muse will not allow me to invest it merely to make more money.'

'No, sir.'

Culpin had to remain unsatisfied in his curiosity. For Oliver was never eager to break the seals, and it was three days before he did so this time. He procrastinated and deliberated; took truant-walks with his sweetheart (like all truancies they on the one hand offered the intense delight of stolen time, but on the other they were fundamentally aimless); he called Amos to stoke the fire; opened and closed a volume of Ovid; lit, sucked and relit a pipe; tinkered with a poem he was writing, and stared ten times out of the window, before at last reading his letters.

A refusal of payment from Saint Petersburg because the colours delivered were not identical with the samples. A reluctance to settle an account since bales contained short measure. Another complaining that a shalloon was 'too loosely woven'. A demand note for five shillings for a stone figure of Cupid. Also, in this unusually pregnant Pandora's Box, was a storm of demands from staplers for instant payment for raw wool. Knowing how every clothier's solvency depended upon receipts reaching him from investments sent all over the world, the staplers normally gave ample credit. 'Do unto others as you would have done to yourself' was a Christian precept reciprocated to keep them all out of debtors' prisons; and which also gave a most bloody axe to wield, if turned upon its head. Conspiring to demand immediate settlement of bills was a well-known way to bankrupt an unpopular trader. Especially at the onset of winter, for Oliver could not possibly expect money from beyond the Alps until spring.

His associates had turned into hawks stooping to destroy him. Sober-suited merchants and bankers in Norwich, London, Leeds and Somerset (well-padded men who gave money for almshouses and grammar schools, and who had plaques and statues erected to memorialise their own generosity) had plotted over his fate, using the magic of their credit-notes and bills, as witches conspire with pins over a figure made of wax.

'The Lord brings deliverance to poor sinners in the end,' Culpin softly remarked as he came by Oliver's side, to comfort and to see if the fire needed attendance.

'Ah, Culpin, you're an excellent loyal fellow, but I'm afraid that the troubles besetting us are because the best of the weavers have stayed with my father – as is natural and admirably loyal. What I have left in my cottages are scamps and scoundrels who skimp their work, punishing me because they are discontented and not realising this makes their own position worse. There is no more market for soldiers' woollens, and that's the reason for it – there is a lull in our wars. They must either weave better cloth, for the satisfaction of the fine ladies abroad and in London, or instead indulge their passion for defacing the coinage of the realms and for illicit brewing, to support their domestic economies.'

'Unless the manufactories come,' Amos muttered. Then he announced more loudly, 'We are an ignorant lot, is poor servants, who do not know the ways of business. But if you'll pardon me, the warnings is that they are incensed about Miss Wylde, sir.'

'*Nonsense, Culpin,* many a man cares for his housekeeper!'

'Yes, sir.'

The woeful Culpin gave great attention to the fire. Then he added, 'It is well-known that ours is one of the disaffected districts of England, sir. It is forever being found necessary to bring soldiers here to quell rebellious subjects. Either the people will be driven by their poverty and their animosity to the government to sinfully clipping bits of gold from coins deposited with them by gentlemen like yourself, sir, and stamping out fake money, or they will purge the district of what, some say, is an evil spirit that dwells amongst us, bred from our collective sin. A Jew that I spoke to – only on behalf of your business – said that in his religion Miss Wylde would be described as being possessed by a "dybuk". He also said it was an "incubus". An evil ghost from the past that lives in a body and makes it do all manner of things that are out of keeping with a life of Grace. Of course, I do not believe such superstitions, but there are many who do.'

Oliver, after he had brooded over this, tried to express his worries for Anne's safety. 'Anne, creditors are closing in on us, they consider our liaison . . .'

'Neither the Dutchman nor any others care if we are immoral or not! They all have the same interest – they all "piss in the same pot", as we say – all they think of is to get hold of your father's money, by making him feel compelled to pay your debts. Therefore they must make sure that you have plenty of them.'

'Well, I have ample money owing me. I have only to collect it from abroad, and could try to cross the Continent myself before winter sets in. I suppose the staplers can be persuaded to wait for a while.'

Anne saw that if Oliver left, he might not ever return. It was the very instability of their lives, sometimes happy and sometimes quarrelling, that made her long the more for him to stay with her. 'You could avoid the creditors by making over Lower Laithes and your other possessions to me,' she remarked.

He looked at her sadly. 'Then we will never marry, because if we did so they could claim "your" property as my debt. My son will always be a bastard.'

'You will be able to pay them off soon, and then we can wed.'

'What do *I* want with it all?' Oliver said impatiently. 'Take it then! You can have Lower Laithes and everything else.'

'But if they find out you have given property away, they will say that you disposed of what is rightfully theirs, to avoid paying your legal bonds. "Sell" them to me, properly.'

So a written agreement was made through a lawyer, stating that Miss Wylde would receive Lower Laithes for the sum of £5 with revenues from cottages and from timber in Blood Wood, 'as recompenses for her care and diligence about my business'.

In what was now Anne's house (and which was growing steadily shabbier, through lack of servants), Oliver despondently consumed his way through wine, port, and small beer. Irresponsibility, his shedding of his possessions upon Anne Wylde, and this new form of his enslavement to her, actually gave him some peace of mind – especially when he saw how boldly and well she could bear it.

It was not his drinking that annoyed Anne so much as his long silences. Sometimes, recognising the disquiet caused in her by his drunken gaze, he said (either looking painfully directly at her, or at other times mysteriously beyond), 'I want to see Benjamin Tim.'

'That would bring unhappiness to us all,' she prevaricated.

In such scenes Anne, being without logical answers, would pretend anger. (The mixture of frustration with pity that she felt at his impotence and shabbiness was usually quite enough to inspire her annoyance.) Tears would then dampen Oliver's eyes. They knew that one of them would have to be the first to leave the room, and they became practised at the game of angry exits.

Oliver's excuse was generally to see about the ale in the cellar. (God bless Mary Pickles who had left such a store of it!) On the way he might stare into Blood Wood for a while, perhaps moved by the music of wind in the boughs, or by their flickering which made it look as though the stars were racing madly about the Heavens. Or maybe he glimpsed the spies who these days were always nearby, (acquaintances of Culpin, go-betweens to Mr Van Broyes), lurking and accosting people in taverns.

He dreamed up schemes to save his fortune. His father's sulphur springs at Upper Spout had not been a success because the climate was too bleak to attract frail ladies. Israel Merrybent's activities behind the Hellenic façades were attracting only seditious radicals and meat-stealers, hence also the attentions of Dick Almighty. It had become a place of ill-repute, though the soldiers who were sent up

166

there never found anything, because their red tunics shone for miles across the moors and their clatter was broadcast ahead of them through the hamlets. Oliver planned to reclaim this little Parthenon, and to heat it with coal dug from the moor. He thought of prospecting for coal in Blood Wood, just as other clothiers, suffering hard times, were doing. Horsfall had told him that young miners could be imported from Scotland and made 'indentured apprentices', so that they had to accept their masters' terms and were as firmly enslaved as Negroes from Africa.

The only practical outcome of Oliver's deliberations was that night after night he took his violin, left Lower Laithes, plunged into the wood and visited a house where an untemperamental woman, who laughed and did not blame him for anything, sold ale or even let him have it on credit. 'You cannot be cheated wi' ale!' Oliver sang out in this tavern. 'Them that buys beef, buys bones; them that buys land, buys stones; them that buys eggs, buys shells; but them that buys ale, buys nowt else!' As night progressed he drank more, sang even more idiotic ditties, took his naps by the fireside, and recalled with nostalgia the days when, like Tim Bobbin, he never worried for a moment where he would lay his head. The journey home became more and more difficult to make. He began to be proud of himself again because he was a daring reckless fellow, Tim Bobbin's second self.

One night after he had gone too far with his boasting, a big quarryman allowed Oliver to overhear him say, 'John Wylde, the mason, has been found dead. Frozen on a heap of stones he'd set aside to build a wall with.'

The group watched, out of the corners of their eyes, Oliver fidgeting with his tankard.

'He died of the Melancholy,' another declared.

'He was the best mason of all in these parts. I used to cut the stone for him. Why, how he could choose it! He knew exactly what would suit, and could measure dimensions at a glance. He just held his hands out, and it'd be right size. They'll be coming to view his work in future days, yet see how he was served in his lifetime!' Their eyes slid even more towards Oliver. They regarded him as people do a man about whom they believe that he follows a different, secret and irrational order when he is alone with his wife, and so cannot be trusted.

'Nobody would go tell his daughter, because she's living like a queen wi' a bankrupt piece-maker who has pretensions, though he can do nothing without his father and is under her heel into the bargain. A "poet", so they say, though no gentleman or parson'll subscribe to his verses – and yet they're too fancy for homely singing either.'

'Yonder fellow's looking sickly!'

Oliver rushed out. The dawn, a sodden red flower dripping upon the hills, refreshed him. As he returned determinedly to Lower Laithes it began to rain in the woods, hammering the boughs like a thousand shuttles banging and making a single melody. Sneaking under the rain came the smell of woodsmoke and he imagined the comfort of the fire. Yet he felt that he was not in a fit state to tell Anne his news. He wavered, looked for an excuse, and found it when he spotted a stranger's horse tied in the yard. So he went away again.

Between the oaks and beeches were misty vistas, speckled with gold. The remaining leaves clustered like yellow lanterns upon the boughs, whilst the rest swirled over the stream and paths. There was a satisfying odour of decomposing leaves. Fungi had recently appeared, livid upon all the rotting places: sickly orange trumpets like pigs' ears, erect pink spotted horns, and grey clustered slimy things that seemed to belong more to the bottom of an ocean. Oliver climbed until the trees changed from oaks to birches and he could look down upon the singed brown tips below. The tiny, metallic autumn leaves of hawthorns pattered around him like showers of gold coins.

He knew that it was all beautiful, even the seasonable rotting things, yet he could not feel it. Was Oliver, also, becoming a victim of Melancholy? (For so many were.) The more he stared, the more he was convinced that beauty had vanished for him. Permanently. Her grave was in the enclosures and the foundations of manufactories. He blinked, and shook his head, as if some quick movement like that would skim off the world's deadening veil. He consoled himself by thinking that the truly lovely had always been haunted, if not by aching sadness, then certainly by nostalgia. As if what was called 'beauty' was in fact a faded ghost, a memory, from the womb. Though he must face the present, with its 'consummate villainy', its 'disgrace and reproach that bowed his face to the earth', yet just like John Wylde (and like many other men in these days, though all entirely unknown to Oliver), his yearning was still for Paradise: for a half-remembered tantalizing mother-land where the world's beauty truly existed.

He reached the moor, where it was cold, wet, lonely and greasy. Oliver walked here to avoid the reproaches of starved weavers living upon the lower slopes: in recent days other mills had been burnt, and more images of Anne Wylde made out of wax, straw and bits of wood, mainly by children or by peddlars, to be sold at fairs. Was he as weak and contemptible as they had suggested in the public house? He himself so often felt that he was only half a person and that he was adrift: his other half was Anne Wylde. Perhaps they tore at one another with hooks because they were grappling to be united. Perhaps the reason that they both acted selfishly was because they felt this lack of being bonded together. Their selfishness was a perverse attachment, for they were doing whatever they could to attract one another. It was like looking into a mirror, and clawing at the reflection.

Amongst the bogs he saw an isolated cottage, known to him by its secret reputation, and which at last put a *practical* idea into his head. When Oliver came close, a loom clattered peacefully in an upstairs room, the children ran out to finger the fine worsted of his coat, and the housewife stood on the doorstep, suckling a young pig at her breast. The animal was satisfied. With its long-lashed bright eyes it peeped out of her blouse without any of those kicks and wriggles natural to a piglet. The woman, having this substitute for the baby of her own that had died, also looked contented. She glanced at Oliver, then stared dreamily beyond him at the patches of dark water glittering amongst the rushes around the cottage. You would not guess that she had just been hurriedly shifting a heavy loom to cover what had been hidden under the stones of the kitchen floor.

Her attention regretfully flicked back to him, as if she had been reminded of a duty. 'What does *thou* want?' she asked, unwelcoming. Her voice grated, her throat having been made coarse by the moorland wind.

'My name is Oliver Greave, I'm from Lower Laithes . . .'

'I know that. And I hear that trade with merchants down London or wherever is not what it was.'

But she stepped aside (frightening the pig into making a desperate stab at her), indicating that he might enter the cottage. He walked into a warm smell of new-made oatcakes which were drying upon strings stretched above the fireplace. Yarn hung on a distaff. A peaceful scene, apparently showing that all the family was usefully employed. Yet a child, after stroking Oliver's arm in wonder, pointed her finger at her open mouth, with the habit of begging. Because Oliver pulled nothing out of his pockets, she and the other children returned to their work: this consisted of trampling a freshly-woven piece in animal and human urine, in order to bleach it. The loom did not cease to clatter until the woman shouted up the ladder, 'There's someone 'ere to see thee!' She looked Oliver up and down a few more times, then solemnly added, 'A man.'

Whilst the weaver descended, the woman stared some more at Oliver and then asked bluntly, 'Does something ail thee?' He could not answer.

The weaver, when he appeared, puffed and panted with a great show of weariness. He displayed his dusty hands. 'I didn't know we had a visitor,' he humbly and courteously excused his slowness. 'It's growing over such a dull day, and I'm getting so old that I can hardly see. But I've woven eight yards! Been at it since daylight. If it's fine tomorrow I'll have to be spreading dung on my enclosures instead of going to hear the preacher. 'Tis a terrible hard place this for us to make a living. It never lets us forget we are descendants of Adam, expelled here from th' Garden of Eden for our sins.'

'You look decently prosperous.'

'Looks deceive! If yonder pig does not live to fatten we shall starve this winter. But as thou can see, women are sometimes of use to us! Is there a purpose to your visit?'

'I am suffering financial embarrassments and I have been told that you are coiners. We might help one another.'

The weaver ceased to be humble. 'I must ask you to leave my house, sir.'

'I was sent by Mr Horsfall.'

'I do not know a Mr Horsfall. I'm sorry, sir, I must ask you to go.'

'Do you know Israel Merrybent? – He is in my father's employ.'

'I do not know him either, sir. We are merely poor people struggling to make our honest living up here where the world is so unkind.'

Oliver left, shamefaced, pitying these poor weavers whom he had apparently slandered, and muttering his apologies. But when he was a hundred yards across the moor a different woman came to the door and called him back. It was Bridie! She had learnt much more English here. 'It is all right, sir!' she whined. 'They did not know you were desperate. But perhaps it is now our turn to employ you!' Oliver went back to the cottage.

'What you accuse me of is a hanging offence,' the weaver said. 'For aught I knew, you might have been a customs' man.'

'I quite understand. Look, to ease my unhappy prospects I am eager to take part in your business.'

'You must deposit gold pieces for us to clip, then.'

'But I have no gold. That is why I have come here!'

'I have told you our way of doing trade. You must lend us your own gold pieces for us to clip the corners from and stamp out new ones. Then we will return your money, with interest even though devalued – for those who'll bother weighing it. Or we will invest it quietly for you in our own concerns. We are the bankers for the common people and many of us wish to escape our miseries and buy passages to the Americas. But now you are wasting our time.'

Bridie laughed. 'Can you give the young master work and let him earn his bread with his sweat, as we do? He can drain the wet moor for us and spread dung on the fields whilst you go listening to sermons!'

The weaver's wife doubled up laughing, so that the pig fell out of her bosom and squealed across the floor, chased by the children. 'He's got some fine cloth and boots to keep out the rain! Would you like the job, sir?'

Bridie repulsively rubbed herself against him. 'Come and lie with me and I'll give you a clipped guinea for it!'

'No other whore would *give* you money to go with her,' the housewife mocked.

'I'm so grateful that Mistress Anne took me in out of the cold!'

Oliver pulled away, frightened. He walked backwards towards the door, turned and left as fast as he dared, without indecently running, whilst their laughter rolled after him. He made not towards the open moor by which he had slyly come, but towards the nearby packhorse track – the busy traffic of which was of advantage to the coiners who wanted to transport and take delivery of gold without attracting attention to travellers who elsewhere would be unusual. Though

Oliver was avoiding people, yet this was the quickest way home. His destiny, after all, still awaited him, at Lower Laithes at the foot of the hills exactly where he had left it on departure the previous evening.

(11)

It was a long while before Anne could weep for her father. Then at last, after his funeral, the preparing for which numbed her grief, unexpectedly she was convulsed with such tears as she had never experienced before. Cried so that her chest hurt. When she could produce no more because her voice was broken she kept up a strangled sobbing, trying to save herself from the pain in her chest, throwing her head from side to side, up and down, her capless untidy hair this way and that, in a fit that consumed her whole body. It caused Oliver to fear for her heart, her lungs, and her sanity. But she had to exhaust herself. Then she slept with her head upon Oliver's chest, and he, though with an aching arm under her head, bore it happily.

Searching John Wylde's house before creditors claimed it, Anne found the frail insect-like spectacles through which her father had peered to understand Voltaire, Tom Paine and Socrates. She also had taken to Lower Laithes the large brown painting of seven gentlemen, uniformly Puritan, balefully staring over the filled-in well. As it had frowned over all her childhood and growing up, she had become nostalgic for it.

Anne was not the only unhappy one in Lady Well these days. When she rode out in elegant mourning clothes on her fine black gelding, she witnessed such misery as she had never thought possible in this self-satisfied place. Instead of the prosperous tradesmen of a few years ago, now, after the intervention of a few savage winters, and a peace in Europe, the moorland tracks were full of shuffling weavers and returned soldiers who with no hope of work were turning over the brambles in case there might be a few sour blackberries left untouched. They set traps for rabbits or they stared wistfully into streams that had already been fished bare of trout. Hundreds had left the district and ruined cottages stood about the moor: the main roof-beams sagged, the tiles slipped and let rain in, rotting the floors, freezing in the slates so that when the thaw came the stone split and crumbled.

Israel Merrybent's wife died of cold and hunger. Or was it from that painful lump, solid as a stone, in her chest? No one knew, or cared. Except, yes, Israel, who though he had done nothing but curse her since their courtship was over, was distraught. He took his breast-like bladders of whisky from place to place, hungry, weeping and from habit muttering soothing fragments of his old curses under his breath as if they might summon the ghost of his former 'happiness'.

There was a woman who used graciously every Sunday to give charity to the poor outside the church, and (because her husband was purchasing one loom after another), was cultivating a manner for the time when she hoped to pass by in a carriage; she had now lost her husband in the army and was reduced to scraping dried dung from drovers' highways and from commons, taking it from door to door to sell it for fuel. She spat at Anne's gelding. 'The mighty, too, shall be fallen!' she shouted.

Coal pits were all that flourished, like sulphurous pustules breaking out of the sweet hill's surface. What were they hewing coal for? Anne did not know, but seeing the tips she felt sure there would soon be too much unless there was found some new use for it. Around one place Anne came across a group of unhappy battered people flapping like distressed birds that had lost their chicks. The miner had descended the shaft (which was simply a hole a hundred feet into the ground), and had his breath taken away by fire-damp. As they pulled him back he was too dizzy to hold the rope and he fell again, breaking his bones. He was an old man who had spent his life as a weaver and was now forced to become a collier. His wife, crippled with arthritis and insane with pain, had come out into the confusion of rain and wind on the moortop. There was also his newlywed daughter and her husband; several small children, five years of age upwards, who had just begun to work in the pit; and the son, who descended to make a rescue but was overcome by the fumes of the mine and fell with his father into the water. Apart from the weeping old woman there was an awed, tense silence when Anne arrived. The son-in-law was going down next. He defeated the fumes by telling them to drop him rapidly, and was able to load first the father, then the son into the basket. The casualties looked like messy crushed fruit. Red juice, pumping out of them, swamped their rags and smeared their black flesh. The old collier's wife forgot her suffering and with cramped limbs tried to wash her unconscious husband's forehead in rain and spit.

Anne could not speak. She gave them the one guinea that she had on her. They did not answer. She rode off into the rain, haunted by the sulphurous stench and by a woman's words shouted after her: 'They look like niggers, don't they? But black slaves have an easier life than miners, dressed up in silks wi' powdered wigs. Gentlefolk dress animals to be better than us!'

Anne next went to Lady Well. Some weavers of old-fashioned woollens were arguing in the street with a group of wool-combers (engaged in making the new worsteds). The former said that the furnace in the combers' shop would someday burn Lady Well to the ground, and it would be a judgment on them for changing their methods from using cold teasels. Others talked of the well cleared by Esther Kershaw, which had now performed a third miracle: a family that lived lower down the hill and who used to be sickly from drawing contagious water from a choked spring were now enjoying their first autumn without illness. The rim of the well, which Esther had built up with stones, had become a place where people leaned to gossip, and with idle peaceful gestures improve Esther's masonry. They had rediscovered their old pastime of reading fortunes by watching the water's winged spirit – a tiny fly – flit about the surface. Old people and children spent pleasant hours and days thus. They had begun once more to hang rags (fragments of clothing from sick people) on nearby hawthorns and votively to offer old nails, brooches, horses' shoes and coins to the water-spirit. Doubtfire described them as 'superstitious whimsical persons idling their hours waiting upon a fly as it imbibes the panacean dews'. He had appealed to his bishop for help to restrain the people, or at least for him to pay a visit and overawe them; but His Lordship, forgetful of Christ, replied that Lady Well and its moors was 'no fit place for a gentleman', and had refused. So Parson Doubtfire ill-temperedly smashed more of the church windows, shouting out that 'the brutish inhabitants of Lady Well are not worthy of the Gospel of Jesus Our Saviour.' Bright blue chips of Mary's gown and scraps of Christ's red garment still glittered on the path. Finally he had the temerity to paint out Saint Uncumber, though he feared that the women would throw stones at him for it. He next wanted to remove the cross from the tower, saying it was an 'ornament

175

of superstition and idolatry', and he had ladders already placed; only, he could find no one who would climb them.

Anne found Doubtfire at home, dissecting a corpse. It was that of Dick O'Lovely, who had died of starvation against an enclosure wall, with only his violin for a companion.

'Our most famous local fiddler was blind,' Doubtfire said, 'quite sightless.'

'Him, *blind*?' Anne questioned. 'He could find his way everywhere!'

'I have just Examined his eyes. There could never have been sight in them.'

'I think our Dick O'Lovely saw more than most of us. Especially those responsible for ruining us and bringing such misery upon Yorkshire. Mr Doubtfire, many of those dependant upon Mr Greave are now beggared. Two hundred weavers and a thousand spinsters are suffering.'

Though it was a cold day, Doubtfire sweated with embarrassment before her. 'Ah yes, I have seen much Evidence of it. I was called only yesterday to the Bedside of a Valuable weaver who had Died for lack of food. His wife and children were most Distressing. I was entertained in my scientific Interests by the appearance of the body. When the Grieving widow leant upon the stomach, it ejected air and Appeared to make the Signs of Life.'

Oblique ideas, half-escaping his attention, slithered across the back of Doubtfire's mind. A thought of flesh, which our souls must inhabit as our prison and punishment because we are sinful. Merely thinking of flesh's satisfaction filled Joseph Doubtfire with foul horror, yet there before him was the beautiful Anne Wylde, only an arm's length – and yet also an ocean's space – away. Whilst all around and around and around were the foul grass, flowers, birds, and animals, at their cavortings.

'At least our clothier's satires and the many affecting compositions of his muse must bring you delight,' Doubtfire suggested.

'No so much as you suppose,' Anne answered.

'Why so? Surely he will confer lasting Celebrity upon our great Emporium of the woollen Trade!'

'Because two hundred weavers and a thousand spinsters are starving.'

'Ah! And Oliver Greave's muse is responsible, for because of her he

Skulks in Holes to avoid his debts? Evidently genius is not always accompanied with Prudence in everyday concerns! Let it be a lesson to him to leave the Lord to account for His miseries and not interfere. Oh, but this is a most Sinful spot of a Sinful country, and surely the Lord is known by the Judgment He executes?'

'Mr Doubtfire, could we set up a charitable school for the weavers whilst they are unemployed, for them to study and think about the Bible and be taught economy and given flour for their wives to learn to bake it?'

'*Think* about the Bible? Why should they think on it? 'Tis doctrine that we must all *accept*.'

'To learn it then, if you wish. We could offer them food to encourage them to come, for they would tend to stay away, suspecting our motives.'

'And who would subscribe to it?'

'The Snawdens, the . . .'

'Your servant Amos Culpin has been struck with a strange providence, Anne Wylde. He has cut off his own Members, cast them into a Fire and come to my house seeking comfort, leaving so much Blood that his way may be traced by the cakes of it. "Why have you treated yourself so barbarously?" I asked. He answered "I have had one wife and baby that died long ago, and 'twas more than enough of the joy of flesh to satisfy me." He said that lately he had a vision that he could not be Saved unless he Dismember himself and go on a pilgrimage to Jerusalem. I fear Amos Culpin will meet his Maker under the surgeon's hands, and not in Jerusalem. There is Filthiness of the spirit everywhere to be Cured, before you teach them to bake! Amos confessed to me some antecedent Filthiness that drove him to this Extreme. Thus, the parts that were Abused have Smarted by the hands of the same person, and that is why I say that the Lord is known by His Judgment.'

'God's love is sometimes in *our* hands to discharge as we can.'

'*Woman, are you questioning my Ability to interpret God's will?*' The parson's hand was forgetfully raised against her. Then he remembered himself, and let it fall unaggressively upon his table that was littered with the heart, liver and empty stomach of Dick O'Lovely. Anne left hurriedly, sick of the stench of formalin, analysis and death.

She next went to Makings. There they were crowded into the

kitchen for a special prayer-meeting to 'save the countryside from poverty'. All those who considered themselves The Elect were present.

Benjamin Greave stood on the table and declared, 'The Lord it appears 'as now sent His check upon our walling and improvement of the wastes! But no doubt He has His good reasons for favouring instead th'impulse for "democratic liberties", as some have a mind to call it, and that are bringing ruin to our times, to the Age in which we live! So as we must abide with it . . .'

Dick Almighty impatiently scrambled up next to him, livid with exasperation. For, far from accepting that God intended 'a check upon our walling', he had decided that God's province was Heaven, whilst it was up to himself – with a little aid from other sensible men – to do something about the world in which we lived. He had therefore called a meeting of the Society For Prosecuting Felons to discuss 'the propriety of petitioning the government and the King for funds to employ the deserving but distressed poor of the township known as *Lady Well* in enclosing the waste called "*Raven's Hill*" for the benefit of some Gentlemen of the district'.

Though Dick's great heroic efforts to provide 'honest labour' had not met with success, had in fact (unknown to Dick) stopped a good way short of reaching the ear of the King, yet his eloquence still did not fail him. In his opinion the clothier's speech was far too dry for the times, which required a 'full-blooded, honest rhetoric', especially if it was to reach a royal ear; and this he delivered, shouting over his belly, 'I'll tell thee what, my friends! If the Lord has taken away thy dinner, He has also in His wisdom given thee the brains to think of a way to get it back again! Listen to what happened to me – for 'tis a parable. My dinner was stolen. Yes, *my* dinner was stolen, only the other day.' Dick paused, letting an eloquent and weighty silence impregnate the room. 'Would I hunt the villain (for you know the manner of thief-catcher that I am) to the world's end, have him transported and hung, and tie the noose myself? On this occasion, no. "I was expecting it," I lightly told the assembled company ('twas at my own inn). "For I exchanged words with the Devil himself upon that very subject this morning."'

The kitchen-congregation was astonished.

'How's that, then? It's said that you pretend concern for the poverty o' the weavers.'

'Licking his chops the while, His Awful Majesty, Satan, otherwise known as the Devil, otherwise known as Beelzebub, sagaciously remarks in my own, my very own ear, "Be assured thy meal will be stolen from thee by twelve o'clock!" "Then," I smartly answered him (for I have almost as much experience as the Devil himself in apprehending villains!), "I warrant I'll discover the culprit by four in the afternoon!" "How's that?" asks the King of the Nether Regions – puzzled by my clever devious devices, of course. Whereupon I proceeds to sprinkle deadly poison upon the meat – that the Devil might have his disciple with him more quickly.'

There was laughter. (Laughter at a prayer-meeting!)

'I left the room then for them to think about my words. On returning one hour later, I found, as I expected, my joint replaced.' Almighty smiled upon his audience: such an innocent, confident, unapprehensive smile, unlike an adult's and more typical of a babe who has made the happy discovery of a full breast.

Patience Helliwell sidled close to Anne. 'Women also are allowed to preach amongst us, Miss Wylde. You'd happen enjoy that. Would you like to address us with a few words of prayer for Mercy and Grace?'

'No.'

'Because "the Lord is known by His judgment" – so I was told by our Parson today. I do not see any purpose in praying to Him, if what He wants is what I see in Yorkshire today. Only the practice of love can do anything for it.'

'That is what we are doing – praying for God's love.'

'You do not need to pray. Either you have love in your heart, in which case it will come out of itself, or you have it not. There is no use in praying.'

'If the *old parson* was alive, you'd be whipped i' the stocks for saying less than that.'

Then Benjamin Greave came up, so Patience melted away, feeling sure that *he* would be able to reprove the 'careless witch'.

'I dunna want to see thee in this house!' Benjamin thundered.

'Mr Greave, you must do something for the weavers and spinners under your care.'

'What does thou think we are at today, then? We're praying so hard that I'm in a muck-sweat with it! Ar't'married to my son yet, Whore of Babylon? *Thou'rt* architect of all our troubles! Thou'rt maker of 'em! Go do something yourself – get out of my house! The weavers'd be prosperous and peaceful if it was not for your interference. Get out! Thou'rt a demon! I'll leave nothing to thee nor thy bastard progeny, so there's no call for you to be hanging around Makings! Thou'rt not to be the vessel of *my* heirs! Get out of my house! Get out! Out!'

'All you will achieve is to make your legacy sterile.'

'Are you cursing me now? It was always known thou'rt a conspicuous witch. Jezebel! Get out o' my house! I say, get out o' my house!'

Anne could think of nowhere and no one else to turn to. A few days later, and without saying anything to Oliver, she took three hundred pounds that was intended for his creditors and secretly bought several cartloads of raw wool for those cobwebbed, dusty looms of Lady Well.

When Oliver was summoned to the Bankruptcy Court, Anne Wylde for the first time left her native district. In the lowland city of York she felt as though she had tumbled into a pit devoid of all that she loved; she was stark and alone when removed from Lady Well's moors and heather. Also she suffered a sickening conscience, thinking that this bankruptcy had somehow been brought about by her own unconscious desire for her lover to be sacrificed.

In the Court, Oliver felt strangled and drowned by the brown box in which they placed him, looking up steeply to the bench of three judges. It was hot and still; he could smell the varnish blistering, and hear it pop. Through a tall window, he could see the avenging crowd outside. Israel Merrybent was there with a peddlar's tray of long-legged, black-haired dolls. To entertain children, some of his customers strung up these Anne Wylde figures on toy gallows.

'Your creditors claim that, using Anne Wylde, you have secretly purchased wool with £300 that rightly belongs to themselves,' a judge declared, with all the weightiness that his robes and state gave him.

'It was with her own money spent to save the weavers from starving,' Oliver answered 'This was only after many other schemes for their relief had been raised or tried, and none of them had come to anything. I have seen women in this county gnawing bones that were discarded by a rich man's dogs. Other females, often elderly, hire themselves out like ponies to carry loads of cloth for miles over hills and dales. Even children whose parents can afford to send them to a dame's school subscribe a penny a week to the expenses of their own probable funerals during the next epidemic of typhus fever. To describe Yorkshire today, an author's pen would need to be dipped in gall.'

'A pretty speech! The weavers starve because of Greave's mismanagement of his affairs whilst he is devoted to foolish poetical flights of the imagination: or versifying, to state it plainly. Let him put his business straight first!' one of Oliver's accusers interrupted.

Oliver, born in wealth, had not, until he heard the intensity with which these men spoke, realised how determined the ordinary person is to get money. Nor how vehement this mundane passion can make him in his hatred of art, of radical aims, and of anything in which money is not the prime purpose.

'It is also accused that you have made over possessions and rents to Miss Wylde, in order to impede your creditors,' a judge said.

'They were payments to her because I am in her debt.' Oliver added, 'For her services,' and a titter rustled by.

'As your muse?' his accusor sarcastically suggested.

Oliver nervously picked at a blister of varnish.

One of the creditors shouted, 'It makes no difference that Anne Wylde received payments and rents, for as she is married to Greave, what she has is due to us! He is guilty of concealment!'

'Are you married to Miss Wylde?'

'No, I am not.'

'He married her in secret down London!'

Anne Wylde was brought into court.

'Have you ever been to London town?'

Anne was feeling only homesickness. 'I have never travelled out of my native valley until today, sir. York is a very fine town, full of very fine buildings, and a beauteous river such as I have never seen in ...'

'Are you married to Oliver Greave?' they interrupted her sternly. 'Swear your answer.'

Anne swore that she had entered into no contract other than for her business and housekeeping services. The court admitted that indeed she did not bear herself like a married woman. Lawyers then pushed forward dated inventories and contracts, in penmanship looped and artistic to the point of illegibility, and which after scrutiny (producing a scratching sound like the scurrying of mice), convinced the judges that property had been made over to her before the declaration of Oliver's bankruptcy.

The weakness in her case was the £300 payment for wool. That did not belong to her.

The judges retired. Two of them wished to acquit Oliver, but the third said, 'If we keep him in York Castle for a while, we might discover something from him that will lead us to the coiners with whom he has been dealing. It is not an easy matter to apprehend these criminals, for in the Lady Well district – a region of savage moorland and a still-barbarous people, one unvisited by any reliable clergymen – they have formed what they term a 'Society For The Prosecution of Felons', the aim of which is *not* to give support to our honest soldiery! Its real purpose is to ensure that there are brought to court only those criminals guilty of offences that the local gentlemen wish to prevent – that is, ones against their own property, or concerned with the stealing of cloth, especially from where it is hung out to dry in the open air upon tenter frames. For woollen cloth is the chief love of that district. In other words, Gentlemen, The Society For The Prosecution of Felons exists mostly to safeguard exemption for coining, in which they themselves are involved.'

Oliver's prison smelled of urine, damp and fear-sweat. Amongst the straw, the stained walls, and the monstrous shadows, there was a fierce struggle for food, for a drier corner free of draughts, or for the gaoler's favours. There was continuous coughing, and muttered swearing. Oliver watched one 'sinner' drive himself crazy by masturbating all day on his wet straw, his gaolers and companions having long abandoned him to the Devil. The prisoners had an unforgettable pallor which Oliver could not imagine any amount of sunshine removing. They were resigned, shunning visitors and light as if fearing what these might bring, more than what they suffered already. Oliver was a man of the free air and spacious moorland, and to have the door locked upon him caused him instant fear, panic and pain. He did not dare dwell on the thought of his future days. He did not dare imagine the moors. Yet he was determined that Mr Van Broyes and the other traders would not get the better of him, nor of his father.

Meanwhile Benjamin Greave met his son's creditors. They saw an aged fool with red eyes.

'My son writes telling me not to have dealings with you because you are aiming at destroying me through his trouble,' Benjamin told them, bluntly.

The clothier had so much admired his son for this action, deciding that he was not so attached to a woman's skirts after all, and it made his sorrow doubly hard to bear. Unhappiness had now bent him to look like some poor moor-edge farmer, subject to the whims of weather, trade and sickness, in shabby clothes, and with a grey skin, lined and grimed. When he was a young man this was apparently to have been his lot; strange how fate had brought about, at least, the appearance of it.

'I'll tell ye what I'll do. So long as you keep it secret from him, I'll pay £10,000 to acquit him of his debts.'

Oliver, as soon as he was released, without warning, rushed to Anne. She saw him pale, frail, vulnerable, and too nervous to smile after the time that had separated them. She was overwhelmed once again by her feelings, of protectiveness mixed with admiration for the strong innocence that kept him erect through his troubles in an alien world.

Only later did Oliver visit Makings, sure that justice had prevailed and that it was now in his stars for reconciliation with his father. But Benjamin Greave, because he had heard that Oliver had returned first of all to Anne Wylde, withdrew into his resentments and refused to see his son.

The loving couple remained in peace for some weeks until, one day when Oliver was out, an agent of the creditors called; a lean nasty man with a horrid forcefulness, and old greasy neglected clothes polished by squatting on benches. He peered around Lower Laithes possessively, like a bailiff, and he would not give his name.

Anne said, 'Darkness is descending and I do not nowadays have a boy to accompany you over the moors. Please come to the point, sir.'

The man seemed to think that the last thing he should be expected to do was to explain himself to such as her. After a silence which he intended to be unnerving, he leered at her and replied, 'Let me express myself this way: you should not make such a display with your black gelding, nor with your other possessions, Miss Wylde. For there is a revolution on the Continent that will sweep away all those with despotic pretensions, and I expect that even in this savage corner of England you have heard of it. More likely here than in other districts, in fact. This place is notorious for disaffection.' He paused, then added threateningly, 'I myself like to wear the cap of liberty when I can.'

'Don't let your masters hear of it, then!'

He became more animated. 'But the danger of rebellion seems diverted in this valley! I was expecting distress, and found weavers supplied, even after the heavy judgment against Mr Greave, with wool. I wondered how they have obtained it?'

'Perhaps you would rather find poor people, to be recruits in spinning mills?'

'Manufactories are the agencies of progress and reason, like the revolution in France that will free the passages of capital and trade from royal impediments. You and your black gelding, Miss Wylde, are an interference to the time of plenty that is at hand. Your sort are rotten posts which pretend to stop an ocean, to prevent the future, and if your creditors do not sweep you away, some more bloody hand will do it.'

'I heard this talk from my father years ago, sir.'

'John Wylde has already profited from manufactories!'

'Other men profited, not my father, and so it will be when you have built for my poor weavers. Only the worst and most designing will flourish. They are better off when I care for them in their homes.'

'"My weavers", is it? Then you admit that, whilst you have debts to bear, you are providing wool for them?'

Knowing that he was driving her to the edge of her self-control, he keenly watched her features.

Anne screamed, 'What would you expect of us? To rot in the gaols in which you would so gladly have thrown us?'

'I do not think I need to wait for Mr Greave,' the stranger said, and left.

When Oliver returned, Anne told him, 'A visitor called to talk of revolutions. Your creditors are planning to throw you in prison again.'

'I will go abroad before I will be returned there! Anne, today I met Nicholas Horsfall obstructing my path. No, let me tell you how I felt! I know he is not always trustworthy, but he was such a bold handsome sight – red jacket, white wool trousers, red sash, boots and the skull-and-crossbones on his hat – he made me feel guilty about the face that I myself turn to the world! He talked to me of going abroad. He told me it would be his pleasure to help me into a commission in the 17th Dragoons, as a return for all that my father has done for him. Don't be startled! I shan't accept, but ...'

'You could not live abroad. You love too much "the wind on the hills, the scent of heather, and the crack around the fire at a moorland inn". That is how you expressed it to me once.'

Oliver shrugged. 'We are always strangers on earth, wherever we are – expelled from Paradise. We are in a foreign land all our lives. It is called "*woman*". We are conceived inside that foreign garden. We spend all our lives as aliens within her, first as mother then as wife, never quite understanding her customs or her language. It does not matter if I live in Yorkshire, Greece or France. Compared with that first fact of existence, I am no more a stranger in one place than I am in another.

'But first I want to see my son.'

Anne would do anything to prevent a meeting between Oliver and the 'by-blow', the bastard, the curse whom he took to be his own child. She would lie to him, she would divert, she would act forgetful, she would pretend anger. Finally, as the weeks went by, she could devise nothing further to frustrate his curiosity and his wish. Together they followed the paths that Anne had often secretly taken.

When Aunt Pity saw Oliver, she without a word took the key of the shed and led the couple to it ... Anne walking a little behind, so as not to let him see her expression, read her thoughts, or observe her conflict about this creature that was hers and yet not hers; that she saw one moment one way, the next another; this ferrety animal she wished to hate, yet for which love was torn out of her unwillingly in pain-pangs like yet another birth.

The imprisoned child heard visitors arriving, and though only two years of age he drummed on the door, in anguish to be freed of the terror of being alone. But when it opened he was equally frightened of the strangers (including the one who was his own mother) and he dived at Aunt Pity's well-known skirt. Then that seemed insufficient and he scrambled back into the familiar corner of his shed, to his straw, a spinning top, and a crude rocking-horse.

Anne picked the child up, hiding her tearful face by kissing his hair (which struck Oliver as being so unlike his own). When she had given sufficient comfort, she tried to hand the boy to Oliver, whilst still averting her head.

The child struggled free and stood between them, for a moment glaring at his 'father'. Then on tottering but determined legs he made arrow-like for the garden.

Autumn sunlight brought the gold out of everything and before him rose gilded banks of flowers, some erect, some fallen. A red admiral butterfly paused for a moment, its broad crimson wings panting upon a Michaelmas daisy. The face of the tiny infant turned brutal. '*Peter!*' Anne shrieked. For with an expression of ferocious intense evil that Oliver, at least, had never before seen on a human, the child snapped his hands together and crushed the butterfly. Smiling and proud for the first time, he held up his chubby palms smeared with the remains of the red admiral.

'Come and live with me at Lower Laithes, Aunt Pity,' Anne tearfully pleaded.

'Nay, not there, lass,' Pity said. 'I'll not!'

As they returned home, Anne continued to hide her thoughts, and also her face, because she knew that it displayed her pain at the necessities that overwhelmed them. Though they believed themselves to be so close that they were as one body, both lovers had discovered the poignant agony of realising that in extremes there was little help they could give one another. There was nothing Oliver could say. He did not even precisely understand what ailed his beloved.

There was only one comfort he could offer. And so they lay together through the mid-morning, apparently deep in their sweetest love. But Anne was still from time to time turned away from him. Until at last she cast off into forgetfulness, she sailed from mortal life, and then 'Oh . . . oh . . .' she murmured; it turned to wild grunts, and finally she was whirled away. Whilst Oliver entered through that bushy door into that familiar room paved with gold and precious stones, fountains playing, that was like a vision by a saint or a martyr. When it was over, he still kept his eyes closed. Anne saw that he was absorbed in himself, and did not want to come back from wherever he was. When eventually he looked into Anne's eyes he experienced vertigo there, too. As if he was looking down wells of clear water right to the earth's centre. As if they were mirrors of infinite reflection, back . . . back . . . back. . .

Afterwards, her mind pacified, or at least her thoughts blanked out for a while, she bore his resting body, his head upon her breast, with more than usual patience, as if she gave particular importance to this moment. From time to time they shifted position, limbs glued with sweat, yet neither wanting to move apart. Neither wanted to admit how fragile was their hold upon one another. Soon they came together again. Each time Oliver penetrated, Anne was whirled into a desire for him to go deeper, deeper. Quite without reason, and out of what well of her being she did not ever understand, the word 'Kill' came upon her lips, as softly as a sparrow landing upon a bough; and she could not help but whisper, '*Kill, kill!*'

She did not know whether it had been a suicidal longing, or too great a desire for life. For life's ultimate challenge, its extreme expression, is to death to overthrow it.

Anne dressed and Oliver watched in quiet contemplation of her movements.

'What are you looking at?' she asked, sharply. As it was obvious, and he felt that he had the right, he did not answer. 'What are you staring at?' she repeated.

He crimsoned. 'Do you think I have no right to look at you, who has caused all my pain?'

Although she thought that his failings were weaknesses, and not wicked, yet Anne at this moment remembered how sometimes she had secretly resented the patience he required of her, wanting her to mother him. She knew he was no Apollo! Also, recalling her father's death, her Aunt Pity's frailty in old age, the loneliness and the obstinacy all about her, and the poverty of the weavers, she felt powerless to help anyone, no matter how much love she gave. She felt a painful hollowness in her breast. 'Do not blame *me* for your downfall,' she answered – bitter words, though she could still feel his semen within her. 'I cannot do anything for you any more. I expect you will go abroad and leave me, in the end.'

Oliver could not bear that look which showed her to be so separate from himself – mentioning his 'downfall' like any greedy trader or magistrate; talking coldly of his 'leaving'. He could hardly imagine that a few moments ago they had been glued together, searching for cooler places upon one another's bodies and yet not able to part.

'And "Hell hath no fury like a woman scorned!"' he answered sarcastically.

'Women become "furies" because if they do not attack, they always are the ones left with the suffering.'

'You have killed the joy between my father and myself,' Oliver said coldly. Immediately, he crimsoned with shame, and had to obliterate it. Also, her unwanted truths caused a desire for violence to rise like sickness choking and tightening his throat.

His first blow fell on her neck. As she went down he shouted, as if his cries would drown the blow, 'All my dear father's hopes and ambitions ruined! Oh, if you had never left Lady Well, never been born, Anne Wylde!'

She lay on the floor, a bloody mess. A dead body, his love.

Oliver flew around the house in a panic. When he recovered slightly he placed a sheet tenderly over her. She looked pathetically young and frail. What was most horrible was that the murder had been such a simple, brief act – like killing a sparrow.

An hour later Oliver left, wearing a suit of thick kersey cloth, with stout shoes and a simple bag, so that he looked like a peddlar, or a merchant of the middling sort. He walked away a few steps. Then ran back towards her. He could not believe that an hour ago Anne was alive – that she had ever been alive. But neither was she yet dead for him. Not really, no not really. He could shake her and she would wake up. Yet he could not bring himself to touch her now. Perhaps she had merely left that body, and she would come in through another door, tomorrow, or the day after that. Yes! No! He tried to drive the truth in by banging his fist on his forehead. He wrenched himself away. He stepped a few yards again into the bright cold wintry garden, his life over, yet going on. Anne, oh Anne. Forced himself to tear away. Stumbled, found his feet and went into the wood. He could even now feel the impression of her body as if she was still snuggled sweetly and happily against him: his twin, his own self. He was stamped with that arm flung around his neck whilst she slept, that thigh resting peacefully between his buttocks, her toe against his ankle, her forehead comfortably into his left shoulder as if it had found a socket for itself there. Her body-scents still covered his skin, and he could smell them clearly.

Yet his suffering was for the time being frozen, and lacking pain, except for one moment of agony when he longed, most vividly, to retrieve their past hours. For the sheer sake of remaining upright, he shook that moment away.

Following the river, he forced impressions into his memory and lingered at favourite spots to absorb one last, slow taste of his native hills. He surveyed, too, those manufactories where the women spun, row upon row of them at machines; emblems of the new times that had killed his love, blighted the Greaves' trade, and driven the salmon and trout from the river, which now contained only the reflections of these long, dark palaces in its waters.

Then he pulled himself together to think more positively of the unwanted freedom that lay before him. He realised that he had now only his own lonely self to care for. From then until he reached the stopping-place of the stage coach he walked hastily, with his head down, stubbornly fighting off grief by thinking of his future.

Two days later Anne woke up, with Dick Almighty and the apothecary at one side of her, Earth and Jenny Loveless at the other.

(12)

Nicholas Horsfall's family troubles began when his ancestor, an abbot, was hanged in the porch of his own church for taking part in a pilgrimage, during that earlier century when 'sin' first wore the dress of Catholics. Aghast at the wickedness of men's doings, the Abbot had turned to feminine things: he had become a Marian. But his devotion to 'Our Lady' softened his defences against the worldly, so he was easily trapped, convicted, and executed. His niece, Margaret, in her turn horrified at Catholic Marian suffering, slipped out of danger by marrying the Protestant Horsfall. Then a hen became agent of the family's ruin: because this Horsfall tenanted a farm for which one fowl per annum was paid in extra rent and the Protestant refused to submit to this feudal obligation, whereupon the Lady of The Manor (a vicarious *Lady of The Heavens*) persecuted, or at any rate sued, him (for she received eight hundred hens annually this way). She won her case – for the judges were in her favour and patronage – whilst Horsfall, stubbornly pursuing justice, ended in the debtors' gaol. He tried to escape, so both his legs were fettered. He lay in the mire at the bottom of York Castle for six years, never able to remove his clothes, and eventually they had to be cut from him. All for a hen. Meanwhile his estate fell into ruin. His daughter, called 'Mad Mathilda Horsfall', or 'the Crazy Horsewoman', rescued the family home by presenting its mortgages and bills to her husband as (undeclared before their marriage) her dowry.

The Horsfalls had been Catholic or Protestant, rich or poor, skin-flint or generous, martyrs, heretics or rulers, as the centuries dictated, to an extreme degree. With such aristocratic ancestors, what wonder that Nicholas Horsfall looked down upon Benjamin Greave who had no history but a scramble for a living upon the soaked moors, and for God's Grace in mean nonconforming chapels?

Nicholas Horsfall one winter's day rode out of his dilapidated mansion, with its mortgaged flaking stone, to visit Benjamin Greave.

He wore his cavalry uniform, as if going into battle. His bright red coat looked vivid as freshly shed blood against the snow, which was drifted in the lanes, whilst new flurries that made one dizzy to look at dropped into a silence that swallowed them upon the white banks and altered slopes. The streams were frozen. Nobody who didn't need to showed out of doors, and cottages had their shutters fastened. There was an expression of terror in the eyes of the few who struggled about the countryside, either because hunger forced them to search, or because they were pack-horsing illegal whisky, or gold coins hidden in rolls of cloth. Even the locked shutters on the roadside houses seemed to emphasise the fact that these were outcasts. Fires glowed wherever they gathered to warm themselves – knowing that in this weather no one was likely to chase them from taking wood or, if they could, from finding a rabbit to eat.

Horsfall, wearing his usual contemptuous expression for the world (unless it was one at war), found Benjamin Greave dreading, fearing, and as cowardly as he expected an old man (even a rich one) to be, when left alone in winter.

'A ship went down near Yarmouth with all hands lost, God help all the sufferers!' the old fellow remarked. Greave had now formed the habit of wringing his hands. 'I'm worried if I had some cloth aboard. If so, you may pray the Lord's help for our weavers, for I have no money for them. I've not seen the snow lie up to the eaves like this for seven years! My barns are full of stuff that I cannot get rid of, and I daren't get my folk making more. There'll be some frozen toes and nipped fingers in our cottages this season! The servants cannot get to chapel and church to pray for release, so I have put up with them reading sermons in my own house. You never heard such wailing – I can't imagine who fathered such hymn tunes as they sing today. I don't know where to escape to, what wi't'plagues of business, and manufactories growing up everywhere taking the trade from me. On top of it all I'm worried about that lad of mine, my son. Oh, what a woeful world is this.'

'Oliver has deserted to the Continent to escape his debts. Not a worthy or noble action.'

'He left me to die in the winter like a dog!'

'The worst is, that if you do, your inheritance will then go straight to his woman and her bastard progeny.'

The old man gripped Horsfall's arm tightly. For once in his life he whispered. 'They have such, do you think?'

'It is thought that a son is hidden in some cot on the moors, and for sure the bastard'll emerge later to claim your fortune.'

'Has Oliver married the Wylde woman before he left?'

Horsfall stuffed his pipe with tobacco that he helped himself to from the mantelpiece. 'You must take care of your money!'

Ironic advice, considering the Horsfall's traditionally spendthrift ways, and Benjamin's thriftiness.

'Will thou be trustee of my will, then? I'll send for my lawyer straight as there's a thaw, and make a new one.' Benjamin Greave was still wringing his hands.

'Anything I can do by way of return to you would be very little.' Horsfall's spurs struck sparks from the stones as he moved to light a taper at the fire.

'Would you root out my son and discover whether he says he is married to Miss Wylde? I'll pay you for it.'

'I already know that Oliver has gone to Brussels. It is worthwhile, you know, for a gentleman to employ spies in the times through which we are living. I will gladly follow him. There is no need of recompense, I have enough of those from you already.'

'Ah, if only you were my son! Or if only I had a daughter. What perfection it would be to marry your old family to my humble clothier's fortune. Would you do something for me?'

'Your wish is my command. I am your humble servant in all things.'

'What a winter this is! I've not seen a weaver coming down from the hills for weeks.'

'What can I do for you, old friend?'

Horsfall was impatient to learn 'the worst': one never knew what the 'eccentric old piece-maker' might want.

'The work at Lady Well church has been at a standstill for I don't-know-how-long. Nobody seems to get on wi't, though I leave instructions. They're more interested in reading 'bout Tom Paine, I think, instead o'making worthwhile improvements to their church. Would you see to the design of my monument? No one has more knowledge of what's tasteful in art and tombstones, and I was relying on Oliver for that job. Art and frippery and hanging on to a woman's skirts are the only things he's any talent for. I feared that he'd desert me, afore long!'

'Nothing would give me greater pleasure than to assist in the design of your tomb.'

'You're a good fellow! What do you say that I should do, then, to preserve my fortune?' The old trader's face took on the incandescent trusting look of a child.

'I'd advise you not to leave it direct to your son, but to his daughter Betty and her male children when she has some. It will then stay in your line but be in no danger of diversion to Anne Wylde and her bastards.'

'There's but one fault wi't'plan, Mr 'Orsfall. Betty's a sickly creature. What if she dies before marriage and without issue?'

'Surely she will last that long!'

'I aren't so certain. I haven't seen her for a long while. She is away staying with an aunt since my son disgraced himself.'

'The important thing is to be assured that the inheritance does not pass either to Anne Wylde, or to Oliver's creditors. If Betty dies issueless before the age of twenty-one, then there is no way to cheat a malignant fortune.'

'Oh aye, but there is though! I'll leave my money to thee, Nicholas Horsfall, before I'll let my enemies get hold of it. I always thought that Oliver sharing my business would bind us together in a symbol, for all t'weavers, of the family happiness and prosperity of the whole valley under the fatherhood of trade. But now I see my interest'd be better spent on thee.'

'That is too much! I do not seek payment for what I have done!' Horsfall put his cheerful, youthful arm around the old man's shoulders, and it made Greave feel so protected! 'You have crossed the Rubicon of old age, Benjamin Greave! You are defenceless and in need of looking after.'

'You've been more of a son to me than my own lad and you must have some security in the end as reward for your pains. You would be doing me a service, even then, by helping me "cheat a malignant fortune", as you say. And yet it may not come to that! If my son is in wedlock with Anne Wylde, he might still have legitimate progeny in whom I can invest my immortality.' Benjamin paused, ruminating. 'And thou's made a mistake or two, investing in foolish manufactories. Aye, if only the old could teach the young!'

'If he married her, any children would still be of the blood of Anne Wylde.' Horsfall hurriedly pointed out.

'But how am I to tell if my son and Miss Wylde are wedded or not? If I ask him outright, he's bound to give me a crooked reply.' Benjamin laughed. 'Thou'lt never get a straight answer from someone who's been brought up in our trade.'

'Write a letter for me to deliver, saying that you would be more glad if she were his wife, than anyone else on earth. Then he will tell you, either quite truthfully that he is already married to her, or he will promise to wed her on the instant. No other device could encourage a more spontaneous heartfelt response.'

Benjamin Greave's eyes became damp with admiration. 'No one knows like you Horsfalls how best to defend a family line!'

One dry, sunny day in Brussels Oliver passed a gardener watering a lawn and the sudden smell of wet grass transported him home. Oh, those moist, milky Yorkshire nights, full of the music of water, of streams, rain, and the never-ceasing sound of the wells and springs! The pangs of homesickness were as physical to him as gallstones. Anne Wylde's guilty, incredulous murderer, slinking through the alleyways of a foreign city, was filled with a vision of banks of fox-red grass, of bracken rising in the autumn sunlight, of grey boulders carved by streams into softly-rounded hips and breasts, of the fraternity of the inns, and especially of the friendship of that elusive maker whom he loved, Tim Bobbin.

Everywhere in Oliver's life there was still the spirit of Anne Wylde; she who had never harmed anyone. This way, that, he tore, distracted, and yet looking for distraction. He stared transfixed in an agony of knowing that he could not escape his guilt and loneliness. Should he kill himself?

Oliver Greave spent much of his time composing letters, literary essays and poems. He never sent his epistles, because a critical glance later showed him that they had not expressed his heart. And his work would probably never be published, for where now was his access to gentlemen-subscribers? Still, he wrote. He was trying to give expression to something inside himself that did not seem to love him and his career in the world; at frightened moments, he named it 'conscience'

– a chariot driving him to Hell. Oliver wrote because when not doing so he became a prisoner of himself, of that inescapable person the murderer of Anne Wylde, and he fell into silence. The nearest he came to happiness was in writing.

In efforts to struggle free of the brake upon him, he began many days two or three times. He would return to his bed hoping to frustrate the prospect of another day of failure, and rise to start again, forcing himself to a second breakfast and a further run at those manuscripts, those longings. Such fresh starts and failures played havoc with his night's rest. Working and sleeping in short bursts destroyed his sense of day and night.

Not only was his eating irregular: as he had never been forced to look after himself, but always found that some woman was preparing his meals, his cooking was bad and he swallowed it quickly so as not to have to taste it – thus further ruining his digestion.

However, his poetical digestion was working better in this silence and isolation. His confused thoughts burrowed down into his soul and there restored themselves, becoming articulate. These illuminations would take him by surprise. They hung before him in the air only for a moment, and if he did not write them down instantly, they evaporated. They were like pictures from some ancient Tomb, broken into by grave-robbers, fading quickly in the light. However when he did grasp them, he wrote a new kind of poetry.

> All night upon my thigh I've felt her hand
> Which rested there, those years ago.
> Oh, Heaven is that woman's charms!
> No golden apple trees, no
> Angel-crowded vistas, you can keep all those,
> Whilst I spend eternity in her arms!

Horsfall had to wait for a month before the weather made it possible to travel to find Oliver, and Benjamin Greave was kept on tenterhooks. Twice Nicholas Horsfall received urgent messages to go to Makings. He expected to find the clothier dying. But the first call was merely to consult yet again over the phrasing of his letter, and the second was to remark that the sudden spring weather looked as though it would last; the sodden fields were drying out, the roads had regained their firmness, and a cargo of Russian pine on order since autumn for his mausoleum had arrived, so surely it was possible to reach Brussels? Horsfall laughed off his annoyance and realised that the sooner he crossed the Channel the sooner he'd enjoy peace from 'the boorish old chaw-bacon'.

Oliver's room (when Horsfall found it, through the post office where the poet went daily in futile hope of letters) reeked of dissolute living. It was musty, smelling of tobacco and stale food, and untidy with manuscripts and books. The Captain found it disgusting.

Horsfall first handed over the gold sent by Benjamin Greave. 'It must be a fine thing to be a gentleman abroad!' he laughed. 'You should be more cheerful, enjoying your free hand with the ladies, and no prying faces. What sport *are* you up to these days?'

Oliver, who had phrased so many fine sentences, now could hardly speak, but could only turn crimson. (The Captain was not surprised to find a refugee from justice nervous.) 'We English find Brussels on the whole . . .' he got out, and choked. '. . . Articles of convenience are dear . . . the price of fish . . .'

Then, 'How is Anne Wylde?' he blurted (whilst trying to cover some papers).

'Surely you are not pining for your English mistress amongst all these foreign fruits, my friend? I saw such beauties strolling near the harbour for the sailors to take their pick. I don't want to upset you – but, you know, they say the witch was unfaithful. Don't be angry with me, old fellow! It's only gossip. You remember what we are like for that in Lady Well. It is rumoured that she was enjoyed by a whole gang of sinners one Lammas Day, and that as a result she has a child hidden. A fine infant, too, coming from elegant stock, they say.'

'What happened to Anne Wylde?'

'Do you have some tobacco, old friend?'

Oliver fidgeted around his room until he found tobacco. Horsfall rummaged through his pockets. 'Have you a pipe?'

Oliver rooted in drawers and found a clay pipe. Horsfall packed it and sucked away. 'It is very dry,' he remarked.

'Anne Wylde?'

'Ah! Your father has entrusted me with a letter for you.'

Oliver rushed to break the seal. No, he could not believe what was happening to him . . . oh yes he could . . . he could . . . When, flushed with excitement and confusion, he looked up, he caught Horsfall again taking in the details of the room.

'My father says that he wishes I would marry Anne Wylde, for she would be more agreeable to him than any other woman! Is she alive and well then?'

'This is uncommonly dry tobacco, old friend ... why shouldn't she be?'

'Wait a moment and I will compose a reply!'

Oliver rushed into another room. As he tried to sit down, he knocked over a chair. Once seated, he could not write. He got up, danced about, grabbed the pen again, and cut himself in trying to sharpen it.

Horsfall meanwhile rummaged through Oliver's papers. There were lists of phrases: 'Nobody believes it ... *pas un ne le croit.*' 'My shirt is dirty ... *ma chemise est sale.*' 'I love you with all my heart ... *je vous aime de tout mon coeur.*' And literary utterances, evidently part of a novel. 'Little does he feel the sad variety of pain, the curse attendant upon family and home, who never knew misfortune and is surrounded with pleasure.'

Oliver re-entered. 'Anne Wylde is well, then?'

'Why shouldn't she be, old fellow? Upon my word, you are too excited! At about the time you escaped ... left ... some ruffian knocked her down, and (not for the first time in her life) left her for dead. Oh, it's all right, she recovered! The justices are still searching for the culprit. They have a few clues. But you would not know about that ...'

Oliver grabbed and kissed him.

'In God's name you are too enthusiastic, fellow! It comes from living amongst foreigners. Look, sir ... you must be needing employment.'

'Indeed, sir! It's kind of you to think of that! Though only until I return to England to marry Anne Wylde. For I cannot come straightaway, I must be circumspect ... the justices, you say ...'

'I'd stay where the garden is still fresh, if I was you. She is after all no more than a common girl without ancestry or, I suspect, even dowry. You should think higher of yourself, my friend, and not forget what you will doubtless be heir to one day! Give me your ear, for I have a plan for you, old fellow. I'm profiting from what I've learnt from the old clothiers of our district, for one cannot rub shoulders with them and not gain by it, and though my first manufactory was burnt down by plotters against their King, yet I am still a cloth-factor, in a small way of business, and I'd make it worth your while to extend my interest abroad.'

'I'm sure I can form a most perfect judgment of what foreign people consider to be perfection in English woollen goods. On the other hand, my wish is to return straight to England to marry Miss Wylde.'

'Best be circumspect, old friend.' Horsfall winked. 'You never know what the justices might invent. And I will provide you with the means to stay abroad, whilst you consider the matter.' Horsfall offered his hand and Oliver shook it.

'You are a true friend,' Oliver said.

The poet's visitor departed, leaving him to his frightening excitement, and not knowing what to do with himself; to his plans for returning to England, to the apprehensive hesitations engendered in his mind by Horsfall, and to his exiled scribblings.

Benjamin Greave tore open Oliver's reply even before he had wished Horsfall good day. '*What do you make of that?*' the clothier asked.

The Captain read: 'It always used to be my intention never to marry. Not to be unhappy, or that I thought no woman so deserving, but because I found a single life preferable. That is, until I met Miss Wylde, for since then I have been in entire happy agreement with your presently expressed wishes.'

'*I still cannot tell whether the lad is wedded or not!*' Benjamin Greave shouted.

Everything these days was unsettled; why, the whole of Europe was 'on fire with revolution'. Or so Benjamin Greave's visitors were always telling him – as a way of explaining the 'difficulties' of selling cloth. All property and inheritance was threatened by seditious traitors; whilst at home in Lady Well the Society For Prosecuting Felons had found it necessary to demonstrate their loyalty to 'the Constitution and the King' by burning publicly an effigy of Tom Paine.

Determined in such times at least to find the truth about his own heirs, Greave rode over to Aunt Pity's cottage. The spring sunshine cheered him; as did the sight of farms, because they were mostly his own property. His tenants had recovered from the winter, he was glad to see. They looked thinner, and it was good for them, he thought, to get rid of a bit of fat. There were fewer of them, and families were better off for being rid of a few dependent old folk. Benjamin set foot on Black Hill. He had not been so far up on the hills since he was a young man, collecting whinberries and courting young ladies. Little had changed since: here a quarry had been cut, there some reprobate or gallow's-bird-in-hiding had thrown up a rough cottage near a watercourse. This constancy was a relief, because he more habitually looked down into the valleys where he was offended by the sight of alteration and new building, nothing but building and more building – manufactories for spinners that were getting as large as palaces.

Dried grasses rustled as he descended to the old woman's cottage. Aunt Pity hobbled out and silenced the dog. To Benjamin Greave, she looked no older than in his youth (and she'd seemed an old woman then), when they used to tease her. But he was glad to see that she was none the worse for it, and nowadays she was left in peace. He remembered how when she lived in Lady Well he and the other children used to visit her with their stomach pains, headaches, bleeding limbs, and she would go into her dark cellar, or out to her garden, for aromatic leaves. Women also came, for private consultation or with complaints about their husbands, so she had become the counsellor and keeper of all the secrets of the town.

'Are your hens laying yet? It must have been a hard winter up here!' he shouted down the hillside, with the condescending jokiness of the persecutor who is hiding his conscience from his victim.

'They lay most of the year round, for me.'

'You must have bewitched them, then! There's truth in the old rumour, after all.'

'I do no more than talk to them because I'm lonely. But never mind my hens. What can I do for you, Benjamin Greave?'

'How do you know who I am, when you can't lift your nose off the ground?'

By now he had reached the door. He walked into the house as if he owned it. (Perhaps he did: he was not sure any more how much property was his. Only lawyers knew things of that kind.) Sharp-eyed,

199

he looked around. He would dearly like to know the secret of her red dye. If he found that out, he might profit from setting up a commercial manufactory. What were those dried-up plants on the table there?

'I can tell folks by their voices ... and their smell. You stink of money and of wool-oil. You always did. You're the same as your son.'

'He's been here then, has he, a time or two?'

'A time or two, as you say. Benjamin Greave, what are you doing to the hawthorn?'

'She has taken *herself* off, I am told, without the necessity of the aid of respectable and devout men. I don't know where she is.'

'Nay, I mean the hawthorns upon the hill. It looks very bleak there now.'

'Ah! We are felling them to make room for improved grazing.'

'It will bring ill-luck on you all.'

'They say it is the hawthorns that bring the bad luck, not the honest men who do away with them, you old witch!'

''Tis the hawthorns that preserve us.'

'That's right! For we use cuttings of the old trees to plant new ones in the form of hedgerows for enclosures. So all things are improved for mankind thereby.'

'You cannot take only what *you* want of the old spirits.'

'You old fright! They say that after the first Christians came you went to the civilisation of the Arabs, together wi' everyone else not fitted to being a monk, and left Christianity in darkness for a thousand years. What does tha' answer to that?'

Pity answered nothing.

'And what brought my son to this desolate place, visiting an old witch?' Benjamin next asked. At last he sat down, rinsing his hands in invisible water, and his eyes still prying for secrets in the dark corners of the cottage. He noticed some apothecary's mixing-bowls and retorts, battered and foolish-looking as the tools of scientific investigation often look when they drift into the kitchens of old women.

'I expect you know.'

'It wouldn't be because he's got a child hidden, would it?'

'Eh, Benjamin Greave, always worrying about what you're leaving behind and who's going to get it – like a dog with its droppings. You get madder and madder:

> "As foolish as monkeys
> Till twenty or more;
> As bold as lions
> Till forty and four;
> As cunning as foxes
> Till three score and ten,
> They then become asses,
> Or something . . . not men!"

'You know the old rhyme. Whoever has your wealth will only spend it for you as fast as if they've set fire to it, not having worked for it. They'll not consider you!'

'We must all think of what we leave behind, though.'

'We leave the memory of our good deeds. Unless we do bad ones. And they're remembered, just the same.'

'You talk like a parson. I never expected that, for I thought you'd be full of the Devil's words. Has he a son left here or not?'

'Can you see any child?' Aunt Pity poked at the fire. 'Though it's warm outside, it's still cold within until June up here.' As she grumbled, she turned her neck sideways to peer at him, because he was wringing his hands, and peeping around her room. He tried to control himself.

'Maybe you've an infant hidden somewhere. It'd be a terrible fate for the lad if he hasn't been christened.'

'Poor creature!'

Benjamin shouted loudly and angrily, 'I have to learn if I have a grandchild, and whether 'tis a boy or girl, to know where to leave my fortune, you old crow!'

'Poor creature!'

Greave realised that he would not get a better answer. 'Well, if I have no grandson, I know what to do for my heirs!' he shouted and left, hoping that he was leaving in the air a threat menacing enough to prise open Pity's secret. She did follow into the garden. But there she merely sang to her hens.

Benjamin climbed back on to the moor, breathless and annoyed. He trod carelessly. One foot sank into a hollow covered by grass, and his old heart raced from surprise and fright. God help him, there was lying, betrayal, disillusion, disloyalty to th'government and poverty for th'weavers on either hand, whilst even the ground underfoot could not be trusted! What it was to be old and suffer this. If only the Empress of Russia would take more shalloons ...

He sat down on a bank whilst his thumping breast quietened down, and a haze spread across his eyes. As it cleared he saw a viper coiled, small and very neat, upon a stone. It raised its head and slithered, moving daintily as a maiden dressed in her best and going to her first hiring-fair. The glowing yellow underbelly and the dead-leaf back were shifting with eerie silence and smoothness. Benjamin froze, very frightened. The snake raised her delicate striped oval head, sensing with exquisite pleasure and tasting the air with sharp flicks of her tongue. Benjamin knew that he ought to remain still, but he instead panicked and scrambled up the bank. Before he had even raised his arm off the heather, the viper struck, and vanished as if ashamed of what she had done. Benjamin stared at the undignified wriggle disappearing into the heather, as though wishing to call her back, to change her mind and retrieve her poison. Then, seeing his arm already swelling, he sucked and spat but it steadily swelled and became numb.

He rushed to the nearest cottage, which was Elkanah Beanland's. Slithering clumsily in his hurry through mud and stones, Benjamin banged on the door.

'I thought it was robbers coming, Mr Greave! But you're always welcome, man, to sup with me!' Elkanah shouted.

'Find me a horse! I've been bitten by a snake!'

'A snake! You can ride my nag if you like, but the woman yonder's the one to heal you. Go see her, and put your trust in God.'

'I've just come from there, you old fool! You must pray me God's speed to Makings, Elkanah. I cannot go back to Pity's house.'

'Has thou offended her, Mr Greave? Happen the snake was one of her familiars, Mr Greave!'

'Happen so! Stop shouting in my ear! Where's your *horse*, man?'

Elkanah turned his face towards the blank moor, and whistled so that his whole cheek turned blue. An old nag appeared out of a hollow where she had been enjoying the sun. 'Look at her staring at us!' Elkanah shouted. 'She's a tired old girl now, and like me she's none too secure of her legs on *this* earth.' He cupped his hands and yelled, 'Thou'd better hurry up, see! Mr Greave the master's been bitten by a snake!' The mare shook her ears and trotted casually down the slope. 'Come on old lass, you've got the grandest man in this valley to ride on your back, he'll reward you for it, I'm sure . . .'

'I'll give you five pounds if I get home and recover.'

'Nay, I want none of your money, man! Just say a prayer to the Lord for my old horse. Maybe, after all, she'd enjoy being buried decently, something of that sort to send her off. We all want that if we can afford it, don't we, Mr Greave! Let's help you up, Mr Greave! Thou's looking a bit green.'

Benjamin, lopsided and fainting, cantered away on the tired old mare. It seemed to take all afternoon to reach Makings, where he fell into the arms of Patience Helliwell.

(13)

It was a long while before Anne realised that Oliver had left the country. (It was a long time before anyone knew of it.) She did not mind too much that he had struck her, as most men did that to women, but she was resentful of his having run away. Then she forgot it in her longing. During the hazy days of her recovery she would imagine that he was in the next room, or that he must be one of those vague figures at her bedside. She once mistakenly touched Dick Almighty's hand, and realised what she had done when she saw him blush – his round face like a sun setting in water – and felt his desire.

As the autumn advanced, and the woodlands shivered to pieces as if they would never live again, the more she thought: I am recovering, and it is not I that am collapsing, but the world around me.

Although she had rents from the farms, she would not touch them (other than for necessities and to pay the bills of the apothecary) because she felt that they were really Oliver's. She could have had revenues from felling Blood Wood, but she would rather starve than touch the trees. Everyone but Earth and Jenny left Lower Laithes. Whilst Jenny often worried what eventually might become of her, the Negro, who had always been tossed about the world without regard for his wishes, never gave it a thought.

When Anne was well enough to go out, she realised that during her sickness she had travelled rapidly in the direction of old age. Her back had begun to stoop, just like Aunt Pity's, and even if from time to time she remembered to straighten it, yet it soon sank over again. Time however brought no relief from persecution. Children and weavers still shouted after her, 'Jezebel shall be eaten by dogs!' and ''Awthorn, 'awthorn, burn int' fire!'

So she was glad to return to her rooms. Anne's loneliness transformed the appearance of things. Clock, carpet, door, the gowns in her wardrobe, had turned into stubborn strangers full of hostile silence and stillness. She tried to fill the aching freezing space of her mind by staring, staring out, clock, china tea-service or the shoe casing her foot. In her transfixed gaze they retreated, an inch, a yard, and then floated away into mist. She blinked and they snapped back again, leaving her head spinning. She attacked them at last, violently throwing her shoe across the room, and it clattered against the wall. At least it was a sound! But it was like a shriek in a foreign tongue.

She could not think why Oliver did not send a letter to her. Perhaps some tragedy had occurred. But she knew his scrupulousness with language: more likely, she told herself, he was writing and tearing up the pages for lack of some nice poetic phrases. At certain times she visualised him so clearly that she felt sure he must be thinking of her at the same moment – as if his concentration was forcing his image complete across the seas, hills, cities unimaginable to her, and the wide green estates of England, France or wherever he was.

The only love, she knew, that she would ever have. The poor woman would go to her door, sometimes in the night, and stare around pathetically sure that he was approaching out of that blankness muffling her senses – smothering her even on a summer's day, though birds were singing.

Anne sometimes tried to concentrate herself and magic her image to him. The effort tired her and left her with that aching time again, there merely to be filled. She had played the part of a poet's muse for so long that without it she felt no more than an old rag: the muse's dress, tossed aside into a hedge. She was looking more and more like an old witch, too. Her tall frame became gaunt and stooped, her nose hooked, her eyes sunken and sharp.

Her first winter alone arrived. It was a vicious one, and, whilst the young ones frolicked like puppies in the snow, she for the first time suffered that common old-person's meditation that she might not survive this particular season. Gulleys were levelled and outlines thickened with drifts. Objects stood sharp and dark against the sun. Hardly anyone or anything moved, except during the short midday thaw, which was so slight that the melted frost merely hung in still globes and had not time to fall before the cold tightened its grip again. For only an hour each day water trickled out of the drifts. Its runnels wove the fields, then stiffened, and were creased with ice. The ice came into the house, lining the windows, thickening on bowls of standing water, forming a crust on Anne's chamberpot and skimming newly-washed floors. It mocked her, reminding her that she would soon have to leave this place which she could not warm or clean, where she could not pay for servants. The icicles seemed to glitter with grinning faces. The muses tumbling off the ceiling now mocked her – Erato, the naked inspirer of love poetry with her saucy grin, and Melpomene, the darkly-painted lady of tragedy, scowling deeply. 'Know thyself!', carved over the door and growing moss, mocked her. For she did not know where exactly to look for 'herself', only feeling vaguely that it was not in her own breast, but in some unknown foreign place with Oliver.

The true thaw came, but did not change the silence, for it arrived as a moist warm fog, like piles of wool before it is spun. Anne felt even more maddened and imprisoned. She could see nothing, and all she heard was the banging of hammers in the fulling mill. Bang! Bang! The insistent unceasing hammering of trade as if driving nails into nature's coffin.

One Sunday, when no one was at work, Anne told Earth to fetch his spade and hatchet and they went to the fulling mill, finding their way by touch amongst eerily dripping boughs where all was soundless but for the church bell clanging monotonously. (Twenty times, to announce that it was the twentieth day of the month.) The Negro was good at feeling his way. He would go a few yards ahead before he turned, grinning, twirling the spade and hatchet in the air. His look was devilish and frightening, and he was so ragged, with his torn tunic, and only a silver collar to remind of his previous pampered state. But Anne had not allowed fear to rule her life before, and so she advanced boldly. Earth skipped ahead, touching the trees – their moss luminous upon the grey day – until he was almost out of sight, then he waited for her to catch up.

They came to where the stream poured over a weir to drive the hammers of the mill. There was hardly any light in the water and it went over fleshy, grey and thick, like a collier's muscles, and with a sullen pounding at the bottom of the fall before thundering under the building. Anne told Earth to attack the bank of the weir hanging above the wood. The Negro looked horrified. But when Anne began with the hatchet, he laughingly joined her, as if this was the slave-revolt in San Domingo. Earth was tireless, his spade and his muscles one everlasting pendulum.

The sluggish water trickled over the bank. Soon it moved faster, carrying stones and soil tumbling as Earth gladly helped it on its way. It became a cascade, roaring in its escape through the trees, finding a way round the mill, and in at the windows where piles of cloth were waiting for tomorrow to be fulled.

The two conspirators, who could barely understand one another through language, communicated, as they had never done before, with looks directly into one another's faces. Anne held out her arms. They held hands, then danced and skipped round one another on the bank top that was crumbling more and more under the power of the stream. As they returned to Lower Laithes, the Negro chuckled to himself.

On Monday the workmen, finding their wool ruined and no water-power to drive the hammers, at first suspected Loveless and the combers. But Earth's naked footprints were seen leading along the banktop, so men went with dogs to Lower Laithes.

They found the Negro digging in the garden; he was making a stand against the encroachment of weeds, and destroying completely what was now no more than a palimpsest of the ornate borders, in his hope of creating a plot for vegetables. As they gave chase, other men, boys and dogs joined in, leaving their looms thinking that Benjamin Greave, made generous by an unexpected profit, had restored one of the forgotten saints' days. A trumpet and a tin whistle were produced. They were arguing about whether fiddlers and mummers should be called forth, when the Negro ran into a tenter field, ruining the fifteen shilling's worth of drying cloth in which he got tangled and making them forget all else in their fresh anger with him. But when he was cornered, and they had called off the dogs, his captors fell silent: for they had not yet thought what to do with him.

'Let's peg him in the stream, since he has ruined its use for us, and set the dogs on him as they used to wi' beasts – wi' bulls and bears – in grandfather's day!' said Joshua Binns. So two held Earth's arms and pushed him triumphantly through the lanes.

'Yon poor animal's tired, let him be!' an old weaver shouted over a wall.

'Nay, we're having sport as in grandfather's day!' an apprentice answered. And another young man: 'Nay, you'll not be against a bit of sport.' A fresh generation of tormentors was evidently growing up to replace Binns and his friends, who were getting stiff in their limbs.

They took the Negro to a place just above the mill. The water was freezing cold and the weavers could not think how to get into the stream to peg him there. 'Let him go, we've had enough of him now,' one said.

'Are we to be defeated for lack of a bit of invention?' Joshua exclaimed. 'Where's thy spirit? We've always found a way before, we Yorkshire folk!'

To the Negro's waist they tied a rope with two leads, one of which was taken across the stream near a bridge, thus dragging Earth to the middle. Before he could scramble on to the far bank, the other length was used to tether him in mid-current.

The young man's first instinct was to climb on to one of the boulders, and though it was slimy he made progress, fascinating his persecutors with the way in which he gripped with his toes.

Because the water was so cold, the dogs at first merely barked up and down the bank. But eventually one bold rough terrier plunged in and the rest followed. The pack's excitement made the spectators forget the sporting chance they had intended to allow the Negro. Back and forth across the stream, throwing stones, banging drums and blowing trumpets, they built up a competitive frenzy; for the one with the least pity would prove to be the boldest inventor of torments, and so each cultivated pitilessness in himself.

The Negro squatted on a stone, his head tucked into his arms: as a victim he was boring. Whilst the dogs snarled and leaped, he chafed his rope upon the edge of the rock. When he was free he sprang up the far bank, his slender legs working and his ribs beating like a panicking young deer as he disappeared into the trees. The weavers and dogs were too tired to give chase, and no one ever saw Earth again.

For Anne's part in ruining the mill and the wool, Dick Almighty fetched her to the stocks. Considering the sedition, arson and malicious wrecking of manufactories taking place in Yorkshire, it was amazing that he did not make a greater example of her – at least bring her before magistrates, who would remand her to York castle. Lady Well inhabitants might indeed have been delighted by that, enjoying bonfires and fireworks for a week.

As it was, the mild punishment that she received left them wondering who they were more furious with – Anne Wylde or Dick Almighty. There seemed to exist a conspiracy between the victim and the Constable who brought her along the roads. In fact Almighty was actually seen to defend her, as the populace shouted, 'Jezebel's being fetched to the dogs!' and when women, as heartily as men, ripped Anne's petticoat, and plastered mud on her head.

The stocks were in sight of John Wylde's house, which was now inhabited by the Methodist manager of a spinning mill. 'We have seen some changes, you and I, Anne Wylde, but I don't think we've improved things none,' Almighty remarked in a kindly way. His limbs were now almost as stiff as the old oak bars of the stocks, and he panted as he lifted them, replacing them over her with a tenderness that seemed improper coming from a thief-catcher. He might have been a lover placing a coverlet upon his sweetheart.

'It is but the way the weft is shuttled across the warp,' Anne answered, whilst she did what she could do to make herself comfortable.

'I beg your pardon? As always, you talk in riddles and henigmas. You are too clever for us simple people. That is why you have ended up in the stocks.'

Almighty patted his stomach with a gesture of irritation that was familiar to all rogues. He had no patience with mysteries and he punctured those cloudy devils as soon as they were apprehended. But the patting-of-his-stomach was no more than a habit and he did not intend any malice to Anne Wylde by it.

'The warp is what is given in our lives. Call it fate. The weft is what is woven across it by fortune. Every moment – such as this one – is made of the meeting of the two.'

'And how did you come to comprehend the symbols of the first weavers: of Athena, Penelope, Ariadne and Aphrodite?'

'I have had the time for thinking.'

Almighty finished his work and turned the big key in the lock with a gesture of artisan satisfaction which was second nature to him. But afterwards he hesitated, apprehensive of the behaviour of his Lady Well flock during his absence. Though fortunately, because the rain was tearing through the alleys, few people bothered to come out.

'It will not be a long day,' Almighty promised, with a sweetness quite untypical of him. Yes, there was dampness on his eyes. Yet he could think of no further excuse to linger.

Anne, left alone in her soaked rags, with rain running off her matted hair, realised that a stage of her life was finished. She adjusted to becoming just such a beggar and scoundrel of the highways and wastes as she was now shown to be; no more than a poor woman fastened into heavy wooden stocks. Whilst Lady Well looked equally beggared. Before her was the church stripped by a mad parson. Over there was the 'new well', where a few loiterers despite the rain were watching flies, or searching for the blood in the water that would foretell war. In vistas between buildings Anne saw a scattering of burnt farms on the hillsides.

Dick Almighty often returned anxiously to inspect his charge. He excused himself for being solicitous by saying that he was on his way to the apothecary's, whilst the second time he was 'going to meet an informant to illegal brewing'. Both visits, however, followed immediately after shouts and jeers from over-excited spectators. During mid-afternoon Dick released her. He came dragging by the ear a travelling ex-soldier. The Constable told the crowd that the stocks were now needed for this 'villain, scofflaw, miscreant and son of Belial', who, though warned thrice of his offence of lingering in Lady Well, yet had stayed longer than the churchwardens would suffer. Besides, the soldier had a snuff box with the seditious word *Liberty* engraved upon it. This Almighty had pocketed – as evidence. (Incidentally, it was made of silver.) 'Do you not know that in the King's England you can be transported in chains for life and hung after being made to suffer a multitude of torments, for uttering that dread word *Liberty*?' he bellowed at his victim, as much to frighten the folk of Lady Well into giving up any republican objects made of silver and gold that they might possess, as for the soldier's benefit.

Almighty let Anne go, with that same desiring gentle touch that he had shown once at her bedside. Then, in case his sentiment was observed by some malicious observer as sharp-eyed as himself, he compensated for it by threatening the 'sinning pole-cat of a soldier' with a whipping before he left town. Jangling the keys of the stocks and the lock-up, Dick guarded Anne safely out of Lady Well. Yet, uniquely for him, he said nothing all the way. When she had passed quarter of a mile beyond the boundary she turned and saw him watching her. She waved, and he returned it, still solemn and thoughtful.

Almighty that very evening sent around his servant-boy to call together at his inn the most powerful body in Lady Well, the *Society For Prosecuting Felons*. He placed the deeds of the Adam and Eve and of all his other properties on the table, and instructed the company to scrutinise them most carefully. Moreover, he provided them with the first round of ale free of charge. 'Gentlemen,' he announced, 'I have spent too many long, painful, sad years as a widower. I am therefore in immediate want of a real, good, handsome prime wife, and any single woman possessed of attractive charms wishing to better her condition is bound to consider my offer a most advantageous one. For her only duty in addition to the usual affectionate ones, will be to give directions to servants – as I have no children. Now sup your beer, gentlemen, and think on it, before you decide what you shall do.'

After they had lingered awhile to see whether Dick Almighty was offering a second round of free ale and decided that he was not going to do so, Joshua Binns rose and answered, 'I think I speak for the whole company of us when I say that should you, Mr Whitely, meet with a spouse as beautiful as the Goddess Diana, who may bring you children as the vine bringeth forth grapes . . .'

'What, at his age?'

'He might get Anne Wylde!' Jabez Stott sniggered.

Binns continued '. . . Your possessions, real, personal, and funded in a proper bank, as well as in other places that some of us know of, are sufficiently ample for the support o't'same, as appears from th'papers and deeds you have so honestly and in keeping with your genial, upright, God-fearing, righteous, law-abiding character placed afore us.' The weaver cast his shrewd narrow eyes over his confederates. 'I therefore move that we, the Gentlemen of the Society For Prosecuting Felons, print and publish advertisements for Mr Whitely's benefit and that we all contribute to th'expense, as a mark of our esteem for our beloved Constable, innkeeper and sin-catcher . . .'

'As amanuensis to the Society I move that I herewith draft it!' interrupted Jabez Stott, who was impatient to exert an influence. 'In fact I've already noted a wording, on a piece of paper.' He paused to receive the agreement and congratulations of the Society. But it was not forthcoming because being Yorkshiremen they wanted to see some substance in the gesture before offering praise. So Jabez continued, 'After Mr Whitely's words, as already expressed to us, it runs thus: "Private personal application is requested to be made and none but such as can give testimonials of a virtuous highly respectable character need apply. Time of application to last until he, Dick Whitely, be suited." How's that? I am used to penning advertisements for my master.' Now that he had got his speech out, Jabez was nervous and baffled.

'Put in that I'll be at home every Monday.' Dick Almighty patted his stomach, this time affably and beamed with satisfaction. He had saved himself perhaps three shillings in expenses for printing and advertisements and he had received the renewal of their acclamations. 'Well, gentlemen,' he wittily, God-fearingly and uprightly concluded, 'I owe no person anything but *love*, and I warrant I'll keep open house the day I am married!'

After her release, Anne planned to move into a cottage. Though poor she still decided not to sell any of the fine things in Lower Laithes, wanting all to remain as Oliver had left it, for when he returned. She took only some fine linen for her bed. Anne and Jenny covered the furniture and fastened the shutters. Paint flaked from the muses, who were still unpaid for. Damp rose up and mildewed the classical legs of escritoires and tables. A small bird had got in through a broken window and died; it was so weightless that a slight draught from an opened door blew it across the floor. Behind the two women, moving through the house, shade lapped the rooms, window by shut window, a tide of darkness, until only a few chinks of light stabbed the bared breast of an antique figure, or a honey-coloured piece of stone.

Anne gave Jenny a guinea, which was all she could afford, and made up the rest of her wages with gifts; a heavy shawl, a bundle containing whinberry and blackberry jam, oatmeal cakes, and a flask of rum. The women, now so equal, parted in the weed-filled garden. Spring was in spate. Birds sang freely, whereas for so many months only their sharp alarm calls had cut the misty silence. Over the hills, the weavers and the wild animals were moving about happily, free of ice and starvation. A soapy froth of bright new green was incandescent upon field, moor and trees, and the dew glittered like church glass.

Anne attempted to embrace Jenny. But even at this tender moment, her servant kept some distance from her. Anne first thought that it was out of respect. Then she realised it was because her breath was no longer sweet.

Anne went to a cottage on the top-side of Blood Wood. Walls fended off the moor and its predatory creatures from her poultry, herbs and vegetables. It was not the poorest type of cot, but it was simple. The ground floor was paved and there were ample passage-ways, a covered well in the kitchen, two bedrooms with floors of oak planks, and on one wall she placed the brown painting of the men who had filled in the well. A thing that she especially liked at this place, in contrast to Lower Laithes, was that the animals and poultry wandered close around it, so their scents mingled with those of herbs and wild flowers.

Jenny instinctively made towards Lady Well, where there were walls to shelter her, and where someone might take her in as a servant. She actually had work in Dick Almighty's Adam and Eve in mind, when she saw pinned on the door a copy of his advertisement. She asked a passing tradesman to read it to her. Circumspectly, Jenny did not rush in. Instead she sat in the graveyard to think up a plan of campaign. When she had considered for a quarter of an hour she went to the apothecary. 'You want a rubbing bottle?' he asked her. No; she risked most of Anne Wylde's guinea on a comb, a little mirror, and some cosmetics. She took these back to the churchyard and propped up the mirror. But what could *she* do to beautify herself? She had never thought of such a thing since she was a child, and at Lower Laithes where mirrors were available she had hardly ever bothered to look into one because it always disheartened her. Nor could she expect to charm a man with her speech.

But she would not need a clever tongue with Mr Whitely, she realised, for he would do all the talking. He was as powerful a man as any woman could wish for, and if she *could* win him, she would be as obedient a wife as any man could want, and his most faithful servant even though he did not ask for that. On the other hand, if it was as Mr Almighty said and she could be more than servant and live like Anne Wylde...! After a while, Jenny plucked up her courage, arranged her shawl as she had often seen Anne do, and went to knock on one of the rear doors of the inn.

Anne soon grew into one of those mysterious women, like her own Aunt Pity, who appear to give all their love to the plants in their garden, and to their hens. By the age of thirty she had turned into an 'old crone'. The skin receded from her bones. Like her Aunt Pity's it had few wrinkles, but as it pulled tight it made her features even sharper. Her eyes seemed brighter, her lips became more prominent, and the movements of her limbs more gaunt. She formed a habit of walking outside her house, even in night or fog, as if in a daze, staring at nothing, not recognising, thinking of no one knew what. She stayed alone, until she found two foxcubs deserted by their mother and, with that tenderness for vulnerable wild creatures that had typified her when she was a child, she raised them as her companions.

Oliver still did not return. Why did he not come back to Yorkshire? At thirty-five when, people thought, she should be ashamed of her desires, Anne was nevertheless longing for her lover's touches.

On better days, as the age of forty approached, she would peep at some old weaver, disturbing him once again with a return of the power she once had over his sleepless nights; and he might smile back, foolish in his years, blush, and talk.

Anne would not go into a manufactory. She would rather work with the gangs of labouring women. (She had no weaver menfolk for whom she could spin.) They gathered stones out of the enclosures. They scared birds. They weeded crops, sacks over their shoulders to absorb the rain. The men who employed Anne looked now not at her beauty, but at her hands to see if she was used to work, and at her shoulders to observe whether she could bear loads. They were no longer shy of her face; instead they stared with indifference or distaste at this old person, afraid that she might call on them for assistance. Anne found no joy in looking at herself, either. But thankfully, month by month her increasingly bowed back made her less able to peer into her mirror, and gave her no encouragement to hang her glass upon a lower nail. She had become like Aunt Pity who had passed away, how long since? – it was after Peter escaped and fled.

Anne was reduced to going to the slaughterhouse gate for blood to make puddings. Around her the flock of poor women (all belonging to Lady Well, all known to her, and many of whom had once served her) squabbled like starlings, with harsh voices and elbows sharp as beaks as they fought to get in when the gates were periodically opened for them to scoop up the blood running from the hanging beasts. The fights amused the butchers, which was why they locked the gates and only opened them for short periods.

Sometimes they would have sport at the expense of one of their apprentices or cattle-boys, by sending him to face the roaring flood of women. One day, these massed, bloody gorgons were laughing at the mincing, timid footsteps of a youth at his first day's work and Anne recognised Michael Loveless. His words when she had gone to collect Jenny, years ago, rang through her mind: '*I know someone who ate meat last Quarter Day.*' The terrified lad inserted his key into the lock and the women mimicked it obscenely.

'That must be the black milk of a witch still on thy lip, for it cannot be a moustache!' Esther Kershaw shouted.

Anne was wracked by her desire to protect him, yet was too weak to do anything. Then a huge old woman, with a scarf hiding her skull and a smile upon her pox-marked face, stepped forward and lifted the boy into the air. It was Mary Pickles. Michael thought that the hungry monster was going to gnaw the flesh off his bones or throw him to the oxen, but soon he realised the tenderness of her touch. As he relaxed, high above the raging females, the savage terrified animals and the rivers of blood, he began to cry, not now from fear but from nostalgia for long-forgotten tender womanhood.

Fortunately the men could not see him, and the women took no notice as they rushed past to the blood. Mary Pickles put the lad down and he ran away.

A few months later he was transported to Van Diemen's land for setting fire to spinning mills.

Anne stayed by the gate, where her eyes met those of Mary Pickles. 'My fine house is no use to me any more,' Anne said, and then (not wanting to talk about the past), 'How do you make your puddings?' When Mary described her method, Anne shook her head. 'Pour your oatmeal into the blood when it is warm,' she told Mary. 'Together with salt, eggs, and cream if you have some, adding marjoram and thyme, and then put beef suet in by the handful.'

Thus the two made friends. Mary was invited to Anne's cottage to collect marjoram, and they talked until the stars were out – the four eyes of the foxes glinting under the sofa. (A place they would not leave until the visitor departed; when, with turns and timid hesitations, they frolicked around their mistress.)

In a few more years, Anne was to be found every afternoon climbing the barrow on Raven's Hill, to stare in the London direction and see if Oliver was coming. She went there so often that the lane came to be called Fox Lane because of her two animals gliding and scurrying through the laneside gorse.

She began this habit after one occasion of extraordinary irrational certainty that her lover was arriving. So she had hurried up the barrow and started southwards, her eyes screwed up (for she could not see well any more) until darkness came.

The next midday, disturbed, she found herself walking several times around her cottage; one moment hesitant and the next feeling compelled to rush to some bush or tree as if Oliver might be behind it, until eventually she felt assured that she *would*, this time, find him from the mound. She stared so keenly into the distance that her eyes ached. Yet if for a moment her glance strayed elsewhere she soon switched her attention guiltily back to the horizon. She might have missed him in that one moment when her glance was absent! Day after day she suffered pangs of hope and disappointment. Sometimes she raced downhill to greet a mere stranger, who decided that she must be the local madwoman.

She could not bear to leave the hill before darkness fell: the lean half-blind old woman with the foxes. Lingering where there was naught but rock, gorse and heather, a wistful look on her face and about her bearing, she frightened and disturbed many a traveller who came upon her by surprise. At all times before her imagination, when at work amongst the stones of the fields or in her bed, was her vision of this one road – the boulders softly eroded like bales of raw wool, the rough herbage, the changing birds and flowers of the seasons, the Clay Slack Chapel over there, and, under her, the barrow where the ancient people also went to meet their dead.

One day on her way to Raven's Hill Anne saw that workmen were taking down Making Hall. They would not talk to an old woman, for they were too busy, or too dusty and wanting to get to an alehouse. But at last a man of her own age was troubled by a memory of something in that tallow-coloured flesh of hers, working upon her frame like the strings of a rickety loom, and he exclaimed, 'Anne Wylde! Well, well! What a dance *you* have led us through your life!'

Anne anxiously pulled at the joints of her fingers, in which she now suffered arthritis. 'That is all over now. Tell me, what is happening to Makings? It is Oliver Greave's property.'

'Nay, lass, it is Horsfall who has bested since the Old Man wove himself to th'far end. You must talk to Horsfall about it.'

The mason's eyes turned inwards, sadly. 'Betty Greave died, Benjamin left her everything, but failing any issue of her body, then all to Horsfall who is building a mansion in the new style, out of the stone. He is a powerful man now is Mr Horsfall, for he has friends in London, and, they say, all over the world. Greave never even got his own tomb made because he left it in the charge of Horsfall, and died sudden. You shouldn't be such a recluse, you should fight and then thou'd know what everyone else knows. Lawyers have done this work, I suppose! As Saint Luke says, "Woe unto ye lawyers, for they mak' only trouble with their wills." There was a man in Lady Well once left nothing but two worn suits to three sons. There has been some cackling in Hell over that legacy, too, I fancy . . .

'Do you want a reminder of the old place?' the mason added. 'Come with me.' He led her through the rubble. 'It's just a carving done by someone in the old days, I thought myself that maybe it was from the hand of old John Wylde.' He put into her hands the sculpture of Perseus slaying Medusa which had once been fixed over the porch.

Anne took the carving to her cottage and placed it over the mantelpiece. The place was full of mementos. Oliver's tobacco tin, still holding a few dusty bits of tobacco just as he had left it; a piece of door-lintel carved by her father; some bits of jewellery that she never wore.

She went outside to prowl and poke thoughtfully around her garden. It was spring and the primroses were breaking forth. As she prodded her fingers in the moist earth, piled it up to keep them comfortable, or removed little grass-plants, she muttered to her flowers, and to her foxes. These two darted and leaped around her, never still. 'Has tha' got fleas, then?' Anne used to say to them, so often that, she reflected, if they had been humans they would have been bored by her. Perhaps it was a good job that she had little human company!

Her first sign of a person approaching was when first one, then the other, fox stiffened and vanished into the banks and undergrowth. It was a long while before Anne heard or saw anything. Yet she too felt apprehensive. She had a habit of fearing who might be coming for her, although she had now been left in peace for years.

Jenny was approaching down the road. Anne's one-time maidservant was dressed in fine clothes, though a little bedraggled, and she was a good deal plumper than she used to be. But Jenny was crying. She could say nothing; she merely blubbered and mumbled. All that could be got out of her was that she wanted Anne to accompany her to Lady Well.

The two women, taking short cuts across enclosures, walked there in an hour. Jenny snivelled the whole way and Anne realised it was useless asking questions.

Before the Adam and Eve, Dick Almighty stood upon an empty barrel. Workmen, directed by bailiffs, were removing the inn's contents and piling them into a cart, whilst Dick Almighty harangued a crowd that had gathered. He saw Jenny and Anne at the back of it, but it made no difference to what he had to say, though his confidence was diminished a little.

'Gentlemen!' (There were many ladies present also, but Dick took no account of that.) 'I have made the first mistake of my long life! And I have been ruined by it – by that and by my generous disposition towards our native poor, of which you all have knowledge and have perhaps benefitted. As you all know I took a woman into my house and bed, to be my wife. I gave her love and all else besides, and now I have been ruined by it. For Jenny who seemed so meek and well-suited, turned into a veritable harridan! A strumpet, a Jezebel, a Messalina and Delilah rolled into one, a wanton hetaera, a lascivious wastrel!' His voice rose as he cried over the heads of the crowd, to the hills. 'Whatever possessions she has not forced me to sell to pay for her excesses, she has smashed in her rages! It is as if she has been waiting for *me*, her poor victim, for the whole of her life! I frankly admit that she has ruined me, and so we are both turned out of doors to beg.'

Jenny cried quietly to Anne, 'He struggled for hours upon hours to bring himself up. He used his hands until he was sore, and was puffing and blowing. But no matter how he went at it nor what I did to entice him, Dick Almighty could work up nothing bigger than a baby's finger!'

Anne was about to laugh. But Jenny gave out a loud and tragic cry – the first time in her life that she had ever raised her voice: 'All I ever wanted was a strong and manly husband!'

(14)

Anne Wylde, Mary Pickles, Esther Kershaw, Jenny Loveless and others were working in one of Horsfall's enclosures. They were carrying stones from the field to its outer edge – jagged rocks used only for the foundations of the dressed-stone walls that were now more and more cast like intricate lace over the Yorkshire hillsides. The rough edges cut the women's hands. The gang was paid according to how much they shifted. Fools to themselves, each woman tried to prove that she was the strongest and fastest. Anne, Mary and Jenny – three friends – stayed aloof, which often led to fights with the others. Bitter, foolish battles in which, rather than exchange blows, clothes and hair were torn. Tiredness made their heads reel and clogged their brains. They were absorbed by the work's rhythm, tugging out the boulders and carrying them along the web of tracks.

It was autumn. Silver mists lay, became frayed into long strands, floated upwards, and vanished as the mornings wore on. The woods were shivering to pieces. Dewy blackberries and whinberries were ripening on the banks and hedgerows, hanging close to their mouths, beckoning them as they came to their work. The air glittered with winged and wandering seeds. Sometimes there was a light but threatening frost in the mornings; soon they might, after all, be well advised to search for work in a spinning mill.

Anne looked knowingly at one newly-erected manufactory to which, no matter what happened to her, she would never go. It was Horsfall's. It had lewd statues of naked women in 'the antique style' around its portals, and above them a motto in Latin that few could understand – *Labor Omnia Vincit* (a corruption which had been suggested by Doubtfire of *Amor Omnia Vincit*). On the roof was a clock-tower – a gift making it unnecessary for anyone in Lady Well to own a clock, and also benefiting Horsfall because it reminded every-one that time and duty, especially the duty to arrive at his spinning mill, was of primary importance. At the foot of the tower was the workers' entrance, where was placed a large Bible of which the foreman turned a fresh page every day. The canal in which so many had invested, hoping for a great highway linking Yorkshire with Lancashire, stopped there at the mill. For though Horsfall had encouraged the use of his land for 'the cut', when it reached his own building he unexpectedly refused to allow it to go further; so the only revenue available to the canal company was in transporting coal to Horsfall's, and his products away from it, on the Captain's own terms.

The women saw men in ragged soldiers'-jackets coming over the hilltop. They had scars or dirty bandages, and some were limping or on crutches. To help them face the women they were drunk, and though not hurrying were sufficiently menacing to cause the more alert and suspicious females to keep hold of their stones.

The men lined up by the largest piles on the field's edge, and repeated loudly what they had been saying over and over again for many hours in a hush-house. 'We soldiers have fought for you in France or Spain, and now we need our work back. 'Tis only fair, because you can go to the spinning mill!'

'All guilty rogues should be whipped!' sang out Anne's own son, Peter. Though they did not recognise one another, and he now called himself 'Jonas Pity'. He was tall, like Anne, but neither beautiful nor kind, and a bully. After escaping from the shed he had worked for a farmer, excelling at killing, butchering and being cruel to animals. He was soon drifting about the moors, joining but soon leaving various gangs, and sometimes when he was drunk boasting that he was descended from Benjamin Greave of Making Hall – a rumour that he himself did not believe when he was sober. After falling for the wiles of a recruiting sergeant 'Jonas Pity' discovered that he would pine away with homesickness within a week of being away from Lady Well, whereupon he deserted and returned to the hills that he loved, determined never to leave them again. His deepest philosophy, often quoted by him, was, 'All guilty rogues should be whipped.' He went about mostly with two dogs (descendants of Aunt Pity's), which were so large and fierce that everyone guessed his reason for having them was because he believed he had enemies; these animals were the only ones to which he was kind.

The women appeared to be short of an answer, yet the men were waiting for one. Eventually Esther taunted them, 'Thou's never been a soldier, Jabez Stott, for you couldn't bear the slaughter!' whereupon a stone was thrown at her. Mary Pickles flung one back, and a battle began with the men returning a hail of rocks from the pile that the women had taken a morning to lift painfully out of the enclosure.

'Let 'em lie and we'll pick them up for you!' Jabez shouted. He had been such a fine looking man, a virgin bloom upon his skin, until he followed the army, and now his teeth were broken in a vicious leer.

The women took to their heels. But Anne Wylde stayed. If a stone had struck her head, she would not have minded; but it is such that the stones always avoid. She let the poor laughing soldiers and her unrecognised son's dogs surround her. Then they did not know what to do with her, for she looked so old that she roused only compassion. She walked off slowly leaving them 'triumphant' in the field, herself beyond caring what she would now do for bread.

All the other women, like mice seeking their holes or stores of seeds, had scattered towards what comforts they could hope for, or even half-hopelessly imagine. Mary Pickles went to the Cloth Hall to hire herself for carrying bales on her shoulders across the countryside. Jenny Loveless entered the poorhouse – it was better to be imprisoned than to starve through another winter.

(She would not return home: she had tried that once before. 'The worst of daughters is, they always come back,' Jack Loveless had remarked in his dry, philosophical manner – he did not mean to be cruel. It had been on her mind to retort, 'Michael will for sure not come back, for he has been transported!' But she said nothing. She had shouted out once before in her life, when the bailiffs had removed Dick Almighty's goods, and it had only brought the culminating humiliation to one who, after all, had been kind to her. Although Jenny had not yet even got her bundle over the doorstep, she turned away, and her father was just too slow in expressing his regret. He did not utter another word until she had turned the corner, by which time she had hardened her heart, so that when he chased after her she would not speak to him.)

When Jenny reached the poorhouse she saw husbands and wives being separated in tears and for ever on the doorstep of old age. But she herself was one of the lucky ones. For Jenny met there a man who was adept at breaking or shaping all human laws and regulations: her husband, Dick Almighty! He was so thrilled at their being reunited that his confidence and skill in manipulating worldly affairs magically returned. He not only broke the rule that kept the sexes apart, and slept with her for comfort and warmth that night and subsequently on all others: he also arranged a welcoming dinner.

That very day he wrote a letter to the Society For Prosecuting Felons.

'Sirs! Last night I dreamed that you sent me a small parcel containing plum pudding, apples from what as you know used to be my own orchard, some game fairly paid for and not poached, and two trouts even though these be very rare now in our native streams. For a long time my inflamed and sorry eyes have been a stranger to sleep. I now desire an increase in my growing faith in human kindness by sending a little of the above which will prove that dreams come to pass as they did in former times. Your attention to these broken hints will much oblige your poor afflicted pauper, in truth, Dick Whitely.'

After Jenny had been in the workhouse for a few months, reconciled and happy with her husband whom, she at last realised, she could trust to be her protector, her secret little nest of happiness was brutally destroyed, as callously as the shelters of robins and thrushes are by bird-nesting boys. For the master pressed her into signing indentures to work for five years in a spinning manufactory; and Dick Whitely, with innocent hope and trust in the benevolence of The Coming Age, let her go, thinking her youth more important than the comfort of his own declining years.

After the battle with the soldiers, Esther Kershaw, like an escaped hare, went straight to the moors. As a hare makes its form in the grass, so she had learnt to contrive comfort out of turf-stacks, abandoned, unfinished or burnt buildings, peat-gulleys and the leesides of walls, of flocks of sheep or of cattle. A rain-stained Bible was her companion, and for amusement she read the signs of the wind, sky, flowers, berries and shifting flocks of birds. With these aids she prophesied everything, from a hard winter, or the burning of a mill, to the Second Coming. She instinctively turned every day towards the weak midday sun, to store warmth in her cheeks for the approaching winter, or for energy to survive the Apocalypse. Unlike other travellers she never varied her pace, since she was without appointments. She walked something between slowly and quickly. She was weighed down with all her possessions, either worn or carried upon her back. Esther only bothered to move at all in order to stop her limbs locking together, and to convince herself that her life was not without purpose. Though she set off in a direct line southwards, it would always eventually (sometimes after months) become a circle, usually turning westwards after the sun, thus bringing her back to Lady Well – where she never stayed for very long, being saddened because the Baptists had built a chapel over the well to stop its use by 'pagans'. At first Esther had followed the rivers. But now that manufactories had been built along them, the way was so sulphurous, dangerous and churned with mud, and the watercourses so unfit to drink or to bathe in, that she kept to the moortops for as long as she could find whinberries or trout, and could lay nooses of animal-gut to catch rabbits and hares.

But she survived mainly by being encased in the shell of her preaching, for which people gave her food, shelter or money. She took up her stations at busy cross-roads, holding her Bible open at Revelations – not to read from it, for she knew her texts by heart, but because to have a book in her hands made her feel like an educated preacher rather than a vagrant. She told the weavers and merchants who were hurrying by before winter came on that her husband, too, had like themselves been storing up goods and credit as if for more than his earthly stay; but to what fires had it led him?

With the wooden emphasis of all those certain that they have been Elected or Saved, Esther shouted that *she* was the one who had uncovered the pure springs of Christ, and had encountered the great succouring White Cow, even if only in dreams.

Why did Oliver Greave procrastinate for so many years? Was it simply because of his indecisive nature? Or was his long-damned instinct to follow his wanderlust so strong as to overcome even his love? Oh, how can anything except his muse comprehend a poet's will! Or so Oliver Greave excused himself.

Sometimes he missed boats as if he had actually contrived to do so. At other times he allowed wars and skirmishes to intervene – or imagined that they did. The complications of Horsfall's business caused Oliver to wait, in which period there would develop, as if by malign influence, further difficulties that demanded to be resolved before his return. Sometimes (it must be confessed) a lady delayed him. For he could not live without a female body warm against him, even though it did not offer true love. At such times the ache of Anne Wylde's absence momentarily receded. The act of love linked his hidden and his conscious worlds. Without it Oliver would never have known what strange ambiguous forces lay within him, rushing upwards out of deep pools; his inner being was a theatre for mad, hidden gods, who emerged at his copulations. Also, as he grew older his hair vanished, his stomach sagged and his windiness increased, so he developed scares for his virility and had to prove himself.

For a multiplicity of reasons, without ever trying to correct what he was doing, Oliver allowed women, wars, misunderstood departure times, floods, storms, business, drunken stupors, revolutions, even the guilt of his own impotence in this matter, to cut off his daily-renewed ambitions to return to Yorkshire.

All over Europe he stumbled into revolutions, or the intentions for them. He remembered what Loveless had told him in Yorkshire about finding the true muse for the times in such causes. Yet their energy baffled as well as intrigued him, in his own queer state of doing practically nothing to improve upon his fate. In revolution was there embodied a rational ideal, its hour come round at last? Or, on the contrary, a bursting out of instinct?

He drifted across land and sea finding a fresh delight in travelling without baggage, friends, family, or the encumbrances of loyalties. On many a dusk when he passed by lit windows where families were settling to meals, or to playing cards, or to musical entertainments, and when he was inclined to be sad and sorry for himself as he sought brief shelter under a bush or the lea of a rock, and in a strange place, he fought his mood by reminding himself of the advantages of his state. He enjoyed a necessarily keen sense of the whole world around him, and he was rewarded with an independent, naked, fresh, innocent watchfulness. He realised too that the whole of mankind similarly was discovering a new and naked identity. Everywhere man was breaking out of old enclosures, in politics, in philosophy, in religion; whilst as a poet he happily observed here and there the common man's language being freed into literature (Tim Bobbin's dream). He even saw his own Nature Muse make her entrance into poetry.

Yet, paradoxically, the more keenly Oliver appreciated Nature, the more horribly he was haunted by a feeling that She had departed. He would dash here and there – from bush, to meadow, to the edge of the sea – staring fascinated at some beautiful thing that filled him with *despair*. Beauty was a chimera. If one touched it (as he often did – leaves, fruit or flowers), the loveliness was damaged even by one's own gentle hands. To comprehend beauty was dangerous and frightening. He felt he was at the edge of a terrible ocean in which he might be drowned and torn to pieces.

In this mood he journeyed as far south as Greece, just as he had always longed to do. There he found the real sun, that had for so many years burned and glowed as a dream in his northern belly. Now it was hung in a hot, featureless cage of light. There was a sky of such fierce blue as he had never before experienced, either in pigment or glass; he felt that if he hit it, it would clang like a steel shield.

Oliver Greave, this man of complicated thoughts, appeared amongst the Turks, and the Greeks whom they enslaved, merely as a typical English traveller. In his blue worsted coat and his three-cornered hat he stood back from things with a peculiar mixture of shyness and arrogance, yet doing no harm, not cheating or robbing anyone, and interested mainly in comfortable beds, the times of ships, and in ruins. Hesitating on quaysides or in confusing and brutal markets, and amongst broken temples, he had always Pausanias, his ancient guide to Greece, in his pocket. But time and again he was disappointed. He so rarely found the glittering erections to Demeter or Athena, Zeus or Apollo. Instead he saw perilously collapsing piles being quarried to build mosques, Christian churches and houses. The 'greatest civilisation ever known to man', had been reduced to sterile stones in a land that had now lost its oak groves and its rivers of classical times, and was white and dry as a sun-bleached prehistoric skull: the shelter of vipers, kites and spiders. Whilst the Greeks cared nothing about their ancient past but were, like the rest of Europe, interested in revolution, freedom, and a 'rational' future.

Oliver, even before his beloved monuments, could still feel Anne Wylde all over his skin. So eventually, eventually, he *did* return to Yorkshire along the roads from the south. He now saw his past life, indeed the whole of his own materialistic age, as if it was one of those dreams that are unintelligible in the moment that you awake from them but become steadily clearer in meaning. He felt that he was only waiting for some clarity that was hiding round a corner (as his muse had once seemed to do) to jump out and replace the confusion.

When at last he reached England it seemed so *green* – it was as if nature conspired to create a cheerful harmony for his homecoming. Until he reached his native valleys in the north, and what a foul mess he saw there! Smoke was rising from a chaos of spinning mills and cloth manufactories. The hills were darker. They were glowering like damp cinders, as if spring would never come to them again. When he drank at streams whose waters had delighted him in boyhood, they tasted of soot. *Reason* had not stopped the ruin of nature! Hanging dramatically upon the hillsides above the manufactories were Methodist and Baptist chapels ostentatiously elbowing out of the way the older, smaller, simpler Congregationalist and Quaker places of worship. One was on the site of a cock-pit, one was where an ancient cross had been, another where had grown a thorn tree 'from the time of Christ', whilst several of the Baptists' churches were built over famous springs so as to make sure that never again could these places evoke their ancient mysteries. At the foot of every steep village was a manufactory, houses crowded in its shadow, and at the crown of the streets was a chapel – so that now the community hung between a symbol of earth or work and of God in His sky.

Only the narrow packhorse-road over the moors was the same, busy with traders scurrying to the rear door of Horsfall's new mansion just as they had once hurried to Makings. Their weaving was still piled over the backs of bandy-legged ponies, even though yet vaster quantities of the new trade was transported in large carts, or by canal barge. Here was the clothier's true symbol: a pony crippled with the weight of sin that God had laid upon his back, just as he loaded an animal with wool! This was the price, for all, of prosperity for some.

At dusk Oliver came across a mad scrawny woman preaching at a crossroads, where laughing merchants made wide sweeps to pass her by. 'As birds perched upon a winter tree all face the same way, backs to the wind so's it'll not ruffle their feathers, so you men of this Age flock all in the same direction, wanting not to be ruffled by the unpleasant blasts of Truth!' Esther Kershaw screeched.

Though no one else listened to her, she did think that she had 'pinned her cross' through the heart of the bowed, prematurely aged stranger paused before her; that she had transfigured and transfixed him, just as the Great Preachers did, John Wesley, William Grimshaw of Yorkshire and Saint Paul.

But then he smiled at her, which made her irrationally angry. So she spluttered and abused him with words from *Revelations*. The stranger laughed even more and Esther grew more angry.

'I am Oliver Greave, Esther!' he interrupted.

She stopped in amazement. 'Risen from the dead! And did you find the Original Paradise on your travels?'

Oliver shook his head.

'You were looking in the wrong places,' Esther said. 'You will find the First Garden not in Africa, not in the Americas, not in the South Seas, but only in your own heart, when all is peace there because you are true to yourself. Then you will always take Paradise with you ...' She paused. 'Oliver Greave, Mistress Anne has been driven off by soldiers ...' Esther flushed and was silenced by the realisation that she could not possibly tell all, and she did not know where to begin. Then she started to tumble over her words. 'She keeps two foxes and has grown terrible strange. She has a cottage yonder down by the rocks, along the stream course, you'll find it by the fruit trees in the garden ...'

Oliver would not stay for any more preaching.

Esther watched him depart. She saw in his back, and in the still-cocky way that he swayed his shoulders, just a ghost of the young poet who had delighted the taverns, and been so wayward. It was as if a faint, invisible flame was still burning there.

After she had reflected for a few moments, Esther thought that she had better forewarn Anne. She packed up her Bible and hurried by a short cut across the flank of the moor.

Though the sun had just set, yet miraculously it appeared to be rising again in the east! Esther saw a glorious rosy light flickering upon the landscape. A sunrise such as she had never witnessed before: the whole eastern sky was in beautifully formed crimson and purple feathers, or maybe like tiny sea-shells, rising out of Lady Well. Instantly she saw the 'meaning' of it. This was from the marriage of Christ with the virgin Anne Wylde, which was spreading cascades of blood as described in Revelations!

So it was not after all true, then, the rumour that Oliver and Anne had been in wedlock! – for otherwise there would be no hymen to burst in clouds of blood. But now Greave would be too late to find a bride, for she was married to Heaven!

Esther hurried to Anne's cottage not knowing what amazement to expect.

From his house Doubtfire watched the flames of his burning church, and he waited for the Inevitable. Soon people were running back and forth, outlined against the Fire like wiry black flies squirming in Pain. Miserable, ignorant Creatures! It was as if the Lord held them with Tweezers and was dipping them in the flames of Hell. They had brought out a fire-machine (patented, but imitated and built nevertheless in a workshop opened by Jabez Stott). It was a long wooden box improvised out of a surplus coffin (for its intended occupant had unexpectedly recovered from typhus fever), already lead-lined so that it would hold water and with a force-pump attached, leading to a copper pipe. The six strongest men of the town were furiously working it, the motions of their limbs like tentacles of the ineffective machine. Others were bringing buckets of water from the fortunately proximate well, inside the Baptists' Chapel. Perhaps the well would now save the church?

'What must it be like to wake in Hell?' Doubtfire calmly wondered. Death, he thought, was no more than a preliminary Sleep to it, containing nothing worse than Nightmares. But when the Parson of Lady Well woke in Hell, his Thoughts could not be a sweet gratitude that his Bad Dreams were over. Waking must be so Horrible that one's first Longing would be to retreat into that Nightmare which one had just escaped. And there would be a realisation that this was for Eternity and without return. Also, even in the most Horrible Dream there is no *physical* Pain, unless perhaps a Discomfort of the bed: a cold draught about the head that makes one dream of snow, or thirstiness that puts one in mind of fruit. Hell must have real Pains, Fetters and Cramps, for which dreams do not console. Perhaps the whole skin would be too sore to touch.

By whom? Doubtfire remembered Demons. They would have green faces, and smiles. Their smiles would be the most Unfortunate thing about them. They would be the once-loved ones, Mocking; though Doubtfire thankfully had no person to love him. But one would be

Mocked also because out of reach of what one loved – the scent of bluebells, that tall strange girl Anne Wylde, brandy, or a Congregation swayed.

His once-submissive congregation had now turned into a swarm of enemies shouting, '*Doubtfire!*' against the crashing slates and timbers. The evidence of someone who had caught him with his tinder and flint, and moreover had actually believed the evidence of his eyes, (for years people had surprised the parson near a burning building, but had suspected him of nothing other than of being custodial) had been passed around Lady Well. They gathered near his door, and three of the Society For Prosecuting Felons came forward, one of them being the magistrate, Nicholas Horsfall. They were bound to take him to Bedlam, and yet it was they who were apprehensive, because it was so rare for them to have to arrest one of their own class.

Doubtfire enjoyed letting them batter for a while on his door. At last he let them in. He was calm, as he had not been for many years, even in his own church. They entered his room, still decorated with its skulls, draped urns, books of devotion, mementi-mori, and cruel steel-engravings of martyrdoms. Everything in Doubtfire's religion had to do with death; whilst the scalpels, microscopes and other instruments of his vocation lay amongst the partially dismembered corpses of animals and birds.

The Parson first became truly afraid when he was taken away in a common cart which smelled of manure, the rough wood giving him splinters: and yet also it could be thought of as some kind of pulpit that jerked and rocked him to Hell. 'Why are you not all a-bed! Get back to your wives!' Doubtfire shouted.

The dark outline of the church crumpled. Its walls swelled and it collapsed in flames that scorched his eyes. Its 'vainly coloured glasses' and its 'idolatrous statues' were finally done for! He saw revealed, like the core of a broken fruit, the firelit rose-coloured remnants of Benjamin Greave's unfinished tomb. Also some kind of red sap was bleeding out of the roof-beams, and Doubtfure remembered Esther Kershaw's apron.

'I am in peace,' Doubtfire told his captors. 'I have but to step off my earthly Seat into eternal Hell!'

'No, I will not have Oliver Greave see me as I am now,' Anne told

Esther. 'It is finally too late. He carries the purest picture of me already in his heart.' As Anne collected her things into a bundle, she could not think what she was doing, and she wept. 'I have nothing, and I have created nothing. The only child I gave birth to is from a rape.' She went out of her cottage, leaving no message but the door invitingly open and candles lit inside.

Oliver was hurrying over the dark flickering hillsides. He felt as glorious as Adonis, Hippolytus, or the sun himself, as he came to his loved one, bearing his experiences as his gift brimming in the chalice of his love. On the way he was confronted by an old woman of the roads – one such as he had met all over England, indeed everywhere in Europe, displaced by war, revolution, or by the pastimes and the gardening-tastes of nobles. Women usually selling clothes-pegs, sprigs of heather, or telling fortunes. What experiences must that old crone have suffered, to double her up like that and make her so uncurious about what is to her right hand or her left! he thought. As he scrutinised her he found such an uncanny echo of Anne Wylde that he thought he must be going mad, and that he'd better hurry on quickly to find the real one.

Anne passed him by, dragging her feet into the dusk without looking at him. How could she, her heart would fail.

She went right out of Yorkshire. No remains of her were over found. No long skeleton, its bones as slender as a bird's, in a moorland gulley after the snows. There are no records of her having knocked at the doors of almshouses. She disappeared as dreams do: when Reason awoke, she had gone. You have seen the dew fade. Though some watch it second by second, no one ever sees where the glittering jewels go to.

When Oliver arrived at the cottage's open door he calmly sat outside amongst the flowers lit by the stars and by the strange red sky. He was most intrigued by how Anne had laid out her garden. It was so simple, and so roughly designed, as if after her period at Lower Laithes she had been swept back in spirit to the artisan world of her childhood. He contemplated their future old age, being wise and venerable together, their reduced circumstances having brought wisdom in its train. As he waited, he anticipated Anne's appearance. He would have the advantage and be able to enjoy her expression as it changed when she saw who was sitting there!

Then a realisation that the place was empty crept over him. His fear was quite unreasonable and yet he knew it would prove justified. He got up and went inside, a smile still lingering upon him, then fading. Looking around in the candlelight – at the pathetic sight of her recently washed pots, the table, the old sculpture from Makings propped upon the fireplace, the chair with a cushion still bearing her, *her* imprint – he was possessed by the uncanny but absolute certainty that Anne would never return.

He sat down, weary. He had made up his mind to come back to Yorkshire, but it was not Yorkshire without her. He knew what his life would be now. Sitting in the corners of alehouses, just as in his youth, but without merriment, alone, hoping to meet anyone who had known her. Musing whether her spirit had perhaps entered that owl's cry; staring at the harebells and wondering if it was there; hearing her dashing about the spring sky in the songs of the larks – above all she would be amongst the larks that she had loved so much. Wondering if the soot had come upon the moors because she had fled. She was like a butterfly hatched in a January frost, he thought. Was she someone I dreamed of? *Or is she dreaming me?* he wondered. As a bough broken from a may-tree in the autumn will sometimes give out unseasonable buds that come to nothing, he thought, so Anne Wylde was born into our time in Yorkshire.

MORE ABOUT PENGUINS, PELICANS
AND PUFFINS

For further information about books available from Penguins please write to Dept EP, Penguin Books Ltd, Harmondsworth, Middlesex UB7 ODA.

In the U.S.A.: For a complete list of books available from Penguins in the United States write to Dept DG, Penguin Books, 299 Murray Hill Parkway, East Rutherford, New Jersey 07073.

In Canada: For a complete list of books available from Penguins in Canada write to Penguin Books Canada Ltd, 2801 John Street, Markham, Ontario L3R 1B4.

In Australia: For a complete list of books available from Penguins in Australia write to the Marketing Department, Penguin Books Australia Ltd, P.O. Box 257, Ringwood, Victoria 3134.

In New Zealand: For a complete list of books available from Penguins in New Zealand write to the Marketing Department, Penguin Books (N.Z.) Ltd, Private Bag, Takapuna 9, Auckland.

In India: For a complete list of books available from Penguins in India write to Penguin Overseas Ltd, 706 Eros Apartments, 56 Nehru Place, New Delhi 110019.